Cathy Williams can ⟨...⟩
books as a teenager, ⟨...⟩
she remains an avid fa⟨...⟩
creating romantic stories and engaging plots, and each
and every book is a new adventure. Cathy lives in
London. Her three daughters—Charlotte, Olivia and
Emma—have always been, and continue to be, the
greatest inspirations in her life.

USA TODAY bestselling author **Jennie Lucas**'s
parents owned a bookstore, so she grew up
surrounded by books, dreaming about faraway lands.
A fourth-generation Westerner, she went east at
sixteen to boarding school on a scholarship, wandered
the world, got married, then finally worked her
way through college before happily returning to her
hometown. A 2010 RITA® Award finalist and 2005
Golden Heart® Award winner, she lives in Idaho with
her husband and children.

THE ITALIAN'S CHRISTMAS PROPOSITION

CATHY WILLIAMS

CHRISTMAS BABY FOR THE GREEK

JENNIE LUCAS

MILLS & BOON

First Published in Great Britain 2019
by Mills & Boon, an imprint of HarperCollins*Publishers*
1 London Bridge Street, London, SE1 9GF

The Italian's Christmas Proposition © 2019 by Cathy Williams

Christmas Baby for the Greek © 2019 by Jennie Lucas

ISBN: 978-0-263-27365-6

MIX
Paper from
responsible sources
FSC® C007454

This book is produced from independently certified FSC™ paper
to ensure responsible forest management.
For more information visit www.harpercollins.co.uk/green.

Printed and bound in Spain
by CPI, Barcelona

THE ITALIAN'S CHRISTMAS PROPOSITION

CATHY WILLIAMS

CHAPTER ONE

'ROSIE! ARE YOU going to focus on what I'm telling you?'

The cut-glass accent was a mix of despair, impatience and long-suffering love and Rosie guiltily dragged her eyes away from the far more stimulating sight below of people coming and going, skis on shoulders, imbued with the unique excitement of being on holiday in the run-up to Christmas.

The luxury five-star resort—a jewel nestled in the heart of the Dolomitic Alps in the Veneto region of northern Italy—was the last word in the very best that money could buy and as good as a second home to Rosie, who had been coming here with her family for as long as she could remember. She could close her eyes and accurately visualise every beam of deep burnished wood, every swirl and curve of marble, the timeless cool greys of the exquisite indoor swimming pool area and the oversized chandeliers dominating the Michelin-starred restaurants.

Right now, sitting in the galleried landing with a *latte* in front of her, Rosie was in prime position to admire the dramatic twenty-foot Christmas tree sweeping upwards by the reception desk, a vision of tasteful pink and ivory and tiny little electric candles. She could almost *smell* the pine needles.

'Of course I am,' she said with a suitable level of sincerity and enthusiasm. Across from her, her sister was on the verge of another of her laborious, long-suffering sighs. 'You were asking me what I intend to do once the ski season is over. I don't *know,* Diss. Right now, I'm just enjoying the ski instructing. It's *fun.* I'm meeting some really lovely people and plus, let's not forget, I'm looking after Mum and Dad's chalet while I'm here. Making sure it…er…doesn't get burgled…or anything…'

'Because burglars are a dime a dozen here in Cortina?'

'Who knows?'

'You can't keep flitting from place to place and from job to job for ever, Rosie. You're going to be twenty-four on your next birthday and Mum and Dad…well, *all* of us—me, Emily, Mum, Dad…we're *all* concerned that it's getting to a point where you can't even be bothered to try and…you know what I mean…'

'Become an accountant? Get a mortgage? Find a decent man to look after me?' Rosie flushed and looked away. She was particularly sensitive on the subject of men and, in her heart, she knew that this was what her parents were worried about—that she was never going to find Mr Right, as both her sisters had. That she was going to spend her life drifting from Mr Wrong to Mr Really Bad Idea to Mr Will Take Advantage. She had, as it happened, been down several of those roads in the past and, whilst she had put a cheerful face on each and every disappointment, each and every one had hurt.

At this point in time, if she never had another relationship in her life again, she wouldn't lose sleep over it. The last guy she had gone out with had been a fellow traveller in India. He had been out there buying cheap

Asian artefacts to sell for a profit in a market somewhere near Aldershot. They had had fun before he had taken a shine to a tall brunette and disappeared with her, leaving only an apologetic note in his wake.

The only saving grace in all these disappointing relationships, as far as Rosie was concerned, was that she hadn't made the mistake of bed-hopping. One guy. That was it. The one guy all those years ago who had broken her heart. She'd been nineteen and finding her feet all over again, having dropped out of university, and he had been there to catch her as she was falling. A biker with a refreshing disdain for convention and the first guy who had been a world away from the upper-class posh boys she had spent a lifetime meeting. She had loved everything about him, from his tattoos to the ring in his ear.

He, in the end, had loved the financial package she came with more than he had loved her for who she was, and had thrown a fit when she had promised to dump all her worldly goods for him. She still shuddered when she thought about what could have been the biggest mistake of her life. Since then, she'd enjoyed life without getting in too deep.

'Whoever said anything about becoming an accountant?' Candice rolled her eyes and grinned, and Rosie grinned back, because Emily's husband, wonderful as he was, could be a little tedious when he began pontificating about exchange rates and investment opportunities.

Still, he earned a small fortune, so he had obviously played the game right.

Whilst she, Rosie, hadn't started playing it at all.

'With Christmas just three weeks away...' Candice shifted and Rosie looked at her sister with narrowed eyes, smelling a conversation ahead that she would not want to have.

'Don't worry, I'll make sure the chalet is in tip-top shape for the family invasion. You know how much I love the whole decorating thing. Plus, I'll make sure there are lots of chocolates hanging on the branches of the tree for Toby and Jess.'

'There has been a slight change of plan. The snow is so magnificent at the moment that everyone's coming over a little earlier than originally planned.'

'Earlier than planned?'

'Tomorrow, as it happens. I'm the advanced warning party, so to speak. I know you and I had planned a couple of girly days together but you know Mum and Dad…they can't resist the slopes and the atmosphere here at Christmas. And there's something else,' Candice said in a rush. 'They're thinking of asking the Ashley-Talbots over for a long weekend. Bertie too. He's something or other in the City and doing quite well, I hear. They think it might be nice for you two to…er…get to know one another…'

'No.'

'It's just a thought, Rosie. Nothing's confirmed. He's always had that crush on you, you know. It might be nice!'

'Absolutely not, Candice.'

'Mum and Dad just thought that there's no harm in actually meeting someone a little less…*unorthodox*.'

'When you say that you're the advance warning party—' Rosie narrowed suspicious eyes '—does that actually mean that you've been sent to start preparing me for lots of lectures on getting my house in order, starting with dating Robert Ashley-Talbot? Well, no way will I be getting involved with him! He's…he's the most *boring* guy I've ever met!'

'You can't say that! You might find that you actually enjoy the company of someone who has a *steady job*, Rosie! Emily and I both happen to agree with Mum and Dad! Give me *one* good reason, Rosie-Boo, why you won't at least give it a go. If you find that you really don't like Bertie, then that's fair enough, but you haven't seen him in *years*.'

'A year and a half, and he can't have changed that much.' Nerdy, prominent Adam's apple, thick-rimmed glasses and a way of getting onto a really dull topic of conversation and then bedding down for the duration.

Rosie looked down. Down to the lively buzz of excited guests, down to the glittering Christmas tree, down to the clutch of leather chairs in the foyer, where a group of three people was gathering some papers, shaking hands, clearly about to leave.

'And—' she turned her clear blue-eyed gaze back to her sister '—I wasn't going to say anything but…but… I'm just not in a good place for meeting Bertie, Diss. Or *anyone,* for that matter.'

On her lap, she crossed her fingers and told herself that this was a perfectly sensible way out of a situation that would turn Christmas into a nightmare. She didn't want Bertie coming over. She didn't want to have to face the full force of her family gently trying to propel her to a destination she didn't want to go because they were concerned about her.

She leaned forward. 'I've had my heart broken while I've been out here.'

'What on earth are you talking about, Rosie?'

'You say that I never go for the right kind of guy?

Well, I did. I fell for one of the guests here. A business-man. As reliable and as stable as…as…the day is long. He was everything you and Ems and Mum and Dad would have wanted for me, which just goes to show that those types just aren't for girls like me. I bore them in the end. It was just a holiday fling but I guess I got more wrapped up in him than I thought I would.'

'I'm not sure I believe you,' Candice said, eyebrows raised. 'It's very odd that this is the first I'm hearing of this and we've been sitting here for what…an hour? What a coincidence.'

'I wasn't going to mention it but I felt I had to when you told me that Mum and Dad were thinking of asking Robert and his parents over for the weekend. I'm just a little shaken up, that's all. I know I've dated the wrong sorts but I really felt that this guy might be the one. I went into it with my eyes wide open and I was hurt. So… I just need a bit of time out to lick my wounds.'

'And where is this mysterious disappearing man right now?' But her voice was hesitant, on the cusp of be-lieving.

'As a matter of fact…'

And there was that group of three again. She recog-nised the elderly couple—Bob and Margaret something-or-other. She had given them both a lesson, filling in for their usual instructor who had called in sick when Rosie knew for a fact he had been suffering from a hangover. They had said were there to try and learn to ski because, although they were in their late sixties, they believed that old dogs could be taught new tricks and, since their daughter loved her skiing, they were up for giving it a try. They were going to be retiring. Selling up. A nice young man, Matteo, would be coming in for a flying visit to do the deal. Exciting times.

With his back to her as he shook hands with the older man, Matteo—or the man she assumed was Matteo, because who else could it possibly be?—was just the candidate for the role of businessman heartbreaker. There was no way she intended to spend her Christmas dodging Bertie, and a broken heart was the only excuse she could find that might save her from that dreadful possibility.

'There he is. Matteo. With that couple about to leave. He's here on business with them. He doesn't know that I'm up here looking down at him. Thinks I'm out on the slopes giving a lesson. He's probably completely forgotten about my existence already.'

She looked at her sister who stared down to the group of three, eyes narrowed.

'*That* creep was the guy who hurt you?'

Rosie mumbled something inarticulate, meant to convey an affirmative reply without going into further detail. Not a liar by nature, she was guiltily aware that she was blackening a perfect stranger's character with her little white lie.

Distracted, what happened next took her by surprise. It was so out of keeping with her cool, collected, elegant blonde sister. Candice was *always* so controlled! But here she was now, angrily rising to her feet, hands slapping down on the table, and then she was hurtling between tables, feet flying at a pace while… Rosie watched, mouth open, horror slowly dawning because she knew that this was not going to end well for her…

She would have to stop her sister before things went any further. She didn't waste time thinking about it. She leapt up and followed in hot pursuit.

* * *

For once, Matteo Moretti wasn't looking at his watch. He usually did. The end of a deal always awakened a restlessness inside him, an impatience to move on to the next thing. True, the signatures on the dotted line were technically not there yet, but that was a formality. Hands had been shaken and, as soon as the horror of the Christmas season was over and done with, the lawyers would be summoned and the finishing touches put to a purchase that meant a great deal to him.

Bob and Margaret Taylor, the most unlikely of clients, were beaming up at him. Bob, yet again, was congratulating him in his bluff, Yorkshire accent for getting past the post.

'Land's worth a bob or two.' He slapped Matteo's arm and winked. 'Can't tell you how many wanted to get their greedy paws on it but you're the first person the missus and I feel we can trust to do the right thing.'

'Honoured that you think that,' Matteo responded with sincerity.

He'd been here at this eye-wateringly pricey resort for the past three days, wooing Bob and his wife. A different type of approach for a very different type of deal.

Around him, Yuletide merriment had been a constant backdrop, getting on his nerves, reminding him that it was high time he did what he always did every single Christmas—escape. Escape to his villa on the outskirts of Venice, which was a mere couple of hours from here.

He worked in London and had a penthouse apartment there, indeed lived most of his life there, but his elegant, yellow-stone villa here in Italy was his bolt-hole and the only place where he felt perfectly at peace. Every year he removed himself from the canned carols, the ridiculous Santa lookalikes ringing bells outside supermarkets and the pounding of crowds on pavements, frantically hunting down presents, wrapping paper, Christmas decorations and all the paraphernalia that seemed to arrive earlier and earlier in the shops with every passing year.

Two weeks away from it all, isolated in his sprawling manor with two trusted employees to cook and clean for him while he worked. God bless broadband and the Internet. It enabled him to avoid the chaos of the festive season while still keeping on top of each and every detail of what was happening in his various offices across the globe. He might live in England but he was Italian and this bolt-hole in Italy reminded him of his heritage and everything that went with it. He threw money at his PA, told her to do as she wished when it came to entertaining the troops at various office Christmas parties and he disappeared.

'Just a couple more "i"s to dot and a couple more "t"s to cross and it's yours, lad, and we couldn't be happier.'

Intensely private and remote, Matteo felt the twist of something highly emotional swell inside him because this was the one and only deal he had ever done that had real personal significance. His background, his childhood—in a way the very reason he was where he was now—all lay in that land he was on the verge of buying and the halfway house within it. It was a place of retreat for foster kids, an escape where they could feel what it was like to be in the open countryside, with nature all around them. Horses to ride, quiet, secret places to go and just *be,* chickens to feed and eggs to collect. An idyll.

So many years ago, but a fortnight spent there, when he had been just ten and about to go off the rails in a big way, had done something to him, had given him something to hold onto. He had found an anchor in a restless, rudderless existence and had somehow held onto that. Bob and Margaret hadn't been in charge at the time. They had come later, and of course he'd kept that connection to the place to himself, as he kept everything of a personal nature to himself. But with ownership of that special place within his grasp… Yes, he felt strangely emotional.

Shaking Bob's hand as they made plans for their final meeting, Matteo was ill prepared for what happened next.

A scene.

A blonde woman bearing down on them from nowhere. The high pitch of her voice was as piercing as the scrape of fingernails on a blackboard. Heads spun round, mouths opened and closed and there was a flurry of activity as stunned hotel employees and guests alike gasped and wondered what was going on.

For a split second, Matteo was utterly lost for words. Next to him, Bob and Margaret were also stunned into immobility.

'Who do you think you are… Matteo whoever you are…? How *dare* you mess with Rosie? People like you should be strung up! And I guess you're going to run away and leave her all broken-hearted. And I bet you won't even look back. You have no morals at *all*! She's been hurt too many times!'

'Are you talking *to me*?'

'Who else could I be talking to? Is your name Matteo?'

'Yes, but there seems to have been some kind of misunderstanding…'

Matteo, already on the back foot, peered around the tall blonde to see a shorter, plump girl, wearing an expression of dismay, borderline panic and acute embarrassment.

For a few seconds, he was utterly nonplussed. She was staring directly at him and she had the bluest eyes he had ever seen. Her hair was vanilla-blonde, a tangle of unruly curls framing a heart-shaped face that was, just at the moment, suffused with colour. Her mouth was a perfect bow shape and her skin was satiny smooth.

Words failed him. He stared. He registered that she was calling his name and then, somehow taking advantage of that moment of weird disorientation he had experienced at seeing her, he realised she was leading him away from the others with a sharp tug on his arm.

'Please, please, *please*...' Rosie was whispering, simultaneously tiptoeing and tugging him down so that she could whisper into his ear, 'Could you just play along with this for the moment? I'll explain in a bit. I'm really, *really* sorry, but all you have to do is...'

Is what? Matteo thought. Through the confusion of his thoughts, he felt her small, delicate hands clutch at his arm. She was so much smaller than Matteo, his tall form and muscular body towering over her.

'Who the hell are *you*?' Matteo kept his voice low, a whispered conversation that he knew looked a lot more intimate than it was. He was thinking fast but was disconcerted by the softness of her body and the sweet, floral scent of her hair. She was much shorter than him and her reaching up to him somehow emphasised the fullness of her breasts, pushing against her jumper, just brushing against him.

'Rosie. Sorry. Sorry, sorry, sorry. I had no idea my sister would rush down here like a tornado...'

'This isn't what I expected from you, son. You know how traditional I am when it comes to treating other people the way you would want to be treated yourself.' This from behind him—Bob's voice, thick with disappointment.

How the hell did the woman know his name? And who was she anyway? His head was clearing and one thing was certain—the ramifications of what was going on were becoming patently obvious.

No deal.

Lengthy unravelling of this mess was going to take time and time was not on his side. Bob was making noises under his breath, wondering whether he hadn't made a dreadful mistake, while his wife was trying to be the voice of reason. The deal was disappearing into the ether. He had no idea who was the woman imploring his help. His assumption was it was some kind of set-up somehow to extract money from him. He was made of money. Public accusations of some kind? Blackmail? Press somewhere waiting in the wings, cameras at the ready?

His levels of anger bordered on volcanic. Of key importance was to take this scene away from Bob and his wife and sort out the consequences later. Damage limitation was essential. He wanted this deal and he was going to do whatever it took to seal it.

And the only thing he could think of doing right now was to follow the lead of the pink-faced girl still looking at him and play along, much as he didn't want to.

He smiled and Rosie went a shade pinker.

'Rosie,' he murmured, spinning her round and edging

them both back to the group, who had fallen silent during their whispered *tête-à-tête*, including the screeching sister. 'You know we talked about this...'

He looked at Bob and Margaret with a self-deprecating smile and anchored the fiery little blonde closer to him so that she was nestled against his side. 'She's gone off the rails because she thinks I'm going to be one of those fly-by-night guys...' He shook his head, leant down and brushed his mouth against her cheek. 'How can I convince you, my darling, that this isn't just a fling for me?'

Rosie looked at him. Her skin burned where he had brushed it with his mouth. His arm, hooked around her waist, was doing all sorts of things to her body, making her squirm.

In the heat of the moment, she hadn't quite appreciated just how stunning the guy was. Raven-black hair, bronzed skin and eyes as dark as midnight. She knew that she was breathing quickly, just as she knew that she wasn't thinking straight. She was conscious of her femininity in ways she hadn't thought possible.

'Um...'

'This feels like the start of something big, Bob,' Matteo said in a darkly persuasive voice. 'I would have mentioned it to you but I didn't want to jinx it.'

'So romantic,' Margaret was saying with approval.

'Isn't it?' Matteo commented neutrally. He tightened his hand on Rosie's waist and gave her the tiniest of squeezes, nudging her ever closer, thigh against thigh, his arm resting just below her breast now.

Rosie felt the tightening of her nipples. She had no intention of catching her sister's eye but she could feel Candice looking at the pair of them and heaven only knew what was going through her head. Candice was astute but it had to be said that this dark stranger, dragged into a charade not of his making, was doing a fine job of pulling it off and her only question was *why*?

'You should head back to your hotel.' Matteo's primary objective at this point was to put distance between Bob, Margaret and the combustible situation unfolding in front of them. 'Long day tomorrow finalising our deal.'

'You're getting a good man in this one,' Bob said warmly, moving in to shake Rosie's hand. 'Glad everything's sorted, lad. Misunderstandings can get out of control! Nice to see you've got the makings of a family man within you. A good woman is always the making of any man.' He chuckled and gave his wife a hug.

Matteo thought it best to speed things along. He had no idea what was going on but the threat of it all blowing up was a distinct possibility and one he intended to divert with everything at his disposal. He mentally bid a temporary farewell to his Venetian villa that was waiting for him the following evening. It wasn't going to happen.

'So they say,' he murmured as he thought ahead to how he intended to squash whatever machinations were afoot. 'Comprehensively' was the word that sprang to mind.

'Hope we get to spend some time with the two of you before we head back to Yorkshire. Family is everything, like I say, and I wouldn't mind raising a glass or two to celebrate young love.'

Matteo murmured, nodded, half-smiled, brushed his lips against Rosie's hair… He exerted every ounce of charm to smooth over the sudden, alarming pot holes that had surfaced on the very smooth road. He walked them to the glass door, where they were waiting to be met, the little blonde still by his side because question time was about to begin.

Rosie watched with mounting dread as Matteo disposed of her sister with ruthless speed. He was the essence of charm, even though his hand on her waist carried the hint of a threat that sent shivers racing up and down her spine. She could hardly blame him. She listened in mutely as he smoothed over Candice's doubts, laying it on thick until Candice was smiling and telling him how relieved she was that things were back on track, apologising for the fuss and then, somehow, laughingly blaming *Rosie* for having given her the wrong impression.

Rosie couldn't believe the way events had transpired. Who knew that her five-foot-ten, ice-queen sister could let rip with such uncharacteristic drama? Candice was the one who flinched if someone raised their voice slightly too loudly in a restaurant. She moaned about people shouting into their mobile phones in public! She'd once told Emily off, when they had just been kids, for laughing too much.

Candice out of the way, Matteo dropped his hand, stood back and surveyed the blonde coldly.

'So,' he said flatly, 'Let's find somewhere nice and cosy and private and have a little chat, shall we?'

Rosie quailed. The man was sexy, dangerous...and from the expression on his face in the presence of his quarry.

'I'm really sorry, I—I know how this must look...' she stammered, only dimly aware that he was leading her out of the crowded foyer. She found she couldn't quite meet those wintry eyes.

'Do you, now?' Matteo purred.

Where was he taking her? She cast a desperate backward glance behind her, back down to the marbled foyer with the tall Christmas tree. The low buzz of curious voices that had greeted the little scene earlier had died down but there would still be curious eyes looking to see whether it might kick off again.

'Where are we going?'

'Somewhere private,' Matteo murmured, voice as smooth as silk and as razor-sharp as a knife, 'Where we can have our cosy little chat.'

'I've already apologised...' Her legs, however, were obeying his command. She stood up and began walking alongside him, hyper-aware of his presence. There was a leashed power to the guy that made her quiver with a combination of apprehension, downright fear and a weird sort of breathless excitement that stemmed from a place she couldn't quite put her finger on.

He wasn't saying a word and seemed unaware of the cluster of well-heeled people around him that parted to allow him passage as if in the presence of royalty.

It was extraordinary.

She had no idea where they were going but eventually they reached a door which he slid open, standing back to allow her to brush past him.

She'd never been into this particular inner sanctum, even though she had been coming to this very resort with her parents for as long as she could remember, before they'd bought their own chalet just a bit further up the slopes.

It was a large, square room, richly panelled, with a gleaming wooden floor that was largely covered by an expanse of expensive, silk Persian rug. A cluster of deep, comfortable sofas was positioned here and there and a long bar extended along the back of one panelled wall. Rosie assumed this was the chill-out area for the senior management who ran the resort, somewhere where they could relax and unwind, away from the clamour of what might be going on outside.

She stared around her and, when she settled her eyes back on Matteo, it was to find that he had made himself at home and poured a whisky for himself. Needless to say, there was no offer of any form of refreshment for her.

'Okay,' Rosie began. 'I know what you're going to say and I'm sorry.'

'First, you have no idea what I'm going to say, and secondly, if you're sorry now, then you're going to be a whole lot sorrier when I'm through with you and your accomplice.'

'Accomplice?' She gazed at him, bewildered, and then wished she hadn't because he seemed to have the most peculiar effect on her. He made her feel as though the room was beginning to spin and if she didn't sit down fast she would topple to the ground in an undignified heap.

'The blonde with a voice that could shatter glass. Sit.'

A voice that could shatter glass? That was a first when it came to a description of her sister. Of either of her sisters, for that matter. Both were tall, sophisticated and impossibly beautiful in an ice-queen kind of way. Whereas she was… Rosie: short, way too plump because of the siren call of chocolate and all things sweet, with shoulder-length blonde hair that refused to be tamed, breasts far too abundant to be fashionable…

She recalled the heat of his hand so close to her breast and shivered.

Conscious of each and every one of those downsides, and aware of those cool, cool eyes on her, she haltingly headed for the closest chair and dropped into it, little knowing what was coming but all too ready to take the blame.

'If that little scene was some half-baked attempt to screw money out of me then you messed with the wrong guy,' he said flatly. He didn't raise his voice or move a muscle but for all that the single sentence was imbued with threat and Rosie shivered and licked her lips.

'I came here to do a deal that means a great deal to me,' he continued, in the same deathly subdued, almost conversational tone. 'Which is why I played along with whatever game you fancied you'd set in motion. I'm going to play along just until my deal is done, and then, let's just say you'll understand the meaning of regret.'

'You can't threaten me,' Rosie objected weakly. 'And that woman was my sister, not an accomplice!'

'Can't threaten you? No, you've got that wrong, I'm afraid. Here's the thing, whoever the hell you are—whatever scheme you and your sister or whoever she was have concocted, you can bury it, because there's no money at the end of this particular rainbow.'

'Money?'

'Did you really think that you would create a public scene to grab my attention, hurl baseless accusations against me to grab the *public's* attention and then somehow manoeuvre me into a place where I would part with hard cash to shut the pair of you up?'

'I have no idea what you're talking about.'

'Don't play games with me, miss!'

'I'm *not* playing games! I honestly have no idea what you're getting at! Are you saying that you think my sis-

ter and I are out to get money from you? Why would
we want to do that?'

Matteo clicked his tongue with blatant incredulity,
reached into his pocket and extracted a card from his
wallet, which he tossed onto her lap. Then he sat back
and crossed his legs.

'How *rude*!' Rosie exploded, her face bright red. 'Is
this how you treat women? How dare you just…just fling
something at me?'

'Spare me the self-righteous outrage,' he returned
smoothly. 'Why don't you have a look at the card?'

Still fuming, Rosie looked at the card, which had just
a name on it and three telephone numbers. She politely
reached forward to return it.

'I'm sorry but this doesn't mean anything to me. Well,
I guess it's your name. Matteo Moretti.' She sighed. He'd
taken the card back and was obviously waiting for her to
expand. His expression was unreadable and she got the
impression that this was a man who knew how to conceal
what was in his head and that it was something he was
accustomed to doing. He emanated a certain amount of
menace but she wondered whether that hint of menace
wasn't amplified by the fact that she was just so *conscious* of him in a way she had never been conscious of
any man in her life before.

Suddenly very much aware of her physical shortcom-
ings, she fidgeted in the chair and tried to get herself
into a suitably more elevated, commanding position.

'I suppose you're someone important, which is why
you think I should recognise your name, but I don't know
who's who in the world of business. You must be rich,
because you think that I'm some kind of master crimi-
nal who wants your money, but you're wrong.'

'Your sister knew my name,' Matteo said bluntly. 'Care to explain?'

'Her name is Candice.'

'Irrelevant. Just answer my question. Time is money.'

Sinfully good-looking he might be but Rosie was beginning to think that he was the most odious guy she had ever encountered. Rude didn't begin to cover it.

'I teach skiing here,' she said stiffly. 'For the season. I happened to meet your…your friends on the slopes. Pierre was supposed to be giving them a lesson but he went out last night with his girlfriend and he didn't show up for—'

'Get to the point!'

'I'm getting there! Bob and Margaret told me that they were here mixing business with pleasure. They told me your name—Matteo. They said you never left the hotel, then they laughed and said that if they didn't get to grips with skiing then you were to blame because they were too busy feeling guilty about you being cooped up inside to concentrate on getting their feet in the right place. Obviously I didn't know it was *you* at the time, but that's how I happened to know your name. It was just coincidence that you happened to be where you were when…'

When all hell broke loose.

Matteo gritted his teeth. 'How much more tortured can this explanation get? I feel as though I'm being made to sample a vision of hell. Are you ever going to get to the point or do I have to bring the police in to question you?'

'Police? How *dare* you?' She glared at him and he stared back at her without batting an eyelid.

'Just. Get. To. The. Point.'

'Okay, here's the point!' Rosie snapped, leaning forward and gripping the sides of her chair tightly. 'I had to pretend that I had broken up with someone, because I didn't want to be condemned to seeing Bertie over Christmas, and I spotted you down there in the foyer with Bob and Margaret and I... I...figured that you were the businessman called Matteo so I lied and told my sister that I'd been seeing you! Is that enough of an explanation for you? I'm really sorry but you were the fall guy!'

CHAPTER TWO

THEIR EYES MET. Matteo was beginning to feel a little unsteady. He had never before heard such a garbled non-explanation from anyone in response to any question he had ever posed in his life. Her mouth was parted and she was leaning forward, her body language speaking of an urgency for him to believe what she was saying.

The woman was distracting.

It wasn't just the breathless, convoluted workings of her brain which he was finding extraordinarily difficult to deal with. It was *her,* the entire package. The second he had laid eyes on her, something inside him had kick-started and now…staring back into her impossibly turquoise eyes…

He shifted, frowning. There was enough on his plate without losing focus over this nonsense. His eyes roved over her flushed face, subliminally appreciating the satin smoothness of her skin and the juicy fullness of her lips. As he watched, her tongue flicked out, nervously licking her upper lip, and his whole body jack-knifed in sudden, heated response.

A libido which had been dormant for the past six months surged into life with shocking force. He gritted his teeth together but he had to shift position because his erection was rock-hard, pulsing against the zipper of his trousers.

Was she leaning forward like that on purpose? Making sure that those lush, heavy breasts were on tempting show, begging to be fondled?

Matteo had a very particular type of woman. Very tall, very slim and very brunette. He went for the career woman, the woman who challenged him intellectually. He liked the back and forth of informed conversation about politics and the economy. He liked them cool, confident and as driven as he was. He'd fought hard for his place in the world and he appreciated a woman who had battled against the odds as well. An ambitious woman with a career of her own was also not a needy woman, and he disliked needy women. He didn't want anyone needing him. He operated solo and that was the way he liked it.

So why was he staring at this woman in front of him with the rapt attention of a horny teenager? She was breathy and ultra-feminine and didn't strike him as the sort who would be winning awards for her thoughts on world finance. She was the antithesis of what he sought in any woman.

Furious with his lack of self-control, he leapt to his feet to prowl through the room, at the same time finishing the glass of whisky he had poured, tempted to help himself to another but resisting the urge.

He had to remove his eyes from the sexy woman on the chair but, when he finally glanced at her again, it was to find that he was still in the grip of whatever ludicrous spell she had temporarily cast on him.

He positioned himself in front of her and then leant

down, gripping either side of the chair, caging her in so that she instinctively drew back.

Her breathing was fast and shallow, her breasts heaving.

'Not going to work,' he growled.

'What are you talking about?' Rosie whispered. 'I've tried to explain what happened.'

'You expect me to believe that I was just some random target? That you really have no idea as to the reach of my power? And, if that's the case, why are you coming on to me?'

Rosie's mouth fell open and she stared.

'I beg your pardon?'

'Don't think that you're going to get me into any sort of compromising situation! I wasn't born yesterday. That garbled nonsense about dragging me into this situation to avoid a guy—unbelievable.'

'Compromising situation?'

'You're a sexy woman but I'm not a fool.' Matteo gritted his teeth, controlling his hands with extreme difficulty, because what he desperately wanted to do was take what was obviously on offer, starting with those luscious lips and moving on to the even more luscious breasts.

'You're telling me that *I'm sexy*?'

'And advertising it isn't going to work. Where's your sister? Lurking behind the door? Ready to take an incriminating photo, perhaps?' He pushed himself away from the chair but his body was still on fire as he strolled through the room, purposefully maintaining distance between them.

Eventually, he sat down. He was still hard, still turned on.

'I can't believe you'd imagine that I was coming onto

you,' Rosie said faintly. The thought alone was enough to suffuse her with colour.

Her? She was the one who had drawn the short straw when it came to looks. Her sisters had always been the ones to turn heads. She, Rosie, had been the girl the boys enjoyed hanging out with. She self-consciously folded her arms over her breasts and then realised that, in doing so, she had simply drawn attention to them.

She wondered whether that would lead to another crazy accusation that she was trying to come on to him. Her skin prickled. He had called her *sexy* and she didn't think that he'd been kidding.

'And it wasn't garbled nonsense,' she belatedly continued. 'If you'd just listen! My family...' Her voice was staccato with suppressed nerves. 'Well, you've met Candice, my sister. They've been a bit concerned about me...they think I need to settle down, find a job, a life partner...'

'A *life partner*?'

'Yes.' She flushed. Why had she launched into this brutally honest explanation? Why hadn't she skimmed over the details? The way he was looking at her, frowning in silence with his head tilted to one side, was bringing her out in goose bumps. She should have left him puzzled about the nonsensical reason for her behaviour because now she would have to confess that the last thing she was was *sexy*. *Sexy* women didn't have their entire protective family twitching with concern about their life choices.

'How old are you?'

'Twenty-three.'

'Let's suspend disbelief for the moment and go along with your story: why are you supposed to have a *life partner* at the age of twenty-three?'

Matteo realised, with frustration, that the woman was doing it again. Distracting him. He raked his fingers through his hair and reminded himself that this was the woman who had probably scuppered his deal, the one deal that mattered even though he had nothing to gain financially from it.

She looked as pure as the driven snow but he knew better than to trust the way people looked. Scratch the surface and there was usual a healthy store of avarice and general unpleasantness to be found.

She was gazing at him with those incredible aquamarine eyes.

Matteo was beginning to think that she wasn't the Machiavellian character he had first assumed, working in cahoots with a partner in crime. For once, his cynicism might be misplaced. He wasn't going to give up the notion willingly, but...he was getting there.

Nor was he convinced that she had been trying to come on to him, he grudgingly conceded. She was either an actress of Oscar winning standard or her shock at the accusation had been genuine.

He was so accustomed to women making a play for him, that the idea of one actively horrified at the thought of it was as novel as discovering a fish riding a bike in the centre of Hyde Park.

No ulterior motive, which just left her explanation that she had started an ill-thought-out act of impulse to escape some guy's advances.

This time, when he looked at her, it was with lazy interest. He was thirty-two years old but his palate was lamentably jaded. This slice of novelty was strangely compelling.

'Aren't you a little young to be told that you need to

start thinking about settling down?' He shifted, making a concerted effort not to give in to the urge to stare at her fabulous body. 'And, conversely, a little old for your family to be the ones giving the lectures?'

Rosie bristled. 'They care about me. Not that that's any of your business.'

'Everything is my business when, thanks to you, the deal I've been nurturing for the past eight months will probably come to nothing. Whether what you and your sister did was a deliberate ruse or not, the upshot remains the same.'

'Bob and Margaret seem very reasonable people, not the sort to jeopardise whatever agreement you reached with them because of a scene in a hotel lobby.' Rosie flushed as her guilty conscience ate away at her. She couldn't understand why he needed any deal so badly when it was obvious that he was made of money. Her parents were rich but she suspected that this guy was in a different league altogether.

'Bob and Margaret are deeply traditional people,' Matteo informed her coolly. 'Church goers with an extremely healthy respect for the family unit, as you may have gathered. My integrity has been paramount to winning their trust.'

'I'm really and truly sorry. I had no idea that my sister would fly down there and let rip. It's not like her at all. She *never* makes a fuss. She's probably at the chalet right now broadcasting our relationship to the entire family.'

'The chalet?'

'My parents own a chalet about fifteen minutes from here.' She stared off into the distance and wondered what the next step was going to be.

Her gaze slid over to where Matteo was still staring at her, his loose-limbed body relaxed and her heart picked up speed. He was so perfect…so stupendously good-looking.

'You still haven't properly explained what went on down there,' Matteo prompted, his voice clipped. 'Now Cupid has supposedly targeted us, you might as well fill me in on this guy you don't want to meet and why you're having to in the first place. I didn't ask for this but it's landed on my lap and I'm going to have to make the best of it. I'll need some personal details about you.'

Rosie looked at him and then found that she couldn't stop looking and, when she looked, her brain went into overdrive and she started thinking about the way his mouth had felt against her cheek.

'I…well…as I mentioned, my family think it's time for me to start settling down—and please don't tell me that I'm too old to have my sisters and my parents fussing around me. I know that. Fact is, Candice came over to warn me that they were thinking of inviting some family friends to the chalet over Christmas.' She grimaced. 'Bertie is their son.'

'And?' Matteo tilted his head and looked at her with raised eyebrows. 'You don't like him? Ex-lover? Bad break-up? Where are we going with this one?'

'You're very rude, aren't you?' She scowled and then, without warning, he smiled at her and all that sexiness was thrown into such stark focus that she was temporarily shocked into silence.

The harsh beauty of his face was no longer forbidding. All of a sudden, Rosie glimpsed at what true sexiness in a guy was all about and in an instant every boyfriend she had ever had faded into insignificance. She had gone out with silly little boys. The glorious specimen sprawled in front of her was just the opposite. He was all man, an alpha male in the prime of his life. She felt faint.

'No one has ever said that to me before,' Matteo drawled. 'Should I be irritated, bemused or intrigued?'

Rosie squirmed. She wasn't sure how to answer that question or whether he even expected an answer. She felt hot and bothered, as if she was coming down with something.

'My parents think that Bertie and I might be a good match and I guess…' She hesitated. 'I acted without thinking. Candice was sitting across from me, ruining my entire Christmas. I just looked down and spotted Bob and Margaret and the guy they said they'd been doing business with, and I knew that you were all leaving, so I…told my sister that I couldn't possibly face Bertie because I'd been having a fling with you, which hadn't worked out and I was all broken up. It seemed safe. You were going and there was no way I thought she was ever going to…do what she ended up doing.'

Hearing it spoken out loud, Rosie couldn't imagine why she had done what she had. Why hadn't she just stood her ground and refused?

She knew why. Because it had always been her nature to follow the path of least resistance and that had evolved into her just going with the flow.

'I should have just told Candice that if Bertie was going to be on the scene then I would make sure not to be there. I should have had a bit more will power. Instead, I acted on impulse, and I'm sorry.'

'I'm getting the picture of someone who lets her family run her life for her. Am I right?'

'Is there anything I can do to make it up to you?'

'You shouldn't make offers like that,' Matteo murmured. 'A guy could get all the wrong ideas.'

Heat coursed through her body, a slow burn from the inside out. Her breasts ached and her nipples, straining against her bra, felt ultra-sensitive, tingling. She imagined the pads of his fingers rubbing them and her breathing became shallow and laboured. She had no experience when it came to this kind of sophisticated, lazy flirting. If that was even what it was. All she could do was stare at him while her mind continued to play with all sorts of graphic, contraband images.

What on earth was wrong with her?

This guy reeked of danger and yet the pull she felt was overpowering.

'So, now that we're an item, what happens next?'

'I…well…'

'In the thick of this relationship, our hot, two-week clandestine fling, where were we supposed to be meeting? My room at the hotel? Your parents' chalet? Neither of the above? It's a mystery that Bob and Margaret didn't jump in with a string of questions about our so-called affair, bearing in mind most of my time over the past few days has been spent with them working on finishing touches to my deal.'

'How am I supposed to know?' Rosie retorted truthfully. 'I didn't stop to think things through.'

Impulse on that scale was unheard of in Matteo's world and it was strangely refreshing to glimpse a life where variables were given a chance to survive. Not for him, and yet… 'Well, we're going to have to come up with some sort of plausible story or else the whole thing falls apart, and I'm not about to let that happen.'

'Because of this deal you're working on?'

'I just need to get past the finishing line.'

'Why?'

'Come again?'

'Why would a deal mean so much to you that you would go along with this charade instead of just calling me out? I mean, you seem to have enough money...'

'You've lived a life of comfort,' Matteo said coolly. 'From that vantage point, it's easy to come out with platitudes about not needing money or having enough of it. Tell me, have you ever told anyone that the best things in life are free? Take it from me, they seldom are. Now, back to my question—what happens next? Your sister is staying with you. Having witnessed our show of love, presumably she expects nothing less than a formal meeting with the man who's head over heels in love with you?'

Rosie's brain was only just beginning to move on from what he had said about her attitude towards money. She was mortified to realise that he was right. She'd led a charmed life and it was easy to take all that for granted when you knew that it would always be there. For all her free-spirited travelling, she would never have fallen very far, because there would always have been a cushion waiting for her.

'She's probably curious,' Rosie admitted.

'And the over-protective family? Will the grape vine be buzzing with news of our whirlwind romance?'

Rosie shot him a sheepish smile and pushed some tangled blonde curls off her face.

'"Buzzing" might be an understatement,' she confessed.

'But at least the ex-lover won't be on the scene now you're spoken for.' He'd felt it again. A charge of electricity, powerful and disorientating. Primal. She represented everything he steered clear of when it came to women, and yet she was uniquely appealing and he had no idea from where the appeal stemmed.

'Bertie was never an ex,' Rosie was obliged to point out. 'Never even came close! Our families have known each other for ages and, somewhere along the line, he got it into his head that he wanted to ask me out on a date. I was seventeen at the time. I've never fancied him but now he's a big shot in the City somewhere and everyone thinks he could be a suitable match.' She rolled her eyes.

Matteo didn't say anything. His dark eyes were lazy and thoughtful. 'So I'll be meeting the family,' he murmured.

'You don't have to. I could tell them that you've been called away on business. Candice has met you. She'll understand.'

'Why will she understand?'

'Because...' Rosie thought that, for someone as forbidding as he was, it was oddly easy to talk to him. 'Because she has two children now, but before that she was a successful lawyer, so she understands the demands of work. She'll get it if you pay a flying visit and then disappear.'

Rosie frowned and sat forward. 'That would work,' she said slowly. 'If you disappear, then there won't be the complication of your meeting my parents and the rest of the family. That way, I can gradually warn them that the big romance isn't actually going as planned. These things happen,' she thought aloud. 'People meet and think that they've fallen in love but it turns out to be a mistake.'

'And naturally,' Matteo said soothingly, 'That's exactly what will happen but, for the moment, that solution is off the cards.'

'Why?'

'Because my deal hasn't been finalised. Bob and Margaret are here for another week. Skiing, having fun and making sure the last details of my purchase are drawn up and inspected via email by their lawyers in London. Until signatures are on the dotted line, we're in love and thinking of building a future together. Once everything's signed, sealed and delivered, then the hasty unravelling of our relationship can begin.' He gave an elegant shrug which implied that that was the way forward and there was nothing she could do about it, whether she wanted to or not.

'It'll be harder on my parents if they actually meet you face to face.'

'Tough.' Matteo didn't bother beating about the bush. 'I didn't ask for this.'

His dark eyes scoured her face. He could read the tension and anxiety there, and of course she had a point. She clearly came from a tight-knit family unit. The less they were hurt by her behaviour, the better, but as far as he was concerned that was not his problem. Matteo didn't allow sentiment to rule his life. It simply wasn't in his nature. He had managed to remain focused, to stay on course with his life—unlike many of the kids he had grown up with, who had ended up either in jail or six feet under. That said, a life spent in foster care had toughened him. He had known what it meant to have nothing, to be a face and a name in a system and not much more. He had climbed out of that place and forged his way in the world.

That brief spell of respite at the place he was in the process of buying had shown him that there were alternatives in life. He had held onto that vision and it had seen him through.

He had realised that the only way to escape the predictability of becoming one of the victims of the Social Services system was to educate himself and he had applied himself to the task with monumental dedication. By the time he had hit Cambridge University, he had been an intellectual force to contend with.

He'd known more than his tutors. His aptitude for mathematics was prodigious. He'd been head-hunted by a newly formed investment bank and had swiftly risen to the top before breaking free to become something of a shooting star in the financial firmament. Money had given him the opportunity to diversify. It had allowed him to get whatever he wanted at the snap of a finger. Money had been his passport to freedom and freedom had been his only goal for his entire adult life.

Money had also jaded his palate, made life predictable. Being able to have whatever and whomever you wanted, he had reflected time and again, did not necessarily guarantee excitement.

He hadn't had a woman in months and he hadn't been tempted.

Now here he was and, in that instant, Matteo decided that he was going to go with the flow and make the best of the situation into which he had been catapulted. Moreover, he was going to enjoy the experience.

'I have a suite here, at this hotel,' he mused. 'Bob and Margaret are at another location, further down the slopes. If I'm the new man in your life, then I'll be expected to be at your parents' chalet with you, I presume?'

'Wait. What? Now, hang on just a minute…'

'It's hardly likely that we're in the thick of a stormy, passionate affair and I'm bedding down on my own in a hotel room while you're miles away in a chalet somewhere with nothing but the telly and a good book for company. Is it?'

'Well, no. but…'

'But?'

'But this isn't a normal situation, is it? I mean, we're not actually involved with one another, are we?'

'You need to follow the plot line here,' Matteo imparted kindly. 'There will be people we will need to convince and no one, not even traditional and church-going Bob and Margaret, will be persuaded that this is the affair of a lifetime if we're crossing paths off and on.'

'Stop being patronising,' Rosie said absently. What did he mean by being at the chalet with her? Sharing a bedroom? She paled at the thought because suddenly her little white lie had taken on a life of its own and was galloping away at speed.

Matteo burst out laughing and she focused on his handsome face and glared.

'I hadn't banked on this,' she said tightly. 'You may find the whole thing hilarious but I don't.'

'I don't find anything hilarious about this situation,' Matteo shot back and, she thought for the millionth time, there was no need for him to remind her that she had brought this mess on herself. 'But here we are. I'm going to move into your parents' chalet today.'

'Candice will know that you haven't been living with me,' Rosie pointed out.

'How?'

'There would be signs of us sharing a bedroom. You would have left stuff behind. Clothes on the backs of chairs. Shaving foam. Bedroom slippers. Aftershave...'

His eyebrows shot up, his expression halting her in mid-flow.

'I have never spent a night in any woman's house and, if I had, I certainly wouldn't have left anything behind.'

Rosie's mouth fell open and she gaped at him. 'You've *never* stayed at a woman's overnight?' He was so arrogant, so beautiful, so sophisticated—she found it impossible to credit that he had never spent the night with a woman.

What woman, she guiltily thought, would let him out of her bed? It was an inappropriate thought but it lodged in her head, pounding with the steady force of a drum beat.

Matteo made a dismissive gesture with his hand that was both elegant and strangely exotic and she watched him from under lowered lashes, fascinated and mesmerised by the strong, proud lines of his handsome face.

'I'm a normal, red-blooded man with a healthy libido,' Matteo told her wryly. 'I work hard and I play hard, but I don't do love, and I never encourage a woman to think, even for a second, that I might.'

'And if you spent a night with a woman...it would mean that you're interested in more than just *sex*?'

'Forget about me,' Matteo drawled. 'The danger would lie in *her* believing that there might be more to it than sex.'

'And yet you're okay with spending time in the chalet with me?'

'Oh, but you're not my woman,' Matteo purred silkily. 'And this isn't about sex. This is a little pretend game that'll be over just as soon as I get what I'm after…'

CHAPTER THREE

ROSIE THOUGHT THAT it was one thing to produce Matteo as a boyfriend, like a magician pulling a rabbit from a hat then yanking him off stage before anyone had time to suss that it was all sleight of hand. It was something else to hold him up to scrutiny, which was what she would be doing by having him in the chalet with her. He would be spun around for inspection, asked questions, quizzed about his intentions. How was she going to deal with all that without cracking? How was *he*?

Her sisters, in particular, had all made it their mission to make Rosie keep them posted on her love life and she had always obliged. They had met a couple of her fleeting boyfriends and had not held back from making their opinions known, politely but firmly. She was so much younger than them and they had never really stopped treating her like the baby of the family.

Hence, Rosie thought with uncharacteristic bitterness, the reason why she was where she was now.

She had bolted from the prospect of having their idea of a suitable partner presented to her instead of standing her ground—but why on earth had it occurred to them that they could actually match her up with someone of their choosing in the first place?

This time, she was going to deal with the situation calmly. If there were too many questions, she would just stop answering. If the quizzing from Candice and Emily went too far, she would tell them to back off.

Matteo was a perfect stranger, but some of his remarks had been a little too perceptive for comfort. They had made her see herself in a different and more critical light than she had ever done before.

She wasn't silly and she didn't feel entitled but she *was* a trust-fund baby in the truest sense of the word and she had felt embarrassed to acknowledge the fact.

'You're going to be held up to the spotlight,' she warned. 'Five minutes with Candice is quite different to several days with my entire family.'

'I can take the heat,' Matteo drawled. 'Can you?'

Rosie looked at him steadily. 'I know what you think of me,' she said, matching him for self-composure and liking the way she felt empowered by it. 'That I live off my parents, and float from one thing to the next and allow my entire family to have a say in my life, but this time round I am definitely going to take the heat.' She grinned suddenly. 'They'll be shocked.'

'Good,' Matteo murmured approvingly. 'Sometimes it's worthwhile to shock.'

'I just have one condition.'

'I'm all ears,' Matteo said wryly.

'I'm the one to do the breaking up.'

Matteo looked at her, at a loss for a suitable response.

'I can tell from your stunned expression that no one's ever broken up with you before, am I right? None of those women you refuse to spend the night with, just in case they get ideas, has ever broken up with you…?'

'Fate has smiled on me in that respect.'

'Well,' Rosie countered drily, 'Either smiled on you or else made you incredibly arrogant.'

Matteo grinned and then he burst out laughing. 'You're the most unexpected woman I've ever met,' he murmured. His eyes were lazy and shuttered and feathered over her like a caress. 'I've never met anyone as honest and outspoken. You contradict your background. So…you want to break up with me. I don't see why not. Maybe it's high time I suffered from a broken heart, and it works for you, doesn't it?'

Rosie nodded slowly. 'I'm tired of my family feeling ever so slightly sorry for me.'

'So you dump the eligible guy and you instantly gain their respect. Well, we'll have to make sure that I'm the very besotted boyfriend, won't we? Now, why don't I check out of my suite here and we can both go to your chalet and begin this game…?'

His suite was breath-taking. Huge, with several rooms, including an open-plan kitchen, fully equipped but, she imagined, seldom used.

'You want this to be a convincing act?' he had put to her as they had emerged from the private room where they had been ensconced for ages. 'You come with me to my suite while I pack my things. Then we check out together. I was here on business when we met. Now that your family are coming over, it's only natural I shift base so that we can be together and meet them as a couple.'

Rosie looked at him as he efficiently gathered his belongings. While he packed, he conducted a series of calls in Italian, phone to his ear as he wandered from bedroom to living area, from bathroom to office, picking things up and tossing them in a case he had dumped on the glass table in the living area.

She got the feeling that he had forgotten about her completely.

'I don't know anything about you,' was the first thing she said when he was finally off the phone and the last of his things had been flung into the suitcase.

Here, in his suite, nerves assailed her. There was something so sleek and so innately *dangerous* about him that she found it impossible to think that they could convince her very perceptive and inquisitive family that they were really an item. Up close and personal, the force of his personality was more powerful, not less. She'd told herself that she wasn't going to be browbeaten by their curiosity and their questions, but how on earth were they going to believe that she, Rosie, bubbly, extrovert and carefree, had lost her heart to someone like Matteo?

Add to that the fact that he really was a stranger and the uphill task of convincing *anyone* seemed insurmountable.

In the act of zipping his suitcase, Matteo paused and looked at her for a few seconds.

She hadn't moved from her position by the door. She looked nervous and he marvelled that a lifetime of privilege—which had clearly been her background, judging from what she had told him—had managed to leave her unscathed. He hadn't been kidding when he had told her that she was unexpected. He met a lot of privileged people. Young and old, and even the most charming—they all had a very similar veneer of confidence borne from the assumption that the world was theirs for the asking. They all spoke loudly and with booming confidence.

Most drew distinct lines between the people who served them and the people on their own level.

Rosie was as skittish as a kitten, open, guileless and honest to a fault, and that surprised and charmed him.

Now, looking at her, Matteo wondered whether he hadn't agreed to this charade because a part of him found her intriguing.

Rosie took a few hesitant steps forward and peered at the half-shut suitcase.

'You haven't brought any ski wear? Or have you stored it somewhere else?'

Matteo strolled to the small kitchen and withdrew a bottle of water from the fridge, which he held out to her. When she declined, he unscrewed the cap and drank.

'I don't ski,' he admitted. He dumped the empty bottle on the counter and hesitated momentarily, then he moved to the sofa and sat down, watching as she followed suit to sit facing him. 'And stop looking so nervous. I'm not going to pounce on you.'

'I know you're not.' She stifled a wave of nerves brought on by him telling her to stop looking nervous. 'We're not in public now. You know a lot about me, but I don't know anything about you, and I'm going to have to if our story is going to be credible. I'm surprised you don't ski,' she admitted.

'There's a time for learning to ski,' Matteo said wryly. 'It's fair to say I missed the slot.'

'Those obligatory school trips to the slopes can be a bore,' Rosie reminisced. 'I guess I'm lucky my parents were crazy about skiing. I can remember staring down fields of snow with little skis on when I was about three.' She laughed, throwing her head back, catching some of her hair in her hand and twisting it into a pony tail before releasing it.

Matteo smiled. 'Tell me more about your family. Your sister is married with two children and was a lawyer before she settled on motherhood...'

Rosie was transfixed by that smile. It was so genuinely curious that she felt her nerves begin to abate. She told him about Emily, sister number two and a chartered surveyor. Also married. Pregnant with her first. She chatted about her parents. Her mother had been a lecturer and her father a high-ranking diplomat before they'd retired three years ago.

'And they didn't approve of past boyfriends,' he encouraged. 'Hence Bertie...'

Rosie grimaced. 'Hence Bertie. Not at all my type.'

'No? And what is your type, Rosie?'

Rosie opened her mouth to recite what she had always taken for granted—that she, free-spirited unlike her sisters, was attracted to other free spirited souls, unlike her brothers-in-law. Except, was she really?

He saved her from having to stumble through an answer by saying gently, 'You're very lucky. Riding lessons...skiing holidays from the age of three...house in the country and *pied à terre* in London. I'm guessing you dated guys your family didn't approve of as a form of quiet rebellion.'

'That's not true,' she countered but she could feel his observations too close to the bone. 'I've always been adventurous,' she concluded unconvincingly.

Matteo shrugged, ready to let it go and surprised that he had been lured into psychoanalysing her when he rarely felt inclined to plumb the depths of any woman.

'You wanted to know about me,' he said indifferently. 'Think of an upbringing as far from yours as it is possible to be.'

Rosie frowned. When she looked around her, all she could see was the trappings of wealth. He was clearly far, far richer than her parents or indeed anyone that she had ever known. He was in a league of his own and she didn't understand where he was going with that enigmatic remark.

He was sophisticated, polished and, if there was something of the street fighter about him, then she presumed that the richer you were the more ruthless you had to be.

'Did you grow up here? In Italy? I heard you on the phone, speaking in Italian...'

'I was born here but my parents went to England in search of a better life when I was a baby.' Matteo paused, uncomfortable with sharing details of his past but knowing that she was entitled to information up to a point. 'There was nothing for them here in Italy and they were young and hopeful. Unfortunately, life did not quite work out the way they planned. My mother contracted a virus shortly after they arrived in England, and was taken into hospital, but by the time they diagnosed meningitis it was too late.'

Rosie covered her mouth with her hand and stared at him. There was a remoteness about his features that mirrored the cool briskness of his voice. He was stating facts with all emotion removed from the recital. More than anything, she felt her heart twist at that. It was a defence mechanism to protect himself from the pain of losing a parent at such a young age. That was something she felt instinctively, just as she also knew instinctively that this proud, arrogant man would not appreciate her sharing her thoughts with him.

In that moment, he was so very human that she wanted to reach out and touch him. She sat on her hands just in case they decided to disobey the warning bells in her head telling her to avoid any such spontaneous show of affection.

'I'm so sorry, Matteo,' she contented herself by saying and he lowered his eyes, thick lashes brushing his aristocratic cheekbones, before he looked at her once again, fully composed.

'Don't be. It's history.'

'And where is your father now?' she asked. 'Does he live over here? He must have been devastated at the time. Did he return to Italy?'

'My father died when I was four and I was taken into foster care. No, he did not return to Italy. I have maintained my links, however. I have a villa on the outskirts of Venice and at the moment I'm in the process of expanding my operations to Naples. Hence my conference call earlier.'

'Foster care?'

'It's of no importance.' He stood up and glanced around, making sure that he was leaving nothing behind.

Rosie thought differently. It was of monumental importance and it gave her valuable insight into this forbidding stranger now phoning down for a porter to come and collect his belongings.

He was so cold, she thought, so contained, and there was a very good reason for that.

He was walking towards the door and she shot to her feet and hurried behind him. Instead of opening the door, however, he stared down at her, his dark eyes shuttered.

'The only reason I've told you what I have,' he stated, 'Is because you have a point. Relationships aren't built on two people knowing absolutely nothing about one another, and this has to be a credible relationship until all the paperwork is done on the deal I'm working on with Bob and Margaret.'

'You haven't told me why it's so important.'

'Nor will I. And I should tell you that you should save the questions if any of them involve further delving into my past. I've given you sufficient information for us to pull this charade off. The confidences end there. The fact is we are not in a relationship. This is a temporary and fictitious arrangement and all we need to establish is a sufficiently credible basis from which we can answer the most straightforward questions.' He opened the door and they walked in silence to the lift, then rode down to the busy foyer.

All the while, thoughts were buzzing around in her head like wasps. He had opened a door and, having peered in, she wanted to have another look.

As soon as they were back in the public domain, he slung his arm over her shoulders, only breaking apart to sign himself out.

There was a background hum of Christmas carols being played which followed them out of the hotel onto the snow-covered slopes.

Rosie had been to many ski resorts with her family over the years but they had fallen in love with this one and had made it their annual destination. The ski resort was situated in the heart of the Southern Alps in the Veneto region of Northern Italy. From here, Venice was a couple of hours away, and she figured that Matteo had probably arranged for his clients to come to this particular resort because it had suited him. He couldn't have picked a more beautiful spot for the uninitiated.

The mountainous, pink and orange backdrop of the Dolomites was picture-postcard perfect, soaring up, commanding the valley and everything nestled inside it. The vista never failed to impress and Rosie stopped and stared at the sight.

'You don't know what you're missing.' She turned to him impulsively.

'Meaning?'

'You should learn to ski. I could teach you.' She laughed at the horror etched on Matteo's lean face and slowly he grinned.

'You don't give up, do you?' he murmured, staring out at the panoramic view with her. Out here, everything was shrouded in silence, and the hue from the rising mountains was quite special. He had always used his Venetian villa as a bolthole. It had never occurred to him that this glorious place existed. But then again, he didn't ski, so why would it have?

He gazed back down to her upturned face. She had dimples when she smiled. She had stuffed a woolly hat on her head and her tangled white-blonde curls trailed in disarray from under it. Wrapped up in countless layers, her small, curvaceous body was tempting beyond endurance and Matteo spun around on his heels, indicating that they should make for her car now.

'What do you mean?' Rosie tripped alongside him, keeping some distance but feeling the impact of his presence slamming into her at every step.

'I mean, others would have tactfully retreated once I warned them off trying to get to know me.'

'That's very egotistical of you.' She swerved into the hotel car park, heading towards the four-wheel-drive car that was kept on permanent standby, as the villa was used by the family out of season as well.

'Egotistical?'

'I don't want to get to know you,' Rosie lied, beeping open the doors and hoisting herself into the driver's seat. She waited until he was sitting in the passenger seat before turning to him. In the late-evening light he was all shadows and angles, and he sent a shiver of fierce excitement racing down her spine. 'I just thought that, if we're going to be stuck with one another for days on end, it might give us something to do aside from arguing, and anyway, it's a shame to be here and not try your hand at it.'

She started the engine and the car shuddered into life.

'I've never had any woman tell me that she has to think of things to do if she's going to be stuck with me,' Matteo said, amused in spite of himself. 'Sure you know how to handle this thing in snowy terrain?'

'The road to the chalet is clear and gritted, Matteo, so there's no need to be nervous—and of course I know how to handle it.' She glanced across at him. 'Don't tell me that you think women can't drive as good as men?'

'Can they, though?'

Rosie heard the lazy teasing in his voice and she burst out laughing.

Her heart skipped a beat. A thread of something beyond excitement suddenly sparked and sizzled in her veins.

'Probably better.' She was focused one hundred percent on the road ahead of her, taking it very slowly, but she didn't want to lose the moment. She liked this. 'Are you scared of giving it a go? The skiing, I mean?'

'Terrified,' Matteo drawled.

'I'll make sure you're all right.'

'Will you, now? That's an offer that's almost too good to pass up.'

They were nearing the chalet—a left-hand turn off the main road and then just a short drive to the warmth of the ski lodge. The drive was short but hazardous, but the car was equipped for all conditions and handled the steep climb to the chalet with aplomb. Ahead, the bright lights were welcoming.

Candice was waiting for them, dressed to go out but making sure she stayed put to ask questions. Having shaken off the snow, hung various jackets and coats and dumped shoes and boots and all the other paraphernalia, Rosie faced her elegant, glamorous sister with a strength of purpose she had never really experienced before.

From behind, she was aware of Matteo approaching, but the touch of his hand on her waist, curving to rest just under her breasts, still made her flush. She hesitantly slipped her arm around him to complete the picture she knew he was striving to convey. The pressure of his palm on her rib cage and the crazy tingling of her nipples in heated response fogged up her brain and she knew that she was beetroot-red.

She wanted to moan and chewed down on her lip in horror, especially when he lazily circled his fingers on the woolly jumper, applying just the right amount of pressure.

She had whipped off the woolly hat and in a matter of a few heart-stopping seconds he sifted his fingers into her hair and tilted her chin so that she was gazing up at him. Then he lowered his mouth to graze over hers... and all those things she had read about in magazines suddenly made complete sense. Lust…desire…whatever you wanted to call it…

She had had one serious relationship that had, in retrospect, been nothing more than the optimism of youth to be loved and a need to be rescued from her abortive university career. It had lasted a matter of months and had certainly not prepared her for the high-voltage charge of craving that shot through her body when his lips met hers. Nothing she had ever experienced had. Confusion tore into her, darkening her eyes, sending a slight tremble through her body.

Her vocal cords seemed to have dried up, but it didn't matter, because Candice was smiling and Matteo had eased into charismatic gear and was saying all the right things, asking all the right questions, giving her cool, contained sister little chance of asking questions back.

'I'd really love to hear about the two of you and how you met.' She glanced at her watch, while from the sidelines Rosie breathed a sigh of relief. 'But I'm going to catch up with some friends I haven't seen for ages. Before the family descend tomorrow evening. By the way, they can't wait to meet you. Hope you don't mind but I couldn't help but share the news with everyone—and get them to hold off on trying to set you up with Bertie.'

'Actually,' Rosie heard herself say, 'I do mind, Diss. It was my place to tell them that Matteo and I are…er… going out.'

'Yes, I suppose so but…' Bright colour poured into Candice's cheeks. For the first time in living memory, she was discomfited by her much younger sister, and Rosie realised that this was what she should have been doing all along. Taking control of her life and owning her decisions.

'It's done now,' she said quietly. 'It doesn't matter.' Oddly, Matteo's hand cupping the nape of her neck gave her a certain amount of strength.

'I do apologise, Rosie. I was just so excited that you'd actually met someone...'

Candice shifted, aware that she was treading in unchartered waters, accustomed as she was to compliance from her younger sister.

'Socially acceptable?' Matteo interjected coolly. He tightened his hold on Rosie and she leant against him, loving the strength he imparted. He was as solid as a rock.

'That's not quite what I meant.' Candice reddened.

'My track record hasn't been great,' Rosie said appeasingly.

Candice gave her a bright, relieved smile and moved towards her for a quick hug before standing back and looking at them both with her head to one side.

'You two make a fantastic couple,' she said. 'I was quite prepared to thump you when Rosie told me that you'd let her down. I can't tell you how happy I am for the both of you that whatever misunderstanding you had has been sorted. I can just tell that you're meant for one another.' She winked at her sister.

'Hang on, Candice,' Rosie interjected, horrified and embarrassed that 'holiday fling' was morphing into 'marriage on the cards'. 'We've really only just met! We're still getting to know one another.'

Candice was laughing, heading for the door. 'That's how all relationships begin, Rosie! Anyway, don't wait up for me, guys. That car could pull a sled in an avalanche, but if I feel too tired to head back then I'll just stay over with Mick and Carol. They've already invited me and they've got oodles of room. I'll text and let you know.'

With which she left in a flurry of air kisses, slamming the door behind her, leaving Rosie alone with Matteo.

'So...' He looked around him. 'Nice place, Rosie.' It was open-plan, big but not huge, and with all the clutter of hectic family life left behind from one holiday to the other—well-thumbed books, games, toys and all sorts of bits and pieces collected over the years. The floors were deep, rich wood and there was a clutter of artwork on the walls, pictures done by Rosie and her sisters. In the sitting area, colourful throws were tossed onto the deep, comfortable sofas, and in the corner the television was rumbling on, volume low, because Candice had forgotten to switch it off.

Looking around her, Rosie saw the place through his eyes. It was the essence of upper-middle-class comfort.

'Can I ask you something?' She waited until he had turned full circle to look at her.

'Ask away.'

'I know you said you didn't want me prying into your private life...'

Matteo realised that her prying was a lot less objectionable than expected. He wondered whether that was because, for the first time in his life, he had opened up about his past with another human being. Of course, he had had very little choice, given the situation, and none of it mattered anyway, because they would be parting company before Santa dropped down the chimney with his sack of goodies, but it was still a little unnerving.

He wasn't the confiding sort and he grimly told himself that he wasn't going to change any time soon. A leopard never changed its spots and his reticence was solidly ingrained. He had always lived his life with the assumption that, when it came to other people and his private life, information was purely on a need-to-know basis.

Like now, was what sprang to mind.

'Then don't,' he informed her silkily.

'I was just curious to find out how you…ended up where you did.'

'Rich and powerful?' He sat on one of the squashy sofas, which was a lot more comfortable than the pale leather ones in his place in London. He thought of that halfway house and the boisterous fun he had had there all those years ago. He'd never thought he would ever laugh again after he'd been put into foster care, but he had. The place had been designed to broaden the horizons of the underprivileged kids who went there and it had worked, at least for him.

'There's that modesty of yours again,' Rosie teased lightly, but her curiosity was getting the better of her fast and she joined him on the sofa, opposite end, but close enough to hear every word he was saying.

'When you're a kid in care, you have to make an effort not to slide down to the lowest common denominator,' Matteo told her conversationally. 'No one has any dreams for you. You have to make sure you have dreams for yourself or you sink to the bottom fast. I was lucky. I was bright. I learned the value of education.' He shrugged. 'I studied. I never skipped class. I set my sights on the only thing that mattered.'

'What was that?'

'Freedom. When you grow up without any advantages, money is the only thing that buys freedom, and by the age of eighteen I'd come to the conclusion that I would just have to make money and a lot of it. I was gifted at maths and got into Cambridge University. Got a first-class degree and was lucky enough to get taken on by a burgeoning investment bank. By twenty-five I'd made my first million. The bonuses were insane, but that life didn't suit me. I don't like taking orders or working for other people. So I jacked it in and began scouting around for companies to buy. Small IT companies, mainly. That's the long and short of it. Rags to riches.'

'Your opinion of me must be very low.' She thought of her cosseted background, the trust fund that kept her going, the university career she had jettisoned because she had been bored stiff.

Matteo looked at her. She had such a transparent face. Yes, he really should have a low opinion of her, but there was something about her…

'You're not the sort of woman I would normally be drawn to,' he was forced to concede.

She raised aquamarine eyes to his, and his jaw tightened, because she was hurt.

'That's not meant to be an insult, Rosie,' he said roughly.

'I know that. It's the truth. What sort of women *are* you drawn to, just out of interest?'

'Career women,' he admitted.

'Of course.'

'We're poles apart,' he reminded her. 'I'm sure you wouldn't, under normal circumstances, go for someone like me.'

'Definitely not.' Rosie tilted her chin at a mutinous angle, pride coming to her rescue, because it cut to the quick that, whether he found her sexy or not—and she hated herself for dwelling on that stupid, throwaway compliment—he would never have given her the time of day if he hadn't been dumped into playing out this charade. 'I'm just shocked at how easily Candice fell for the charade,' she mused truthfully.

'People believe what they want to believe,' Matteo said with a shrug. 'Human nature. Your family want what they think is best for you and someone rich, powerful and wearing a suit fits the narrative.' He looked at her. 'And here's another reason why no one will question this too deeply...'

Matteo looked at her flushed, pretty face ,but then his eyes drifted down to the tightness of her jumper straining over full breasts and the curve of her hips.

The atmosphere shifted. He could feel it and he knew that she would as well. He was just looking, he thought, because he wasn't going to encourage any further complication to an already complicated and annoying situation. He was going to be sticking around for a handful of days and then he would be off, leaving her to assert her independence and damn him for the bastard he really wasn't at all.

'What's that?' Rosie asked breathlessly.

'The most obvious reason of all. Opposites attract...'

CHAPTER FOUR

ROSIE COULD ONLY concede the truth behind that statement. Matteo was sinfully good-looking but he wasn't her type. Take away the dark good looks and the perfectly honed, intensely masculine physique, and what you had was your basic businessman, the sort of guy to appeal to her entire family but not to her.

It was true that she had never met any businessman quite in this one's league but he was still nothing like the free-spirited adventurers towards whom she always gravitated. She shouldn't be attracted to him at all but she was.

But then, he wasn't exactly Mr Typical Business Tycoon, was he?

That background in foster care...

Not exactly your run-of-the mill CEO...

And those cool, cool eyes...seeing everything and revealing nothing...also not typical.

And that thread-like scar...where had that come from? Surely not filling out profit and loss columns with his fountain pen?

'She took it for granted, your sister,' Matteo said conversationally. 'That it was okay to break the news about us in a group family chat without asking whether you might have preferred to do the news-breaking yourself. That par for the course? Because, if it is, then you did well to put her in her place.' He settled his gaze on her.

'I know,' Rosie said simply. She didn't add that his presence had given her backbone. 'The problem is that Candice wouldn't have relayed the information the way I would have.'

'Explain.'

'You heard her. She thinks this is some great romance and that's what she would have told everyone. I would have been a little more realistic. I would have prepared them for the fact that there was a chance this wasn't going to work out. It feels as though things are getting more and more difficult to control.'

'That's the problem when a lie begins to spiral out of control.'

She was hovering.

Things had taken an unexpected turn and he could see that she was uncomfortable with the situation. Her edginess was apparent in the way her gaze was flicking towards him, then flicking away...in the way her whole body seemed alive with restlessness even though she wasn't actually moving around. Underneath the feisty, open exterior, real apprehension was creeping in. The consequences of that little white lie were dawning on her.

'It's also the problem with acting on impulse but, if you think you've been inconvenienced, then I should tell you that the last thing I'd banked on doing was remaining here for longer than strictly necessary.'

'I'm sure you have commitments. It's Christmas.'

'I don't do Christmas. The only reason I'm here at this time of year was because of the timing on this deal.

My only commitment was to retreat to my villa outside Venice and escape the madness.'

'Escape? *Escape?*' Distracted, she angled her bright, blue-eyed gaze in his direction.

'Don't look so bewildered.' Matteo's eyebrows winged up. 'Not everyone is in love with the festive season.'

'You have no family...' Rosie said slowly.

'Don't go there,' Matteo told her, voice dropping by several degrees.

Rosie frowned. 'It must be a lonely time of year for you,' she said simply and Matteo vaulted to his feet and frustratedly raked hands through his hair.

'What is it about *stay out of my private life* that you don't get?'

Rosie didn't apologise. Her mind was busy with images of him in foster care. He had given her a sketchy description of what it had been like but she knew that it probably would have been far more soul-destroying. He had expressly set up No Trespass signs and he had made it clear that the only reason he had said anything at all was because he'd felt it necessary.

Except...her heart went out to him. She knew that she was going where no doubt angels feared to tread, but there was a generosity of spirit inside her that found it difficult to leave the subject alone.

'Everyone needs to talk to somebody about the distressing things that happen in their lives.'

'I don't believe I'm hearing this! I don't think you quite understood...'

'You don't want to talk about it.' She shrugged but her clear blue eyes were stubbornly fixed on his face as he towered over her, looking down, expression forbidding.

'No,' Matteo said with angry force. 'I don't.'

'Which says a lot.'

Matteo leant over her, hands on either side of her, depressing the soft sofa cushions and caging her in. His face was dark with enraged incredulity that someone had dared cross the boundary lines he had laid down. Did the woman have *no* limits when it came to saying what was on her mind? Matteo was accustomed to people editing their behaviour around him. Her lack of interest in following those rules left him practically speechless. From the second she had appeared in his life, normal rules of behaviour had been suspended.

'Don't make me regret having told you what I did.'

'Why would you regret it?'

'Are you hearing a word I'm saying?'

She held his outraged stare. 'You're accustomed to everyone doing what you tell them to do, aren't you?'

Matteo stood up but remained standing in front of her. 'Yes, I am!'

'Okay. You win! I won't ask and you don't have to tell me anything. Would you like something to eat? Drink?' She stood up and swerved around him, heading to the kitchen and straight to the fridge to peer inside.

As always it was crammed with food. A lot of optimistically healthy options that were probably past their sell-by date. She had been staying at the chalet since the season had begun and she was an impulse shopper. Things in attractive jars always held so much promise but often it was the easiest way she ended up taking.

He was still scowling when she looked at him quizzically. 'Well?' she snapped. 'You don't want to talk to me about anything of any importance, so we can talk about food options instead. I know you'll think it's safer. What do you want? I can make you something.'

Matteo wasn't into women cooking for him. In fact, he actively discouraged it, just as he always made sure that a night of pleasure never turned into breakfast together the following morning.

'I usually just eat stuff that comes out of boxes or cans but I don't suppose you do.'

'I don't,' Matteo said flatly. He paused. 'You ask a lot of questions.'

'So do you.' Her azure eyes were innocent and her voice was sincere because she meant it.

'Show me the rest of your house.'

Rosie shook herself back to earth, hesitating and on the cusp of barrelling past his Keep Out sign but reluctantly accepting that, if he wasn't into sharing, then he wasn't into sharing. They meant nothing to one another and she would have to put her curiosity to bed because it wasn't going to get her anywhere.

She gave a perfunctory tour: open-plan living area with a huge, modern fireplace and lots of comfy chairs, perfect for settling in for the long haul—just her, a book and the fall of silent snow outside. The kitchen, which was the hub of the house, and a study in which her father occasionally worked, although now that he had retired those instances were few and far between. He had forgone offers of consultancy jobs and opted for quality time with his family instead.

Wooden stairs led to the floor above: six bedrooms all leading onto a broad landing that overlooked the space below. Next to her, Matteo's silence was oppressive, and she wondered what was going through his head.

She found out soon enough.

'So where is our bedroom?'

About to head back downstairs, head still buzzing with unanswered questions, Rosie spun around on her heels and stared at him with consternation.

'You can choose which bedroom you'd like,' she told him politely. 'Mine…' she nodded in the direction of the bedroom at the end of the long, broad landing '…is down there.'

'Well, I suppose that's where I'll be dumping my bags.'

He headed down at pace towards her bedroom and, as he flung open the door, she was right behind him.

She'd waved an arm to indicate the bedroom floor, only opening the first door and standing back while he'd looked inside like a prospective buyer doing a tour of a house. Now, with him standing in her bedroom, her personal space, she felt invaded. She was on show here, with all the little pieces of her childhood for him to see. A framed photo of her on her first horse, with her dad proudly standing next to her. The ridiculous chair in the shape of a big, pink heart which had been her favourite when she'd been about eight, and which her parents had stashed away in their attic, shipping it over when they'd bought the chalet years before. Pictures of her family over the years.

'You're not staying in *my* bedroom,' She folded her arms and watched, tight-lipped, as he strolled through the bedroom, peering at this and that and ignoring her. He had dumped his bag on the ground like a declaration of intent that sent a chill of forbidden excitement racing up and down her spine.

He commanded the space around him. He was so tall…so muscular…so *there*.

'Oh.' He spun round and stared right back at her. 'This is exactly where I'll be staying.' As if to confirm what he'd said, he picked up the designer bag and flung it on the mattress of her four-poster bed.

It landed with a soft *thud* and then sat there, challenging her to remove it.

'But…'

'No *buts.* You got me into this mess and, now I'm in it, for better or for worse you're just going to have to suffer the consequences. We're supposed to be an item. Hot off the press, so to speak. Your sister is going to be extremely suspicious if she thinks that we're not sharing a bedroom. Particularly given the fact that she probably assumes that you've been sharing my suite at the hotel while we've been conducting our torrid affair.' He glanced at his watch then back to her, where she had remained hovering at the doorway to her own bedroom, almost as though, having asserted his authority, *she* was now the guest in her own space.

'I can tell her that we're in separate rooms here out of respect for Mum and Dad.'

'That's ridiculous.'

'You don't know my parents!'

'Are you telling me that you would be exiled to the Arctic wastes if they discovered that we were sleeping together?' He pinned his eyes to her reddening face. 'Right. Enough said on the subject.'

Rosie's face was a picture of dawning dismay. Their love-at-first-sight scenario invited enough questions without those questions reaching fever pitch because they were in separate bedrooms, like a Victorian couple.

'Now,' Matteo declared, jettisoning the subject as if suddenly bored with the whole thing, 'I would come down and have something out of a box or a can with you, but right now I want a shower, and I have a stack of emails to get through, so I'll have to forfeit the feast.'

He reached for the button on his trousers and Rosie stared open-mouthed for a few seconds before gathering her wits.

'I hadn't banked on this,' she said tightly and he stared at her with disbelieving eyes.

'And I hadn't banked on it either,' he informed her coolly. 'Right about now, I should have been getting in touch with my housekeeper and readying her for my arrival. Instead...'

Instead, she mentally filled in, *here you are, sharing a room with a woman you don't know, who keeps getting on your nerves with her constant questions, caught up in a crazy game of make-believe.*

'If you're sure you're not hungry...' she muttered, inching a couple of steps back, eyes still fixed on him. She didn't want to, but she couldn't help feverishly wondering what he looked like underneath the expensive clothes. Bronzed and sinewy, she imagined, every cord and muscle defined. She felt faint thinking about it and, when she contemplated the prospect of sharing her bedroom with him, she went into a positive mental tailspin. She eyed the *chaise longue* by the window.

'You can make that up.' She nodded in the direction of the *chaise longue*. 'It's very comfortable.'

Matteo didn't say anything. He glanced at it, his hooded silver eyes revealing nothing. 'Like I said,' he drawled, 'I'll do without the food. Now, unless you have no objection to seeing me strip off in front of you...?'

Colour high in her cheeks, Rosie fled, shutting the door behind her.

In the quiet of the kitchen, she hastily prepared some pasta for herself, making good use of a number of tins. Comfort eating. Her head was full of the ramifications of her very small, practically invisible little white lie. Everything had snowballed and now here she was, with the sexiest man on the planet upstairs in her bedroom. Her nerves were shredded. When she thought of Matteo, everything inside her went into meltdown. Physically, she felt faint when she closed her eyes and pictured him in all his over-the-top sexiness. He was just so breathtakingly *beautiful*.

But it wasn't just confined to the way he looked. If that had been the sum total of it, then she could have steeled herself against the impact, because a good-looking guy without personality was just a cardboard cut-out to be admired without any threat of him getting under your skin.

No. Matteo's extraordinary effect on her was all wrapped up in the power of his personality, his air of command, and now that she had eked out a couple of personal details the fallibility she could sense underneath the cloak of arrogant self-assurance.

He posed questions, he ignited her imagination, he stirred depths of curiosity she'd never known she possessed.

Absorbed in hectic speculation, she ate without thinking—the pasta, some salad that looked dangerously close to needing last rites performed then a slab of chocolate dessert that was just the thing to settle her mind.

She was startled when she heard the sound of the door opening and then there was Candice, shedding outer layers of snow-covered gear as she breezed into the kitchen, pink-faced and smiling.

'I really miss the little monsters.' She headed straight to the fridge to pull out a bottle of mineral water. 'But—' she looked at Rosie with a grin '—some time out is a wonderful thing. Had a ball. So nice to catch up with that crew. Where's Matteo?'

'He's…um…working.'

'Working?' She kept her eyes fixed on Rosie's flushed face as she drank from the bottle before lowering it. 'Where? In Dad's office? Surely he can pack in the work for a few days…if he's head over heels in love with you?'

'Well, you know how it goes when it comes to men and…er…work.' Rosie offered vaguely. Her sisters had always had the ability to pin her to the spot with their penetrating blue eyes and she was pinned to the spot now, unable to move forward and incapable of shuffling back.

'Tell me.'

'Lucien works all the hours under the sun, or have you forgotten?'

'He's a surgeon,' Candice responded drily. 'Lives depend on him. It's early days for you both, Rosie. I would have expected him to have made a little time for you, especially considering the time of year, when most businesses are operating at a much slower pace.'

Rosie remained steadfastly silent. A fierce defensiveness for her so-called boyfriend suddenly kicked into gear allied to the stubborn need to stand her ground. Where had that come from?

'He isn't where he is because he's a slacker, Candice,' she said without the usual note of apology in her voice. 'Sometimes work can take over, and not necessarily because lives are at stake. Lucien might save lives on an operating table, but Matteo and how he runs his businesses can affect the livelihoods of lots of people who work for him.'

Candice stared.

'I consider myself duly told off. Second time for the evening. The only reason I sound nosy...' She sighed. 'Okay, I've researched the guy,' she confessed, 'And he's big stuff, Rosie. Somewhere at the back of my mind, I recognised the name, but I honestly thought I was mistaken because I couldn't believe that someone who doesn't even breathe the same air as we do could... well...'

'Find me attractive? Thanks very much.'

'It's not that at all!' Candice said quickly. 'I can't help being protective of you—he's out of your league, Rosebud. For a start, the sort of women he dates...'

'I know. He likes high-powered career women.'

'So he told you? I'm impressed with his honesty on that front, at least. Of course, Emily's heard of him, and so has Robert. But, from everything I've read and heard, he's so far up the pecking order that you literally have to be a billionaire to have much personal contact with him at all on the business level.'

Frankly, Rosie couldn't help thinking, the more Candice elaborated, the less likely it seemed that someone like Matteo would even glance in the direction of someone like her. Not unless they had temporarily taken leave of their senses. Christmas madness. Except, he didn't do Christmas.

'But of course,' Candice continued, flipping open the bin and dumping the plastic bottle into the recycling section, 'Opposites *do* attract, I'll give you that.'

'They do...' Rosie smiled to herself, remembering what Matteo had said earlier.

'There's no accounting for people when they fall in love.'

Fall in love? Was that the story doing the rounds? And was it spreading like a forest fire beyond the family unit?

'Well…' She laughed lightly and managed to galvanise her body into action, walking across to sit opposite her sister, wishing she had opted for a restorative glass of wine, for some Dutch courage would have done wonders right now. 'I don't know about *falling in love*…'

'What do you mean?'

'Relationships aren't all about *falling in love*,' she asserted, glancing away.

'That's not what you've always maintained,' Candice told her drily. She paused and delivered a searching look to her sister. 'I don't want you to get hurt,' she said quietly. 'And I'm very much afraid that you will. I just don't think you're tough enough to handle a guy like Matteo.'

Into the brief silence came the last voice either of them expected to hear.

'Maybe that's what I find so charming about your sister.'

They both looked up to see that Matteo had silently pushed open the kitchen door and was now lounging in the doorframe.

How long had he been there?

Rosie tried to remember if she had said anything incriminating and was certain that she hadn't.

He'd showered and changed into a pair of faded jeans and an old tee shirt and he looked drop-dead gorgeous—easy, relaxed, wildly sophisticated and with that edge of danger about him that made her whole body go on full alert.

'Maybe,' Matteo continued, 'It's a breath of fresh air to be with a woman who isn't as tough as nails and doesn't want to spend every minute of her time discussing the state of the world and how it should be fixed.' He strolled towards Rosie and then remained standing behind her, his hands on her shoulders, lightly caressing her neck and feathering shivers of pleasure through her body.

He leant to brush his lips on the nape of her neck and she nearly passed out.

She had never seen Candice out of her depth but Matteo unsettled her, Rosie thought. It was his self-assurance, his bone-deep confidence that his opinions carried weight. He didn't *allow* anyone to take advantage of him and, before they thought that they could try, he made sure to establish the lines of command.

'And what makes you think that your sister will be the one to be hurt?' he enquired coolly.

'Exactly.' Rosie finally entered the conversation but her usual spirited response was seriously compromised by the continuing, caressing motion of his fingers on her neck. 'Candice, please don't worry about me.'

'I intend to take very good care of your sister.' Matteo's voice was still cool.

'Really?' Candice's eyebrows shot up. 'I mean, I hope so. We all do.'

'Why would I say it if I didn't mean it?'

'But,' Rosie interjected, 'It's only been a couple of weeks so...we're taking each day as it comes.'

'And you were always the impulsive one, Rosie,' Candice teased. 'Is love changing you already?'

'Don't be ridiculous!' Rosie spluttered. How much deeper could the hole she had dug for herself go?

'I know it's not wedding bells yet!' Candice laughed and stood up, her movements graceful as she strode towards the door. 'But please don't forget to give me ample warning so that I can start planning my outfit!'

Rosie managed to stammer out something, grateful that Matteo seemed to be taking it all in his stride, and it was only when the kitchen door was shut and her sister well and truly gone that Rosie looked at him with alarm.

'You should never have encouraged my sister to think that there was more to this than there is!' was the first thing she said, leaping to her feet, irritated at Matteo's composure as he helped himself to a bottle of water from the fridge.

'We should head up,' was all he said.

'Why on earth did you come down here, anyway? I thought you said that you had a mountain of emails to get through!'

'The prospect of working suddenly didn't seem quite so enticing.' He circled her and stared down at her for a few seconds until she reluctantly lifted her eyes to his.

'I was trying to ease the way to us breaking up,' she confessed. 'Until you came along and demolished all my efforts. Why couldn't you have just taken the lead from me and backed me up when I started insinuating that this was probably just a fling?'

Matteo shrugged. 'Maybe I'm so arrogant that the thought of being written off as a fling dented my ego.'

'I don't believe you,' Rosie muttered.

'Maybe…' he murmured.

Rosie didn't know what was going through his head, but his expression wasn't the expression of an arrogant alpha male with a sore ego.

'Just maybe it got on my nerves hearing your sister

assume that a man like me could never look twice at someone like you.'

'I'm not asking for your pity.'

'If you don't assert yourself, you'll be walked over.'

'Thank you very much for the words of advice.'

'You've stood up to your sister once. You can do it again. Try it a few times and you might find that it becomes a way of life.'

'You don't like me prying into your private life, Matteo, and I don't like you thinking that you can analyse me.'

'But you've set a precedent. Don't get me wrong,' he grated. 'Your life is none of my business but it affronts something in me when I hear you being treated like a kid who needs other people to look after her. You're not a kid.'

'I know that,' Rosie muttered grudgingly. She sneaked a glance at him from under her lashes. 'I did actually stick up for you when she told me that it was strange for you to be working when you should be desperate to spend time in my company.'

'Did you, now?'

Rosie could see the speculation in his eyes at that admission. 'I thought it might be a good idea to let her know that work came first with you.'

Matteo burst out laughing, his grey eyes darkening with appreciation. 'More of those foundations being laid down.'

'It might have been if you had got on board with me instead of branching out and doing your own thing.'

Matteo shrugged, the smile lingering on his lips, and began heading towards the door. 'I'm hitting the sack. Coming?'

'I'll… I think I'll stay down here and finish tidying the kitchen,' Rosie told him. For a while she'd forgotten the prospect ahead of sharing her bedroom with him but it was all coming back to her now at great speed. On the spot she decided that she would stay out of harm's way in the kitchen, at least long enough for him to fall asleep so that when she finally joined him he would be dead to the world.

She couldn't picture him being dead to the world, though. In fact, she couldn't imagine him sleeping. More lying still with his eyes closed but primed to leap into action at the sound of a pin dropping.

'Don't wait up. There's linen in the cupboard on the landing for the *chaise longue*.'

'Sure.' He didn't bother turning around to look at her but left the kitchen, shutting the door behind him, leaving her to take as long as she possibly could filling the dishwasher, wiping the counters and in the end going through the contents of the fridge and binning everything that no longer had any lifespan left whatsoever.

It was after midnight by the time she finally headed up to the bedroom and she was dead on her feet.

So he was going to be in her bedroom. That meant nothing. She was going to be cool and composed because he was right—she wasn't a kid and she was going to stop behaving like one. She was the only one who could determine the direction of her life and her choices and she was going to remember that.

This felt like a crucial moment for her. She was at a crossroads. She either carried on in no particular direction, escaping her family's well-intentioned guidance by drifting from one job to another, or else she buckled down and asserted herself. It was odd that a perfect stranger had been the one to bring her to this point.

He told her things that she didn't want to hear but it was thanks to him that she had actually stood up to Candice instead of backing away. She had always been treated like the baby of the family and she had followed through, fulfilling their expectations, becoming the family member happy to drift through life while other people got on with responsible living and grown-up decision making.

When she stood back and looked at it through objective eyes, she was mortified.

From now on, things were going to change. They already had.

Filled with the rosy glow of assertiveness, Rosie pushed open the bedroom door and there he was on the *chaise longue*, semi-reclining, and it looked painful. His laptop was open and his legs looked as though they weren't quite sure where they should go. Over the end of the sofa? Uncomfortable. On the ground? Likewise. He was way too tall and too big for the piece of furniture to which he had been consigned but the fact that he had obeyed orders touched her.

He shifted his big, muscular bulk as she walked in, drawing attention… Forget about the inadequacies of his makeshift bed, the guy was semi-naked.

Low-slung, loose-fitting jogging bottoms. That was it. He was half-naked and she stood by the door, shamelessly gaping for a few seconds, before walking in and shutting the door behind her.

Thank God he hadn't switched on the overhead light. Instead, he had swivelled the angle-poise lamp by the bed in the direction of the *chaise longue*. Rosie hoped that in a half-dark room the beetroot red of her cheeks wouldn't immediately be visible.

'You took your time,' Matteo said, now standing up and stretching before dumping the laptop on her dressing table.

Rosie's vocal cords had dried up. She cleared her throat and stared straight past his spectacular, burnished bronze body to the window just behind him. Seemed a safer option. That said, he still managed to intrude into the entire periphery of her vision. He was so tall, muscles densely packed, the flat lines of his stomach tapering to a narrow waist and spirals of dark hair arrowing down...

'There was a lot of tidying to do in the kitchen,' she croaked. 'You... I see you've made yourself comfortable on the *chaise longue*.'

Matteo glanced over his shoulder and grimaced. 'I'm not sure that *comfortable* would be the appropriate word.'

Rosie had expected complaints. Maybe a show of resentful acceptance of the boundaries she had laid down, possibly even fully fledged refusal to accommodate her wishes. But his voice was remarkably even and she felt something...quite different from those waves of taboo attraction. She felt the stirrings of affection.

She glanced at her lovely king-sized bed and Matteo followed the direction of her gaze.

'I'm in your house,' he said, walking to the window and back to the sofa, exercising his long limbs. 'The bed is yours.'

'I'm half your size.'

'Rules of the house apply here,' Matteo drawled drily, flexing his muscles again and then sinking back down onto the *chaise longue*, his dark eyes pinned to her face as she remained hovering like a visitor in her own bedroom. He grinned. 'Relax. There's no need to start thinking about playing the self-sacrificing martyr by giving up your bed for me, Rosie. If the shoe was on the other foot and you were in my house, I'd be sprawled out on the bed and you'd be trying to squeeze into the clothes hamper in the bathroom. It's late. Forget I'm here and go to sleep.'

CHAPTER FIVE

THE BEDROOM WAS empty the following morning when Rosie woke up. In that moment between sleeping and waking, she had a brief respite when she actually forgot about Matteo being in her room at all, then she shot up into a sitting position and squinted at the *chaise longue* which was as tidy as though it had never been slept on. No rumpled linen. No pillow tossed onto the floor and no six-foot-two, drop-dead gorgeous Italian scrunched up asleep.

No Candice either.

There were messages waiting for her the second she checked her phone, including a lengthy voicemail informing her that one of the kids had come down with hand, foot and mouth disease.

'Absolute nightmare!' Candice had sounded rushed and a little frantic on the voicemail. 'It's only a passing virus, and Toby will be over it in a couple of days, but of course Lucien is freaking out, so I've caught the first flight out, darling. Don't despair, though! I'll be back at the end of the week with the gang—and don't let that hunk of yours go anywhere! Lock him away if you have to! Everyone's dying to meet him!'

A long text message from her mother warned her that

they, too, would be delaying their arrival so that they could lend a hand with two-year-old Jess while Candice was playing Florence Nightingale to her elder brother.

Probably a good idea to give you a little more private time with your young man! her mother had messaged, with a winking face next to it. *So you can breathe a sigh of relief, darling.*

With several skiing lessons booked for the day and behind time, Rosie raced through the room, flinging on the appropriate gear, and headed down, taking the short flight of stairs two at a time and screeching to a halt by the kitchen door. Matteo was in the kitchen. It was a little after eight, but he looked bright-eyed and bushy tailed, as though he had had a splendid night's sleep.

'Coffee?' He greeted her equably, shutting the laptop which was in front of him on the kitchen table.

He was in a black polo-neck jumper and faded black jeans and he took her breath away.

Rosie blinked.

'How long have you been up?'

'A couple of hours. Hard to say.' He stood up and strolled towards the kettle to switch it on.

'Because you didn't manage to sleep well on the sofa?' Rosie inched into the kitchen, then told herself that it was ridiculous to feel uncomfortable in her own space. She needed to eat something before she shot out or she'd faint on the slopes. Her tummy was rumbling.

'It was a challenge,' he threw over his shoulder, 'But I've never been one to shy away from a challenge.'

Rosie had a vision of him on the *chaise longue*, half-naked, dwarfing it and yet accepting without complaint that that was his designated sleeping spot, and she felt it again—a stirring of tenderness that was disconcerting.

'Well, you're in luck,' she offered brightly. She headed for the bread bin and extracted a sandwich loaf that was, thankfully, fresh enough to pop into the toaster. 'Candice has had to rush off back to England because Toby has a virus.'

'Hand, foot and mouth,' Matteo murmured and Rosie looked at him with surprise.

'How do you know?'

'I was in the kitchen when she was heading out of here.'

'You were?'

'Like I said, sleeping was a challenge. I threw in the towel just in time to catch her before she left. She explained the situation.'

'Right.' Rosie hesitated as it dawned on her that there was no need for Matteo to stay at the chalet at all because there would be no one around to observe the lovers in action. He could return to the hotel and check himself in for however many nights before the family descended.

The chalet would feel very empty without him there, she thought, and just as quickly she banished that thought from her head. She had been in it on her own for weeks and it had been absolutely fine.

She had been ensnared by his personality and by the way he looked, and she had probably been a bit lonely without realising it. The instructors and all the young people working in the hotel were very friendly, and there was a brilliant social life on tap for anyone who wanted to dip in and out of it. There were always things happening in various groups in the evenings, depending on who happened to be working what shift. But many of her friends had paired up and she could only think that

Matteo had lulled her into enjoying time with a guy on her own.

She had to remember that this was an artificial situation, though, and it annoyed her to feel that nudge of disappointment at the thought of him not being around.

'So I guess you've worked out what this means,' she said casually, offering him some toast, which he politely refused, even though he didn't appear to have eaten anything. There were no dirty plates to be seen and she had a feeling that he wouldn't have been meticulous about washing, drying and putting away anything he'd used.

'What?' Matteo strolled back to the chair and swivelled it so that he could watch her as she buttered her toast and then stood pressed against the counter, looking at him.

'You can return to the hotel and stay there until the family show up. I mean, Candice won't be here, and Mum and Dad are hanging back with her so that they can help with the kids while Toby is poorly. Emily and Rob will come later as well. It'll be a sudden onslaught but in the meantime there's no need for us to pretend because there will be no one around to see us.'

'No can do.'

'Sorry?' Rosie had bitten into her toast and she chewed it slowly. One slice. She'd be starving in an hour but thinking about all those career women Matteo was attracted to had got her thinking that she could do with shedding a few pounds and redirecting her love of chocolate into something else. Celery, perhaps.

'Bob and Margaret are still around,' Matteo elaborated. 'They're not staying at that hotel but they're there on a regular basis, enjoying one of the restaurants, drinking in one of the bars. There are only so many watering holes in this resort. Since the whole purpose of this arrangement was to convince them that we're the happy couple, it's hardly going to do if they spot me back at the hotel without you.'

'I hadn't thought of that,' Rosie admitted.

Which brought her to another realisation and that was that they would now be here, in this lodge together, without Candice and her entire family around to dilute the situation.

She dropped the toast into the bin and looked at him in consternation.

'Don't worry,' Matteo drawled, 'I'll make myself scarce.'

'That's not what I meant.'

'You have a face that's as transparent as a pane of glass. I have a mountain of work to get through, as it happens. This deal isn't the only thing on my plate at the moment. I'd planned on having time out at my villa in Venice to work solidly over the Christmas period, but now that that's been shot out of the water I'll have to get as much done as possible before your family get here.'

'At least you won't have to sleep on the sofa now.'

Matteo didn't say anything. The night had been a hideous lesson in physical discomfort and not because he was averse to sleeping on anything that wasn't a feather mattress. Growing up in a foster home, there had been no luxuries. He had become accustomed to a single bed with a mattress that seemed about as thick as a pound coin.

No, his discomfort had stemmed from the fact that he was way too big for such a delicate item of furniture.

And, as if that wasn't bad enough, he had been aware of her tossing and turning and then, at some point in the early hours of the morning, she had stumbled past him to go to the bathroom, mostly asleep, and after that getting back to sleep had been impossible.

Her body…

Even under the baggy tee shirt and the shapeless shorts he had glimpsed luscious curves that had sent an ache of desire straight to his groin. There was something about the light in this part of the world… The luminosity had penetrated through a crack in the curtain and as she had yawned her way past him, oblivious to his presence because she'd been dead to the world, the shadowy outline of her heavy breasts had been clearly visible.

His erection had been hard and immediate and he had had to suffer in silence, gritting his teeth while his imagination had taken flight.

Never had he felt such an intense craving to have any woman. It had shocked him and had been intensely unsettling because he hadn't been able to control his response.

If he'd managed half an hour's sleep for the entire night, he would have been surprised.

'You can have one of the guest bedrooms,' Rosie elaborated, breaking eye contact and then hovering. 'They're all made up and I can just replace the linen before the family arrive later in the week.'

She couldn't read his expression. If he always seemed to know what she was thinking because her face was 'as transparent as a pane of glass', then reading his thoughts was about as easy as groping a way forward in dense fog wearing a blindfold.

Right now, he was staring at her with hooded eyes, pinning her to the spot, even though she knew she had to run because her first client was in forty-five minutes.

'Good idea.' Matteo dropped his eyes and glanced at the laptop.

Her cue to go, Rosie thought. Enough small talk.

'I'll be on the slopes until this afternoon,' she said, edging past him to the door. 'And then I might go out with some of the gang this evening. So I won't be in your way.' They were talking to one another as though they were strangers and, although she knew that this was to be expected, given the fact that there were no witnesses in the vicinity to make judgement calls on their relationship, she couldn't help but miss the easy, teasing banter he was so good at whenever they were in public view.

'That's not going to work.' He caught her wrist, stopping her in her tracks.

A sizzle of electricity zapped through her and she froze. She wanted to shut her eyes because he was so clever at reading what was in her head and, right now, what was in her head was *I want this man.* She licked her lips but her mouth was dry and she couldn't seem to get any words out.

'Want to know why?' Matteo was gazing at her flushed face.

He rubbed the pad of his thumb absently over the softness of her inner wrist.

He could feel it. He could sense a physical response rippling through her, mirroring his.

This was playing with fire. He wasn't on the lookout for a relationship with anyone and certainly not with a woman who was as soft as meringue, no sharp edges, no defence barriers. Despite her wealthy background, she was so sweetly disingenuous that he would be crazy to go there.

He banked down the tide of images flooding his

mind—pictures of her in bed naked, her plump, ripe body opening up for him.

He dropped her hand and sat back. 'You keep forgetting that we're supposed to be an item.'

'I don't think that Bob and Margaret will be partying at a club.'

'That's not the point. I expect glad tidings of our hot and heavy relationship have already reached the ears of most of your fellow clubbers. How's it going to look if you show up without me?'

'You could always come.'

'I'm not big into the club scene.'

Rosie distractedly rubbed her wrist where he had been touching it. 'Well, if everyone has heard all about us, and I honestly don't think that's the case, wouldn't it be a good idea if we were to do something outdoorsy?'

'Like gyrating on a dance floor at two in the morning?' He raised his eyebrows and Rosie shot him a reluctant grin.

'Everyone's too tired after being on the slopes all day to stay out until two in the morning. Gyrating.' Her smile widened. 'You sound like an old man.'

'I'm old compared to you,' Matteo told her irritably. 'I'm thirty-two. You're twenty-three. I've lived a life of responsibility. You've had the pleasure of doing just as you've always pleased without fear of consequences.' He paused, hating himself for wiping the easy smile off her face. 'It's what makes you who you are,' he said roughly. 'And that's no bad thing.'

'What do you mean?'

'I happen to like the way you approach life, as though each day is filled with the promise of something new and enjoyable.'

'It often is.'

'Is it?' He shrugged. 'You could be right but it's an optimism that usually gets ground into dust by the time reality takes over.'

'What do you mean by reality?'

'Work. Responsibility. Life in general.'

Rosie was so tempted to reach out and touch him. There was a vulnerability there and she was sure he wasn't even aware of it. He'd had a tough life and Lord only knew what sacrifices he had had to make along the way to get where he had.

'How did you get that scar?' she asked suddenly, expecting him not to offer a reply. She had done what he seemed constantly to be telling her not to do, namely push past his boundaries to invade his inner sanctum.

'Fight.' He smiled at her. 'I was a teenager at the time. Fights happened all the time. Someone had a knife and I got in the way of it.'

Her heart twisted and she backed towards the door. 'I should be going.'

'And I need to carry on with this work. What time are you wrapping it up with your lessons?'

'Last one at three.' Rosie knew she had to go and yet she didn't want to leave. Every small entry into his life felt magical. 'I need to go and buy some food,' she said, fidgeting. 'I've been lazy when it comes to buying stuff. It's easy to live off junk food because we get discounted prices at most of the cafés around here. One of the perks of being a ski instructor.'

'I noticed a lot of greenery,' Matteo remarked, enjoying the way she blushed, which was something that never failed to surprise him.

Rosie grimaced. 'I know. I always think that if I buy

lots of lettuce and vegetables then I'm going to actually eat them. I should. I should never go anywhere near chips or burgers.'

'Why?'

'Can't you look at me and tell?' She laughed and then sobered up when her eyes collided with his and she saw that he wasn't laughing along with her.

His expression was…darkly hungry.

She shivered, a core of excitement reaching fever pitch as he continued to stare at her. By the time he lowered his gaze, her nerves were in crazy freefall and there was a heat between her thighs that made her want to rub them together.

'No, I can't, as a matter of fact,' Matteo intoned in a driven undertone that was quite unlike his usual lazy drawl.

'I'll see you later.' Rosie fled. Any longer in his presence and she would start having heart palpitations. Could he see the effect he had on her? For a minute, just then, she had seen something in his eyes that had sent her pulses racing out of control. It was an attraction that had gone to her head like incense. He'd wanted her. She was sure of that.

Her mind was all over the place for the rest of the day. She waved at Bob and Margaret, who were trying out the slopes on their own. She discovered that Matteo had been right to think that news of their whirlwind romance had done the rounds. She had to think fast on her feet when questions were asked, building a picture of a relationship that had been clandestine. He'd been busy wrapping up a deal and she'd been busy with her ski lessons so they had enjoyed snatched time together and things had gone on from there.

Fortunately, due to the nature of the business, there were a lot of arrivals and departures and the few friends she had made who had been there as long as she had, doing the season, seemed to have such frenetic social lives after their duties were done, that they accepted her stammering explanations without delving too deep. Indeed, the thought of 'snatched time together' had struck her girlfriends as wonderfully exciting.

She was pleasantly tired by the time she saw off her last client. She was preparing to head back to the hotel to dump her stuff and change when she happened to glance to her left and there he was. Her heart skipped a beat, then it skipped a couple more as he made his way towards her, dressed in ski gear.

'I didn't think you skied,' she said breathlessly when he was standing in front of her.

She didn't think it was possible for anyone to look as good as he did in ski clothes. Aside from a thin orange strip along the top, he was dressed completely in black. His sunglasses were propped up and he hadn't shaved. She could make out the shadow of stubble on his chin.

At this hour, the slopes were emptying out, and from the resort below she could hear the distant strains of Christmas carols being played. Something about the stillness in the air seemed to trap the sound and hold it within the confines of the mountains rearing upwards, red, gold and white in the fading light.

'I don't.' He flashed her a smile. 'But you had a point when you said that some outdoor time together might be a good idea. Bought the gear, so here I am.'

'It's a little late…' Her skin was burning. 'But… I guess I could take you through the ropes. I mean, it's not as though you actually *want* to learn to ski.'

'Who knows?' Matteo murmured. 'With the right teacher, I might find I have untapped talent.'

Nervous as a kitten, and aware of her roundness thanks to the layers of ski gear, Rosie went through the paces with him.

'Feet together...take it slowly...keep the skis parallel... No, not quite like that. Here, let me show you. Don't forget to keep your eyes ahead! Are you scared of heights, by the way? Will you be spooked in the cable car?'

Rosie had never had so much fun. She was in her comfort zone and, as she laughed and tried to give him some handy tips, she caught herself telling him about when she had first taken to the slopes. It was the one thing she was better at than her sisters.

'They were clever,' she said, eyeing the distance between his skis, 'But I was always the sporty one.'

'I'm surprised you didn't think about making a career in it,' Matteo murmured.

'I'm a good skier,' Rosie laughed, 'But I'm not great enough to compete on an international level!'

'There's more to making a living in sport than practising it at an international level.'

This as they were making their way to the car, Matteo having managed to get hold of a personal driver to bring him down from the chalet.

Rosie paused for a fraction of a second and looked sideways at him.

'You mean like a sports teacher or something?'

'I mean...'

Matteo stopped and turned to look at her so that she was obliged to stop as well and stare up at him.

'The key thing is to find what you enjoy, because chances are you'll probably be good at it, and then with a favourable following wind you can make a career out of it.'

'You enjoyed making money and you were good at it so you made a career out of it?'

'I enjoyed the thought of being free. Money was just my passport to getting there. I've bought food.'

'Sorry?' Rosie's brain was lagging behind, dwelling on what he had said.

'Food. You said you needed. I've bought.'

Rosie felt a tingle of pleasure and for a few moments, a real sense of *contentment.* So this was what her sisters had, she thought with a pang. Someone to laugh with. Someone who bought food. Someone to open the car door for them.

She'd never had that.

This was just an illusion, and she didn't want to get sucked in, but it was hard when he was chatting to her as they slowly bumped their way back up to the chalet, which was in darkness by the time they got there.

Around them, the snow blanketed everything in white. The air was dry and cold. The house, however, was toasty warm as they entered, shaking off the snow and dumping coats, gloves, scarves and boots in the spacious cupboard by the front door.

The intimacy of their surroundings, just the two of them in the house, hit her with the force of a sledgehammer as they headed towards the kitchen, Matteo with two carrier bags in his hands.

He switched on lights as they went. He'd dumped the outer layers and was down to a thermal tee shirt that clung lovingly to his muscular torso.

'I'll just go and get changed…showered.' She was trailing behind him and she didn't give him time to look around, carolling gaily as she veered off to the staircase. 'And I'll pop a towel in the guest bedroom for you!'

Not that there's anything to worry about, she told herself. *He might have glanced at you with a show of interest but you're not his type. And he was the perfect gentleman last night. So making a point of telling him about the towel in the guest room is at best not very subtle and at worst a hint that you are downright terrified of sharing a bedroom with him when there's no sister conveniently lodged two rooms along.*

He had unpacked the carrier bags and the contents were laid out on the kitchen table in ceremonial fashion.

Rosie relaxed and grinned. She looked at what was there: tomatoes, some vegetables, duck eggs, an assortment of expensive pâtés, smoked salmon, various cheeses, an enormous box of the finest Swiss chocolates and a gateau that instantly made her mouth water.

'You don't need to watch what you eat.' Matteo followed her gaze to the gateau.

Rosie ignored him. She was so conscious of his presence that the hairs on her arms were standing on end.

'Duck eggs?' She held the blue box up to him.

'That was a mistake,' Matteo admitted.

'It's a very interesting assortment of food and thank you very much for going to the trouble of buying it. I'm not sure what I do with some of these ingredients. Maybe we should just have a salad for our supper.'

'There's bread,' Matteo informed her.

'I guess you don't cook at all?'

'I try and avoid it.' He found himself telling her that cooking had been *de rigueur* at the children's home when he'd been growing up and the very fact of that had instilled a healthy dislike for anything to do with pots, pans and food preparation.

What he didn't add was that he'd suffered from the realisation over the years that pots, pans and food preparation was what at least some women enjoyed doing in an attempt to whet his appetite for more than just the dishes they had lovingly prepared.

He watched as she fetched plates and busied herself opening the packets he had bought.

Did that count as food preparation? Nothing went into preparing a cold meal. It was ready in under half an hour and, looking at the spread, Matteo found himself wishing that he was about to eat something hot.

'Do you…enjoy cooking at all?' he queried, opening a bottle of wine.

It was a little after six. Early for supper, but it was dark outside, with flurries of snow reminding them of the time of year.

'I wouldn't say it's the love of my life.' Rosie had tactfully stuck the gateau out of sight and she eyed the array of pâtés, cheeses and smoked salmon with a distinct lack of enthusiasm.

He'd obviously bought the sort of food he personally enjoyed.

'This wouldn't be your choice of food?' he quizzed and she looked at him sheepishly.

'I've always liked food that's a bit more…more…'

'Tasty?'

'This is all very good.'

'Wine will improve the flavours. Hang on for five secs.'

He disappeared and returned a few minutes later with two bottles of champagne.

'Forgot I bought these at the wine merchant.' He opened a bottle, found glasses, poured them a glass each and then returned to his seat.

Rosie was ashamed at just how good this felt, sitting here with this guy, eating a meal together, almost as though they weren't caught up in a charade, a game of make believe.

She was uneasily aware of how slender the line could be between reality and fantasy.

This felt real.

This felt more real than any of the passing connections she had ever made over the years with guys and she knew that it was because, very quickly and purely because of the situation, they had shared things with one another. He had shared his background—reluctantly, she knew—but still...

She had opened up to him, he had listened and somehow he had seen right into the very heart of her. That had promoted a feeling of...*closeness*.

The champagne was excellent. The best money could buy.

'I thought you had planned on working all day,' she said a little drowsily after champagne had been drunk and a dent made in the food.

'Bob and Margaret weren't available for comment.'

'I saw them on the slopes.'

'Did they approach you? Ask any questions?'

'They were too far away, but you were right about my friends seeming to know that we're involved. When this started, I had no idea that it would grow legs and start running away from me.' She sighed.

'Like I've said before...' Matteo fetched the gateau from where she had earlier hidden it behind the canisters of sugar and tea '…once you start lying, it's impossible to know where it's going to end up.'

'You must hate all of this.' She looked at the slab of cake in front of her and was indecently keen to tuck in. He produced two forks and gently pulled the plate between them.

'Care to share?'

Rosie's eyes widened. This felt truly intimate. They weren't touching one another—not even their forks touched!— yet as they at the slab of cake it felt weirdly *intimate*.

'You asked me whether I was hating all of this,' Matteo mused.

Her eyes were even more amazing up close, he distractedly found himself thinking. She couldn't quite meet his gaze and he knew, with the instinct of a man well versed in the way women reacted, that her response was a physical one. The champagne had relaxed her but she was still wary. He could sense it. He could almost smell it.

What would she do if he touched her? He found the thought of that so erotic that he had to grit his teeth together to ease the ache in his groin.

'You must be.'

'I should be,' he admitted, 'But I suppose that a change is as good as a rest.'

Rosie wanted to feel relieved at that, but all she could think was, *You're enjoying the novelty of the situation. The novelty of being with someone like me. You've practically said so yourself.*

She didn't want to be a novelty but she wasn't going to give that away.

'I've put you in the room to the left of the staircase,' she said, changing the subject.

'There's a towel on the bed,' he added politely and she blushed.

'I'll tidy in the morning.' She staged a yawn which turned into the real thing. 'I'm exhausted. I always am in the evenings.'

'And yet you wanted to go clubbing tonight.'

'It was optimistic.'

'You don't have to try and run away from me,' he said kindly, which made her blush even more. 'As this evening has shown, we're two adults perfectly capable of passing the time of day together without any major disagreements. I'm going to stay up for a couple of hours, finish some emails. I think, if we can agree to stick to this routine until your family show up, life shouldn't be too overwhelming for us. Wouldn't you agree? And, as soon as my deal is signed, we can begin the process of... disentanglement.'

CHAPTER SIX

ROSIE STARED UP at the ceiling. She hadn't drawn the curtains and the silver light, the reflection of the moon shining down on endless white outside, illuminated everything in the bedroom.

This had always been her favourite time of the year—the run up to Christmas. The entire resort was a winter wonderland of tiny lights, Christmas trees and carols booming through the village, ratcheting up the excitement. Every year, the entire family would meet for a week at the chalet and it would mark the beginning to the countdown for them. They would put up a tree and the board games would come out. Family time.

She should have been alive with anticipation. Instead, she eyed the empty *chaise longue* and realised that her thoughts had been entirely occupied with Matteo.

At a little after one in the morning, he would be sound asleep in a proper bed instead of lying awake, cramped and uncomfortable, on a sofa that she, inches shorter, would have found a challenge.

She thought about him bedding down without complaint and then waking up and busying himself on his computer at some ridiculously early hour in the morning, also without complaint. She knew that he would have spent his entire time at the chalet falling off a sofa in the middle of the night, perfectly accepting that, if that was his designated sleeping area, then so be it.

He had a childhood without any luxuries. As a small boy growing into a young man learning how to be tough and ambitious enough to ignore the siren call of violence—all that had prepared him to accept discomfort should it come his way. He might be worth billions now but she got the feeling that the past he seldom discussed was never forgotten.

Caught up in the fruitless exercise of thinking about him and trying to work him out, she finally decided to get out of bed and head down to the kitchen for something to eat.

She'd barely touched a thing all day and the gateau was beckoning.

The chalet was in darkness as she made her way downstairs to the kitchen. Through the vast glass doors, she paused to take in the expanse of snowy white outside.

She shivered, feeling the chill, because the central heating had switched off at midnight. She should have slung on a bathrobe but satisfying her rumbling tummy had been far too pressing. Plus, she was sick of thinking about Matteo and then mentally asking herself why she couldn't put him out of her mind.

She'd managed to find every excuse under the sun for her relentless absorption with him, starting with *It's perfectly understandable, considering the way we were thrown together* then going on to *It would be unnatural for me not to think about him* and *There wouldn't be a woman alive who wouldn't be thinking of him if she was sharing a house with him...who could ignore someone who looks the way he does?*

She didn't bother turning on the kitchen light due to the unfounded suspicion that it might filter all the way upstairs to where Matteo was sleeping and alert him to the fact that there was someone downstairs.

As a consequence, she banged her foot against the edge of one of the chairs and hopped in agony for a few seconds until the pain subsided, then she opened the fridge and knelt down to inspect the contents.

She wanted to resist the cake but the alternative of eating whatever remained of the options Matteo had generously bought didn't tempt.

She reached out to cut a sliver of the gateau which Matteo had shoved in the fridge, not bothering to remove the knife he had earlier used to cut it, when the sound of his voice coming from behind her almost shocked her into having a heart attack.

With a yelp, she scuttled back and shot to her feet, heart pounding and mouth dry, and she spun round to look at him. The kitchen was still in darkness but to her horror that didn't last long because he banged on the switch and the room was flooded with light.

Never had Rosie felt more conscious of her state of undress. The tee shirt might be baggy but she was excruciatingly aware of the heavy weight of her bra-less breasts pushing against it, and her shorts were tiny. Way too small.

For a few seconds, she couldn't speak at all. She studied him, her thoughts in frantic disarray. She'd glimpsed him without a shirt on but this time... The man was *awesome*, she thought weakly, so very tall, so very well built. So very, very under-dressed. Not only was he half-naked, but the safe option of tracksuit bottoms had been jettisoned in favour of boxers that revealed long, muscular legs and a stomach as flat as a wash board.

'What are you doing here?' she managed accusingly. In timely fashion, she reminded herself that this was, actually, *her* house and he was the guest so why should she feel as though she'd been caught red-handed stealing the family heirlooms? How was it that he somehow found it so effortless to exert control and thereby give the impression that he owned everything around him even if he didn't?

'I heard a noise.'

His voice was terse and, reading into that abrupt response, Rosie could only imagine his annoyance at finding his sleep disrupted yet again.

'I made sure to be quiet!'

'Noise travels around here.'

They stood and stared at one another and, suddenly conscious of herself, she crossed her arms over her breasts and was disconcerted when he followed that gesture. Was he trying to embarrass her on purpose? She swung away but the heavy silence was getting to her.

'I just came down to get something to drink.' She thought of the gateau and silently bid farewell to the chunk of lovely, comforting calories. 'Are you just going to stand there? I'm sorry if I woke you up. I had no idea I made any noise. I banged my toe but I didn't think I yelped loud enough for you to hear.'

'I might as well get myself something to drink as well now that I'm down here,' Matteo muttered, moving forward with the quiet grace of a panther to open the fridge and extract two bottles of water, one of which he handed to her.

Instead of walking towards the door, he remained standing next to her, unsettling in his masculine beauty, holding her transfixed gaze until her legs began to feel wobbly.

Water in hand, she began backing away towards the door, eyes on him the whole time.

'I thought someone had broken in.' He moved towards her, his voice lacking its usual cool self-control. He sounded as though he needed to clear his throat.

'That's rare over here.' Rosie breathed, watching wide-eyed as he stopped in front of her. There was nowhere else to go so she remained where she was, staring up at him and trying hard to play it cool when her pulse was racing and her heart was slamming against her rib cage. 'You could sleep with the doors open and no one would break in.'

'You have the most amazing eyes,' Matteo murmured.

'Matteo...'

'I like it when you say my name in that breathy little voice.'

'Matteo, don't.'

'I'm not doing anything.'

But he was. Right now, he was. He was lifting one hand to sift it through her wildly tousled fair curls. Her mouth ran dry. She badly wanted to touch him but she had no idea how this kind of game went. He traced the outline of her mouth with his finger, then cupped the side of her face and stared at her for a long moment until her head was swimming.

'What's going on?' she whispered.

'As if you don't know.' He laughed softly. 'Haven't I told you how sexy I find you? I'm attracted to you, *mia bellissima*. And it's mutual, or are you going to deny it?'

'You're a good-looking man,' Rosie prevaricated.

'Would you like this good-looking man to kiss you?'

Rosie nodded, an unfamiliar, but powerful heat running through her body.

He lowered his head and the kiss…took her to heaven and left her there. His mouth was cool and when he inserted his tongue she reached up on tiptoe and wrapped her hands around his neck to pull him down closer to her.

A little groan escaped her. Her breasts felt heavy, her nipples sensitised to the point of painful. She ached for him and curved her body in a wriggling movement that invited him to slip his hand underneath the tee shirt.

For a second, Rosie stilled, but only for a second. He brushed her waist with his hand while he continued to ravish her with a never-ending kiss. Of its own volition, her body seemed to have closed what little gap there had been between them.

Lost in a world of sensation, and feeling as though her body was alive for the very first time, Rosie only realised that he had gently propelled her towards the kitchen table when she bumped against the edge of it.

He eased her apart from him and kept his eyes locked to hers when he began to slip the tee shirt up.

Mesmerising eyes, Rosie thought. Bottomless and fringed with indecently long lashes. Inch by inch the tee shirt was lifted until she was standing in front of him, her breasts exposed.

She felt a surge of feminine power when his nostrils flared as he looked down at her body.

She reached behind to prop herself against the table, clutching the edge with her hands and leaning ever so slightly back so that her body was inclined towards his, towards his heated, appreciative gaze.

He cupped her breasts in his hands and massaged them, simultaneously rolling his thumbs over the stiffened peaks. The groans became restless whimpers.

She wanted much more than this.

She wanted everything.

And suddenly, she realised that she was never going to get what she wanted. She was never going to get anything deep or significant with this guy.

Was this her?

Everything that was rooted in principle and tradition flared into life and she caught his hands in hers and looked at him with troubled eyes.

'I'm not sure I can do this,' she said on a miserable sigh, and just like that he dropped his hands and she lowered the tee shirt. 'I know we're adults, and this is what adults do when they fancy one another, but I'm not sure this is...*me.*'

'You're not...sure?'

'I've only had one serious relationship, Matteo, and that was a long time ago and it didn't end well. I thought we were going somewhere, heading somewhere, but it turned out that he was using me. Maybe not to start with, maybe there was something genuine there at the beginning, but in the end the family money, the trust fund... it all meant more to him.'

'What does a relationship you had years ago have to do with this?'

There was genuine bewilderment in his voice, and that threw her, because in her head the two seemed to be tied together, but why? Did he have a point? Did one bad relationship have to influence every relationship thereafter?

Confusion seeped in. She wondered what, exactly,

she was looking for. Permanence? Of course, she came from a secure and loving background. Her parents had been with one another for a lifetime and beyond. But did that mean that the only route open to her was with a guy she would end up marrying and settling down with?

What about the benefits of just having fun? Despite all the adventures she had had on her travels, hadn't she been at pains to avoid the greatest adventure of all—getting involved with someone? Opening up to them, whatever the outcome? Relationships had lasted five minutes because split decisions had been made that he wasn't the one.

'If you have to turn this into a drama in five acts, then maybe I misjudged things.' Matteo's voice had cooled and he stepped away from her, leaving behind an icy-cold void. 'I'm sorry.' His eyes were as dark and as deep as a glacier.

'Matteo…'

'I'm going to head up, Rosie. I'll see you in the morning.'

He spun round on his heels and soundlessly left the kitchen. In his wake, she subsided onto one of the kitchen chairs and thought, but she couldn't make sense of any of her thoughts. Matteo came from a different world from hers and not just in the material sense. He was hard, tough, had dragged himself up by the bootstraps and had battled whatever adversities he had faced to do it. He had money now but he had learnt from his experiences and now lived his life accordingly.

Something inside her shifted, adjusted and settled into another place and she began heading up the stairs, straight to the bedroom where he had been put.

He was up, lounging on the bed with his hands clasped behind his head, staring at the ceiling.

She could see him in the silver light filtering through the windows because, like her, he hadn't drawn the thick curtains, preferring the distant view of craggy, soaring, snowy mountains.

'I know I'm soft,' Rosie began, walking into the room, fired up.

'What the...?'

'Just let me say what I have to say!'

'Go to bed, Rosie. I'm not in the mood for a raging sermon from you. You don't have to justify your decisions to me.'

'I know I'm soft. I've been spoilt. I don't take anything for granted, believe me I don't, but that doesn't mean that I'm not aware of all the privileges I've grown up with. Maybe you think that that has something to do with me wanting the fairy-tale ending when it comes to romance and you could be right. My big relationship ended with a whimper but don't you dare tell me that you don't see what that has to do with anything.'

Matteo had sat up and she was propelled towards the bed—towards *him*.

Against the white bed linen, his burnished gold body, the deep, rich colour of someone in whom exotic genes ran like a thread of gold, was a powerful, lithe reminder of his intense masculinity.

'We're *all* affected by our pasts.' She perched on the edge of the bed and stared at him. His face was in shadow but she knew that he was watching her. She just didn't know what he was thinking, but when did she ever? 'You are. You haven't had *my* past, but you're as affected by yours as I am by mine. Our pasts are what shape us, and I'm not going to have you tell me that you have no idea what one broken relationship has to do with anything. You don't let anyone into your life because of what you went through. You don't like Christmas, and there would be a reason for that somewhere, buried in your past. So, I was hurt once and I never want to be hurt again.'

'You've said your piece and I've listened, Rosie. You should go to sleep now.'

'I'm attracted to you.'

'Don't go there,' Matteo warned in a dangerously low voice. 'I don't like game playing.'

'Isn't that what we've been doing ever since we met one another?'

'Wrong phrasing. I don't want any woman thinking she has to play games with me.'

'I'm not,' Rosie told him abruptly. She felt a surge of empowerment from her decision taken with eyes wide open. 'We're attracted to one another, and it's not about whether this will lead anywhere or not. I *know* it's not going anywhere. I *know* I'm not your type and you're not mine. So I'm not going to be hurt. I'm going to have fun.'

'What are you saying?'

Reckless daring swept through her in a *now or never* moment as she pulled the tee shirt over her head and stood in front of him, fighting hard not to succumb to crippling self-consciousness.

He wasn't saying anything but his silence wasn't the silence of someone politely about to channel her out of the bedroom and that was encouraging. The silence was still and thick with electricity.

She stepped out of the rest of her clothes and for a few seconds squeezed her eyes shut.

'Come.'

One word and it was enough.

This was a situation far removed from both their comfort zones and, if she only subliminally recognised the danger that particular novelty carried, then Matteo was all too aware of it.

Novelty, in his rarefied world, was a scarce commodity. He'd suffered the indignities of being the poor kid at a rich school, where he'd earned a scholarship to board at the age of thirteen. He'd learned the hard way to ignore every single thing that wasn't worth taking on board and that had included all manner of insults and verbal abuse. Ambition, an intellect that was in the stratosphere, an ability to take risks…all of those things had propelled him onwards and upwards, and he had had no time to relax…until now.

He'd made it. He had more money than most people could dream of. Enough to turn his back on work and live on a beach, drinking cocktails, for the rest of his life. But, in the cold light of day, there was a part of him that acknowledged that he was *bored*. What else was there to get? He could have anything he wanted. Any *woman* he wanted. All those top-notch career women, brainy, beautiful and independent, would still do anything he asked. He could read it in the way they looked at him, the way they listened to what he said, even in the way they sometimes played hard to get.

But she was right. His past had made him the person he was today, locked in a controlled world where he called the shots and there were no unpleasant surprises on any front—material or emotional.

Then into his safe, predictable and obscenely wealthy life this woman had parachuted and she was nothing like any woman he'd met before.

On paper, she made no sense. Life had taught him

to walk away from poor little rich girls with their aggrieved air of entitlement and their healthy trust funds. He had no time for anyone for whom life was easy. His admiration was reserved for those who had faced at least some of the tough mountains he had had to conquer. Most of the women he had dated had worked hard to climb the ladder of success. They had gone beyond the call of duty and battled in a world that was largely, and stupidly, male dominated. Some had made marks that would live on after them.

There was no way that Rosie Carter could possibly qualify for any of those categories. She came from a privileged, private-school background but she surprised him at every turn. It had taken guts to do what she had just done. She was a breath of fresh air and he wanted her more than he had ever wanted any woman in his entire life.

Temptation had never looked so irresistible.

Rosie pushed her fair, curly hair behind her ears and stared at him. Her heart was pounding like a sledgehammer in her chest. It was chilly in the room, but her body was on fire, as if someone had taken a match and lit a bonfire under her feet.

He flung back the duvet, inviting her in, and she could see that he was completely naked. Her mouth went dry and the fire burning up inside her went from sizzling to molten.

She stifled a groan as their bodies met and she felt the push of his erection against her.

'I don't get it,' she whispered. 'I can't seem to help myself.'

'What's going on here,' he said, 'Is something that neither of us had banked on. There's a chemistry here that defies logic. Like you said, I'm not the sort of guy you're accustomed to dating and the same goes for me with you. Sexual attraction has a way of defying logic.'

Rosie's breath hitched in her throat at the feel of his hand gently smoothing her thigh, circling just by her crotch. She moaned softly and lay back, eyelids fluttering shut, parting her legs just a bit more so that he could nudge the dampness between her thighs with his knuckles. It was gentle, seductively rhythmic, and her breathing quickened in response.

'You have no idea how much you turn me on,' Matteo rasped shakily, tugging her so that he could plant a series of kisses on the side of her neck. 'You're breathtakingly sexy.'

'So are you.' Rosie's eyes were hot and drowsy as she caressed the side of his face before cradling the back of his head with her hand and pulling him into a kiss that melted everything in her body. His mouth was cool and firm and the feel of their tongues meshing was indescribable.

It was a kiss she never wanted to end. She curved into him, her body pale and smooth in the dim light.

He didn't talk but he didn't have to. His appreciation of her body was in the way he touched her and the hot fire in his amazing eyes.

He bent to suckle one throbbing nipple, drawing it deep into his mouth, tasting and feasting while sensations spiralled in her, making her wriggle and writhe underneath him.

She'd never wanted anyone so badly. Had never come close.

Her body was flushed and tingling all over when he eventually straightened. The contrast in their colouring was dramatic—she so pale, he burnished gold. He stepped off the bed and she could see that he was rummaging in his wallet for a condom. He dropped it on the wooden table by the side of the bed and looked at her with brooding intensity for a few silent seconds.

'What are you doing?'

'I'm looking.' He held himself in his hand and absently pleasured himself for a few seconds.

.Without thinking, she reached up. On cue, he stepped towards her, and she traced the sinewy ridges of his erection with a trembling finger, starting at the base and working slowly to the tip, which she circled until his fists were clenched at his sides in an attempt to maintain some semblance of self-control.

He finally caught her wrist and breathed deeply.

'Any more,' he said roughly, 'And I'll come—and when I come I want to be deep inside you.'

He slowly joined her back on the bed but, instead of kissing her, he lowered himself to her belly and kissed her there, along her rib cage, while she trembled under the caress.

He circled her belly button with his tongue and then darted it into the sensitive hollow there before moving down lower to her panties, in an intimacy she had never experienced before.

She fought against snapping her legs shut and, as if sensing the impulse, he placed both flattened palms on the inside of her thighs, holding her open for him.

That very first sensation as he began to nuzzle the dampness between her legs was electrifying.

She wanted to thrash around, arch up against his questing mouth. The breath caught in her throat and then what emerged was a guttural groan of utter pleasure as he began working his tongue along the slippery groove that shielded her clitoris.

When he delicately began tracing the delicate, throbbing bud of her clitoris, she fisted her hands and moaned against her knuckles. It was exquisite. Transporting. She began to move against his mouth, finding his rhythm and matching it to her own.

She couldn't stop the shattering force of her orgasm. It ripped into her and she spasmed against his mouth, stifling her cries of pleasure, reaching to curl her fingers into his hair so that she could press his face harder between her quivering thighs.

The strength of her orgasm left her weak, flushed and drowsy and it took her a few moments before she surfaced.

'I'm sorry,' she uttered, dismayed, but he was smiling.

'For what? Enjoying yourself?'

'This wasn't what was supposed to happen.'

She wrapped her arms around him and buried her face against the side of his neck because there was something shockingly intimate in what had just taken place, at how her body had reacted.

The freedom she had felt at that moment of coming made her feel as though her soul had opened up.

Suddenly, she wanted *more*, but she wasn't too sure what.

She tentatively rested her hand on his lean, firm buttocks, then stroked him. He flipped her over and positioned her so that she was lying on top of him. Like this, his pulsing manhood against her was a powerful reminder of the chemistry uniting them against all odds. She had just had an explosive orgasm, and her body wanted a repeat performance, but this time she wanted him inside her, moving deep and hard.

X-rated thoughts made her feel faint. She arched up so that her heavy breasts dangled invitingly close to his mouth and their eyes tangled in the subdued darkness.

'Very sexy,' Matteo murmured shakily and, when he contained her breasts between his hands, squashing them gently together, he couldn't contain a groan of utter pleasure.

That did something to her. A strain of wanton recklessness that she had never known she possessed sizzled through her with lightning speed.

She angled her body lower and levered her nipple into his mouth, propping herself up so that he could suckle on it while she watched. It was erotic, giddily so. Very slowly, she began to move against him, sinuously and seductively, inching left to right, and then in small, circular motions that heightened his responses and brought a flare of scorching lust to his eyes.

In the end, he couldn't stand it any longer. He groaned, pulled her down to him and then kept completely still for a few seconds, breathing himself back into a place of some self-control.

'I need to be inside you,' he said hoarsely. 'You're driving me crazy.'

That was music to Rosie's ears. She felt as though she was waking up, stepping into the real world, for the very first time in her life. She watched him heave himself off the bed, every movement clumsy and uncoordinated, testimony to the fact that, whatever he was feeling, it had complete control over him. He donned protection, easing the condom over his erection, taking time because of his size.

She was aching for him…couldn't stay still. She whimpered as he levered himself over her and then the whimper turned into a cry of intense satisfaction when he finally pushed into her.

He moved slowly at first, driving deeper into her, and then faster, holding them both at bay until, on one final thrust, he groaned and she felt him swell inside her. Indescribably turned on, she wrapped her legs around him and let wave after wave of pleasure surge over her. Their bodies were as one. She could never have imagined feeling so close, so united, with anyone.

Spent, her breathing took its time returning to normal, but then she sighed happily and wriggled against him.

Her head was against his chest and Matteo trailed his fingers through her hair, sifting free the tangles. Her warm breath puffed against him. She had one thigh across his and he felt her dampness. She was so soft… sexy curves and bountiful breasts…with an eagerness that was as sweet as the summer sun.

For the first time in his life, Matteo felt exposed. Had sex ever been that good? He had only just come down from a high and he wanted to go there again. He had no inclination to head straight for the shower. His mind wasn't moving on to other things. There was no creeping urge to free himself from the presence of another body sharing his bed.

Disquieted, he eased himself back with a frown and lay flat to stare up at the ceiling and, immediately sensing the shift in atmosphere, she pulled back as well.

The urge to get her back close to him, pressed against him, was strong but Matteo resisted, asserting control over a situation that seemed to have pulled against the reins and galloped off in directions unknown.

'I know you're going to say that this was a mistake,' Rosie began and he turned to look at her.

Matteo thought that she would do well to steer clear from mind reading because she couldn't have been further from the truth. If what had just happened between them was a mistake, then he had been well and truly caught in the grip of it, and furthermore wanted a repeat performance. What was going on? He had encouraged the situation. He would be the first to admit that. He had wanted her and he had finally succumbed, had laid his cards on the table, made a pass, did what came so naturally to him. He just hadn't predicted that their love-making would be so explosive. Disturbingly so.

'You have no idea what I'm going to say,' he managed.

'I can tell from your silence…'

'I wouldn't call it a mistake.'

'Then what would you call it?'

'A complication. I'd call it a complication, and now we need to think about what we're going to do about it…'

CHAPTER SEVEN

'WE DON'T HAVE to do anything about it,' Rosie said, mouth down-turned as she stared at her pale hands clasping her knees. 'You're right. It shouldn't have happened. These things do.'

But never, Rosie thought with a rapidly beating heart, *to her.* In *her* world she'd become friends with some guy, there would be a little bit of flirting, but nothing, in the end, would lead anywhere—because sooner or later she would lose interest and there had never been the driving physical need she had felt with Matteo.

Nothing like it.

In her world, nothing had ever happened. No lights had been ignited. No breathless excitement. No *wanting* so big that it drowned out all the little voices urging caution.

In *her* world, she thought, life had never really been lived.

And, now that she had tasted what living to the full felt like, it was going to be snatched out of her grasp, because what had been momentous for her had been routine for him.

'Not to me,' Matteo said seriously. He reached to clasp her hands and held them in his, and Rosie relaxed a little.

The last thing she wanted was for him to see how vulnerable she felt.

'What do you mean?' she asked cautiously.

'I mean…' Matteo raked his fingers through his hair and frowned, as though trying to get his thoughts in order. 'Life doesn't spring surprises on me.'

'What, never?'

'Never.' He paused and looked at her. 'We don't come from the same world,' he said flatly. 'I may have as much money as I could ever want now, but life is more than just the sum total of the present. Life is a series of small sums, adding up to the person we eventually become, to the way we deal with what life throws at us. You have always lived your life in the exclusive conclave of the wealthy. You, I am sure, have always been open to surprises because there was always a comfort blanket waiting to break your fall if the surprise didn't turn out to be a good one.'

Matteo felt safe saying that. Black and white he could deal with. Grey occupied unknown territory and something inside resisted the threat of dealing with it.

Rosie blushed. 'That's not fair.'

'No, I don't suppose it is, but you can see what I'm getting at.'

'Yes. You're going to tell me that I'm not the sort you're attracted to because I don't have a hot-shot career in the City. Not everyone does and hot-shot careers aren't what they're cracked up to be. Have you any idea how stressed out some of those women are?'

'Stress can be an issue,' he murmured.

'I would rather be outside teaching sport than cooped up in a building popping anti-depressants because I'm finding it hard to deal with the anxiety.' Rosie wasn't going to roll over and play dead.

Matteo grinned, eyebrows raised, expression so unconsciously sexy that it was making the blood in her veins hot with a resurgence of desire.

How was it possible to be so fiercely turned on by someone who was in the process of giving her her walking papers because she wasn't suitable? But she was and she shifted uncomfortably.

'You don't have to bang the drum for people who don't wear power suits.' He shrugged. 'My point is that neither of us anticipated this but it doesn't mean that...'

'That?'

'That I didn't want it to happen and don't want it to happen again.'

'What are you saying?' She licked her lips and registered the way his eyes followed that tiny movement. With hunger. The same hunger she was feeling inside her. Like a match set to tinder, it ignited a series of popping explosions inside her.

Matteo Moretti, self-made billionaire, had come to this five-star Italian ski resort for one reason and one reason only—to close a deal that meant a lot to him.

He hadn't banked on suddenly having his life go off the rails because of her. One minute he had been politely shaking hands with his prospective clients, the next minute he had been on the back foot trying to justify bad behaviour of which he wasn't guilty. He'd been forced into a situation not of his making because of circumstances he could never have predicted. He wanted to do what it took to make his deal happen, and what that took involved a pretend romance with the least likely woman on the planet, as far as he was concerned.

So far, so bad, but on top of that here they were. Unlikely lovers. Had she expected that? She'd certainly acknowledged his massive sex appeal but no way had she projected that thought further into the realms of actually making love.

Now he was being honest and telling her like it was. He'd enjoyed what had happened between them. He wanted more, but there were a lot of conditions attached to that and a lot of sub-clauses he wanted her to understand.

She wasn't his type. She led the sort of privileged lifestyle he had commandeered for himself and made his own but his respect was reserved for people who had fought their way up, as he had. He dated bankers and lawyers and she was an intellectual lightweight—she would be the first to admit it. She'd never been in the league of either of her sisters and she'd packed in trying to be years ago, roughly around the time when her form teacher had kindly suggested to her parents that she focus on sport and arts and crafts.

Rosie was at a crossroads. Back away and put that one night down to a fantastic experience, never to be repeated, or else do what he wanted to do and prolong that one night for just a tiny bit longer, until the charade was over and they went their separate ways. An amicable break-up, initiated by her, between two people who had fallen for each other in haste but had thankfully come to their senses before any permanent damage could be done.

In a flash, she trawled back through the years and could see that her rebellious behaviour, her travelling and changing jobs and all those brief, barely notable liaisons with unsuitable boys had been as predictable as the rising and setting of the sun. He'd been right when he'd said that a comfort blanket of financial and emotional security had made all her choices safe. None of his choices had ever been safe. He would always have had a lot to lose and that dangerous edge to him was so appealing.

For the first time in her life, she knew in her heart that to follow him to where he was now pointing would be the most challenging and exciting choice she would ever make. It was so far out of her comfort zone that she had no idea where it might lead.

Not together in some happy-ever-after scenario, was the thought that flashed through her head. *But would she still be in one piece...?*

'I know what you're saying,' she said in a rush. 'You don't want this to be a one-night stand but you want me to remember that it isn't going to be anything more than a brief fling.'

Matteo was looking at her carefully, his silver eyes hooded and watchful.

He was waiting for her to accept his proposal on his terms. No involvement.

'I'm not looking for any kind of relationship,' he told her flatly. 'Here we are and the sex was fantastic.'

'Have you *ever* been interested in having a relationship with someone?' Rosie asked with genuine curiosity.

'That's not on my radar.'

'Why?'

'Why? Because everything I've ever seen has taught me that romance and all the fairy-tale nonsense that accompanies it comes with a lamentably short lifespan. I prefer to hedge my bets where the odds are better for a successful outcome.'

'Making money.'

'Works for me.' His voice hardened and she was reminded of the gaping chasm between them.

Common sense was making her question how she could be attracted to a guy who was so brutally honest when it came to his intentions.

'We *are* going to be stuck together for a few days more…' she began, yielding to the riptide of physical attraction.

Matteo's slow smile was the smile of the victor and he angled her so that their bodies were pressed together, stomach to stomach, her generous breasts squashed against his muscled chest.

She rested the palm of her hand firmly on his chest, just in case he thought that she was a rag doll, helpless and obedient. He was so staggeringly sexy, so stupidly good-looking, that she knew without a shadow of a doubt that women would trip over themselves to get an invite into his bed. 'And I get it. You don't have to warn me that you're not interested in a relationship with me. I'm not interested in any kind of relationship with you either.'

'So you're not into flowers, chocolates and romance?'

'I never said that. I'm just not interested in flowers, chocolates and romance *with you.*'

'I like that we're on the same page.'

'I can keep things separate,' she assured him, ignoring the shadow of doubt that whispered over her skin. 'Business is the fact that we have to present a certain front for a short while, and pleasure is…'

'What happens when the lights go off?' He traced the side of her cheek with his finger and she shivered, eyelids fluttering, body responding instantly to that gently, teasing caress. 'Or on…' he murmured seductively. 'Either way works for me.'

'What works for me,' Rosie told him, 'Is some sleep. I

have to teach tomorrow and then in the afternoon there's a little Christmas thing for the kids at the resort.'

'A Christmas thing?' He frowned.

She remembered what he'd said about Christmas not being his thing, but it was *her* thing, and if he was to convince her sister that they were an item, and by extension her family who would be trooping over only days from now, he would at least have to pretend to enjoy the festive season.

'It's no big deal.' She shrugged. 'You don't have to come but it'll only be for an hour or so. My sister will be there and some of her friends.'

'I'm getting the picture. If I'm a no-show, doubts might start being cast on our love-struck, whirlwind relationship.' He shrugged. 'I think it's fair to say that the rewards when we get back to this bed will more than compensate for sitting through some festive carols...'

Matteo was unprepared for what awaited him later that evening. Rosie had disappeared to work promptly at ten, and he had closed the door and settled down to make full use of the seldom used office, but having set up camp he instantly realised that his focus wasn't totally what it should have been.

Responding to emails had taken longer than usual because he caught himself sitting back, chair pushed away from the desk, contemplating what the night held in store for him. He'd spent a lifetime winning at everything he undertook but this victory felt so much sweeter.

The woman had cast a spell. He'd told her things he'd never divulged to anyone else. He'd opened up in ways that were hardly earth-shattering in the great scheme of things, and pretty routine by most people's standards, but which were earth shattering *for him*. He was a man who never confided. There had never been any pillow talk. People had no right of entry to his private life, he had long concluded, and if along the way some might have been offended by the rigidity of his Keep Out signs, then he really didn't care.

But there was something about this woman…

He told himself that there had been a perfectly good reason to confide in her. They were supposedly in a serious relationship and he had found himself on the back foot, having to explain his intentions to her sister, to his clients and to her family when they rolled up. It made sense to fill her in on some of his background, if only for the sake of verisimilitude, and it wasn't as though he was ashamed of his past. It had made him the pillar of strength and single-minded purpose that he was, hadn't it?

That said, Matteo was uneasily aware that something had shifted inside him, although he couldn't quite put a finger on what exactly, or how seismic the shift was.

So it was a relief when, at a little after four, the time arranged to meet Rosie at the resort for festive fun, he abandoned his work and headed down to the five-star hotel.

He smiled when he remembered her earnest attempt to teach him how to ski. He figured there was no harm in having another lesson.

He took a taxi to the resort and was deposited at a scene of outlandish Christmas extravagance.

At least, as far as he was concerned.

For a few seconds, he stood and stared. The hotel was lit up with hundreds of thousands of lights. He thought that up in the heavens, a million light years away, some alien life forms would be wondering what the hell was going on down here on planet Earth because the light display would surely be visible from outer space. The glittering, twinkling lights were weirdly hypnotic against the soft fall of snow and the whiteness of the landscape.

There were flurries of people everywhere, entering, leaving, skis on shoulders, holding hands with their kids. Evidently, this was something of a popular tradition. He steeled himself to sit through whatever lay ahead, now that he was here, and dialled Rosie's mobile, which remained unanswered.

Someone jostled him from behind, laughing and wishing him season's greetings in Italian, and that galvanised him into joining the throng of people heading into the hotel.

His irritation levels were rising fast when he heard her from behind, and he swung round.

He had already concluded that coming here had been an error of judgement. He was uncomfortable with the chaos and the over-the-top Christmas decorations everywhere. He had somehow expected the festivities to be of a more sombre nature: a choir singing carols in a dining area cleared of tables, perhaps. Instead...

He was scowling as he swung round, already formulating how he could politely make his excuses and clear off back to the chalet and wait for Rosie there.

And there she was. Santa's Christmas helper—red-and-white-striped tights, knee-high black boots with red *faux* fur at the top, small mistletoe-green dress with matching red fur swishing round the hem and at the cuffs of the sleeves, and a jaunty red-and-green hat set at an angle under which her flyaway, curly blonde hair peeped out with unruly abandon.

His breath caught in his throat and he stared.

'You're...' he managed to say hoarsely, raking his fingers through his hair.

'An elf. I know.' Rosie laughed but she was blushing madly because he was making no attempt to conceal the hot appreciation in his eyes. She'd seen him standing there, so perfectly still and watchful while the crowds swarmed around him. His tension was evident in his rigid posture and, from behind, she had pictured him frowning, irritable, about to glance at his watch. All of those things.

The guy didn't do Christmas, and why would he when he had spent his childhood in a children's home? Yes, maybe there had been the usual celebrations there, but without family it would still have been a lonely time. She hadn't thought but, hot and bothered as she was by the way he was looking at her, she still managed to reach out to circle his arm with her hand and draw him away from the centre of the vast lobby where pandemonium reigned.

'I'm sorry,' was the first thing she said when they were in a corner which was relatively quiet and she could hear herself think. There was still too much hubbub around. She pulled him into one of the smaller rooms where Tim, one of the managers, held his briefings with the ski instructors every morning. She shut the door and turned to face him, back to the door.

'I'm sorry,' she repeated quietly, and Matteo frowned, then strolled towards the large rectangular desk and perched against it, long legs extended and linked at the ankles.

He was such a specimen of pure physical perfection, she thought helplessly. Black jeans, black ribbed jumper, black coat—inappropriately non-waterproof and so stupidly elegant. He removed the coat and dumped it on the desk behind him.

'What are you sorry about?'

'I shouldn't have asked you to come here.'

'I don't recall you asking and, just for the record, I'm not in the habit of doing what other people tell me to do unless I want to. I'm here because I chose to come.'

'But you don't do Christmas.' She didn't back away from saying what was on her mind, doggedly bypassing the uninviting expression on his face. 'And this is the most Christmassy a place could get. You must hate it. I don't suppose,' she continued, tenderness sprouting shoots as she thought of him young and alone in a home without the jolly family chaos she had had growing up, 'That Christmas was great in...er...when you were growing up.'

'Is that the sound of you feeling sorry for me?'

'Yes. Is that a crime?' Rosie tilted her chin at a stubborn angle and folded her arms.

'You always say what's on your mind, don't you? I'm here, and I'll bet Bob and Margaret are somewhere in the throng of people. No need to pull out the sympathy card.' He thawed and appreciatively ran his eyes over her. 'I like the outfit, by the way.'

Rosie reddened. 'I don't think elf outfits were designed for my particular shape, but I promised. Barry, the guy in charge of the entertainment over Christmas, has always been good to me.'

'Good? In what way *good*?'

He looked at her with sudden, brooding intensity. He had no idea from where it had come, but out of the blue a spark of white-hot jealousy had suddenly ripped into him. He thought of her warmth and her voluptuous sexiness curling against his body and all thoughts of her sharing herself with someone else, anyone else, sent his brain into instant meltdown.

It was disconcerting, bewildering. He had never considered himself to be a jealous person. A man who was jealous was a man who lacked the sort of iron-clad self-assurance which he possessed in bucket-loads.

Never had he gone out with any woman and paid the slightest bit of attention to lovers she might have had in the past or, for that matter, to any men who might have come on to her in his presence. He had always had the supreme confidence of a man who knew in his gut that he had everything it took to keep a woman glued to his side for just as long as he wanted her there.

Why would he ever have been jealous of any other man? Emotions, like every other aspect of his life, were there to be controlled. A childhood in which control had always lain in the hands of other people, with rules and regulations there to be obeyed, had resulted in an adulthood where he made his own rules and regulations and was controlled by no one.

And a childhood devoid of the love of a parent, where efficiency had come a poor second to love and affection, had nurtured in him a healthy wariness when it came to his heart and handing it over to anyone. Frankly, that was something he would never do.

So, with those two factors firmly in place, why the attack of irrational jealousy?

'You're not *jealous,* are you?'

Matteo lowered his fabulous eyes for a split second and, when he next met her headlong stare, his expression was as controlled as always.

'I don't do jealousy.'

'There's an awful lot of things you don't do.'

'I do sexy, little red-and-green elf outfits.'

'If you don't *do* jealousy, then why does it matter how Barry is good to me?'

Rosie folded her arms and gazed at him, mouth set. She had never been one to let anything go. Yes, she was non-confrontational when it came to her family, because the path of least resistance had always been the most convenient one to take, but in all other respects she could be as stubborn as a mule when it came to getting answers to questions she asked. And Matteo Moretti seemed to have an amazing knack when it came to arousing her curiosity. Five minutes in his company and she could feel a thousand questions piling up in her head.

She imagined him jealous of her—possessive, guarding her with caveman-like, finger-crooking ownership—and, much as her logical brain instantly revolted against the sexist image, a very feminine part of her twisted with simmering excitement.

'You're doing it again,' Matteo said with exasperation. He shook his head. 'Has it occurred to you that, if we're supposed to be the loved-up couple, the last thing I need is an intrusive old flame entering into the picture and trying to pick up where he may have left off a couple of months ago?'

Simmering excitement was replaced by full-blown anger and Rosie took a step closer to him.

'First of all,' she hissed, glaring, 'How dare you imply that I'm the sort of person who lets a guy *pick up where he left off* as though I have no mind of my own? Do you honestly think that I'm that sort of woman? For your information, Matteo Moretti, I'm extremely selective when it comes to men! I've been on my own, even though I've had boyfriends, for *years*!'

'And then I come along?' Matteo asked speculatively. 'My mind is beginning to work overtime.'

What could she say to that?

'I didn't foresee…what happened between us.' Rosie suddenly found herself on the back foot.

'Even though you're extremely selective.'

'We were thrown together in a highly charged situation…'

'I was very happy to be the perfect gentleman and sleep on the *chaise longue*, although the ground would have been more comfortable.'

'Yes, well…'

'Let's drop this conversation. It's not going anywhere.'

He reached out, curled his fingers into her unruly, vanilla-blonde hair and tugged her gently towards him.

With helpless fascination, she watched as his mouth descended, and she closed her eyes and whimpered as his cool lips met hers. She curled her fingers onto the waistband of his trousers and felt herself slowly being propelled backwards, ever so slightly, until she bumped against the table behind her.

They were in a public place. A room that was only vacant temporarily because everyone happened to be outside, where the Christmas choir would be starting shortly. What on earth was she doing?

But right now, right here, he *owned* her body and what he was doing with it was turning her on so much she was melting from the inside out. He was kissing her, his tongue lashing against hers…cupping her bottom, massaging it with his big hands…pressing against her so that she could feel the rock-hardness of his erection bulging against his zipper.

Neither heard the door opening behind them. Rosie was certainly oblivious to everything until she heard her mother's shocked voice and then Candice laughing with genuine delight. At which point, she shoved Matteo away. When she looked at her parents—at her entire assembled family, because Emily was there as well— she just wanted the ground to open and swallow her up.

'What are you doing here?' She gasped. 'You're not supposed to be here for another couple of days.'

'Surprise, surprise!' Candice trilled. 'We couldn't wait to come over as soon as we could, and thank goodness that beastly virus was over sooner than expected! We just had time to dump our stuff at the chalet and here we are! Harry spotted the pair of you vanishing into this room so we thought we'd give you a happy surprise!'

Happy surprise? Rosie thought in horror. Of all the adjectives she could come up with, *happy* wasn't one of them. And whatever happened to that old-fashioned courtesy of knocking?

She cleared her throat but her father was already striding towards Matteo, and Rosie could tell from the expression on his face that he wasn't going to oh-so-politely pretend that he hadn't seen them a hair's breadth away from doing more than just a bit of kissing and groping.

She was hot with mortification. She'd always been a daddy's girl and she hated the thought of him being shocked at what he would consider inappropriate behaviour, given the surroundings. They were in a resort in which they'd all been well known as regulars for many years.

'Dad…'

'So you're the young man Candice has told us about!'

'We were just about to go back outside,' Rosie said weakly. 'Great that you're all over! Hi, Em. Is everyone here? The kids and Lucien and Robert as well?' Her voice was letting her down badly, but that was only to be expected, given the nightmarish turn of events.

'Rosie, I'd like to have a word with your young man on his own.'

'Dad…' She cast a panicked sideways glance at Matteo who, after looking momentarily disconcerted, had somehow managed to gather his composure while hers was still all over the place.

Her tall, beautiful mother, so much alike to her two eldest daughters, had opened her arms for a hug and Rosie walked towards her even though her heart had plummeted. Her dad could be ferocious when the mood took him, and especially so when it came to his daughters.

'Ken…' Debbie Carter said in a warning voice, halting him in his tracks. 'I'm sure Rosie's young man would like to relax before the cross examination begins.'

'Besides.' Emily was joining the family circle. 'Lucien and the kids are waiting outside with Robert.'

Rosie stifled a groan of utter despair.

But, Matteo, she noted with grudging admiration and relief, seemed to have everything under control, making suitably polite noises, clearly unfazed that they had been caught in the middle of a groping session worthy of a couple of horny teenagers.

'Just one question, young man,' her father eventually boomed. Whatever Matteo had been saying, she hadn't clocked all of it, because her mother had been chattering away a mile a minute about this and that.

'I've looked you up on the Internet, although I've heard your name before.'

'Of course.' Matteo accepted the recognition with a sweeping lack of false modesty.

'You're rich,' Ken tabulated on his fingers, 'You have a history of going out with beautiful, high-flying women and yet here you are with my baby.'

'Dad!' Rosie couldn't have got any redder but her father paid absolutely no notice to her horrified interruption.

'I don't take kindly to anyone dabbling with any of my daughters.'

'Don't blame you,' Matteo returned equably, giving Ken Carter as good as he got without any show of disrespect. He certainly wasn't in the least intimidated by the older man. 'If I had a daughter, I would certainly not want anyone fooling around with her feelings.'

'I *am* here!' Rosie interjected in a high voice, breaking free from her mother and moving to stand between the two men.

They couldn't have been more different physically. Matteo, tall and so dramatically good-looking. Her father, short and rotund, but with the sort of fiercely determined face that advertised why he had managed to get as far as he had.

'My intentions towards your daughter are entirely honourable.'

'Are they?' Ken growled.

'Honourable enough to ensure an engagement ring will soon be on her finger.'

The silence that greeted this statement was so complete that they could have heard a pin drop.

Then screeches of delight came from her sisters, who

rushed towards her, warm pleasure from her mother, who was trying to get a word in edgeways, and a grunt of approval from her dad, now shaking Matteo's hand vigorously, warmly, clapping him on the back and announcing that a weight had been lifted from his shoulders.

'She's my little baby,' Rosie was aware of him saying, while sick perspiration began rising from her toes upwards. 'Needs someone to look after her. Glad she's found that person.'

In a daze, Rosie was vaguely aware of her family all leaving the room *en masse*. Lucien and Robert had apparently chosen to stay outside with the kids, who were in seventh heaven, because Santa was due to make an appearance.

In her elf outfit, and shorn of all festive spirit, all Rosie could think was, *what the heck has just happened...?*

CHAPTER EIGHT

THE REMAINDER OF the evening passed in a blur. Rosie mingled with all the guests, entertaining the kids as Santa's jolly helper while frantically trying to keep her eye on a roaming Matteo. Roaming where and doing what? She wished she had eyes on the back of her head and consoled herself with the thought that he couldn't do any more damage than he had already done.

Engaged? Diamonds on fingers? What on earth had he been thinking?

She fumed internally, because a complicated situation had suddenly got a whole lot more complicated, and yet...

Something inside her burned with treacherous heat at the thought of being engaged to Matteo, wearing his ring on her finger, looking forward to a lifetime of making love with him and finding out more and more what made him tick.

From the very moment he'd entered her life, a curiosity had been awakened inside her that she knew, realistically, would never be sated. Whatever mess he had landed them both in, whatever *further* mess—she had started the ball rolling with her little white lie—this was and never would be a real relationship, one in which sharing and confiding played a part, in which discovery was part of the package.

She was one of the last to leave, because the staff were asked to volunteer for tidying up duties, and it was after eight by the time everything was more or less in order and normality had been restored.

She was standing uncertainly by the Christmas tree in the foyer, fiddling with her hat and wondering how her overwhelming family could be swamping her one minute and nowhere to be seen the next, when a dark, amused and familiar voice said from behind, 'The elf looks somewhat worse for wear.'

Rosie spun round, heart picking up pace and body racing into fifth gear at the sight of him. *He* certainly didn't look the worse for wear. If anything, an evening spent immersed in the Christmas spirit appeared to have relaxed him, although he was so clever at projecting a public face that she wasn't sure whether this was accurate or not.

He'd shoved up the sleeves of his shirt and her eyes were helplessly drawn to his powerful forearms, liberally sprinkled with dark hair. Her mouth went dry and for a few seconds she forgot that she was fuming and angry with him, and had been all evening for the extravagant lie he had told.

'Where's...everyone?' she asked.

'Gone to a French restaurant for dinner. *En masse.*'

'They didn't tell me that that was the plan.'

'That's because I assured them that we would be far keener to break bread together, just the two of us.'

'You're right.' Rosie was proud of her composure as she began walking towards the cloakroom so that she could retrieve her coat, bag and everything else. 'We need to talk.' She felt a lot less jumpy saying this with her back to him. The second he was staring at her with those amazing eyes, her thoughts began going haywire and she couldn't seem to string a coherent sentence together.

She disappeared into the cloakroom and emerged back in sensible clothing but feeling just as dishevelled.

'Let's get something to eat,' Matteo drawled, lounging against the wall with one finger hooked into the waistband of his trousers. 'Long, meaningful conversations are always more productive over food. Where do you want to go?'

Rosie couldn't think of doing anything as relaxing as eating when her mind was buzzing with all sorts of angry, confused thoughts, but she was ravenous. There had been a lot on offer in terms of canapés, but those had been out of bounds to the staff, and she had been too wired to eat any of the leftovers once the tidying had been done. Her stomach growled.

'I'm not actually hungry,' she returned coolly.

'Let's go to the restaurant here. The food is decent enough, from what I recall. And, before you start trying to convince me that you couldn't eat a thing, your stomach has just given you away. You're right, we have to talk, and I won't be doing that standing here outside the cloakroom.'

He pushed himself away from the wall and looked down at her and while she was dithering, loath to give in to his calmly spoken statement of fact, he spun round on his heels and began heading towards the flight of stairs that swept up to the restaurant on the mezzanine floor.

Gritting her teeth with frustration, Rosie pelted behind him, caught up with him. She had a moment of feeling utterly awkward when they were shown to a corner table in the restaurant because, although the coat, scarf and long, black cardigan were all in place, underneath was the elf outfit which wasn't exactly appropriate wear for a serious conversation.

However, there was nothing to be done about that, and she reluctantly surrendered the coat and long, winding scarf to the *maître d'*, making sure to keep the cardigan tightly pulled around her as she took her seat.

Her breasts felt huge, pushing against the stretchy outfit. She had removed the jaunty hat but her fair hair was all over the place and she ran her fingers through it now, trying to get it into some kind of order, her blue eyes very firmly fastened to Matteo's dark, lean face.

'I can see that you can't wait to tell me what's on your mind.' He lounged back in the chair, summoning the waiter over with the smallest of nods and ordering a bottle of Chablis without bothering to look at either the waiter or the wine list, instead keeping his gaze very firmly pinned to her flushed face.

'Can you blame me? How could you?'

'Why don't you take the cardigan off? You must be hot.'

'Thanks for the concern, Matteo, but I'm just fine. And you haven't answered my question—how could you tell my parents, *my whole family,* that we're going to get engaged? How could you pretend that this is actually a serious relationship!' Tears of frustration sprang to her eyes and she rapidly blinked them away.

The waiter came and poured the wine and she muttered what she wanted to eat—the first thing she spotted on the menu that she liked, knowing that she wouldn't do justice to the food that would be placed in front of her.

Matteo leaned towards her, his voice low and cool. 'When I met your sister, I got an idea of how your family operated. She flew down to attack me out of nowhere because she mistakenly thought that I had led you on and broken up with you. She was as ferocious as a tiger looking out for her cub. When you told me that you had lied about being involved with me in order to get out of an uncomfortable Christmas spent with your family trying to match-make you with some guy you weren't interested in, well, needless to say I had never come across a situation like that in my life before.'

Rosie reddened, knowing just how that made her sound—feeble, childish and not in control of her own life.

'We've been over all of this before,' she muttered with simmering resentment. 'It still doesn't explain why you said what you said.'

'Rosie.' He raked his fingers through his hair and sat back, sipping some of the wine and looking at her carefully, as though doing his best to marshal his thoughts. 'Your sister was just the tip of the iceberg. You are surrounded by family who clearly feel it's their duty to protect you.'

'It's not that unusual.' She squirmed and when she met his eyes his expression was remote.

'In my world, it's very unusual.'

With a tug of compassion, Rosie reached out, but he didn't take her hand and she withdrew it and returned it to her lap.

Of course, he wouldn't understand her family dynamics, she thought, ashamed because she had thoughtlessly put her foot in it. Again.

'I'm sorry, Matteo…'

Matteo held up his hand impatiently to cut short her stammered, sympathetic interruption. 'No need to be. I'm getting accustomed to your outbursts of sympathy. It's irrelevant. The fact is that your father, in particular, is extremely protective of you. I'm guessing that's because you're the baby of the family.'

Rosie shrugged and lowered her eyes. 'We have a lot of shared interests,' she admitted. 'My sisters have never been interested in sport and I was always the one he took to football matches. He used to tell me that it was the best relaxation he could think of after slaving away in an office five days a week.'

He, more than her mother, had been the one to indulge her nomadic lifestyle, she was now forced to concede. Her mother had made lots of noises over the years about her settling down, but her dad had always been the one to overrule those small protests.

Now, she wondered whether it hadn't been partly because her father, born into privilege, had had his life conditioned from an early age. He had been sent to the right schools and gone to the right university and maybe there had been a part of him that had always longed to rebel. Just a little. And that part had led life vicariously through his youngest daughter who had always been a free spirit.

Perhaps that was why, when Bertie had been presented as a possible suitor—her dad had climbed on board that wagon with the rest of the family—it had panicked her because everything had suddenly seemed very serious. A serious, suitable candidate to rescue her from her enjoyable but essentially irresponsible life.

If she hadn't been so panicked, she would never have

done what she had done—told that little white lie, never realising what the consequences might be.

'He was never really worried by all those dalliances you had in the past, was he, *cara*? Your father?'

'What makes you say that?' She lifted startled eyes to his and frowned.

'It was a conclusion I reached off my own bat,' Matteo admitted. 'And he said as much to me when I had a conversation earlier on with him.'

'What?' She stared at him furiously and he stared right back at her without blinking an eye. 'What were you doing talking to my dad?'

'Don't be disingenuous, Rosie.'

'What did he say?'

'Exactly that. You deserved to have some fun. You were never academic like your sisters, and if you wanted to stretch your wings a little then he could more than afford to indulge you. But he finally reached the conclusion that it was time for you to discover the joys of leading a more grounded existence, so to speak.'

'You had no right to discuss me behind my back!' she snapped, her voice steeped with dismay. 'And I'm not just a carefree twenty-something!'

'Aren't you?' Matteo questioned and that hurt. For a short while, she couldn't speak at all, and it was a relief that their starters were being positioned in front of them, small, tasty dishes, because it relieved her of the need to say anything.

'You think I don't find that an attractive trait?' he asked gruffly, and her eyes shot to his face.

'What are you talking about?'

'You're like a breath of fresh air and I think I may have mentioned that to you before,' Matteo admitted with rough sincerity. 'I've never met anyone like you in my life before.'

'What does that have to do with…anything? Matteo, it would have been so much easier if you hadn't said what you had. Relationships come and go, and if this one crashed and burned, then…'

'Then it would have joined all the rest of your relationships that had crashed and burned in the past?'

Rosie gazed at him with down-turned mouth.

'Why should you care?' Her voice was so low that Matteo had to strain forward to hear what she had said.

Good point, he thought uncomfortably. There was no reason why he *should* care. He just knew that what he had seen in her during the short time he had known her had fired up in him something strangely protective. Her entire family had descended and when her father had cornered him he had reacted utterly on impulse. For once in his life, Matteo had been galvanised into behaviour that was alien to him.

The only thought that had run through his head was, *they know who I am and they're already predicting the outcome. Another failed relationship, and this time one deserving of even more tea and sympathy because of who I am.*

Underneath the sunny, plucky exterior was someone both sensitive and oddly brave. She needed to find her place in the family dynamics and suddenly he had been driven by the urge to help her along.

Matteo wasn't going to delve further into his motivations. Introspection never got anyone anywhere because, when it came to the crunch, action and not thought was what mattered.

But tugging away at the back of his mind was the notion that perhaps not everyone fought the same battles he had. It wasn't always about carving out a place for yourself in the world of money. Sometimes, there were other forces at work. It didn't mean that the fight was any the less significant.

He shrugged. 'Maybe I didn't care for either the idea that I would be just the sort to take advantage of an innocent like you, because of the person I'm reported as being in the media, or the idea that you would be disingenuous enough to walk straight into a trap from which you could only end up hurt, requiring your over-protective family to go into rallying mode.'

'So you decided to become the knight in shining armour?'

'That wasn't the intention but I'm happy to go along with the description.'

'Except,' she said ruefully, 'That still leaves us the problem of breaking up from a so-called serious relationship where we're about to get engaged.'

'No,' Matteo corrected, 'That leaves *you* walking away from a serious relationship where we're about to get engaged. That puts *you* firmly in the role of heartbreaker.' He grinned. 'I have a feeling that if you play your cards right your family will have a lot of respect for your decision.'

'Why would you do that for me?'

'Maybe I think you're worth it.'

Rosie nodded with a thoughtful frown but inside her nerves were all over the place.

What did it mean?

They had been thrown together because of her rash outburst and she had assumed, from day one, that they were so dissimilar that, even having slept together, there was no way he could ever find her interesting. Not really.

And vice versa, naturally.

But a tiny voice now asked…did they actually have what it took to have a relationship? A proper relationship?

A curious thrill rippled through her, the thrill of the great, big unknown, of an adventure waiting to happen.

'Yes.' She unconsciously glanced at her finger and wondered what a diamond ring would look like on it, then she closed her hand into a fist and banished the thought, because this wasn't real. There would be no genuine 'for ever after' relationship. He'd felt sorry for her. Underneath the tough exterior, she couldn't have found a nicer guy even though she didn't think he'd thank her if she pointed that out.

'You have no idea what kind of Pandora's box you've opened,' was what she said instead. 'My parents aren't going to be casual about this. My mum will already be planning what outfit she'll be wearing, and whether it would be too premature to have a chat with the local vicar, and they'll both be debating whether they should have a marquee on the lawn like they did for both my sisters.'

She closed her eyes and contemplated the dreadful scenario unfolding in front of her. 'But you're right. You're such a catch, they'll respect me for turning down your proposal.' She smiled, a wide, sunny smile. 'A passing fling, well, they would have been sympathetic, but a full-blown marriage proposal—I'm not sure if they'll know quite how to react.'

'You're fortunate,' he said in a husky undertone and

Rosie glanced up at him in bewilderment. 'You have people who care deeply about you.'

'They care so much that they don't understand that there were times when I felt stifled,' Rosie said bluntly. She felt as though something inside her had toughened up. The girl who had rushed into a little white lie to spare herself the annoyance of Bertie, his nerdy persistence and irritating habits was gone for ever. In its place was someone slowly realising that she needed to be in charge of her future, stronger, more assured, more focused.

'There were times when *I* didn't realise just how stifled I felt.'

'So you took to the hills and ran as fast as you could?'

Rosie laughed, marvelling that he could be so perceptive. 'They were always terribly understanding about my academic failures.'

'Maybe they shouldn't have been,' Matteo said mildly. He reached forward absently to graze her knuckles with his thumb.

'We're having a deep and meaningful conversation,' Rosie remarked and then wished she hadn't because he immediately withdrew his hand with a frown.

'We're discussing a way forward with this,' he responded quickly. 'I took this charade past the bedroom door and into the bed.'

'You slept on the sofa,' Rosie was quick to remind him. She wanted him to reach out and take her hand again. She missed the warmth, the feel of his finger casually stroking her bare skin. 'And you would have carried on sleeping there until your deal got signed and you were free to leave.'

'I opened the Pandora's box,' Matteo said drily. 'But let's forget about who did what. We weren't having a deep and meaningful conversation. We were discussing what happens next and how best to deal with the fallout.'

He shifted, uneasy and suddenly restless.

The logic of his argument was reassuring. 'Let's face it, Rosie—when I walk away from this, I won't have any further contact with you or your family. You will be the one left to handle the inevitable post mortem. It's to your advantage if you're given a helping hand in tackling the aftermath.'

'Of course.' She linked her fingers together and stared at them. That told her, she thought, just in case she started getting any ideas. She doubted he even realised the subliminal warning. 'What if word gets out?'

'What do you mean?'

'Social media is everywhere. People with mobile phones taking pictures. What if someone you work with finds out that you somehow got yourself engaged while you were over here on business? And then got cruelly dumped?'

Matteo grinned. 'I like the way you're going to cruelly dump me. I'd bet that there might be a few women out there who would enjoy hearing that.' He became more sober. 'Go ahead and be as heartless as you like. I don't care what other people think of me.'

Somewhere along the line, food had been eaten and wine had been drunk. Matteo hadn't really noticed. He had been way too absorbed in the woman sitting opposite him, absorbed to the exclusion of everything else, and that in itself was a source of wonder because he couldn't recall the last time any woman had commanded that sort of attention from him.

Work absorbed him. Women relaxed him. Not this

one. His life had been a rollercoaster ride since meeting her and it surprised him to acknowledge that, as hair-raising experiences went, this one was pretty exhilarating.

He watched her with brooding intent, his keen eyes noting everything about her softly appealing face, from the delicate tinge of colour staining her cheeks to the glittering blue of her eyes and the fullness of her parted mouth. Then he thought of her in bed, naked and eager, her full roundness, her heavy breasts, such a sexy contrast to the angular women who constituted his usual diet. He felt himself harden at the thought of her.

'I envy you not caring what other people think of you,' she was saying as their eyes tangled. 'If I had half of your indifference, we wouldn't be sitting here right now.'

'But you wouldn't be you if you had half of my indifference and who says that I'm not enjoying myself sitting here right now?'

Her tongue darted out, moistening her upper lip, and Matteo had to stop himself from groaning.

'Stop doing that,' she whispered, lowering her gaze, but almost immediately returning greedy eyes to his lean, handsome face.

'Doing what?'

'Staring at me…like that.'

'Like what?'

'You know.'

'Oh, I know.' He laughed under his breath. 'I just want to hear you say it.'

'You're looking at me as though you could…'

'Eat you?' He raised his eyebrows expressively. 'It's exactly what I want to do, *mia cara*. I want to feast on your body, suckle your breasts until you're squirming underneath me, and then I want to take you until you cry out and beg for me to never stop.'

'Matteo!' She squirmed and looked around her, red-faced.

'Let's get out of here.'

A thought suddenly struck her. 'We should. We can't have the whole troop return to the lodge to find that your things are in the spare room!'

'Don't panic. I removed myself for the night, not for the long haul, and if the bed isn't made quite as it should be then who's to say that we haven't spread ourselves around the house in our uncontrollable need to pleasure one another, irrespective of whether it's your bedroom or not?' He burst out laughing as crimson colour stole into her face. 'Don't look so shocked. It happens.'

He beckoned across a waiter with a crook of his finger and tossed his credit card down without bothering to check the bill. 'I'll enjoy showing you the ropes.'

Rosie had no need to ask what he meant and she blushed furiously, her whole body going up in flames with anticipation and excitement.

'Come on.'

'Where are we going?' she asked, breathless, cardigan still pulled tightly around her as she followed him out of the restaurant. Instead of heading towards the cloakroom so that she could fetch her coat, they headed towards the reception desk where she was greeted like an old friend.

'I think we can spend the night here, don't you?' He slid her a sideways glance.

If he wanted their pretend relationship to hit the gossip grapevine fast, then he couldn't have chosen a more efficient method. They all knew her here at the hotel, and sharing a room with him...?

A flare of adrenaline-charged excitement coursed through her. She felt faint and she had to look away as he sorted out the most expensive suite for them.

'This is crazy. Mum and Dad...everyone...will be expecting us to show up at the chalet after dinner.'

'Mum and Dad and everyone else will be raising their glasses to the wildly enamoured couple. If you're planning on forging a way forward as someone with a voice, then you could start using it right now. Besides, I can't wait, and I don't want to get back to the chalet to find myself bogged down making small talk until midnight.'

'I can't wait, either,' she confessed, as they made their way to the lift, on a heated sigh. Her hand was trembling as she extracted her mobile phone and punched in Candice's number. She sent a text because she didn't know if she would be able to sound controlled should a conversation ensue.

The lift doors opened and as soon as they had whirred shut behind them he pulled her to him. His head descended and his mouth crushed hers hungrily, his tongue plundering her mouth until her legs felt as weak as jelly and she had to cling to him for support, like a rag doll. She pushed her hands underneath his clothes, finding bare, warm skin, and she shoved them up to rub his flat nipples. His body was hard and sinewy. She wanted to explore every inch of it, to feel every corded muscle, sinew and tendon.

In a minute, she thought weakly, the lift doors were going to open and they would be faced with some shocked faces, but they made it to their floor in privacy, and by the time he was unlocking the door to the suite with the gold-and-black card she was desperate to get rid of her clothes.

They stumbled into the huge sitting area, bodies urgently pressed together. He was stripping along the way, blindly leading her in the general direction of the bedroom until he abandoned their stumbling progress and swept her off her feet, kicking open the door.

The bedroom was bathed in the peculiar glow only falling snow outside could cause and he left the curtains open. She was on the mattress of the super-king-sized bed without even realising how she had got there, and she hastily propped herself up on her elbows, watching as he stripped off.

He was so glorious he took her breath away. So glorious that nothing else mattered. Not her family, not what other people might start thinking, not the aftermath of this madness waiting to catch her out.

The only thought in her head was, *I want this guy more than anything.*

The wretched elf outfit had to come off but he stilled her frantic hands as she began to scrabble with buttons, the zip and various bits of Velcro, all of which seemed to be oddly positioned in ridiculously unreachable places.

'I want to see you do a striptease,' he murmured, his voice as dark and as seductive as chocolate. 'I want to enjoy watching you. You have an amazing body.'

He held out his hand, their fingers linked and then she was on her feet and he was on the bed, places reversed. He, utterly naked, and she…

Bit by bit the clothing was removed and bit by languorous bit she began to enjoy herself. Initial nerves were replaced by brazen relish. His eyes on her were such a turn on and she was wet and on fire by the time the last strip of elf costume had been flung to the ground.

She sashayed her way towards him and stood by the side of the bed, and he sat up to slip his hand between her thighs, parting them, feeling the wetness there against his hand. Then he gently parted the delicate folds of her womanhood and flicked his tongue along the groove, finding the stiffened bud of her clitoris with ease.

Rosie moaned and arched back, automatically opening her legs wider to receive his exploring tongue. She moved against him, hands reaching down to press his head harder against her so that he could taste her even more thoroughly.

As he licked, he caressed the soft flesh of her inner thighs, stroking lightly until she was going crazy with desire. She wanted to come against his mouth and yet she never wanted the rolling waves of sensation to end.

He took her so far and then pulled her down to the bed to join him. This time, their love-making was fast, hard and furious and her orgasm was explosive, coming even as she felt him arch back and groan loudly, succumbing to his own release.

She was utterly spent when he eventually positioned her onto her side so that they were facing one another. She looked at him drowsily, smiled and stroked the side of his face.

'We're not in a trap.' Matteo kissed the side of her mouth, the angles of his lean face thrown into shadow because his back was to the window. 'So the charade went a little further than originally intended but is that such a bad thing?'

'What do you mean?'

'I mean this...us.' He swept his hand along her thigh

and she shivered. 'This ridiculous chemistry... So, we're chalk and cheese and what we have isn't going to last. You know that and I know that but for now... God, I want you, *tesoro mio*. When I think of you, I want you, and I want you immediately. I touch you and I don't want the touching to end. This charade...why don't we enjoy it for what it is and forget about tomorrow?'

CHAPTER NINE

ROSIE DIDN'T WANT to think it but she did anyway: *this is perfect.*

She and Matteo were standing on an incline, looking down at a Christmas extravaganza. It was a little after seven and the slopes were ablaze with lights. The sound of laughter and kids screeching with excitement were only just drowned out by the harmonious singing of the Christmas choir, who were perched on a makeshift stage just outside one of the five star resorts in radiant reds, whites, *faux* furs and boots.

For the first time in days, the snow had stopped falling, conspiring to provide a picture-postcard image of what the perfect December evening should look like.

Of course, she guiltily acknowledged to herself, the reason it was perfect was because Matteo was standing next to her with one arm carelessly slung round her waist. They were both drinking mulled wine and Rosie was heady with happiness.

She'd never thought that it was possible for her to be quite so happy. Her family adored Matteo. After her father's initial misgivings, they had all succumbed to his charm. He could hold court without seeming to and what she might once have considered the hugely annoying trait, being just so self-assured, she now found deliciously mesmerising.

It was really no wonder her entire family had been sucked into his magic circle. She could only imagine their giddy relief at the fact that she was supposedly engaged to a guy like him, settled with someone of whom they heartily approved.

She didn't want to think about how they would react when it ended. She didn't want to think of all those scary tomorrows and what they might herald. Three days ago, he had dangled that carrot in front of her: enjoy the chemistry they shared and forget about tomorrow. She had grabbed that carrot with both hands. She was going to live for today. She was going to savour the excitement, the wonder of being with an unsuitable guy who still, somehow, managed to make her blood boil hot in her veins. She was going to enjoy losing herself in the glory of his love-making. Beyond that, anything could happen. In theory.

'Miss your family not being here?' Matteo inclined his head to murmur into her ear and Rosie shivered and looked up at him. In the reflected glow from all those thousands of lights that illuminated the snow-covered slopes, his face was all shadows and angles.

She thought about it. 'Normally I would,' she confessed. 'But I'll be seeing them on Christmas Eve when we…er…when I go back to England. It's unusual for me to be here at this time of year. It's because I'm instructing.'

She gulped down some of the mulled wine. Would Matteo be returning to England with her? And would he be spending Christmas with her entire family at her parents' country house in the Cotswolds? Or would he be going his own way, doing his own thing? She didn't want to ask the question because she was afraid that the answer might not be to her liking. The deal with Bob and Margaret had been signed and now there was nothing binding him to her, aside from the chemistry.

In his *let's enjoy this and forget about tomorrow* suggestion he had failed to clarify what counted as 'tomorrow' and she didn't want to press him for an answer.

'Are *you* going to miss them?' she asked teasingly. 'I expect you've found it all a little…chaotic. It always is when we all get together, especially with the kids, and especially at this time of year.'

'It's been an experience.' Matteo shrugged. 'This would not be how I would usually spend the run up to Christmas Day but, as experiences go, I am certainly glad I've had it.'

'That's good,' Rosie said uncertainly. She laughed. 'I think.'

'I'll certainly be glad to have the place to ourselves once again.' Matteo lowered his voice and brushed his lips against her cheek. 'There's something unnerving about making love when outside there's the danger of two little people banging on the bedroom door and demanding interaction in whatever game they've decided to play.'

'They liked you,' Rosie said.

'Don't sound so shocked,' Matteo commented wryly, leading her down towards the lit slopes where the carollers were finishing the last of their repertoire. He still had his arm around her waist and she was leaning into him.

'I bet you never come into contact with anyone under the age of…let me think about this…maybe twenty-one?

The average age for new recruits to join a company after university?'

'You forget,' Matteo surprised himself by pointing out, drawing her closer against him, 'That I grew up surrounded by a lot of kids. When I hit twelve, I was given the task of looking after a number of the younger ones.' He laughed at the surprise on her face. 'And don't tell me that you're sorry because you've suddenly remembered my very different childhood.'

'You took care of the other kids?'

'It was company policy, so to speak. You would be surprised at how many of them were off the rails by the time they hit six.'

'You don't like talking about your past.'

'I've never seen the point of dwelling on things that cannot be changed.'

'Have you ever confided in anyone?'

'By anyone, you mean a therapist?' Matteo burst out laughing. 'That touchy-feely stuff isn't for me.'

'There's a lot to be said for that touchy-feely stuff,' Rosie said pensively. She shivered as his hand crept under her thick, padded, heavily insulated jacket to caress a sliver of skin under the waistband of her ski trousers. 'I'm a great believer in sharing…what's on your mind.'

'I know.' Matteo grinned down at her. 'You're excellent at letting me know all the highways and byways of what you're thinking.'

'Do you find it boring?' She stiffened and pulled away from the light caress.

'You'd know about it if I did.'

'How? Would you tell me?' She looked up at him seriously, wishing she could read his face, wishing she had as much insight into the workings of his mind as he obviously thought he had into hers. Wishing that the playing field was a little more level.

'I wouldn't have to.'

The carollers disbanded and normality returned, although skiing was now being replaced by *après ski* and the crowds were dissipating, with clusters of warmly wrapped people hiving off in whatever direction their various resorts, chalets and hotels lay.

The loss of that background carolling suddenly made the cold, wintry slopes feel very quiet, very still. 'I meant have you ever confided in any of your girlfriends in the past?'

'No,' Matteo said abruptly.

Rosie ventured boldly into the unknown. 'You've never felt close enough to anyone to talk to them about your past?'

'I'm trying and failing to see where this conversation is heading.'

'It isn't heading anywhere.' She sighed.

'Good,' he said silkily. 'Now, where do you want to eat? Are you hungry? We could always skip an elaborate meal and head back to the chalet. I'm looking forward to having the place to ourselves.'

'So you've said.' She kept her voice as bright as she could but this time it felt like an effort.

He was looking forward to an empty chalet because without anyone around he could, taking his time and without fear of interruption, do what he did best. Make love. Wonderful, stupendous, fabulous sex. But that was where it ended. He wasn't interested in being alone with her so that they could share anything more significant than their bodies.

Rosie hated herself for letting her thoughts stray into that dangerous territory. She was determined to think and live in the moment but her heart clenched in disappointment and frustration.

'Eat, I think.' She needed a bit of time to get back into the right frame of mind, away from the barrage of muddled thoughts assailing her. 'The café in that resort halfway down the hill is very good. Although it might be packed.'

He *had* confided in her, Rosie thought as they slowly made their way past busy, brightly lit restaurants, cafés and boutiques, past the laughing, chattering crowds. He had told her stuff about his past, but did she occupy a unique position because of that? Or had he said as little as he possibly could simply because, in this game of theirs, he'd decided that she needed, at the very least, to have some sketchy background information about him?

And the information had been delivered without the benefit of emotion. He had simply told her facts about himself without telling her how those facts had impacted on him, made him the person that he had become.

It wasn't his fault that his omissions had left her more curious rather than less.

The café was crowded but a table was miraculously produced for them from thin air. She had noticed that he had that impact on people and it wasn't simply because he oozed wealth. It was a combination of his striking good looks and his cool assumption that the duty of everyone around him was to jump through hoops to give him what he demanded.

That curious blend of urbane sophistication and dangerous, wrong-side-of-the-tracks toughness inspired awe, fascination and a healthy respect in everyone he met.

She couldn't imagine what it might be like to work for him. He had offered her a job in one of his companies as a way to becoming independent once they returned to London but she had immediately turned him down. It had felt like a salve to his conscience for any discomfort he might subconsciously feel when their time was up. But, when she thought about him no longer being in her life at all, she felt sick. He had made her question her life and her choices and that had been a good thing, long overdue, but had his offer been genuine? It would certainly be useful, at least to start, if she were to enter the work force as opposed to returning to full-time education, which was also an option.

And she might get to see him. He wouldn't vanish completely out of her life. He would still be *there*. Maybe, subconsciously, by offering her a job, he had been thinking the same thing...?

All those questions were finding air time in her head as she sat down so it was hardly surprising that the woman's voice from behind her took a while to penetrate.

She wasn't expecting it. She wasn't expecting anyone to recognise Matteo and she spun around as he stood up, his silver-grey eyes revealing nothing, although he was smiling at the tall, striking brunette weaving her way towards them.

Rosie watched.

An old flame. That was the thought that raced through her head. The woman was in her thirties, with a sharp, dark bob. She was very tall, very slender and very pale.

'Bethany.' Matteo made the introductions, his voice formal and polite. 'This is... Rosie.'

'Rosie...' Bethany's curious brown eyes looked at Rosie, gauging, intelligent, speculative. 'Have we met anywhere? I don't believe I recognise you. Are you and Matteo…?'

'Tell me what you're doing here, Bethany. Didn't think you found much time to take to the slopes. Join us for a drink?'

'Quick Chablis? Rob's going to be joining me in twenty minutes. You remember Rob, don't you? Melstorm? Head of Asset Management at Frazier and Co? We're an item now.' She flashed an enormous engagement ring in their general direction and sat at the chair Matteo had pulled out for her.

At which point, Rosie was relegated to spectator.

It wasn't so much an intimate catch-up as a conversation about finance and what was going on in their relative worlds of law, asset management, mergers and acquisitions and big business. Names were bandied about and small in-jokes made that elicited the sort of secret smiles from the brunette that made Rosie's teeth snap together.

Chablis finished and about to leave, Bethany finally turned her attention to Rosie and asked pleasantly what she did for a living.

'Don't tell me,' she drawled lightly, head tilted to one side as though trying to work out a conundrum, convinced that the right answer would be found. 'Maybe company lawyer for one of those start-up companies? Dylan Sync, maybe? If this rogue's dating you—and I gather he must be, because it's not exactly his thing to be in the company of any woman he isn't dating unless he's in an office wearing a suit—then you surely must be big in the corporate world.'

Rosie stiffened, sensing an attack under the glossy smile.

'I must be the exception to the rule because I... I'm currently employed as a ski instructor at the resort a little further up the slopes.'

'You're a *ski instructor*?' Bethany stared at her as though she had suddenly grown two heads and then she burst out laughing. 'I don't believe it!' She waggled her fingers in a little wave at the fiancé who was obviously behind them 'Matteo Moretti and a ski instructor! That's a first. You must have something special, my dear!'

'I suppose I must have.' Rosie realised in that instant that Matteo wasn't going to intervene, he wasn't going to stand up for her, and that hurt because it put everything in perspective. 'What do you think, Matteo?'

'I think it's getting late and it's probably time we headed back to the lodge.'

'How did you two meet? I'm curious.' Bethany's eyes darted slyly between the two of them.

'How we met is irrelevant,' Matteo drawled. 'Good luck with the wedding, Bethany. Should I expect an invite to land on my doormat in due course?'

'Oh, I shouldn't think so, Matteo.' Her brown eyes cooled. 'I don't think Rob would like that very much. Ex-heartbreakers always pose a threat.'

Then she laughed again and said to Rosie, 'Have fun with Matteo, Little Miss Ski Instructor, but be warned—he's not a guy who likes sticking around for any length of time!'

'Don't worry about me.' Rosie bared her teeth in a stiff smile. 'I won't be leaving this with a broken heart.' She saw, from Bethany's face, that her jibe had hit home. It wasn't in her nature to be uncharitable, but this time it felt pretty good.

Little Miss Ski Instructor? No way was she going to get away with that dismissive insult.

But this was the sort of woman Matteo enjoyed and not just for her novelty value. This was the sort of woman who appealed to him on an intellectual front. Rosie had watched the way they had talked to one another, their conversation on a level she could barely keep up with. They had friends in common, work in common—an interest in the business of making money in common.

'Apologies,' Matteo said, turning to her.

'Why?'

'You were uncomfortable. I had no idea Bethany would be here.'

'If you thought that I was uncomfortable, then why didn't you say something?'

'Say something?'

'I get it that she was an ex-flame, and you had lots of exciting catching up to do about the stock market and which dull company was doing what, but it got personal, Matteo.' Rosie's heart was thudding so hard, it was making her giddy. 'She was just plain nasty to me and the least you could have done was to say something. When did you two break up anyway?'

Matteo looked at her narrowly and in silence. 'Where are you going with all this?'

'I'm not *going* anywhere. I'm reacting just the way any other woman you were sleeping with would react!'

Pinned to the wall, Matteo experienced a surge of searing discomfort. She never backed down. He should know that trait of hers by now. She was persistent with him in a way no one else was. She didn't wince or back away in the face of his obvious, unflinching disapproval. He didn't want to discuss Bethany, or any of his ex-girlfriends, for that matter. She should be able to suss that out. He knew that she did, but she just kept crashing through his boundary lines as though they didn't exist.

What was it with the woman? Did he need this?

'How would *you* feel if some ex-flame of mine showed up and was rude to you? How would *you* feel if I just stood there and didn't say anything?'

'I wouldn't have a hysterical outburst,' Matteo returned grimly. 'I also wouldn't expect you to rush to my defence.'

'Well, you might have rushed to mine!'

They stared at one another in silence and Rosie was the first to look away. She was feeling so many things. Hurt, disappointment and most of all the sinking knowledge that he felt nowhere near for her what she felt for him. She'd let herself get carried away, had let her imagination play tricks on her, and she was paying the price now. He wasn't going to defend her because he didn't see the point.

'You did a pretty good job of taking Bethany down a peg or two.' Matteo shifted, deeply uncomfortable with the raw emotion of this conversation, yet seemingly unable to shut it down the way he knew he had to.

What was she looking for? He was no one's knight in shining armour. He'd never applied for that job and he never would, and he knew that she deserved better than someone whose entire life had geared him towards turning away from rescuing damsels. But something twisted inside him at the expression on her face.

'You're right. I did.' She paused and looked him in the eye. 'Would you have told her that I was your girlfriend, Matteo? If she hadn't jumped to the conclusion off her own bat? Or would you have passed me off as the ski instructor you were having a drink with because you'd just had a good lesson and wanted to say thank you?'

'Don't be ridiculous,' he said, flushing darkly. 'Why is that women can fixate on one small thing and magnify it to ridiculous proportions?'

'It's patronising to stereotype women and to try and diminish what I'm trying to say. I'm not fixating on *one small thing*. I'm being perfectly reasonable.'

'I can't believe I'm having this conversation.'

'You mean you don't *want* to believe that you are, because the only talking you're interested in doing is between the sheets.'

'It works, doesn't it?' he grated, crashing into the barrier of her arctic coldness and not knowing how to deal with it, because he had become so accustomed to her soft, sweet accommodating nature. She was so ultra-feminine. He angrily wanted to backtrack and rush to her defence, as she'd wanted, just so that he could have her back.

But maybe this was for the best. In fact, it *was* for the best. This was supposed to be fun. He wasn't interested in having to justify his behaviour to anyone. He'd never done that in his life before and he wasn't going to start now.

'You might think it's terrific being repressed,' Rosie said through gritted teeth, getting angrier and angrier by the second, 'But it's not. It's just sad and I feel sorry for you. And, if you don't want to be having this conversation, then that's fine. I'll head back to the chalet and you can do whatever you want. Stay here at the hotel. You've signed your precious deal so there's really no reason for us to carry on with this any more.'

She didn't rush or run off, and anyone might have thought that she was simply getting up to go to the bathroom, but she wasn't looking at him as she weaved her way towards the door, heading straight for the cloakroom so that she could collect her padded jacket.

Would he follow her? Rosie didn't know and she didn't care. She knew that he didn't *do* so many things, of which emotion was obviously one, but his indifference to her feelings hurt her beyond belief.

She thought of Bethany and she felt a rush of pure misery. It was one thing knowing that he went for women like that but it was another thing actually to be confronted by one of them.

That unexpected meeting had really brought home to her that to Matteo this really was just a game and she was no more than a passing indulgence.

Whilst for her…

She couldn't be casual about him the way he was about her because she had made a crucial mistake in her dealings with him. She had somehow managed to pretend that she could be as tough as he was. She had forgotten that she had a heart, and that hearts got broken, and hers was breaking now because she knew, without a shadow of a doubt, that she had stupidly gone and fallen in love with the man.

From pointing at a random stranger in the foyer of the resort, a stranger clearly removed from the festive chaos all around him, she had galloped towards heartbreak. He had seduced her with his wit, his charm, his intelligence and with those glimpses of someone he was at pains to conceal. He had thrown her tantalising titbits about himself and about his childhood and she had gobbled them up and wanted more. What had started as a charade because he wanted to complete a deal, and he needed to go along with the pretence of a relationship with her in order to get there, for her had become an obsession.

And now they were lovers and everything was...*a mess*.

She knew that he was behind her before he said, in a low, gritty voice, 'You don't get to make outrageous statements like the one you just made and then run away.'

'Go away. I don't want to talk to you.'

'Tough. You opened a box and now you don't get to shut the lid until we've gone through all the contents.'

Rosie felt the chill of an imminent break-up whisper over her. Pride came to her defence.

'You're right.' Somehow, they were outside the hotel and heading towards the car. Her feet had propelled her in the right direction and she hadn't even noticed. She wasn't looking at him as she headed to the car and she was revving the engine before she deigned to glance in his direction, and then only briefly. ' I thought that I could do this. I thought I could have a fun fling with you, but you're a stranger, and having a fun fling with a stranger doesn't make me feel good about myself.'

'Where is this coming from? One crazy encounter with an ex?' He frustratedly raked his fingers through his hair.

'It's not about your ex, Matteo. It's about the fact that I don't know you. You keep everything to yourself.'

'You know more about me than any other woman I've ever gone out with.'

And that was why she had deluded herself into thinking that what they had was somehow special. He'd opened up about his past and she had read all sorts of things into that. She'd been wrong to do so.

'Because, as you pointed out,' she said coldly, 'You

had no option because of the situation. You were desperate to get your deal done. You had to pretend to be my boyfriend and so you ended up having to share a few details about your past to keep the fiction believable.'

She laughed shortly. 'You couldn't take any chances that Bob and Margaret or someone from my family might ask a question, only to find out that I didn't know a thing about you aside from your name. You shared what you did because you didn't think you had a choice. I don't even know what your deal was all about or why it was so important to you! You never shared *that,* did you?'

'Want to know about the deal, Rosie?'

'Nope. You can carry on being as secretive as you like, Matteo.'

She wasn't going to beg. She'd made the biggest mistake of her life falling in love with him and she only had herself to blame because he had been honest from the start about his intentions: sex, fun and nothing else. She'd chosen to ignore the hand in front of her because trying to rearrange the cards into a different, more exciting hand had been too tempting to resist. In the end, it was always going to come back to the same place, though. They were never going to have a relationship, not the sort of relationship she craved.

It was going to end but she wasn't going to cry, plead or declare her undying love.

They were back at the lodge. She'd barely noticed the short drive. Now, she flipped open the door and jumped out, landing squarely on pristine white, then she trudged to the front door and opened it to let herself in without bothering to look back at him.

'Jesus, Rosie…' He pulled her towards him as she was

striding off towards the kitchen. 'The deal…' He shook his head and scowled. 'They own a farm.'

'You don't have to share, Matteo. I told you that.'

'It's no state secret.'

'Then why act like it was?'

'It's who I am.'

Rosie didn't think much of that answer and her expression said as much.

'They're very particular about…the plot of land that this farm sits on. The land is valuable. It wouldn't be impossible for a developer to get planning permission to stick up a load of executive houses with manicured lawns and double garages. It's in a prime location in the north of England.'

Rosie opened her mouth to repeat that he could keep his story to himself, because it was too late, but curiosity got the better of her.

'Why would making more money by developing land matter so much to you, Matteo? Haven't you got enough?' She wished that she could pigeon-hole him as a greedy capitalist but it didn't work. He had got under her skin by being complicated.

'There's a…for want of a better word…facility there that provides…' He shook his head and stared at her in silence for a few seconds.

'A facility?' Rosie prompted coldly. Was this his idea of a concession? He didn't want to explain his past to her. He had brushed their relationship aside, when put to the test, because for him it didn't actually qualify as a relationship. She had asked him about the deal but did she really care about it? She had cited it because it had been the first example to come to mind of something else he felt compelled to keep silent about. It would be just something else to do with making lots of money. As if he didn't already have enough. He wasn't interested in talking about what she wanted to talk about, which was his emotional past. *That* was very firmly off-limits!

'Maybe *facility* is the wrong word,' Matteo said brusquely, heading for the kitchen. She followed him, marvelling at how he somehow managed to convey the impression that he was master of all he surveyed, even though he was a visitor in her parents' chalet.

He was firing up the coffee machine, his back to her, and there was tension in his posture. When he finally looked at her, his lean, beautiful face was closed.

'Bob and Margaret,' he said quietly, 'have a place on the grounds that provides a working holiday for...the kind of kid I used to be.'

Rosie's heart skipped a beat and she stared at him.

'It's partly educational, with facilities for learning various crafts, but there's also a football field, tennis courts and horse riding on tap. The quality of the buyer is very important to them because they don't want those facilities to be scrapped. There is an enormous amount of acreage and, whilst they concede that some might be developed, they insist as part of the deal that the main place for foster kids remain intact. Naturally, it wouldn't be a legally binding situation. More of a gentleman's agreement.'

'And gentlemen don't lead young girls up the garden path, play with their feelings and then dump them without further ado. You could have told them the truth, which was that you had no idea who I was.'

Matteo shrugged. 'Why waste time on laborious explanations that would still have probably left a sour aftertaste in their mouths when another, far less onerous solution presented itself?'

'You intend to…develop some of the land?' She was enthralled by what he was saying, sliding deeper into love with him, as helpless against her own emotions as a piece of driftwood blown across stormy seas.

'I intend to develop quite a bit of the land,' Matteo told her. 'I intend to expand on the facilities there so that more underprivileged kids can come and stay there and see that there's life beyond the bleak walls of whatever foster care situation they're struggling with. I will ensure that the best of professionals are at hand for educational purposes. I will make it the sort of place… I would have benefited even more from as a youngster. So there you have it, Rosie. Has it lived up to the hype?'

'Why did you tell me?' she asked quietly.

Because I love you, was what she hoped he would say.

'Because you deserve to know,' Matteo told her roughly. And that was as far as he was prepared to go.

His wintry-grey eyes collided with hers and just for a moment…just for a second…something stirred inside him, one of those confusing, inexplicable, seismic shifts that only seemed to happen in her company, a strange feeling of disorientation that defied common sense.

He gritted his teeth together, despising himself for that fleeting loss of self-control.

The truth was that this crazy charade had not panned out the way he had foreseen.

It should have been easy, controllable. He never allowed himself to enter into situations he couldn't control. It was too much like opening the door to a room without knowing what was happening behind it, and there had been way too many of those doors in his childhood.

A sheen of prickly perspiration broke out over his body and he scowled.

Memories. Who needed them? He'd done a great job of banking down on them over the years, locking them away, always moving onwards and upwards, refusing to be dragged back to a past that was no longer relevant.

Had they begun to wriggle free when he had started dealings with Bob and Margaret?

The land with the care facilities on it—had that kick-started a trip back in time which seemed to have picked up pace just recently?

Or had the woman in front of him somehow opened that door, letting them flood out?

And, if that was the case, how the heck had it happened? Matteo wasn't going to stick around analysing the situation.

'I deserved to know?' Rosie questioned.

'We were where we were because I wanted that land. It's only fair, in the end, that you know the reason why it meant so much to me.'

And no one could accuse Matteo of not being fair, she thought bitterly. He'd been the perfect gentleman who'd kept his distance, and slept on a bed of nails in her bedroom because she'd asked him to, and thereby had opened the first crack in her heart. And he'd been as fair as anyone could be when he'd warned her that he 'didn't do love'. Or sharing. Or jealousy. Or confiding. Or Christmas. He certainly hadn't led her up the garden path with phoney promises about a future that was never going to happen!

And he was being fair now. Giving her the explanation she'd asked for, digging a deeper hole into her heart and showing her just how complex a man he was.

He'd been a gentleman, and he'd been fair and honest, and now it was over because she wanted much more than a fair and honest gentleman. She wanted the whole package, but she was never going to get it, and she couldn't pretend that sleeping with him for a bit longer, until he got bored of her, was better than nothing, because it wasn't.

'Thank you for that,' she said with a stiff smile and keeping her distance. 'I'm glad you told me. I would always have been curious. I've enjoyed being with you Matteo. It was all so unexpected…the turn of events… but I've grown up. I partly have you to thank for that but I can't carry on making love to you until we both get bored. I feel like I'm facing a new chapter in my life and I want to get on with it.'

This was exactly as it should be, Matteo thought. So why wasn't he feeling good about it?

It had to end and, the longer it carried on, the higher the chances of her getting hurt. She wanted more than he was ever going to be able to give her.

He wanted a stiff drink. He wanted to punch something. That lack of control was as powerful as a depth charge and he detested the weakness it represented.

'You need to. We had fun but it's time for us to go our separate ways. What will you tell your family? What are your plans moving forward?'

Rosie shrugged and met his dark, shuttered eyes without flinching. Fear of the future gripped her like a vice.

'I'll think of something. It's not your concern and, don't worry, I wouldn't dump you in it. Now, if you don't mind, I think I'll head up.'

'Take care, Rosie. I'll be gone by the time you wake up tomorrow morning.'

CHAPTER TEN

FOR THE FIRST time in her life, the frenzied excitement of a fast-approaching Christmas day left Rosie feeling flat and miserable.

True to his word, Matteo was gone by the time she awoke the following morning. She'd barely slept but she must have dozed off at some point because surely she would have heard him leaving the house? Naturally, he hadn't slept with her, and the bed had felt as vast as an icy ocean. How had she managed to become so accustomed to the warmth of his body next to her in such a short space of time? Didn't she have *any* inbuilt defence mechanisms that could have come to the rescue? How had she been so ill-equipped to deal with this situation?

She stayed at the ski lodge just long enough to pack her things. Her parents had a housekeeper who came to clean when the place was not in use, and usually Rosie would have made sure to do some rudimentary tidying before she arrived, but this time she hadn't the heart to do anything but plaster a phoney smile on her face and do the rounds with all her friends at the hotel and on the ski slopes.

Then she headed back to London, to her parents' apartment, which she had always used as a base whenever she was in the country.

She looked around her through new, wide open eyes. She was a woman in her twenties who had always thought that travelling the world was a courageous and daring way of life. Her sisters, in her view, had been solid, grounded, unadventurous souls who had buried themselves in having careers when there was so much world out there waiting to be explored.

Thanks to Matteo, all those notions had been turned on their head.

Since when had it ever been courageous to live at home with Mum and Dad when you didn't have to? Since when was it a daring decision to live off a trust fund and sneer at the tedium of responsibility?

It was an ordeal to face her entire family when she returned.

She spent two days in London, catching up with friends, seeing everything in a whole new light. Then she headed up to the Cotswolds, where her mother was in the thick of Christmas preparations, bulk-making mince pies and Christmas treats for the entire family while her dad sheepishly read the newspapers and watched from the side-lines.

Emily, Candice and entourage were all going to be spending Christmas Eve at the Cotswold mansion where her parents lived.

'Darling, it's such a shame that that gorgeous young man of yours can't join us for at least some of the Christmas celebrations,' her mother sighed when on the first night they all sat down for a family dinner at the kitchen table. 'Surely he could have spared a day or so even if he had to disappear for Christmas day?'

'Work commitments,' Rosie had muttered vaguely. 'You know how it goes…'

She needed some breathing space before she told her parents that the whirlwind romance had crashed and burned. She planned to tell them the truth. She would reassure them that she didn't need protecting, that she wasn't a kid any more. She had decided that she would return to university to study sports science. The ski season and teaching at the resort had pointed her in the direction which she now intended to go. Lots of mature decisions had been made and that chapter she had talked about had been opened. She just wished she felt better about it because right now, right here, staring at her reflection in the mirror a mere couple of hours before her sisters descended in a flurry of excitement, presents and stockings that would sneakily be hung for the kids once they were asleep, the world felt like a very lonely place.

Downstairs, her mother would be getting everything ready for the meal of the year, the crowning glory that was the turkey for Christmas Day. It would be put in brine and, at the crack of dawn in the morning, it would be all systems go and Rosie would be expected to be her usual self—excitable, up early before everyone else, fussing over the Christmas tree, the food and everything that would need doing before her sisters, the kids and the other halves woke up and trooped downstairs.

Bubbly, sparkling Aunty Rosie was her designated role and she would have to live up to it or else invite curiosity and anxious questioning. All that was going to happen soon enough, post-Christmas Day and Boxing Day, once she had had time to get over some of the raw pain. Once she had got her thoughts in order. Once she could manage to go for five minutes without thinking about him, which she did constantly.

As soon as she started thinking about him, her body did what it was accustomed to doing—it tensed up, all her muscles contracting and her nerves going into overdrive. And her brain did what it had also grown accustomed to doing—it began wandering down all sorts of pointless dead ends marked *what if?* and *if only.*

She was bracing herself for an evening of pretending to be jolly when there was a bang on her bedroom door and her mother pushed it open, giving Rosie just enough time to get her face in happy mode.

'Darling, there's a surprise downstairs for you.' Her mother smiled. She was wearing a red-and-white apron which was dusted with flour. Underneath it, in a pair of jeans and a long-sleeved tee shirt, she looked twenty years younger than she was.

'Father Christmas come early? Drawn by the smell of your mince pies?' Rosie forced a smile and stood up. She was dressed and ready to start the evening in a pair of culottes and a fitted stretchy top with lots of sparkle and glitter, as befitting a Christmas Eve gathering. She was counting on the clothes to give the right impression just in case her expression ended up letting the side down. 'Have the girls and kids arrived already?' She glanced at her watch with a frown. 'It's not yet six. I thought they were going to pile up around seven. Sorry, Mum, I should be downstairs helping you!'

'Don't be silly, Rosie. Too many cooks spoil the broth. And no, your sisters aren't here just yet. No, guess again.'

'I can't guess.'

'Your young man has shown up out of the blue. Isn't that wonderful? He's come bearing gifts, which is sure to go down well with the little ones.'

'What young man?' It took some seconds to register

who her mother was talking about but, even when she had, she still couldn't quite believe her ears.

'How many have you got, Rosie?' Her mother chuckled. 'I can't possibly be seen like this. I'm going to have a quick shower—give you two love birds time to catch up. Your father has disappeared down to the pub for a drink so you won't be disturbed!'

Debbie Carter looked at her daughter seriously. 'I'm so thrilled for you, Rosie. You deserve a decent, lovely chap and I think you've struck jackpot with this one. I told him that I thought he was too busy with work to pop up here but he said that work would just have to take a back seat. Not many business moguls adopt that sort of attitude! I despaired of your father back in the day, when he was sometimes far too busy to remember that there was such a thing as *family* waiting for him to appear! Which makes Matteo such a rare find.'

Rosie contorted her face into something she hoped might pass for a smile and not a grimace of despair. Truth to tell, her heart was beating so wildly in her chest that she didn't have time to think about anything much at all.

'Maybe,' she muttered inaudibly. It was too late to climb out of her glittery, sparkly outfit but she felt like a fool as she went downstairs to the sitting room, to where, she had been told, he had been directed with a glass of wine.

And there he was. Behind him, the Christmas tree which she had helped decorate was awash with tiny white lights and heavy with ornaments that went way back to when she and her sisters had all been kids. Rosie could recognise each and every one of them. The curtains of the big bay windows were pulled back and the outside lights illuminated a panorama of stretching gardens and the light fall of snow, nothing like the sweeping fall that had covered the ski slopes, but still somehow graceful and strangely romantic.

Rosie walked over to the window on trembling legs and briskly yanked the curtains shut.

She had to sidestep a ridiculous mound of presents, all professionally wrapped and covering most of the ground by the tree and spreading in front of the sofas.

She had closed the door behind her, because there was never any telling in her parents' house just who could come bombing into any room without warning, and now she turned to him and folded her arms.

'What are you doing here?'

God, he looked so spectacular, so gorgeous, that she could feel her heart going into freefall.

He hadn't shaved and the roughness of dark stubble covered his chin. Looking closer, his eyes were ringed with slight tiredness. She wondered whether all those important deals had been keeping him up at night.

Conscious that she was hardly looking her most sophisticated in her sparkling attire, Rosie remained standing by the window, as tense as a piece of elastic stretched to breaking point. She'd barely had time to get her hair in order when her mother had barged into the bedroom and it fell in feathery, unruly waves around her heart-shaped face.

'I've come…to talk.'

'Talk about what?' She glanced at all the presents strewn on the ground. 'And why have you brought all this stuff?'

'Because it's Christmas.' He smiled crookedly and

took a step towards her, but then stopped, as though uncertain.

'You don't do Christmas,' Rosie said scornfully.

'There were a lot of things I never did until I met you,' he said in a low undertone that she had to strain to hear.

'I can't deal with this, Matteo,' Rosie whispered. 'I don't want you here…spoiling Christmas for me. I just can't handle pretending that everything's fine between us in front of my family. We broke up, for good reasons, and I've begun coming to terms with what I'm going to tell everyone—because, as you've seen, they're still in the dark.'

'I…understand.'

'You've ruined everything coming here with all these presents. My family are going to be doubly upset when I break it to them that it's over between us. They're going to be horribly confused because one minute you…you're showing up pretending to be Father Christmas and, the next minute, you're just a part of my history and you've moved on with your life.'

'Not if I can help it.'

'Don't!'

'Come and sit on the sofa with me. I can't have this conversation standing a hundred miles away from you. I need you…to be closer to me.'

'It's not going to work.'

'I'm not here to try and revive what we had. I haven't come to try and persuade you into carrying on with any charade because I still…want to sleep with you. Because you still haunt my dreams.'

He sat on the sofa and waited, his fabulous eyes focused on her with such unwavering intensity that she could feel her body burning up as she stumbled towards the sofa and sat down, pressed up at one end, because any closer would have made her already fast-dissolving nerves dissolve even faster.

'Rosie.' There was urgent sincerity in his voice and, more than anything else, more even than the brutal impact of his physical presence, that made her still, made her focus her wide blue eyes on his. 'I let you go and I should never have done that.' He raised his hand to halt any interruption, even though she had no intention of interrupting because she had been thoroughly silenced by the tone of his voice. 'I…was afraid.'

'Afraid? *Afraid?* Matteo, there's no way I… I can believe that. Isn't being afraid just one of the hundreds of things you don't *do*?' Bewilderment nudged a way past her defences. She felt as though she was suddenly standing on quicksand.

'Used to be.' He pressed his thumbs briefly over his eyes and then looked at her with none of his usual self-assurance.

Rosie had no intention of melting but she knew that she was straining towards him, closing the gap without really realising it. She had pressed her hands on the squidgy sofa and was leaning forward.

'Don't say anything you don't mean, Matteo.'

'I'm not. This comes from the heart, and if I'm not as fluent as I usually am it's because I'm not accustomed to this sort of speech. Rosie, my life, before I met you, was so well-ordered,' Matteo confessed in a roughened undertone. 'No surprises. Relationships, women… I knew how to deal with both. I never wanted any sort of long-term, committed involvement with anyone and I always made that clear at the start of a relationship. I wasn't raised to see the up sides of forming any emotional attachments.'

Rosie was holding her breath. She reached out to cover his hand with hers, her heart softening even as her head tried to be stern and unforgiving.

He didn't remove his hand. In fact, he curled his fingers into hers and tugged her ever so slightly closer to him so that their knees were touching and she could feel the warmth flowing from his body towards her.

'I wasn't abandoned as a baby,' he said roughly. 'My mother—shockingly, in this day and age—died in childbirth. I know this because I was told when I was old enough by one of the carers at the home. I was raised single-handedly by my father until I was four. I remember him. A kind man—this is simply what I have managed to put together over the years using all the resources at my disposal, including hunting down some of the staff who worked there when I was a child, and people who briefly knew him where he worked. My father died at Christmas. He'd left me with a neighbour so that he could go buy some presents. It was an accident. Poor weather conditions.'

'Matteo!'

'It was a long time ago.' Matteo smiled. 'But I suppose you could say that the experience toughened me up. I learned very young that no one was going to rescue me. I had to make my own way in the world and I couldn't depend on anyone. I had lost both my parents. My faith in loving anyone had taken a fatal beating.'

'That's why Christmas is the one time of year you avoid,' she said slowly.

'I have pictures. Not many. Memories.' He sighed.

'When I met you, you couldn't have been more different from the women I was accustomed to going for.'

'As you made crystal-clear,' Rosie murmured. Her mind was taken up with images of a young Matteo, lost, confused and bewildered by the abrupt death of his father, abandoned to fate. Her heart constricted and she had to swallow back tears. He did this to her. Showed her sides to him that made him irresistible. Beneath the harsh, controlled front there was so much humanity.

'I got sucked in without really understanding how. A first for me. And then I met your family, all of them, and what I experienced was also a first. I experienced what it felt like to be surrounded by the closeness of people who cared about you. I experienced what it felt like to be a part of something bigger. It was…disorienting.'

'We can overwhelm.'

'In a positive way.' He angled a smile. 'You're very lucky, Rosie, but not as lucky as I am to have met you. What started out as a charade turned into something else very quickly. We became lovers and it was nothing like I'd ever felt before.'

Keep talking, Rosie thought, *please don't stop.*

'It was…unsettling. When you confronted me after meeting Bethany and laid into me because I hadn't defended you, well, it made me take stock of just how far I'd been drawn into a situation that had somehow spiralled out of control. All my old habits kicked back into gear big time.' He grimaced. 'I was programmed not to care, to focus on what was tangible, namely work. You wanted what was not in the brochure and I told myself that it was for the best that things ended, not just for me, but for you as well. I told myself that you deserved better. Maybe, Rosie, you do.'

'Never,' Rosie breathed shakily. 'I met you and you turned my life upside down in five seconds flat. I didn't want to fall in love with you, Matteo, but I just couldn't help myself, even though my head was telling me all the time that I was being an idiot.'

'You fell in love with me.' He flung his head back for a few seconds, eyes closed, and then when he looked at her there was no doubt in her mind that her feelings for him were returned. The love and tenderness in his eyes brought a lump to her throat. 'I wasn't sure. I'd hoped. Then you left and it felt as though my world had come to an abrupt stop. I was greedy, Rosie. Greedy for you and hungry for the chaos and joy of having an extended family. I thought I'd locked up my heart and thrown away the key, but I was wrong.

'I came here, bearing gifts...lots of them.' He squeezed her slender fingers. 'In a gesture of shameless blackmail. I intended to ingratiate myself until I won you over. Anything, my darling. I realised that I would have done anything.'

He'd brought something else aside from sack-loads of presents but Rosie didn't find that out until later, when the carols were blaring in the background and her entire family was scattered between the living room and the kitchen, with Candice's children weaving between them in a state of high excitement.

He gathered them all in one place and he took out from his pocket that last thing he had brought with him. A little black box.

Rosie watched in stunned silence as he showed her that her beautiful, arrogant, guy...the guy who claimed to have lost the key to his heart...could be breathtakingly romantic after all.

He knelt in front of her, in front of her entire congregated family—including the kids, who had fallen silent for ten seconds—and he proposed.

And what else could she do but say yes? *Yes, yes, yes!*

EPILOGUE

MATTEO LOOKED DOWN at Rosie from the towering heights of a precariously balanced ladder. In his hand he held a star. In his head he was trying to figure out how he was going to get the damn thing to sit perfectly atop the massive Christmas tree that adorned the living room of the townhouse into which they had moved three months previously.

It wasn't quite the countryside, but neither was it the heart of the city. It was perfectly located in the leafy borough of Richmond.

'Please be careful up there,' Rosie said anxiously. 'You look way too big for that ladder.'

'Finishing touches.' Matteo smiled. 'You want everything to be perfect for when the troops arrive in a week for turkey with all the trimmings, don't you?'

He angled the star, waited until approval from his beloved wife was given, and then slowly dismounted. Then he stood back to look at their creation.

Arm around her, he pulled her gently against him. Outside, the darkness was blocked out by thick curtains. Inside, the glittering lights on the tree and the presents waiting to be handed out to family was a Christmas scene worthy of a postcard. Or a fairy tale. Matteo thought that it was certainly *his* fairy tale.

He'd found his princess, even if he hadn't immediately known it, and he had married her. In record time, a mere few weeks after he had proposed in front of a delighted audience of people who were now as close to him as he could ever have hoped.

He smelled the floral sweetness of Rosie's hair and murmured softly, 'Do you wish we could have returned to the slopes and celebrated our first proper Christmas together there?'

Rosie twisted and looked up at him, smiling.

'You know you put your foot down when I suggested popping over for a few days.' She smiled, reaching up to stroke his face.

'Can you blame me?'

'My darling, I'm six months' pregnant. I think travelling is still allowed.'

Matteo rested his hand on her swollen stomach and felt it again, that surge of pride, love, tenderness and a fierce need to protect the beautiful woman who had become his wife.

He'd gone from tough, hard-as-nails tycoon to a guy who was happy to admit that he was vulnerable.

'You can't be too careful,' Matteo growled, swivelling her gently so that they were facing one another. He gazed down at her with love. 'But we'll get there. Maybe next year. Maybe next Christmas. Return to the place where all this began.'

'And maybe bump into Bob and Margaret.' Rosie smiled, thinking of the couple who had been almost as thrilled at their wedding as she and Matteo had been themselves. 'I gather from her email that they're getting quite proficient.' She reached up on tiptoe to kiss him and, as always, the touch of his cool lips made her squirm with sudden desire. 'Who knows? You might get there one day.'

'I intend to.' Matteo grinned and deepened his kiss, his hand curving over her breast, caressing it and knowing that she would be wet for him. 'I can't have you teaching our kids how to ski so that they can taunt their old man that they're better than him on the slopes.'

'In that case, we can get cracking as soon as this baby arrives.'

'And until then…' he ushered her over to the sofa and settled her into it as delicately as if she was a piece of priceless china '…feet up, young lady. I can do more than just stick a star on a tree. Your wish is my command.'

'You're here, Matteo.' Rosie looked at him lovingly. 'I have no more wishes.'

* * * * *

CHRISTMAS BABY FOR THE GREEK

JENNIE LUCAS

CHAPTER ONE

WAS THERE ANYTHING worse than a wedding on Christmas Eve, with glittering lights sparkling against the snow, holly and ivy decking the halls and the scent of winter roses in the air?

If there was, Holly Marlowe couldn't think of it.

"You may now kiss the bride," the minister said, beaming between the newly married couple.

Heartbroken, Holly watched as Oliver—the boss she'd loved in devoted silence for three years—beamed back and lowered his head to kiss the bride.

Her younger sister, Nicole.

The guests in the pews looked enchanted at the couple's passionate embrace, but Holly felt sick. Fidgeting in her tight red maid-of-honor dress, she looked up at the grand stained-glass windows, then back at the nave of the old New York City church, lavishly decorated with flickering white candles and red roses.

Finally, the newly married couple pulled apart from the kiss. Snatching her bouquet back from Holly's numb fingers, the bride lifted her new husband's hand triumphantly in the air.

"Best Christmas ever!" Nicole cried.

There was a wave of adoring laughter and applause. And though Holly had always loved Christmas, striving to make it magical and full of treats each year for her little sister since their parents had died, she thought she'd hate it for the rest of her life.

No. A lump rose in Holly's throat. She couldn't think that way. She couldn't be selfish. Nicole and Oliver were in love. She should be happy for them. She forced herself to smile as the "Hallelujah" Chorus pounded from the organ in the alcove above.

Smiling, the bride and groom started back down the aisle. And Holly suddenly faced the best man. Oliver's cousin, and his boss. Which made him her boss's boss.

Stavros Minos.

Dark, tall and broad-shouldered, the powerful Greek billionaire seemed out of place in the old stone church. The very air seemed to vibrate back from him, moving to give him space. *He* hadn't been forced to wear some ridiculous outfit that made him look like a deranged Christmas lounge singer. Of course not. She looked over his sleek suit enviously. She couldn't imagine anyone forcing Stavros Minos to do anything.

Then Holly looked up, and the Greek's black eyes cut through her soul.

He glanced with sardonic amusement between her and the happy couple, as they continued to walk down the aisle to the cheers of their guests. And his cruel, sensual lips curved up at the edges, as if he knew exactly how her heart had been broken.

Holly's mouth went dry. No. No, he couldn't. No one must ever know that she'd loved Oliver. Because he wasn't just her boss now. He was her sister's husband. She had to pretend it never happened.

The truth was nothing *had* happened. She'd never said a word about her feelings to anyone, especially Oliver. The man had no idea that while working as his secretary, Holly had been secretly consumed by pathetic, unrequited love.

No one had any idea. No one, it seemed, except Stavros Minos.

But it shouldn't surprise her the billionaire Greek playboy might see things no other person could. Nearly twenty years ago, as a teenager, he'd single-handedly started a tech company that now owned half the world. He was often in the news, both for his high-powered business dealings and conquests of the world's most beautiful women. Now, as organ music thundered relentlessly around them, Stavros looked at Holly with a strange knowing in his eyes.

Wordlessly, he held out his arm.

Reluctantly, Holly took it, and tried not to notice how muscled his arm was beneath his sleek black jacket. His biceps had to be bigger than her thigh! It seemed ridiculously unfair that a man so rich and powerful could also be so good-looking. It was why she'd carefully avoided looking at him whenever she'd liaised with his executive assistants—he had three of them—at work.

Shivering, she avoided looking at him again now as they followed Oliver and Nicole. The faces of the guests slid by as Holly smiled blindly at everyone in the packed wooden pews until she thought her face might crack.

Outside the old stone church, on a charming, historical lane in the Financial District, more guests waited to cheer for the couple, tossing red and white rose petals that fell against the thin blanket of snow on the ground.

The afternoon sunlight was weak and gray against the lowering clouds when Holly reached the safety of the waiting limo. Dropping Stavros's arm, she scrambled inside and turned to stare fiercely out the window, blinking fast so no one would see her tears.

She couldn't be sad. Not today. Not ever. She was happy for her sister and Oliver, happy they'd be leaving her today to start new adventures together around the world. *Happy.*

"Whew." Nicole flopped into the seat across from her

in a wave of white tulle that took most of the space in the back of the limo. She grinned at her new husband beside her. "We did it! We're married!"

"Finally," Oliver drawled, all lazy charm as he looked down at his bride. "That was a lot of work. But then, I never thought I'd let anyone put the marriage noose round my neck."

"'Til you met me," Nicole murmured, turning her face up to be kissed.

Smiling, he lowered his head. "Exactly."

Holly felt her own seat move as Stavros Minos sat beside her. As the door closed behind him, and the limo pulled away from the curb, she unwillingly breathed in his intoxicating scent of musk and power.

Oliver turned smugly to his cousin. "How about it, Stavros? Did the ceremony give you any ideas?"

The Greek tycoon's handsome face was colder than the icy winter air outside. "Such as you can't imagine."

How dare he be so rude? Holly thought incredulously. But then, the commitment-phobic playboy famously despised weddings. He obviously was unhappy to be forced to attend his cousin's wedding. And unlike Holly, he didn't feel any compunction to hide his feelings. Luckily, the happy couple didn't seem to notice.

Oliver snorted. "I was going to invite Uncle Aristides today, him being family and all that, but I knew you wouldn't like it."

"Generous of you." His voice was flat.

Holly envied Stavros Minos's coldness right now, when she herself felt heartbroken and raw. Her sister's pressure for Holly to move with them to Hong Kong after they returned from their honeymoon in Aruba had been ratcheted up to an explosive level. Oliver had already quit at Minos International. If Holly stayed, she'd soon be working for the notoriously unpleasant VP of Operations. Or else she had a standing offer from a previous employer who'd moved back to Europe.

But if she was going to leave New York, shouldn't she move to Hong Kong, and work for Oliver in his new job? Shouldn't she devote herself to her baby sister's happiness, forever and ever?

"You really hate weddings, don't you, Stavros?" Oliver grinned at his cousin. "At least I won't have to see your grouchy face at the office anymore, old man. Your loss is Sinistech's gain."

"Right." Stavros shrugged. "Let another company deal with your three-hour martini lunches."

"Quite." Oliver's grin widened, then he licked his lips. "I can hardly wait to explore Hong Kong's delights."

"Me, too," Nicole said.

Oliver nearly jumped, as if he'd forgotten his bride beside him. "Naturally." He suddenly looked at Holly. "Did Nicole convince you yet? Will you come and work as my secretary there?"

Feeling everyone's eyes on her, her cheeks went red-hot. She stammered, "D-don't be silly."

"You mustn't be selfish," Oliver insisted. "I can't cope without you. Who else can keep me organized in my new job?"

"And I might get pregnant soon," Nicole said anxiously. "Who will take care of the baby if you're not around?"

The ache in Holly's throat sharpened to a razor blade. Watching her sister marry the man she loved and then leave for the other side of the world was hard enough. But the suggestion that Holly should live with them and raise their children was pure cruelty.

As of her birthday yesterday, she was a twenty-seven-year-old virgin. She was a secretary, a sister, and perhaps soon, an aunt. But would she ever be more? A wife? A mother?

Would she ever meet a man she could love, who would love her in return? Would she ever be the most important person in the world to anyone?

At twenty-seven, it was starting to seem unlikely. She'd spent nearly a decade raising her sister since their parents died. She'd spent the last three years taking care of Oliver at work. Maybe that was all she was meant to do. Take care of Nicole and Oliver, watch them love each other and raise their children. Maybe Holly was meant only to be support staff in life. Never the star. The thought caused a stab of pain through her heart.

She choked out, "You'll be fine without me."

"Fine!" Indignantly, Nicole shook her head. "It would be a disaster! You have to come with us to Hong Kong, Holly. *Please!*"

Her sister spoke with the same wheedling tone she'd used since she was a child to get her own way. The same one she'd used four weeks ago to convince Holly to arrange her sudden wedding—using the same Christmas details that Holly had once dreamed of for her own wedding someday.

Until she'd realized there was no point in saving all her own Christmas wedding dreams for a marriage that would never happen. If any man was ever going to be interested in her, it would have happened by now. And it hadn't. Her sister was the one with the talent in that arena. Blonde, tiny and beautiful, Nicole had always had a strange power over men, and at twenty-two, she'd learned how to use it well.

But even Holly had never imagined, when she'd introduced her to Oliver last summer at a company picnic, that it would end like this.

Looking at her sister, Holly suddenly noticed Nicole's bare neck. "Where's Mom's gold-star necklace, Nicole?"

Touching her bare collarbone above her neckline, her sister ducked her head. "It's somewhere in all the boxes. I'm sure I'll find it when I unpack in Hong Kong."

"You lost Mom's necklace?" Holly felt stricken. It was bad enough their parents hadn't lived to see their youngest daughter get married, but if Nicole had lost the precious gold-star necklace their mother had always worn...

"I didn't lose it," Nicole said irritably. She shrugged. "It's somewhere."

"And don't try to change the subject, Holly," Oliver said sharply. "You're being stubborn and selfish to stay in New York, when I need you so badly."

Selfish. The accusation hit Holly like a blow. Was she being selfish to stay, when they needed her? Selfish to still hope she could find her own happiness, instead of putting their needs first forever?

"I... I'm not trying to be," she whispered. As the limo drove north toward Midtown, Holly looked out the window, toward the bright Christmas lights and colorful window displays as the limo passed the department stores on Sixth Avenue. The sidewalks were filled with shoppers carrying festive bags and wrapped packages, rushing to buy gifts to put under the Christmas tree and fill stockings tomorrow morning. She saw happy children wearing Santa hats and beaming smiles.

A memory went through her of Nicole at that age, her smiling, happy face missing two front teeth as she'd hugged Holly tight and cried, "I wuv you, Howwy!"

A lump rose in Holly's throat. Nicole was her only family. If her baby sister truly needed her, maybe she *was* being selfish, thinking of her own happiness. Maybe she should just—

"Let me get this straight." Stavros Minos's voice was acidic as he suddenly leaned forward. "You want Miss Marlowe to quit her job at Minos International and move to Hong Kong? To do your office work for you, Oliver, all day, then take care of your children all night?"

Oliver scowled. "It's none of your business, Stavros."

"Your concern does you credit, Mr. Minos," Nicole interceded, giving him a charming smile, "but taking care of people is what Holly does best. She's taken care of me since I was twelve. I can't imagine her ever wanting to stop taking care of me."

"Of us," Oliver said.

Stavros lifted his sensual lips into a smile that showed the white glint of his teeth as he turned to Holly. "Is that true?"

He was looking at her so strangely. She stammered, "A-anyone would feel the same."

"I wouldn't."

"Of course you wouldn't," Oliver said with a snort, leaning back in the seat. "Minos men are selfish to the bone. We do what we like, and everyone else be damned."

"What is that supposed to mean?" his wife said.

He winked. "It's part of our charm, darling."

But Nicole didn't seem terribly charmed. With a flare of her nostrils, she turned to Holly. "I can't just leave you in New York. You wouldn't know what to do with yourself. You'd be so alone."

She stiffened. "I have friends…"

"But not family," she said impatiently. "And it's not very likely you ever will, is it?"

"Will what?"

"Have a husband or children of your own. I mean, come on." She gave a good-natured snort. "You've never even had a serious boyfriend. Do you really want to die alone?"

Holly stared at her sister in the back of the limo.

Nicole was right. And tomorrow, for the first time in her life, Holly would spend Christmas Day alone.

Christmas, and the rest of her life.

Her eyes met Stavros's in the back of the limo. His handsome features looked as hard and cold as a marble statue, his black eyes icy as a midwinter's night. Then his expression suddenly changed.

"I'm afraid Miss Marlowe can't possibly go to Hong Kong," he said. "Because I need another executive assistant. So I'm giving her a promotion."

"What?" gasped Oliver.

"What?" gasped Nicole.

Holly looked at him sharply, blinking back tears. "What?"

His expression gentled. "Will you come work directly for me, Miss Marlowe? It will mean long hours, but a sizable raise. I'll double your salary."

"But—" Swallowing, Holly whispered, "Why me?"

"Because you're the best." His jaw, dark with five-o'clock shadow, tightened. "And because I can."

Stavros hadn't meant to get involved. Oliver was right. This was none of his business.

He didn't care about his cousin. Cousin or not, the man was a useless bastard. Stavros regretted the day he'd hired him. Oliver had done a poor job as VP of Marketing. He'd been within a day of being fired when he'd taken the "surprise offer" from Hong Kong. Stavros was glad to see him go. He suspected Oliver might be surprised when his new employers actually expected him to work for his salary.

Stavros didn't much care for his cousin's new bride, either. In spite of his own turmoil last night, he'd actually tried to warn Nicole about Oliver's cheating ways at the rehearsal dinner. But the blonde had just cut him off. So she knew what she was getting into; she just didn't care.

He didn't give a damn about either of them.

But Holly Marlowe—she was different.

Stavros suspected it was only through the hardworking secretary's efforts that Oliver had managed to stay afloat these last three years. Holly worked long hours at the office then probably nights and weekends at home, doing Oliver's job for him. Everyone at the New York office loved kind, dependable Miss Marlowe, from the janitors to the COO. Tender-hearted, noble, self-sacrificing… Holly Marlowe was the most respected person in the New York office, Stavros included.

But she was totally oppressed by these two selfish people, who, instead of thanking her for all she'd done, seemed intent on taking her indentured servitude with them to Hong Kong.

Two days ago, Stavros might have shrugged it off. People had the right to make their own choices, even stupid ones.

But not after the news he'd received yesterday. Now, for the first time he was thinking about what his own legacy would be after he was gone. And it wasn't a pretty picture.

"You can't have Holly! I need her!" Oliver exploded. At Stavros's fierce glare, his cousin glanced uneasily at his wife. "*We* need her."

"You don't want some stupid promotion, do you, Holly?" Nicole wailed.

But Holly's face was shining as she looked at Stavros. "Do—do you mean it?"

"I never say anything I don't mean." As they drove north, past bundled-up tourists and sparkling lights and brightly decorated department-store windows, his gaze unwillingly traced over her pretty face and incredible figure. Until he'd stood across from her in the old stone church by candlelight, he'd never realized how truly beautiful Holly Marlowe was.

The truth was, he hadn't *wanted* to notice. Beautiful women were a dime a dozen in his world, while truly competent, highly driven secretaries were few. And Holly had hidden her beauty, making herself nearly invisible at the office, yanking her fiery red hair in a matronly bun, never wearing makeup, working quietly behind the scenes in loose-cut beige skirt suits and sensible shoes.

Was this what she'd looked like all the time? Right under his nose?

Her bright, wide-set green eyes looked up at him, luminous beneath dramatic black lashes. Her skin was pale except for a smattering of freckles over her nose. Her lips were red and delectable as she nibbled them with white, even teeth. Her thick, curly red-gold hair spilled over her shoulders. And that tight red dress—

That dress—

Stavros obviously wasn't dead yet, because it set his pulse racing.

The bodice was low-cut, clinging to full, delicious breasts he'd never imagined existed beneath those baggy beige suits. As she moved, the knit fabric clung to her curves. He'd gotten a look at her deliciously full backside as they'd left the church, too.

All things he would have to ignore once she worked for him. Deliberately, he looked away. He didn't seduce women who worked for him. Why would he, when beautiful women were so plentiful in his world, and truly spectacular employees more precious than diamonds?

Sex was an amusement, nothing more. But for years, his company had been his life.

And the reason Holly chose to dress so plainly in the office was obviously that she wanted to be valued for her accomplishments and hard work, not her appearance. In that, they were the same. From the time he was a child, Stavros had wanted to do important things. He'd wanted to change the world.

But that wasn't all they had in common. He'd seen her tortured expression as she'd looked at Oliver. So Stavros and Holly each had secrets they didn't want to talk about.

To anyone.

Ever.

But her inexplicable infatuation for Oliver couldn't possibly last. When she recovered from it, like someone healing from a bad cold, she'd realize she'd dodged a bullet.

As for Stavros's secret, people would figure it out for themselves when he dropped dead. Which, according to his doctor's prognosis, would happen in about six to nine months. He blinked.

All the life he'd left unlived...

Just a few days ago, Stavros had vaguely assumed he'd have another fifty years. Instead, he'd be unlikely to see his thirty-seventh birthday next September.

He would die alone, with no one but his lawyers and stockholders to mourn him. His company would be his only legacy. Estranged from his father, and feeling as he did about Oliver, Stavros would likely leave his shares to charity.

Poor Stavros, his ex-mistresses would say. Then they'd roll over and enjoy their hot new lovers in bed.

Poor Minos, his business associates would say. Then they'd focus on exciting new technology to buy and sell.

And he'd be dirt in the ground. Never once knowing what it felt like to commit to anything but work. Not even leaving a son or daughter to carry on his name.

Looking back, Stavros saw it all with painful clarity, now that his life was coming to an end. And he had only himself to blame. Nicole's thoughtlessly cruel words floated back to him. *Do you really want to die alone?*

Christmas lights sparkled on Sixth Avenue, as yellow taxis filled with people on the way to family dinners rushed past in the rapidly falling twilight. The limo turned east, finally pulling into the entrance of the grand hotel overlooking Central Park.

"This isn't over, Holly," Oliver said firmly. "I'm going to persuade you."

"You'll come with us," Nicole said, smiling as she smoothed back her veil.

The uniformed driver opened the back door of the limousine. Oliver got out first, then gallantly reached back to assist his glamorous bride. Nicole's white tulle skirts swirled in a train with her fluttery white veil, her diamond tiara sparkling. Tourists gaped at them on the sidewalk. A few lifted their phones for pictures, clearly believing they were seeing royalty. The new Mr. and Mrs. Oliver Minos waved at them regally as they swept into the grand hotel to take photos before the guests arrived for a ballroom reception.

Silence fell in the back of the limo. For a moment, Holly didn't move. Stavros looked at her.

"Don't give in to them, Holly," he urged in a low voice. It was the first time he'd used her first name. "Stick up for yourself. You're worth so much more than they are."

Her green eyes widened, then suddenly glistened with tears. She whispered, "How can you say that?"

"Because it's true," he said harshly. He got out of the limo and held out his hand for her.

Blinking fast, she slowly placed her hand in his.

And it happened.

Stavros had slept with many women, beautiful and famous and powerful, models and starlets and even a Nobel laureate.

But when he touched Holly's hand to help her from the limo, he felt something he'd never experienced before. An electric shock sizzled him to his core.

He looked down at her as he pulled her to the sidewalk, his heart pounding strangely as he helped her to her feet. Snowflakes suddenly began falling as she looked up, lingering in his arms.

Then Holly's gaze fell on the lacy white snowflakes. With a joyous laugh, she dropped his hand, looking up with wonder at the gray lowering sky.

Without her warmth, Stavros again felt the winter chill beneath his tuxedo jacket. The world became a darker place, freezing him, reminding him he'd soon feel nothing at all. He stood very still, watching her. Then he lifted his face to the sky, wondering if this would be the last time he'd feel snowflakes on his skin.

If only he could have at least left a child behind. He suddenly wanted that so badly it hurt. If only he could have left some memory of his existence on earth.

But the women he knew were as ambitious and heartless as he was. He couldn't leave an innocent child in their care. Children needed someone willing to put their needs above her own. He knew no woman like that. None at all.

Then he heard a laugh of pure delight, and Stavros looked down at Holly Marlowe's beautiful, shining, tenderhearted eyes.

"Can you believe it?" Stretching her arms wide, laughing like a child, she whirled in a circle, holding out her tongue to taste the snowflakes. She looked like an angel. Her eyes danced as she cried, "It's snowing at my sister's wedding! On Christmas Eve!"

And all of the busy avenue, the tourists, the horse-drawn carriages, the taxis blaring Christmas music, faded into the background. Stavros saw only her.

CHAPTER TWO

THE GRAND TWO-STORY hotel ballroom was a winter wonderland, filled with white-and-silver Christmas trees twinkling like stars. Each of the twenty big round tables had centerpieces of red roses, deep scarlet against the white. It was even more beautiful than Holly had dreamed. A lump rose in her throat as she slowly looked around her.

She'd imagined a wedding reception like this long ago, as a lonely nineteen-year-old, cutting out photographs from magazines and putting them in an idea book each night while her little sister slept in the dark apartment. Holly had been alone, her friends all in college or partying in clubs.

Holly didn't regret her choice to give up her college scholarship and come home. After their parents had died in the car accident on their anniversary, she'd known she couldn't leave Nicole to foster care. But sometimes, she'd felt so trapped, chained by the responsibilities of love. She'd felt so lonely, without a partner, and with a teenaged sister who'd often shouted at Holly in her own grief and frustrated rage.

So to comfort herself, Holly had created the dream book. It had kept her company, until Nicole had left for college three years ago, and Holly had started working for Oliver.

In her romantic fantasy of long ago, she'd always imagined she'd be the bride in the white princess dress, dancing with an adoring groom. Now, as she watched Nicole and Oliver dance their first dance as husband and wife, surrounded by all their adoring friends, she told herself she'd never been so happy.

"They really do make a perfect couple." Stavros's low, husky voice spoke beside her. Somehow, his tone made the words less than complimentary.

"Yes," Holly said, moving slightly to make sure they didn't accidentally touch. When he'd helped her from the limo earlier, her whole body had trembled. It was totally ridiculous. She was sure Stavros Minos hadn't felt anything. Why would he? While Holly, hours later, still felt burning hot, lit up from within, whenever the Greek billionaire drew close. Whenever he even looked at her. She had to get ahold of herself, if she was going to be his assistant!

What was wrong with her? Holly didn't understand. How could she feel so—so aware of Stavros, when she was in love with Oliver?

She was, wasn't she?

But she didn't want to love Oliver anymore. It had done nothing but hurt her. And now he was her brother-in-law, it felt slimy and wrong. She wanted to reach inside her soul and turn off her feelings like a light—

"You arranged the reception, too, didn't you?" Stavros said, looking at the Christmas fantasy around them.

She forced herself to smile. "I wanted my sister to have a dream wedding. I did my best."

Stavros abruptly turned to look at the happy couple, dancing now in front of the largest white-flocked tree, decorated with white lights and silver stars. He took a long drink of the amber-colored liquid he'd gotten from the open bar. "You are a good person."

Again, the words should have been a compliment, but they weren't. Not the way he said them. She tried to read his expression, but his darkly handsome face was inscrutable. She shook her head. "You must hate all this."

"This?"

"Being best man at a wedding." Holly shrugged. "You're the most famously commitment-phobic bachelor in the city."

He took another deliberate drink. "Let's just say love is something I've never had the good fortune to experience."

More irony, she thought. Then his black eyes burned through her, reminding her he knew about her secret love for Oliver. Her cheeks burned.

Looking toward the beautiful bride and handsome groom slow-dancing in the center of the ballroom, the very picture of fairy-tale love, she mumbled, "You're right. They do make a perfect couple."

"Stop it," he said sharply, as if he was personally annoyed.

"Stop what?"

"Take off the rose-colored glasses."

Her mouth dropped. "What?"

"You'd have to be stupid to love Oliver. And whatever you are, Miss Marlowe, you're not stupid."

The conversation had taken a strangely personal turn. Her heart pounded. But there seemed no point in trying to lie. She'd never dared to give voice to her feelings before. She whispered, "How did you guess?"

He rolled his eyes. "You wear your heart on your face." He paused. "I'm sure Oliver knows exactly how you feel."

Horror went through her. "Oh, no—he couldn't possibly—"

"Of course he knows," Stavros said brutally. "How else could he have taken advantage of you all these years?"

"Advantage?" Astonished, she looked up at him. "Of me?"

He looked down at her seriously. "I have ten thousand employees around the world. And from what everyone tells me, you're the hardest working one."

"Mr. Minos—"

"Call me Stavros," he ordered.

"Stavros." She blushed. "I'm sure that's not true. I go home at six every night—"

"Yes, home to do Oliver's paperwork. Never asking for a raise, even though you were paying for your sister to go to college. Which, by the way, she could have gotten a job and paid for herself."

Her blush deepened in confusion. "I take care of my sister because—because she's my responsibility. I take care of Oliver because, because," she continued, faltering, "I'm his employee. At least I was…"

"And because you're in love with him."

"Yes," she whispered, her heart in her throat.

"And now he's impulsively married your sister, and instead of being angry—" he motioned at the winter wonderland around them "—you arranged all this."

"Except for this dress." She looked down ruefully at the tight red dress, wishing she was dressed in that modest burgundy gown she'd selected. "Nicole picked it out. She said my dress was the frumpiest thing she'd ever seen and she wasn't going to let it ruin her wedding photographs."

"They really do deserve each other, don't they?" he murmured. Then he glanced down at her and growled, "You look beautiful in that dress."

Another compliment that didn't sound like a compliment. If anything, he sounded angry about it. His jaw was tight as he looked away.

Was he mocking her? She didn't understand why he would tell her she was beautiful but sound almost furious about it. Her cheeks burned as she muttered, "Thanks."

For a moment, the two of them stood apart from the crowd, watching as the bridal couple finished their dance with a long, flashy kiss. The guests applauded then went out to join them on the dance floor. Feeling awkward, Holly started to turn away.

Stavros stopped her, his dark eyes glittering as he said huskily, "Dance with me."

"What? No."

Broad-shouldered and powerful in his tuxedo, he towered over her like a dark shadow. Lifting a sardonic eyebrow, he just held out his hand, waiting.

What was he playing at? Stavros took starlets and models to his bed. Why would he be interested in dancing with a plain, ordinary girl like her? She looked up at him. His handsome face was arrogant, as untouchable and distant as a star.

"You don't have to feel sorry for me," she said stiffly.

"I don't."

"Or if you think it's a requirement, because you're best man and I'm maid of honor—"

"Do I strike you as a man who gives a damn about other people's rules?" he asked, cutting her off. "I just want you to see the truth."

"What's that?" Half-mesmerized, she let him pull her into his powerful arms. Electricity crackled up her arm as she felt the heat of his palm against hers. She looked up at his face. His jawline was dark with five-o'clock shadow below razor-sharp cheekbones. There was a strange darkness in his black eyes, a vibrating tension from his muscular body beneath the well-cut tuxedo.

"You don't love my cousin. You never did."

She tried to pull away. "You have some nerve to—"

Holding her hand implacably in his own, he led her out onto the dance floor, where guests swayed to the slow romantic Christmas music of the orchestra.

She felt everyone looking at her. The women, with a mix of envy and bewilderment, the men, with interest, their eyes lingering on her uncomfortably low neckline.

Even Nicole and Oliver paused to gape at the sight of Stavros leading her out on the dance floor. Holly felt equally bewildered. Stavros could dance with anyone. Why would he choose her? Had he lost some kind of bet?

Surely this couldn't just be to convince Holly she had no real feelings for Oliver.

But if he could, how wonderful would that be?

Suddenly, Holly wanted it more than anything in the world.

Stavros led her confidently to the center of the dance floor, forcing others to move aside to make way for them. Pulling her against his chest, he looked down at her. She felt his dark gaze burn through her body, all the way to her toes. He looked at her almost as if he—

Desired her?

No. Holly's cheeks went hot. That was a step too far. No man had ever desired her. Not Oliver. Not even Albert from Accounting, who'd asked her on a date a few months ago, then stood her up for some playoff game.

But there was heat in Stavros's gaze as he moved her in his arms.

"You don't love my cousin," he whispered, tightening his hold on her. "Admit it. He was just a dream you had to keep you warm at night."

Could it be true? How she wanted to be convinced! "How can you say that?"

His sensual lips curved. "Because as little as I know about love, it seems to involve really knowing someone, flaws and all. And you don't even know him."

She rolled her eyes. "I've worked for him for three years. Of course I know Oliver. I know everything about him."

"Are you sure?" Stavros said, glancing at the dancing couple.

Following his gaze, Holly saw Oliver give a flirtatious smile to a pretty girl over his wife's shoulder. She saw Nicole notice, scowl, then deliberately step on her new husband's foot with her wicked stiletto heel.

"So he's a little flirty," she said. "It doesn't mean anything."

Now Stavros was the one to roll his eyes. "He sleeps with every woman he possibly can."

"He never tried to sleep with me," she protested.

"Because you're special."

Holly sucked in her breath. "I am?"

"Get that dying-cow look off your face," he said irritably. "Yes, special. His secretary before you filed a sexual harassment suit against him. I told Oliver if that ever happened again, I'd fire him, cousin or not. And he's a Minos man to the core. Like he said, selfish to the bone. Why would he want to risk losing an amazing secretary slaving away for him night and day, just for some cheap sex he can—and does—get everywhere else?"

"Cheap!" Holly had never even been naked with a man before. How dare Stavros imply she offered cheap sex to all comers? She glared at him. "What right do you have to criticize him? You're just as bad. You sleep with a new actress or model every week!"

Stavros's jaw tightened. "That's not true..." Then something made the anger drain out of his handsome face, replaced by stark, raw emotion. "But you're right. I have no right to criticize him. And I wouldn't, except he's trying to take your life. Don't let him do it," he said fiercely. He pulled her closer, looking down at her as they swayed to the slow music. "Oliver is using you. Look past your dream. See him for the man he really is."

Looking back at Oliver, now arguing with his new bride as they left the dance floor, Holly suddenly thought of all the times that he'd stopped her as she left the office on Friday nights, putting stacks of files into her arms. "You don't mind taking care of this over the weekend, do you, Holly?" he'd say, flashing her his most charming, boyish, slightly sheepish grin. "Thanks, you're the best!"

She thought of all the times he'd mysteriously disappear when an unpleasant conversation was required, leaving Holly to do his dirty work for him. And not just work like firing someone. Frequently she'd be left alone to sort out weeping, heartbroken women who appeared at the office, begging to see him, railing about broken promises.

At the time, Holly had convinced herself it was proof of his faith in her that he'd relied on her to handle such important matters.

But now…

She looked at Oliver and Nicole, who'd gone back to sit at the head table. There was still a smudge of white frosting on her sister's cheek. Earlier, when they'd cut the wedding cake, Nicole had delicately fed her new husband his slice, holding the pose beautifully for pictures. Immediately afterward, Oliver had smashed the piece into his bride's face to make the crowd laugh.

Now, sitting on the dais, they were arguing fiercely over champagne. She was trying to pull the bottle away from him. Yanking it back, Oliver tilted back his head and vengefully drank it straight from the bottle.

And this was supposed to be the happiest day of their lives.

Holly's body flashed hot, then cold, from her scalp to her toes. With an intake of breath, she looked up at Stavros as they danced. "My sister—"

"She's made her bed. Now she'll have to lie in it." His hands tightened as he said, "But you don't have to."

Holly desperately tried to remember the feelings she'd once had for Oliver, all the lonely nights she'd spent in her tiny apartment, with only her romantic fantasies about her boss to keep her warm. But those memories had disappeared like mist against the cold reality of this wedding, and the hot feel of Stavros's hand over hers. The dream was gone.

"Why are you forcing me to see the truth?" she said helplessly. "Why do you care?"

Stavros abruptly stopped dancing. He looked down at her, his black eyes searing through her soul.

"Because I want you, Holly," he said huskily. "On my arm. In my bed." His hand trailed through her hair and down her back as he whispered, "I want you for my own."

He was going to hell for this.

Or at the very least, his conscience warned, he shouldn't hire her as his secretary. Because as hard as he'd tried to ignore her beauty—he *couldn't*.

Stavros looked down at her. Her emerald eyes widened. Her curly red hair looked like fire tumbling over her shoulders. Her petite body felt so soft and sensual in his arms.

But he wanted to keep her as his secretary. He wanted to keep her for everything. He wanted Holly more than he'd ever wanted anyone.

Why her? He didn't know. It couldn't just be her luscious beauty. He'd bedded beautiful women before.

Holly Marlowe was different. The supermodels and actresses seemed as glittery as tinsel, cold as snowflakes. Holly was real. She was warm and alive. Her heart shone from her beautiful green eyes. She didn't even try to guard her heart. He could read her feelings on her face.

And her body…

As they'd danced, he'd watched the tight red fabric slide against her ripe, curvaceous body, and his mouth had gone dry as he'd imagined feeling her naked skin against his own. With his hand against her lower back, he'd felt her hips move, felt the sway of her tiny waist. He'd watched her blush and shiver at his touch, and wondered how innocent she might be. Could she even be a virgin?

No. In this day and age? Surely not.

And yet he'd known then he had to make Holly his, if it was the last thing he did. Which it well could be.

His gaze fell to her pink lips, tracing down to her low-cut neckline, where with each sharp rise and fall of her breath he half expected the red fabric to tear, setting her deliciously full breasts free. He repeated huskily, "I want you."

Holly gave a sudden jagged intake of breath. "How can you be so cruel?"

Frowning, Stavros pulled back. "Cruel?"

"All right, so I'm just a secretary. I'm plain and boring and nothing special. That gives you no right to—no right to—"

"To what?" he said, mystified.

"Make fun of me!" Her voice ended with a sob, and she turned and fled, leaving him standing alone on the dance floor.

A low curse twisted his lips. Make fun of her? He'd never been more serious about anything in his life. Make fun of her? Was she insane?

Grimly, he turned through the crowd, trying to pursue her. But other people suddenly blocked his path on the dance floor, business acquaintances desperate to ingratiate themselves, women hoping for a shot at dancing in his arms.

He barely knew what he said to them as his eyes searched the crowds for Holly. His heart was racing and his body was in a cold sweat. Symptoms of his condition? His body shutting down?

All the things he'd never get the chance to do…

All the things he'd never thought of…

His eyes fell on Oliver, chatting with a trashy-looking girl by the open bar. As much as he despised his cousin's boorish behavior, Stavros realized in some ways he'd been just like him.

He'd never cheated or lied to a girlfriend, it was true. But that was hardly an amazing virtue when Stavros's relationships rarely lasted longer than a month. Whenever the pull of work became greater than the pull of lust, or if a mistress demanded any emotional involvement from him, Stavros would simply end the affair.

For nearly two decades, he'd worked eighteen hours a day, building his tech company. Unlike Oliver, he wasn't afraid of hard work. At first, he'd only wanted to succeed as a big middle finger to his estranged father, who'd cut off his mother without a penny and excluded Stavros from the Minos fortune. But by the time he was twenty, he'd learned the pleasures of work: the intensity, the focus, the thrill of victory. He'd become addicted to it.

But the truth was, he still wasn't so different from Oliver. Like his cousin, Stavros had spent all his adult life focusing on money and power and sleeping with beautiful women, while avoiding emotional entanglement. Stavros had just been better at it.

It was a blow for him to realize that Oliver, as weak and shallow as he was, had managed to do something he hadn't: he'd taken a wife.

Two years younger, and Oliver was already ahead. While Stavros had so little time left…

His eyes narrowed when he finally focused on Holly, speaking urgently with the bride on the other side of the ballroom. "Excuse me," he said shortly, and began pushing through the crowds, ignoring anyone who tried to talk to him.

He came up behind Holly just in time to hear the bride tell her angrily, "How dare you say such a thing!"

Holly flinched, but her voice was low as she pleaded, "I'm sorry, Nicole, I'm just scared for you…"

"I don't care what you imagine, or what Stavros Minos says. Oliver would never cheat. Not on me!" Nicole lifted her chin, her long white veil fluttering as her eyes flashed. "You don't deserve to be my maid of honor. I should have asked Yuna, not you! Better an old college roommate than a jealous old maid of a sister!"

"Nicole!"

"Forget it." Her sister's eyes sparkled as coldly as her tiara. "I want you out of here."

Holly took a deep breath. "Please. I wasn't trying to—"

"Get out!" Nicole shouted, loud enough to be heard over the orchestra, causing everyone nearby to turn and look.

Holly's shoulders flinched. She took a deep breath, then slowly turned away. Stavros had a brief glimpse of her stricken face before she walked through the silent, staring crowds.

He turned to Nicole.

"Your sister loves you," he said in a low voice. "She was trying to warn you."

"Warn me?" Nicole's perfect pink lip curled as she lifted her chin derisively. "Excuse me. I've never been so happy."

Stavros stared at her in disbelief.

"Good luck with that," he said, and went after Holly.

He found her shivering in front of the hotel, hopelessly trying to wave down a yellow taxi in the cold, snowy evening. As Christmas Eve deepened, the traffic on Central Park South had dissipated, leaving the city strangely quiet, tucked in to sleep beneath a blanket of snow, as the stars twinkled in the black sky.

When Holly saw him coming out of the hotel, her expression blanched. Turning, she stumbled away, across the empty street toward wintry, quiet Central Park. When he followed her, she shouted back desperately, "Leave me alone!"

"Holly, wait."

"No!"

Stavros caught up with her on the sidewalk near an empty horse carriage, festooned with holly and red bows, waiting patiently for customers. He grabbed her shoulder.

"Damn you…"

Then he saw her miserable face. Choking back his angry words, he pulled her into his arms. She cried against his chest, and he felt her shivering from grief and cold.

"I told her too late. I should have seen… I should have warned her long ago!"

"It's not your fault." Inwardly cursing both his cousin and her sister, Stavros gently stroked her long red hair until the crying stopped.

She looked up at him, her lovely face desolate, tearstained with streaks of mascara as she wiped her eyes. "I'm not going back."

"Good."

She took a deep breath. "Nicole didn't send you after me?"

Stavros shook his head.

Her shoulders sagged for a moment, then she lifted her chin. "So what do you want?"

He came closer, looking down at her as scattered snowflakes whirled around them on the sidewalk in front of the dark, snowy park. "I told you."

Her eyes widened, and her lips parted. Then she turned her head sharply away. "Don't."

"Don't what?"

"Just don't." She swallowed hard, her green eyes glistening with tears as she looked at him beneath the moonlight. "All right, I was a fool over Oliver. I see now it was just a dream to stave off loneliness." Her voice broke. "But you don't have to be cruel to prove your point. I know I'm not your type, but I do still have feelings!"

"You think I'm toying with you?" Searching her gaze, he said quietly, "I want you, Holly. As I've never wanted anyone."

Looking away, she mulishly shook her head.

As she shivered, he took off his sleek black tuxedo jacket

and draped it gently over her shoulders. Reaching out, he cupped her cheek, running the tip of his thumb over her tender, trembling lower lip. "Holly, look at me."

Her eyes were huge in the moonlight as she flashed him a troubled glance. Behind her he could see the snowy park stretching out forever beneath the wintry, starlit night. She said haltingly, "You can't expect me to believe—"

"Believe this," he whispered. And, grabbing the lapels of the oversize tuxedo jacket around her, he pulled her hard against him, and swiftly lowered his mouth to hers.

CHAPTER THREE

EVEN IN HER wildest dreams, Holly had never imagined a kiss like this.

The few anemic kisses she'd had in her life, the forgettable ends of unsatisfying dates in high school and her one semester of college, had been nothing like this.

But then, she'd never been kissed by a man like Stavros.

His lips moved expertly as his tongue swept hers, taking command, taking possession. Held fast against his powerful, muscular body, she felt herself respond, felt her body rise.

Beneath his passionate, ruthless embrace, a spark of desire built inside her to a sudden white-hot flame.

She'd never felt like this before. The memory of her childish infatuation with Oliver melted away in a second beneath the intensity of this fire. A moment before, she'd been heartsick and despondent over her sister's harsh words. But now, she was lost in a sensual dream, her whole body tight with a sweet, savage yearning she never wanted to end.

When he finally pulled away, Holly looked up at him in shock. Behind him, the bright lights of Midtown skyscrapers illuminated his dark hair like a halo.

"Agape mou," he said hoarsely, stroking the edge of her cheekbone gently with his thumb. "You are everything I want in life. Everything."

Her throat went dry. Trying to smile, she said unevenly, "I bet you say that to all the girls."

"I've never said it to anyone." He looked toward the park's black lace of bare trees against the sweep of moonlit snow. "But life doesn't last forever. I can't waste a moment." He looked at her. "Will you?"

She bit her lip, feeling as if she was in a dream. "But you could have anyone you want. I'm so different…"

"Yes, different. I've watched you. You're warm and loving and kind. And so damned beautiful," he whispered, running a hand through her long red hair. His gaze dropped to her low-cut red dress. "And so sexy you'd make any man lose his mind."

Sexy? *Her?*

He cupped her cheek, kissing her forehead, her cheek, her lips, with butterfly kisses. Drawing back, he looked at her. "You're the only one I want."

Lowering his lips to hers, he kissed her again until she forgot all her insecurity and doubts, until she forgot her own name.

When he released her, she was still lost in the heat of his embrace. Lifting his phone to his ear, he said unsteadily, "Pick me up on Central Park South."

"You're leaving?" she whispered, oddly crestfallen.

"I'm taking you home."

"You don't need to take me home. I have my Metro-Card. I can—"

"Not your home." His eyes burned through her. "To mine."

The thought of going home with him, of what that could mean, caused her to shiver as images of unimaginable delights filled her mind. Her breathing quickened. "Why?"

His sensual lips quirked at the edges. *"Why?"*

"I mean…do you need something typed, or…?"

"Is that all you think you are?"

She blushed beneath his gaze. She bit her lip, then forced herself to respond. "You want to seduce me…?"

"How clearly must I say it?" he said huskily. He cupped her cheek, searching her gaze. "I want you, Holly. In my bed." He ran his hand through her hair as he whispered, "In my life."

And those three last words were the most shocking of all.

She stared at him. Once, she'd thought that working all hours and having a secret crush on her boss was the most she could expect out of life. Even earlier today, as she'd watched Oliver marry her little sister, Holly had been sure her future would be one of self-sacrifice, self-abnegation, caring for others, trying to ignore her own loneliness and misery.

Now, in Stavros's arms, wrapped in his tuxedo jacket, looking up at the handsome Greek billionaire's hungry black eyes, she felt like she'd suddenly traded a small black-and-white dream for a big Technicolor one.

His hand tightened on her shoulder. "Unless you still think you're in love with Oliver."

Holly took a deep breath, then slowly shook her head. In all her years working for Oliver, she'd seen only what she wanted to see: his boyish good looks, his cheerful, sly charm. She'd deliberately chosen to be blind to the rest: the laziness, the constant womanizing. "You were right," she said quietly. "It was just a ridiculous dream."

Stavros exhaled. "Then come home with me tonight."

"I can't…" Her heart was pounding. "I've never done anything like that."

"You've played by the rules for your whole life. So have I." His jaw tensed with an anger she didn't understand as he looked up toward the moon, icy and crystalline in the frozen black sky. "The tycoon's playbook. Dating models whose names I can barely remember now. Working twenty hours a day to build a fortune, and for what? To buy another Ferrari?" His lips twisted bitterly. "What has my life even been for?"

Holly stared at him, shocked that Stavros would allow himself to appear so vulnerable in front of anyone. It threw her into confusion. She'd thought of him as her all-knowing and powerful boss. But now, she realized, he was also just a man. With a beating heart, like hers.

"You're not giving yourself enough credit." Gently, she put her hand over his. "You've created jobs all over the world. You've built amazing tech that—"

"It doesn't matter. Not anymore."

"It matters a lot…"

"Not to me."

She took a deep breath. "Then what does?"

"This," he said simply, and lowered his lips to hers.

This time, his kiss was gentle and deep, wistful as a whisper. Could this really be happening? Was she dreaming? Or could she be totally drunk on half a glass of champagne?

Her heart filled with longing as his powerful body enveloped hers.

"Come home with me," he murmured against her lips.

She sucked in her breath, looking up at his handsome, shadowed face. "It's Christmas Eve…"

His dark gaze burned through her. "There's no one else I'd rather have in my arms when I wake on Christmas morning." His hand slowly traced down her cheek to the edge of her throat to her shoulder shivering beneath the oversize tuxedo jacket. "Unless you don't want me…"

Her—not want *him*? Just the ridiculousness of that suggestion made her gasp. "You can't think that…"

His shoulders relaxed, and his dark eyes met hers. "Then live like we're alive."

Live like we're alive. What a strange thing to say.

He was right, she'd followed the good-girl playbook her whole life, Holly thought suddenly. What had being sensible and safe and good ever done for her, except to leave her working overtime for free for a manipulative boss and sacrificing all her dreams to spoil her little sister—only to feel used and taken for granted by both?

"Say yes," Stavros urged huskily, stroking his hands slowly through her hair. "Come away with me. Be free."

A Rolls-Royce pulled up to the curb. She looked at him, her heart pounding.

"Yes," she breathed.

A trace of silvery moonlight caressed the edge of his sculpted, sensual lips as he drew back to make sure she meant it. "Yes?"

"Let's live like we're alive," she whispered.

Glancing back at the waiting car, he held out his hand. "Are you ready?"

Holly nodded, her heart pounding. But as she took his hand, she didn't feel ready. At all.

As she sat next to him in the back of the limo, she barely noticed the driver in front. She didn't notice anything but Stavros beside her. The journey seemed like mere seconds before they pulled in front of a famous luxury hotel in Midtown.

"This is where you live?" Holly said, looking up at the skyscraper.

He smiled wryly. "You don't like it?"

"Of course I do, but…you live in a hotel?"

"It's convenient."

"Oh." Convenient? She supposed her shabby one-bedroom walk-up in Queens was convenient, too. She only had to change trains once to get to work. "But where is your home?"

He shrugged. "Everywhere. I travel a lot. I prefer not to keep permanent live-in staff."

"Right." She nodded sagely. "I prefer that, too."

His lips quirked, then he turned back toward the glamorous hotel, all decorated and sparkling with Christmas lights.

"Mr. Minos!" a uniformed doorman called desperately, rushing to hold open the door. "Thank you again. My wife hasn't stopped crying since she opened your Christmas card."

"It was nothing."

"Nothing!" The burly man swore under his breath. "Because of your Christmas gift, we can finally buy a house. Which means we can finally start trying to have a baby..." His voice choked off.

Stavros briefly put his hand on the burly man's shoulder. "Merry Christmas, Rob."

"Merry Christmas, Mr. Minos," he replied, unchecked tears streaming down his face.

Holding Holly's hand tightly, Stavros led her through the gilded door into the luxurious lobby, which had at its center an enormous gold Christmas tree decorated with red stars stretching two stories high. All around them, glamorous guests walked, some briskly and others strolling, many trailing assistants and bodyguards and holding little pampered dogs. But Holly only looked at the dark, powerful man beside her.

"That must have been some Christmas gift."

"It was just money," he said shortly, leading her through the lobby.

"The doorman—did he do a big favor for you or something?"

As he led her to the elevator, he gave an awkward shrug that made him look almost embarrassed. "Rob holds the door for me. Always smiles and says hello. Sometimes arranges for a car."

"And for that, you bought him and his wife a house?"

Pushing the elevator button, Stavros said again, "It was nothing. Really."

"Nothing to you," she said softly as the door slid open with a ding. "But everything to them."

Wordlessly, he walked into the elevator. She followed him. "Why did you do it?"

"Because I could."

The same reason he offered me a job as his secretary, she thought. "Stavros," she said, "is it possible that, deep down, you're actually a good guy?"

She saw a flash of something bleak in his dark eyes, quickly veiled. He turned his face toward the sensor then pressed the button for the penthouse. "I'm a selfish bastard. Everyone knows that."

But there was something vulnerable in the tone of his voice. "I'm finding it hard to believe that. Unless there's something else," she said slowly. "Something you're not telling me. Is there—"

Her voice cut off as Stavros pressed her against the elevator wall, and hungrily lowered his mouth to hers.

He kissed her with such hot demand that the questions starting to form in her mind disappeared as if they had never been. All that was left was heat. She felt molten with desire.

With a ding, the elevator door slid open.

Gripping her hand, he pulled her forward. Knees still weak, she followed, looking around her.

The enormous, starkly decorated penthouse was dark except for the white lights glittering from a ten-foot fresh-cut Christmas tree, which stood in front of the floor-to-ceiling windows overlooking the sparkling lights of the city below.

Still shivering from the intensity of his kiss, she looked at him. "Nice tree."

Stavros glanced at it as if he hadn't noticed it 'til now. "The hotel staff arranged that."

She looked around the apartment. There were no photographs on the walls. Nothing personal at all. The white-and-black decor looked like something out of a magazine, curated by a museum. "Did you just move in?"

"I bought this place five years ago."

She looked at him, startled. "Five *years*?"

"So?"

Holly thought of her own shabby walk-up apartment, filled with photos of family and friends, her comfortable, beat-up old furniture, her grandma's old quilt, the tangled-up yarn from her hopeless efforts to learn how to knit. "It seems unlived in."

"I hired the top designer in the city." He sounded a little disgruntled. "It's a look."

"Um." She bit her lip, then turned with a bright smile. "It's nice."

He pulled her into his arms. "You don't really think that."

"No." Butterflies flew through her belly as she stared at his beautiful mouth. Her gaze fell to his thick neck above his black tuxedo tie, to his broad shoulders in the white bespoke shirt, down all the way to the taut waistline of his black trousers to his powerful thighs. Butterflies? The crackle in her core felt more like the sizzle of lightning, burning through every nerve.

"Tell me the truth."

Biting her lip, she said, "I think your apartment is horrible."

"Better," he breathed, and he lowered his mouth to hers.

She tasted the sweetness of his mouth, and surrendered to the strength and power of his larger body wrapped around hers. Surrendered? She hungered for more.

Stavros kissed her for hours, or maybe just minutes, holding her body tightly against his as they stood in his shadowy, stark penthouse, beside the lights of the Christmas tree.

Heart pounding, dizzy from his passionate embrace, she pulled away with a shuddering breath. "This doesn't seem real."

"Lots of things don't feel real to me right now." Brushing tendrils of red hair away from her face, he said softly, "Except you."

As he pulled her tight against his body, his tuxedo jacket fell off her shoulders, dropping silently to the floor. His hands ran slowly through her hair and down her back, over her red dress.

Pulling away, her eyes fell to the floor as she warned him, "I don't have much experience."

"You're a virgin."

Her cheeks flamed. "How did you know?" she whispered. "Is it the way I kissed you?"

"Yes. And the way you shiver when I pull you into my arms. The first time I kissed you, I felt how new it was to you." He gently stroked her cheek, down the edge of her throat, to her breast. Her hard nipple ached even at that slight brush of contact. "That made it new to me, too."

Thinking of the gossip about his previous mistresses, all gorgeous sophisticated women no doubt with amazing, gymnastlike sexual skills, she suddenly couldn't meet his eyes. She bit her swollen lip. "What if I don't please you?"

With a low laugh, he gently lifted her chin as he countered, "What if I don't please you?"

"Are you crazy?" Her eyes went wide. "That's impossible!"

His lips twisted with an emotion she couldn't quite identify.

"That's how I feel about you, Holly," he said in a low voice. "You deserve better."

Stavros felt like *she* deserved better—better than the most famous Greek billionaire playboy in the world? But as she looked into his dark eyes, she saw he believed every word.

With a deep breath, she said quietly, "I can't work for you, Stavros. Not after this."

His expression fell. "You can't?"

Shaking her head, she gave him a crooked smile. "It's all right. Working for the VP of Operations won't be so bad."

His jaw tightened. "As you wish. You will, of course, still get your raise."

"I wouldn't feel comfortable—"

"Nonnegotiable." He cut her off. "You've more than earned it by being the company's hardest-working employee for years. In fact, you should be *demanding* a raise, not just accepting it. Damn it, Holly, you need to realize your value…"

Impulsively, she lifted up on her toes and kissed him. It was the briefest of kisses, feather-light, but it felt daring and terrifying to make the first move. As she started to draw back, he caught her, pulling her against him urgently. He kissed her hungry and hard, as if she was a life raft, and he was a drowning man.

Her body felt tight with need. Her breasts felt heavy, her nipples aching, sending electric sparks rushing through her every time they brushed against his hard chest. Tension coiled low and deep inside her, and she wanted him even closer. Reaching up, she pulled his head down harder to deepen the kiss.

With a growl, he lifted her up into his arms, and carried her down the hallway to an enormous bedroom.

The room was huge, but as sparsely decorated as the great room. Shadows filled the room, with a white gas fire shimmering like candlelight in the stark modern fireplace. Next to the windows, an artificial white tree gleamed with white lights.

Setting her down beside the bed, Stavros stroked her cheek. "You're so beautiful, Holly," he whispered. "I never imagined anyone could be so beautiful. Like an angel."

"I'm no angel."

He paused, looking at her in the winter moonlight flooding in through the window. "No." Reaching around her, he slowly unzipped her red maid-of-honor dress. "You're all woman."

Noiselessly, the dress dropped to the floor. Leaving her standing before him in only a bra, panties and high-heeled shoes.

She should have felt cold, standing nearly naked in front of him in the large bedroom. But beneath the heat of his gaze, she felt lit with an intoxicating fire as he slowly looked her over, from her full breasts plumped up by the white silk demi bra, past the softly curved plane of her belly, to her white silk panties, edged with lace. Taking her courage in her hands, she lifted her gaze.

Cupping her face in both hands, he lowered his head to hers and kissed her until the whole world swirled around her as she was lost in the sweet maelstrom of his embrace. His hands roamed feather-light over her body, stroking her breasts, her tiny waist, her big hips, the full curve of her backside. When his hands stroked over the silk bra, she held her breath until he reached around her to unhook the clasp, springing her free. With an intake of breath, he cupped her breasts, tweaking her taut nipples. She shuddered, vibrating with need.

Reaching down, he pulled off her high-heeled shoes, one by one, sending each skittering across the black floor. Pushing her back against the white comforter of the king-size bed, he undid the cuff links of his shirt.

Never taking his eyes off her, he loosened the buttons, and she had her first flash of his hard chest. He dropped the shirt to the floor, and she got her full view of it, in all its tanned, muscular glory. A trail of dark hair led to his flat, taut belly.

He unzipped his dark trousers, and slowly pulled them down his thighs, along with his underwear, revealing his muscular, powerful legs laced with more dark hair. She sucked in her breath as he straightened, and she saw how big he was, and how hard for her.

She wasn't a total innocent. She'd seen pictures of the male form. There had been that sex education course in high school, gag gifts in shops, and working in an office, she'd once stumbled over a coworker watching porn on his computer. She wasn't totally naive.

But in this moment, seeing him naked in all his physical power and brute force, she felt nervous. Swallowing, she pulled the white comforter up to her chin, squeezing her eyes shut, suddenly shaking.

She felt the mattress move beneath her.

"Holly." His voice was low. His hand, warm and gentle, was on her shoulder. "Look at me."

Biting her lip, she looked up at him, wondering what she should do, what she should say. Stavros's darkly handsome face was intense, lost in desire.

"Are you afraid?" he asked in a low voice.

Biting her lip, she looked away. "I don't want to displease you. I—I don't know what to do."

"Holly," he repeated huskily. Slowly, he ran a fingertip down her bare shoulder above the comforter. Just that simple touch caused a sizzle of electricity to go through her. "Look at me. All of me. And see if you please me."

She looked down as he'd commanded, and saw how large he was, how hard and thick and smooth. He wanted her. There could be no doubt of that.

Trembling, she lifted her mouth toward his. Holding her tenderly, he kissed her.

With his lips on hers, all rational thought disappeared again in molten heat, in the rising need that made her forget everything else. She was dimly aware of the comforter disappearing. As his naked body covered hers, as she felt his weight and strength on her, she sighed with pleasure and a sense of rightness—of being part of something, half of a whole. Entwining her tongue with his own, he teased her, toyed with her, made her gasp. The kiss was so perfect, so deep, when he pulled away she was left with a sense of loss and longing.

He nibbled her chin, then slowly worked his way down her naked body with hot kisses, as his hands caressed her bare skin. He licked her neck, her collarbone. He cupped her full, bare breasts and lowered his mouth slowly to the valley between them, making her grip the white cotton sheet beneath her as she felt his hot breath against her skin.

He wrapped his lips around her taut, aching nipple. His mouth was wet and hot as he suckled her, pulling her deep into his mouth, swirling her with his tongue. She gasped with pleasure, closing her eyes.

He moved to the other breast, suckling that nipple in turn, as his hands stroked slowly down her body, caressing her belly, her hips, her thighs. He lowered his head, kissing where his hands had just caressed her, seducing her with feather-light touches that made her skin burn. She felt his fingertips lift the edge of her panties from her hips.

"Do you want me?" he whispered, his voice so low it made her tremble.

"Yes," she breathed.

"Louder."

"Yes!" she cried, her cheeks burning.

Then Stavros suddenly pulled away, looking down at her. And he spoke words she'd never expected. Words that nearly made her heart stop.

"Marry me, Holly." Stavros cupped her cheek, his dark eyes burning in the Christmas-Eve night. "Have a child with me."

Her eyes widened with shock. "Are you serious?"

"I've never been more serious."

Holly couldn't believe it. Even a one-night stand with a

man like Stavros seemed like a dream. But he wanted to marry her? Have a baby with her?

Tears came to her eyes.

"I've shocked you," he said grimly.

"No...yes." Lifting her chin, she whispered, "It's like all my most impossible dreams are suddenly coming true."

Exhaling, he ran his thumb lightly along her cheekbone, brushing a tear away. "Is that a yes?"

"Yes," she breathed.

He smiled, and it was brighter than the sun, even as she saw a suspicious sheen in his black eyes. "You'll never regret it. I swear it on my life."

"I'll do my best to make you happy..."

"You already have." Lowering his head, he kissed her. "I want you, *agape mou*," he groaned against her lips. "I'll want you until the day I die."

She held her breath as he kissed down her throat, to her breasts, then her belly. She shivered, lost in a sensual dream. He wanted to marry her. He wanted to fill her with his child...

He slowly pulled her white silk panties down her legs, and tossed them away. Kneeling between her legs on the bed, he pushed her thighs apart. She felt the warmth of his breath against the most sensitive part of her body, a place no man had ever touched.

Lowering his head, he spread her wide with his hands. For a moment, she couldn't breathe, as he teased her with the warmth of his breath.

Then he tasted her, delicately with the tip of his tongue, swirling against the core of her pleasure. Even as she gasped in shock at the intensity of the sensation, he moved, deepening his possession, reaching around her to hold her tight, as he lapped her with the full width of his tongue.

She cried out, grasping the bed beneath her as electricity whipped through her, causing her back to arch, lifting off the mattress.

He moaned, his hands tightening on her thighs, holding her down as her whole body strained to fly. Her breasts felt tight, her whole body aching with need. Then he pushed a single thick fingertip inside her, stretching her.

Pleasure built inside her, whirling her in every direction, pleasure she'd never imagined. She held her breath, closing her eyes as her head tilted back. Her body arched off the bed as he worked her with his tongue—then, just as she tightened with pleasure almost too great to bear, he pushed a second fingertip inside her. And she exploded into a thousand chiming diamonds, in a million colors, soaring through the sky.

She was only dimly aware as he reached for a condom from a nearby nightstand. But as he started to tear it open, she covered it with her hand.

"No," she panted, still dizzy beneath waves of pleasure.

"No?" He looked stunned.

"You don't need that." She smiled. "Live like you're alive."

Savage joy lit up his dark eyes as he threw the condom to the floor. "This is my first time without one," he whispered, lowering his head to kiss her. "My first time ever."

"For both of us," she breathed, closing her eyes with a delicious shiver as he gently bit the corner of her neck. Prickles of desire raced through her body.

"I'll end the pain as quickly as I can," he said huskily.

Pain? What pain? All she felt was bliss—

Gripping her hips, he positioned himself between her legs. In a swift, deliberate movement, he sheathed himself deeply inside her.

She gasped as he broke the barrier inside her. But he held himself utterly still, holding her as the sudden pang of pain lessened, then disappeared. His weight was heavy on hers, his hard-muscled chest sliding sensually over her breasts as he lowered his head to kiss her, gently at first, then with rising passion as she started to return his embrace.

Only then did he slowly begin to move inside her, thrusting deeper, inch by inch. And to her shock, a delicious new tension began to coil, low and deep inside her belly.

Reaching up to his shoulders, Holly pulled him down tighter against her, wanting him deeper, wanting more. Wanting everything.

CHAPTER FOUR

HE WAS ALREADY deep inside her, so deliciously deep. Stavros fought to keep control as she gripped his shoulders, pulling his naked body down against her. He felt her move beneath him, tightening with new desire.

"Yes," she'd whispered. He shuddered at the memory.

When Holly had told him she'd marry him and have his child, that single word had nearly unmanned him. And now it was almost impossible to hold himself back, when just the feel of her and the sight of her were enough to make him explode. Especially when he was bare inside her, a pleasure he'd never experienced before. He was a breath from losing control.

But he couldn't. Not yet. He set his jaw, desperately trying to keep hold of the reins in a ruthless grip.

Stavros felt like a virgin himself.

He'd spoken the forbidden words that seared his heart, words he'd never said to any woman. Outlandish words, asking her to marry him and have his baby. It was his one last chance to leave something of himself behind. An adoring wife, and a son or daughter to carry on his name.

She should have refused him, laughed in his face. After all, they were barely more than strangers to each other.

Instead, she'd accepted him, as if she'd dreamed her whole life of marrying Stavros and having his child.

All he'd wanted to do was possess her, to thrust inside her, hard and fast. But he'd known the first time would be painful for her. So he'd forced himself to go slow, to take his time, to seduce her. To make it good for her.

When he'd first pushed himself inside her, he'd hated to see sudden pain wipe out the joy in her beautiful face. So he'd held her, until her pain passed, though it was total agony to hold himself still, so hard with need, so deep inside her. But he managed it—for her. He'd kissed her sweaty forehead, her soft cheek, and held her close until he felt her shoulders relax, and a sigh came from her lips.

Now, the raw intensity of his desire for her was almost too much to bear. As he felt her move beneath him, her every gasp of pleasure was pure torture.

She was soft, so soft. And so sensual. He was on a razor's edge of control.

Holly Marlowe was a sensual goddess. He wondered how he hadn't recognized her beauty and sensuality from the moment he'd first seen her, three years before. He should have seen past the mousy bun and baggy, unflattering clothes. He should have known what they really were—a disguise.

She was his now, and she would be his for as long as he lived. She would be his wife. He would fill her with his child—

With a shudder of need, he kissed her lips, tenderly at first, then with building passion. As her hands gripped his shoulders, pushing him tighter against her, he panted with need, beads of sweat rising on his forehead as he continued to thrust slowly, gently, letting her feel every inch of him moving inside her.

The pleasure was incredible. Some of his control began to slip. But he wasn't ready for it to end, not yet. He wanted to make it amazing for her.

He looked down. Holly's face was sweetly lifted, her eyes closed with ecstasy. He almost exploded right then. With a shudder, he gripped her hips and slowly began to increase his pace. Her lips parted as she sucked in her breath, her fingernails raking slowly down his naked back.

When he finally felt her tighten around him as her gasp of pleasure turned into a scream, he could hold himself back no longer. He plunged deep into her, and his own hoarse shout melded with hers, echoing against the windows overlooking the sparkling lights of the city. The white tree twinkled amid the dark shadows of the bedroom, as the clock struck midnight on Christmas Eve.

When Stavros woke, the soft light of dawn was coming through his bedroom's floor-to-ceiling windows. Outside, the wintry city looked gray on Christmas morning.

He'd been lost in the best dream he'd ever had. Holly had been kissing him, and she'd been heavily pregnant. Emotion shone from her vulnerable eyes as she'd told him she loved him—

Now, he looked at the soft, warm woman in his arms. Both of them were still naked beneath the white comforter. He realized he'd slept all night, holding her in his arms. They were still facing each other, their foreheads almost touching on the pillow, her curly red hair stretched out behind her. Even in sleep, his arms had been wrapped protectively around her.

I love you, Stavros, she'd whispered in the dream, her heart and soul in her eyes.

It was just a dream, he reminded himself harshly. Totally meaningless. But in the cold light of reality, he felt her imagined words like an ice pick through his soul. *I love you.*

When he'd imagined leaving her behind after his death, he'd pictured a pregnant wife dressed in black, standing stoically beside his grave.

He hadn't thought of how it might feel to be the widow left behind. How Holly's warm, generous, loving heart might react to all that grief. It could destroy her.

Could? It *would*.

His conscience, buried and repressed for so long, suddenly came out in full force. Could he really be so selfish? Was he a Minos man through and through after all?

I'll leave her all my fortune, he argued with himself.

But Holly wouldn't care about that, not really. After all, she'd spent three years working for Oliver without asking for the raise and promotion she deserved. When she'd walked into his twenty-million-dollar penthouse, with its elegant decor created at great expense by Manhattan's foremost interior designer, she'd been left utterly unmoved.

Holly, alone of all women on earth, didn't seem to give a damn about money.

So his billions would bring her little pleasure. Far from it. With her kind, sympathetic heart, his widow's fortune would make her an easy target for unscrupulous fortune hunters. First and foremost: his greedy cousin and her spoiled sister.

Stavros looked back at Holly, sleeping so sweetly and trustingly in his arms.

I'll leave her with a child, he tried to tell himself. That, at least, was something he knew she wanted.

But a child she would raise alone?

He felt sick. He'd seduced Holly under false pretenses. His dream had only shown the stark truth: he'd soon make her love him. He'd already started to make her care. Her heart was innocent; she had no defense against love, not like Stavros. Only he knew what love really meant: surrender or possession. Being the helpless conquered or tyrannical conqueror. No one came out of it unscathed.

Just the fact that she'd convinced herself, even for a moment, that she could love a man as unworthy of it as Oliver only proved how open her heart was. She was not guarded. She had no walls.

So when Stavros died, which he would before next

Christmas, he would not leave behind him a dignified wife in a black veil and chic black mourning suit standing stoically beside his grave, as he'd imagined.

Instead, he'd leave a broken woman, bewildered and lost, perhaps with a child to raise on her own. For all he knew, she might already be pregnant. Stavros would soon be dead and buried, forgotten. But Holly would remain, a widow with a broken heart, bitterly cursing him as the liar who'd seduced her with false promises of forever and changed her life in ways she'd never imagined.

A razor blade lifted to his throat as he looked at her, still sleeping trustingly in his arms. He had no choice. He had to tell her the truth. Explain about his fatal brain tumor before it was too late for her to change her mind about marrying him.

If it wasn't already too late.

"You're awake." Holly's voice was soft and warm as she drowsily opened her eyes, smiling up at him with love shining from her face. "Merry Christmas."

Stavros looked down at her. His lips parted to choke out the truth. Then he stopped.

He suddenly realized with horrifying clarity that even if he told her about his illness *she would marry him, anyway.*

As that sister of hers had said, taking care of other people was what Holly did best. She gave and gave and gave, leaving nothing for herself. From the time her parents had died, she'd put her little sister first. From the moment she'd started working at Minos International, she'd put Oliver first. She sacrificed herself for others, even if they didn't deserve it.

And if Stavros told her he was dying she would do the same for him. She'd take care of him. She'd hold his hand through chemotherapy appointments. She'd love him. She'd never leave him.

Even if it destroyed her.

"Holly," he said hoarsely, struggling to know what to do, "there's something you need to..."

He felt a sharp pain behind his right eye, so sudden and savage he jerked back from her. The bed seemed like it was swaying beneath him.

Holding the comforter over her chest, Holly sat up with a frown. "Stavros?"

The pain was nearly blinding, spreading through his head, causing a rough throbbing in his skull. He put a trembling hand against his forehead. How long did he have? Even his doctor had hedged his bets when he'd given him the news two days before.

"No one can say for sure how long you'll live, Mr. Minos," Dr. Ramirez had said gravely. But when Stavros had pressed him, he'd admitted six to nine months might be typical for a patient at his advanced stage.

But Stavros wasn't a typical man. He'd always prided himself on it. He'd always beaten others, proving himself stronger and smarter and faster. His tumor was part of him. All his worst sins bottled up into one fleshy mass rapidly spreading through his brain.

"What is it?" Holly cried. "What's wrong?"

Slowly getting out of bed, he stood still, blinking until the blurriness passed and he could see again in the dim early light of his penthouse's master bedroom. Wearily, he stumbled across the room, opened a drawer and pulled on some loosely slung knit pants. He felt as if he was a million years old.

Going to the wall of windows, he stared out at the cold gray city beneath him. So very cold. So very gray.

All these years he'd hated his father as heartless and cruel. All these years he'd despised his cousin as a selfish bastard.

What Stavros had just done proved him to be the worst of them all.

He was dying, so in a pathetic attempt to make his life matter, to be important to someone other than his shareholders, he'd proposed marriage to this trusting girl. He'd taken her virginity. That was bad enough.

But he'd wanted to do so much more.

He'd wanted to crush her heart and spirit and make her suffer with him as he declined, and failed, and died. Clinging to her like a drowning man, like a filthy coward, he'd wanted to drag her down with him.

Most women he knew might have been happy to exchange six months of holding his hand and watching him die for a vast pot of gold at the end. Those women guarded their souls—if they even *had* souls.

But not Holly. He'd seen it in her warm, trusting face. From the first moment he'd taken her arm at her sister's wedding, when they'd danced at the reception, when he'd first kissed her in the snowy darkness of Central Park, he'd seen how quickly her opinion of him had changed, from resentment, to curiosity, to bewildered desire. And finally, when she'd opened her eyes just now in the gray light of Christmas morning in his bed, he'd seen the way her soft emerald eyes glowed. And he'd known.

He could break her.

"Stavros, you're scaring me." From behind him on the bed, the tone of her voice suddenly changed, becoming artificially bright. "You've changed your mind about marrying me, haven't you? You're scared to tell me. But don't be. I wouldn't blame you if—"

"Yes." His voice was harsh as he turned to face her. "I've changed my mind."

"You have?"

Her lovely face went pale, but she spoke the words as if this was exactly what she'd expected all along. As if she'd known her joy and ecstasy could only be a brief fantasy.

Setting his shoulders, forcing himself not to feel, he said shortly, "Last night was a mistake."

Holly's shoulders sagged, and she looked away, toward the twinkling white tree. Holding the comforter over her naked breasts, she whispered, "Was it something I did, or...?"

"I was drunk last night," he lied harshly, knowing the fastest way through this was to hit her at her most vulnerable point, so she wouldn't fight it. One hard painful wrench, and it would all be over. "I mean—" he shrugged, the stereotype of a casually cruel playboy "—let's face it. Like you said, you aren't my usual type."

The blow hit her squarely. The last color drained from her cheeks, leaving her pale as a ghost beneath her fiery hair. She swallowed, tried to speak, failed. She was lost in pain and insecurity and couldn't see past it. Wordlessly, she looked down at her hands, clasped together tightly over the comforter. "I..."

"You should go," he said coldly.

Not meeting his eyes, Holly slowly got out of bed. Picking up her bra and panties, and her crumpled red gown from the floor, she covered her amazing body. Her face held the pure, unmitigated heartbreak of youth, and he hated himself at that moment more than he'd ever hated anyone. Which was saying something.

"My driver will take you home. He could stop at the drugstore, if you like."

"What for?"

"Emergency contraception," he said coldly.

"That's not necessary."

"It's not?"

Stepping into her high-heeled shoes, she lifted her chin. With a deep breath, she looked back at him. "I told you. I can take the subway."

His stomach churned at the bleakness in her eyes. "Holly—"

She cut him off with a harsh gesture. Then she gave a forced smile. "It's my fault. I knew all along you couldn't possibly— I never should have come here."

Holly was apologizing…to him. It took all of Stavros's willpower not to reach for her, pull her into his arms, tell her how he was to blame for everything. But the habits of a lifetime held him in good stead. His hands tightened into fists at his sides. "I'll make sure you still get the promotion and raise you deserve," was all he said. "But it's better we don't work together in the future."

"Yes." Looking back at him, her eyes suddenly glittered with a strange ferocity he'd never seen before. "You're right. Goodbye." She turned away.

But he couldn't let her go, not like this. Not when he suddenly wondered if he'd ever see her again.

Stavros grabbed her arm. "Wait."

"What else is there to say?" she asked, her voice catching.

His fingers tightened over her wrist. Last night had been the most incredible sexual experience of his life—and more than sexual. Their eyes locked, and all Stavros wanted to do was pull her back into his arms. Into his bed. Into his life.

But not at the cost of hers.

He dropped her wrist.

"It's unlikely you're pregnant after just one night. But if anything happens," he drawled, "you'll let my lawyers know, won't you?"

Her lips parted in confusion. "Your lawyers?"

"Yes. If you're pregnant, they'll take care of it."

Her face went white, then red. Then her green eyes narrowed with cold fury. "You're too kind."

Stavros had played the part of a coldhearted, womanizing louse to perfection, insinuating that he would have his lawyers pay her off if there was a child. Insinuating he was too busy and important to even be bothered with such a minor detail.

No wonder she was now looking at him as if he was the most despicable human being on earth.

"That's all." He tilted his head, making his eyes as frozen and gray as the world outside. "Now get out."

With an intake of breath, Holly said in a trembling voice, "I wish I'd never met you."

And turning on her heel, she left his penthouse, taking all the warmth and light with her, leaving Stavros alone in the coldest Christmas he'd ever known.

CHAPTER FIVE

Eleven months later

HOLLY PAUSED IN shoveling snow, taking a deep breath that turned to smoke in the chill air. All around her, sunshine illuminated the snow, making the white blanket sparkle like diamonds.

It was the day after Thanksgiving, and for the first time in her life, she was spending it alone—and in Switzerland, of all places. Farther from home than she could ever have imagined last Christmas, when her heart had been so savagely broken.

She leaned against the shovel. A soft smile lifted to her face as she looked toward the porch. But she wasn't alone, not truly. She'd never be alone again.

Late November snow was nearly four feet deep around the winding path that led from her tiny chalet, just a rustic cabin really, to the sliver of main road. The nearest village was a mile away, tucked in a remote valley of the Swiss Alps, and even that was nearly deserted in winter. The nearest real market town was Zedermatt, where the festive outdoor Christmas market would open today. A friend had begged her to accompany him there this afternoon. Somewhat hesitantly, she'd agreed. Why not enjoy the season?

Holly's days of working long hours in an office, always filled with stress and urgency, now seemed like a strange dream from long ago. Here, there was only tranquility and peace, and of course, snow, but she'd gotten used to that, shoveling the path to her door every day, and listening to the quiet sound of snowflakes each night against the slanted roof.

In the last year, everything had changed. Her old life in New York, the person she'd once been, were all gone. So much lost. But even more gained.

A baby's gurgle came from the small porch of her chalet, and Holly looked up tenderly, with a familiar joy in her heart.

"Are you hungry, sweet boy?" Shoveling the last few scoops of wet snow from the path to the road, she carried the shovel back toward the chalet. She tromped her winter boots heavily to knock off the snow, then climbed the steps to the porch and smiled down at her sweet two-month-old baby, Freddie, named after her own beloved father.

The baby gurgled and waved his arms happily, at least as much as he could do, bundled up as he was in a one-piece winter fleece that covered him from mittens to hood, tucked snugly into the baby seat with a blanket over the top.

"We'll get you fed," Holly promised, smiling. Setting down the shovel nearby, she lifted the baby seat's handle and carried him inside.

Inside the rustic cabin, a fire blazed in the old stone fireplace. This chalet was two hundred years old, with low ceilings braced with hand-hewn wooden beams. The furniture wasn't quite as old, but close. And the place was tiny: there was only one bedroom. But every day since she'd arrived here, pregnant and heartbroken, last February, she'd blessed her former employer, who'd offered her free lodging in exchange for keeping an eye on the place.

Coming inside, Holly set down the baby carrier then pushed the door closed behind her to keep out the frozen air. She yanked off her heavy winter coat and colorful hand-knitted hat, hanging them on the coat rack while she shook errant snowflakes out of her long red braid. Pulling off her boots, she left them on towels placed just inside the door and stepped nimbly into the room, wearing a loose green sweater and snug black leggings ending in thick warm socks.

Unbuckling Freddie out of the carrier, she changed his diaper then wrapped him snugly in a soft baby blanket. Cradling him in her arms, she carried him to the worn sofa near the fire. As she fed the baby, he looked up at her with big wondering eyes, nestling his tiny hand between her breasts.

Holly had arrived here in a panic in February, wondering how she'd ever cope with raising a child on her own. Then she'd remembered: she already had. She'd raised her baby sister when Holly was barely more than a child herself.

After Stavros had coldly thrown her out of his bed last Christmas morning, she'd never gone back to her job at Minos International. She hadn't even gone back to collect her carefully tended plant or framed photos of her sister. A friend had collected them for her, along with her last check.

Holly had had money in her savings account. She'd learned to be careful with money the hard way, at eighteen, when she'd found herself with a little sister to raise and very little money from her parents' life insurance to support them. Ever since, she'd always been careful.

That saved her when, in mid-January as she'd started her job search, she'd discovered the real source of the stomach flu she hadn't been able to shake: she was pregnant.

And the memory of Stavros's words in bed on Christmas morning chilled her. *If you're pregnant, let my lawyers know...they'll take care of it.*

That, more than anything, had destroyed any lingering illusions she'd had about Stavros Minos being a decent human being.

She'd, of course, heard stories about men lying to get a woman into bed. But she'd never imagined it would happen to her. When he'd desired her, Stavros had been romantic beyond belief, seducing her with sweet words, passionate kisses and, most astonishing of all, proposing marriage and having a child together.

But from the moment he'd gotten what he wanted, he'd expected her to disappear.

Holly had known she wouldn't let him make the baby disappear, too. She couldn't take the risk of seeing Stavros Minos again, even accidentally, or letting him know she was pregnant.

So she'd left New York.

She'd been happy in Switzerland. She was lucky. All right, so Thanksgiving, the traditional American kickoff to the Christmas season, had felt a little quiet yesterday, since the holiday wasn't celebrated in Switzerland. Growing up, Holly's mother had always spent the whole day cooking turkey and baking pies that smelled heavenly, while the two girls stretched out in the morning on the carpet of the family room, watching the Thanksgiving Day parade on TV. In the afternoon, during commercials of his football game, their father inevitably wandered into the kitchen, hoping to sneak a taste of mashed potatoes and cranberry sauce, before their mother shooed him away with a playful smack of a Santa-decorated towel.

Christmas had always been Holly's favorite time of year. At least until last year. Now, with her heartbreaking memories of Stavros last Christmas Day, she was almost afraid to face the holidays this year.

Holly steadied herself. She had so much to be thankful for now. This warm, cozy chalet, her baby, her health. And after nearly a year of estrangement, when she'd phoned her sister to wish her happy Thanksgiving yesterday, for the first time her sister had actually answered the phone.

All right, so Nicole had mostly just yelled at her during the ten-minute call. Apparently Oliver had been fired from

three different jobs over the past year, causing the newly-
weds to move from Hong Kong to Los Angeles, then back
to New York, where he was now unemployed. Her sister
blamed Holly.

"It's your fault," Nicole had shouted. "His bosses expect too much. You should be here taking care of things
for him. And for me!"

Feeling guilty, Holly tried to change the subject. "I've
been busy this year, too..." And she'd finally told her sister the happy news about the baby.

But if she'd hoped it would make Nicole forgive her,
or have any joy at the news of a baby nephew, Holly was
soon disappointed.

Her sister had been shocked, then furious, then demanded to know the identity of the father. Swearing her
to secrecy, Holly had shivered as she'd whispered Stavros's
name into the phone. It had been the first time she'd spoken his name aloud in almost a year.

But knowing that secret only seemed to enrage Nicole
more.

"So now you're a baby mama for a billionaire?" she'd
cried. "You selfish cow—you never have to worry about
anything, do you?"

And her sister had slammed down the phone.

At least they were talking again, Holly told herself now,
trying to remain cheerful. It was a start. And who knew
what the future could hold? After all, they were coming
into the season of miracles.

Her baby was the biggest miracle of all. She could never
be sad about anything for long, not when she had him. She
smiled down at Freddie, who was all bright eyes and plump
cheeks. And if, with his dark eyes and black hair, her baby
strongly resembled a man she didn't want to remember, she
blocked it from her mind with harsh determination.

Freddie was hers. He had no father. Holly would be the only parent he'd ever need.

The baby, born a week late in a Zurich hospital, had been over four kilos—nine pounds, two ounces—and continued to gain weight at a healthy clip. As Holly looked down at her precious child, her heart twisted with love such as she'd never known.

And Stavros would never even know he existed.

Holly looked into the fire. She'd had no choice, she reminded herself fiercely, as she'd done many times over the past year. Stavros had made his feelings clear. The morning after he'd seduced her with promises and lies, she'd woken up on the happiest Christmas morning she'd ever known, only to be tossed out with the trash.

After she'd found out she was pregnant, she'd fled New York in fear that his lawyers might try to force her to end the pregnancy. She'd gone to London, where her former employer had made it clear she had a standing job offer. He'd been bewildered when, instead of accepting a high-paying office job, she'd asked about being a caretaker to his family's old chalet in Switzerland.

"It's not St. Moritz, you know," he'd replied doubtfully, stroking his white beard. "The village is deserted in winter. It was my great-grandfather's cabin. It's a bit of a wreck. Are you sure?"

Holly had been sure. And she'd never regretted her choice. She'd made friends with her elderly neighbors down the road, kind people who'd delighted in showering lonely, pregnant Holly with advice and *Älplermagronen*, and since her baby's birth, with babysitting offers and cake. Holly's high-school German was rapidly improving. As far as she was concerned, she'd be happy to live here forever. Happy enough.

How could she ever admit she felt lonely sometimes, or that she didn't think her heart would ever completely heal from her brief affair with Stavros? It would be the height of ingratitude to ever feel sad, when she had so much: home, friends and Freddie.

It was enough. It had to be enough.

She looked down at the sleeping baby in her arms. Stroking his rosy cheek, her heart full of love, she whispered, "I'm going to make your first Christmas perfect, Freddie. See if I don't."

The baby yawned in reply, drowsy and sleepy with a full belly and a warm fire. Carefully, Holly rose to her feet and settled the baby into a small bassinet in the cabin's bedroom. Leaving him in the darkened room to nap, she softly closed the door behind her.

Back in the main room, the fire crackled. Untying her braid to shake her hair free, she went to the closet and dug to the back, where she found a large box.

It was time to reclaim Christmas.

Reaching into her family's old box of treasures, Holly pulled out her grandmother's old quilt, the chipped ceramic Santa cookie jar, a garland of colorful felt stars and the Christmas recipe book with her mother's faded handwriting. Vintage ornaments from her childhood. She touched the hand-knitted stockings, and her heart lifted to her throat.

She decorated the small main room, putting the ornaments on the wooden mantel above the fire, and then stepped back to look. That would have to do, at least until she got a tree at the Christmas market. A lump rose in her throat. She'd make sure Freddie had a wonderful Christmas—

There was a hard knock at the door, making her jump. Then she shook her head, smiling. Who was it? Elke with freshly baked gingerbread? Horst, offering to shovel snow? Brushing off some errant Christmas glitter from her black leggings, Holly opened the door.

And her smile dropped.

"Holly." Stavros's coldly handsome face glowered down at her. His voice was low, barely more than a growl.

Her lips parted in a silent gasp.

"Is it true?" he demanded. Moving closer, he narrowed his eyes, black as night. His jawline was dark with five-o'clock shadow, and his powerful form filled the door, all broad shoulders and muscle. Behind him, parked on the edge of the snowy road, she saw his driver waiting inside a black luxury SUV that looked totally out of place in this rural Swiss valley.

Terror went through her. Her baby. He'd come for her baby! Instinctively she started to close the door in his face. "I don't want to see you—"

"Too bad." Reaching out a powerful arm, he blocked the door, and pushed his way inside.

Shivering with sickening fear, she stepped back as he closed the door behind him. He calmly shook the snow-flakes from his Italian cashmere coat.

He was even more handsome than she remembered. Even more dangerous.

"I heard a rumor." Stavros looked slowly around the cabin, with its roaring fireplace and homemade Christmas decorations. Pulling off his black leather gloves, he tucked them into his pockets and turned to her with narrowed eyes. His voice was colder than the frigid winter air outside. "Is it true?"

"Is what true?" she whispered, with a sinking heart.

Stavros's jaw was tight as he looked right through her. "Did you have my baby, Holly?"

Her blood went cold. Teeth chattering, she stared at him. The man who'd once seduced her, who'd wooed her with words and languorous kisses, was now looking at her with hatred in his eyes.

She tried to laugh. "Where did you hear that?"

"You're a terrible liar," he said softly. "Is it possible you've lied to me for nearly a year?"

Her heart lifted to her throat. It was all she could do not to turn and rush into the bedroom, to grab their sleeping baby and try to run before it was too late.

But it was already too late. She'd never outrun Stavros. Especially with his driver outside. There was no escape.

Her mouth went dry as she tried to think of a lie he might believe. Something, anything. She could say Freddie was another man's son. Stavros knew she'd been a virgin in his bed, but maybe she'd slept with someone else right afterward. A hookup after Christmas! A drunken one-night stand on New Year's Eve! Anything!

But as her eyes met Stavros's, she couldn't force any lie from her trembling lips.

"Who told you?" she whispered, her voice barely audible.

Stavros staggered back, his dark eyes wide. For a split second, he did not move.

Then he took a deep breath. Reaching out, he cupped her cheek. She felt the rough warmth of his palm against her skin. His touch was tender, but his expression was cruel.

"Who told me? Oliver. Who heard it from your sister." He said softly, "He enjoyed telling me. He's never been able to make me feel like a fool before." Blinding sunlight from the window, amplified by the snow, suddenly bathed the hard edges of his cheekbones and jawline in golden light. "But he's not to blame. You are."

Shivering, she licked her lips. "I…"

"You promised to tell me if there was a pregnancy." His dark eyes were aflame with cold fury. "You're a liar, Holly. A filthy, despicable liar."

But at that, sudden rage filled her, chasing away the shadows of fear.

"*I'm* a liar?" she said incredulously.

His lip curled scornfully. "You hid your pregnancy and ran away like a thief—"

Holly was past listening as nearly a year of grief and rage exploded from her heart.

"*You're* the liar, Stavros. When you wanted me in your bed, you promised the sun and the moon! You asked me to marry you!" Her body shook with pain and anger. "But as soon as you were done, you couldn't throw me away fast enough on Christmas morning!"

He started to speak, then abruptly cut himself off. He looked away, his jaw clenching. He said in a low voice, "I had a good reason."

"Yeah, right!" Holly, who'd never lost her temper in her life, truly lost it now. "You'd had your fun and you were done. You didn't care what it did to me. You're selfish to the bone. Why would I ever let a man like you near my son?"

"Son?" He slowly turned to her. Then his eyes narrowed. "I want to meet him."

"No."

"I'm his father."

"Father?" She lifted her chin incredulously. "You're a sperm donor, nothing more. I don't want anything to do with you. We're better off without you." She jabbed her finger toward the door. "Now get out!"

Stavros clawed his hands through his dark, tousled hair. His black eyes looked weary, almost bleak. "You don't understand. I wasn't myself last year—"

"You were exactly yourself," she interrupted coldly. "The lying, coldhearted bastard everyone else claimed you were." Holly was surprised he'd even bother trying to make excuses. It didn't seem like his style. But it didn't matter. She wouldn't let herself get suckered into caring about him ever again. She shook her head. "You're selfish and cruel. Just like Oliver said—Minos men only care about themselves!"

Abruptly, Stavros turned to face her.

"I was dying, Holly," he said flatly. "That's why I sent you away on Christmas morning. I thought I was dying." He narrowed his eyes. "And now I want to see my son."

Stavros wasn't prepared for the shock he'd felt, seeing her in the doorway of the Alpine chalet.

He was even less prepared for the shock of learning that the rumor was true, and he was a father.

A father. And the baby had to be around two months old. All those months of the pregnancy, and he hadn't known. He felt dizzy with the revelation.

Dizzy, and angry. But not just at Holly.

So much had happened over the last year. He'd been unusually emotional last Christmas, convinced he'd been about to die. That must have been why he'd acted so foolishly, seducing her with such wild longing, proposing marriage, even begging her to have his child.

It embarrassed him now to remember it. All that rank sentimentality, the desperation he'd felt for love and family and home.

Thank God, he'd recovered from that, along with the cancer. Holly Marlowe was nothing to him now.

Or so he'd thought. But now they had a child together. That meant they'd be linked forever, even after death.

And looking at Holly now, Stavros felt the same punch in the gut that he remembered from last Christmas. If anything, she looked more beautiful, more impossibly desirable.

Her curly red hair tumbled over her shoulders of her soft green tunic, and the angry pant of her breath showed off breasts grown fuller and even more womanly than he remembered. Tight leggings revealed the delicious shape of her hips and backside. Her emerald eyes sparkled with fury as they narrowed in disbelief.

"Dying?" she said incredulously.

"It's true. Last Christmas I thought I only had months to live."

He waited for her to react, but her face was stony.

"Didn't you hear me?" he demanded. She shrugged.

"I'm waiting for the punch line," she said coldly.

"Damn you. I'm trying to tell you something I haven't shared with anyone."

"Lucky me."

Turning away, Stavros paced, staring briefly at the crackling fire in the fireplace, then out of the frosted window toward the sun sparkling on the snow. He took a deep breath. "I had a brain tumor. I was told I was dying."

"And that inspired you to seduce me and lie to me?"

"Dying inspired me to want more," he said softly. "To make one last attempt to leave something behind. A wife. A child." He turned back to her. "That's why I slept with you, Holly. That's why I said I wanted to marry you and have a child with you. I wasn't lying. I did want it."

She clenched her hands, glaring at him. "So what happened?"

"I couldn't go through with it. I couldn't be that selfish. I knew you would fall in love with me. You were so…innocent. So trusting. I didn't want to break your heart and make you collapse with grief after I died."

She pulled back, looking strangely outraged. He'd forgotten that about her, how she wore her emotions so visibly on her face. Most people he knew hid their emotions behind iron walls. Including and especially himself, notwithstanding Christmas Eve last year, which he still tried not to think about.

"So you said those horrible things," Holly said, "and sent me away for my sake. You're such a good guy."

Her tone was acid. Staring at her in shock, Stavros realized he'd taken her innocence in more ways than one.

He'd kept the secret of his illness entirely to himself for a year. Even when his hair had fallen out, he'd shaved his head and pretended it was a fashion choice. When his skin had turned ashy and he lost weight, he'd blamed it on the stress of mergers and acquisitions.

Until this moment, only his doctors had known the truth. Literally no one else. Stavros had thought, if he ever opened up to Holly about that night, he would be instantly forgiven. Because, damn it, he'd been *dying*.

He'd obviously thought wrong.

"Why didn't you die, then?" Holly said scornfully. She tilted her head in mild curiosity, as if asking why he'd missed breakfast. "Why didn't your tumor kill you?"

Stavros thought of the months of painful treatment, getting radiation and chemotherapy. After he'd abandoned his dream of leaving behind a wife and child, he'd decided to give up his dying body to an experimental new therapy. He'd thought he might at least benefit science by his death.

Instead, in August, he'd been informed by shocked doctors that the inoperable tumor had started to shrink.

Now, Stavros shrugged, as if it didn't matter. "It was a miracle."

Holly snorted. "Of course it was." She rolled her eyes. "Men like you always have miracles, don't they?"

"Men like me?"

"Selfish and richer than the earth."

The scorn in her voice set his teeth on edge. "Look, I'm getting a little tired of you calling me selfish—"

"The truth hurts, does it?"

"Stop trying to put all the blame on me," he growled. "You're the one who has kept my son from me. I told you to contact my lawyers if you were pregnant!"

"I wasn't going to let you force me into having an abortion!"

Shocked, Stavros stared at her, his forehead furrowed. "What?"

"Christmas morning, you told me you'd changed your mind. You didn't want a child. You said if I was pregnant, I should contact your lawyers and they'd *take care of it*!" An angry sob choked her voice. "Did you think I didn't know what you meant?"

Furious, he grabbed her shoulders. "I *meant* I'd provide for my child with a great deal of *money*," he growled. "Damn you!"

As Holly stared at him, Stavros abruptly dropped his hands, exhaling.

Finally, he understood. Since Oliver had phoned him yesterday, he'd wondered how it could be true. Why would Holly not tell him about a pregnancy? Was it some kind of nefarious attempt at revenge for his seduction and subsequent rejection? Holly had apparently kept the news from her sister as well. She'd only told her yesterday, obviously knowing Nicole would tell Oliver and he'd tell Stavros. But why?

Now it was clear. Holly had been afraid. He gritted his teeth at that insult. But now, with her baby safely born, she was ready to claim the fortune that was due her.

Stavros looked around the ramshackle old cabin, saw the cracks between the logs where the cold wind blew. Holly was no gold digger, but any mother would want the best for her child. She was ready for them to live in greater comfort, and who could blame her?

Now that he understood her motivation, Stavros relaxed.

"You have nothing to worry about," he proclaimed. "I will provide for the baby, if he's mine."

"If?" she repeated in fury.

"I want to meet him."

Holly glared at him. "No."

Stavros blinked. "What?"

"You came here to find out if I'd had your baby. Fine. Now you know. Your lawyers probably gave you papers for me to sign. Some kind of settlement to make sure neither I nor my baby would ever make a claim on your full fortune."

"How did you know—" He cut himself off too late. She gave him a cold smile.

"I was a secretary for many years to powerful men. I know how you all think. You're no different from the rest." She came closer, her eyes glowing intently. "I don't want your money. I'll take nothing from you. And nothing is what you'll get in return. Freddie is mine. You will relinquish all parental rights."

"Relinquish?" he breathed in shock. All his earlier smug confidence had disappeared. Surely Holly couldn't hate him so much, when all he'd been trying to do last Christmas was protect her from her own weakness? There was no reason for her to toss him out like this, without even letting him see the baby. Unless—

A thought hit him like hard kick in the gut from a steel-toed boot.

"Is there another man?" he said slowly.

An odd smile lifted the corner of her lovely lips. "What difference would it make to you?"

"None," he lied coldly.

But against his will, he was enraged at the thought.

He'd spent the year as celibate as monk, exhausted after too many hours at the hospital alone, getting medical treatment that sucked away his life and energy. Why had he imagined, just because he'd taken her virginity, that a beautiful young woman like Holly would have spent the last year celibate as well?

For the last year, he'd tried not to think about her, or how out of control she'd made him feel last year. He'd told himself that he'd done the noble thing, the hard thing, setting her free. Since he'd gone into complete remission last month, he'd tried to forget that their night together had been the single greatest sensual experience of his life.

Because Holly made him lose control. She made him weak. He'd couldn't risk seeing her again.

Until he'd gotten the call from Oliver yesterday. Then he'd had no choice.

Because whatever Holly might think of him, Stavros would never abandon his child. Even if he wasn't sure he was ready to be a father, he would provide for him.

His lawyers had warned him if the baby rumor was true, he should immediately ask for a paternity test, and insist that Holly sign papers to recuse herself and her child from any other claim on his billions before he paid her a dime.

His lawyers had never told Stavros what to do if Holly scorned him, his money, and the horse he rode in on.

"You…don't even want my son to know me?" he asked.

She gave a single short shake of her head.

"So why tell me about the baby at all?" he said harshly. "Just to punish me?"

"I never intended for you to know. I swore my sister to secrecy."

Holly hadn't intended for him to know about his son? Ever? Shock left him scrambling. "But my son needs a father!"

She lifted her chin. "Better no father at all than someone who will let him down, and teach him all the wrong lessons about how to be a man. How to lie. How to make meaningless promises. How to be ruthless and selfish and care only about himself!"

Stavros hadn't thought he had much of a heart left, but her words stabbed him deep. He thought of his own childhood, growing up without a father. Having to figure out for himself how to be a man.

Hardly aware of what he was saying, he insisted, "But

what if I want to be in his life? What if I want to help raise him?"

Holly's eyes widened.

Then her lips twisted scornfully. "I've heard that lie before."

"This is different…"

"You might have lured me once into some romantic fantasy. Never again." Crossing the cabin, she wrenched open the door. A blast of cold air flew inside, whipping the fire with its icy fingers. "Please go. Don't come back. Have your lawyers send me the papers." She looked at him coldly. "There's no reason for us to ever meet again."

"Holly, you're not being fair—"

It was the wrong word to use.

"Fair?" Turning, she called out to the driver parked in front of the cabin. "Your boss is ready to leave."

Stavros's head was spinning. He needed time. He hadn't even seen his baby, or held him in his arms. He wasn't sure what he wanted anymore. But Holly was already making the decision for both of them.

She didn't want any part of him. Not as a husband. Not as a father. Even his money wasn't good enough.

Fine, he told himself coldly. He'd keep his money. He didn't need her. Or their baby.

"Fine. You'll have the papers by the end of the day," he told her grimly.

"Good," she said in the same tone.

Stavros set his jaw, glaring at her. Then he stalked out of the cabin without a word, his long dark coat flying behind him as he breathed a Greek curse that left a whisper of white smoke in the icy air. The frozen snow crackled beneath his Italian leather shoes as he passed his waiting driver and got into the back seat of the Rolls-Royce Cullinan.

"Let's go," he growled to his driver.

"Where to, Mr. Minos?"

"Back to the airport," Stavros barked. He'd tried to take responsibility, but she didn't want him in their baby's life. Fine. He'd give her exactly what she wanted. He'd call his lawyers and have them draw up the new papers, severing his parental rights, and giving Holly absolutely nothing.

All my most impossible dreams are suddenly coming true.

The memory of her trembling voice came back to him, whispered into the silent, sweet night last Christmas Eve. Leaning his head back against the leather seat, Stavros closed his eyes, pushing away the memory. Along with how it had felt to have her body against his that sacred, holy night.

But as the Rolls-Royce wound its way back through the Swiss valley, his shoulders only grew more tense. He stared out at the picturesque valley, blanketed by white snow sparkling beneath the sun.

For the past year, he'd hidden his illness from everyone, driving himself harder at work, so no one would know his secret. When he'd gotten the shocking news that he was going to live, he'd been alone in the medical clinic, with no one to share the miracle except for doctors eagerly planning to document the case to medical journals and astonish their colleagues.

Was this how he would spend that miracle? Abandoning the woman he'd seduced last Christmas…and the child they'd conceived together? Leaving a son to grow up without a father, and would despise Stavros as a heartless stranger?

If he did, he truly was a Minos to the core.

His eyes flew open.

"Stop," he said hoarsely.

CHAPTER SIX

HOLLY PUSHED HER stroller through the festive Christmas market in Zedermatt's tiny town square.

Sparkling lights were festooned over outdoor walkways filled with locals and tourists bundled up against the cold, browsing dozens of decorated outdoor stalls, filled with charming homemade items, centered around an enormous Christmas tree in the square. Sausages of every kind, *bockwurst* and *knockwurst* and every other kind of *wurst*, sizzled on outdoor grills, adding the delicious salty smell to scents of pine, fresh mountain air and hot spiced wine called *glühwein*. Smiles were everywhere on rosy cheeks.

Past the eighteenth-century buildings around the square, including a town hall with an elaborate cuckoo clock that rang the time, craggy, snow-covered Alps rose above the tiny valley.

As she pushed her baby's stroller through the crowds, everyone was welcoming. Gertrud and Karin, elderly sisters who ran a bakery in town, made a point of cooing over the baby. Gunther and Elfriede, selling scented homemade candles from their pine-decorated stall, generously praised Holly's improving language skills.

Holly was surrounded by friends. She'd made a home.

So why did she feel so miserable?

Stavros, she thought. Just his name caused her heart to twist. Seeing him had been more painful than she'd ever imagined. And more terrifying. Asking him to give up his parental rights to Freddie, she'd been shaking inside.

Why had she been so afraid? Even if he'd never actually meant to threaten her into terminating her pregnancy as she'd once feared, he'd still made his total lack of interest in fatherhood clear.

So if he'd seemed hurt by her words, it must have only been his pride, injured at being told he wasn't wanted. Obviously. What else could it be?

Dying inspired me to want more. To make one last attempt to leave something behind. A wife. A child. That's why I slept with you, Holly. That's why I said I wanted to marry you and have a child. I wasn't lying. I did want it.

Was it true? Had he really been dying?

She hadn't believed him at first. But a proud man like Stavros Minos wouldn't lie. Not about something like that, something that exposed weakness.

Holly's hands tightened on the stroller handle. It didn't matter. She wasn't going to let herself feel anything for him, ever again. Even if he'd thought he was dying, it was no excuse for how he'd treated her—seducing her, abandoning her!

But if he'd really thought he had only months to live…

Her heart twisted. What must that have been like for an arrogant tycoon to be helpless, facing death? What was it like for a powerful man to feel so powerless?

He'd kept his illness secret. She was the first person he'd told. He'd obviously thought it would make her forgive him.

But even if her traitorous heart might be tempted to feel some sympathy, how could she?

Because in spite of Stavros acting all shocked and upset that she'd never told him she was pregnant, he obviously didn't want to be a father. If he'd really wanted to be part of their son's life, he never would have let himself be scared off so easily today. He would have insisted on sticking around, whatever she said. But he hadn't. As soon as she'd given him an escape route, and told him they wouldn't try to claim any part of his fortune, he'd been off like a shot.

She and Freddie were better off without him. They *were*. Stavros was selfish and coldhearted. She'd never give him the chance to hurt their son like he'd hurt her. She'd done the right thing, sending Stavros away. She should be relieved, knowing he'd never bother her or the baby again.

So why, when Freddie suddenly whimpered in his stroller, did Holly feel like doing the same?

"Here's your hot chocolate." Coming toward her with an eager smile, Hans Müller handed her a steaming paper cup. The young Swiss man was sandy-haired and solidly built, with pale blue eyes.

"Thank you," she said, turning to him with a smile. "You're too kind."

"I would do anything for you, Holly." He looked at her. "You know that."

Sipping her cocoa, she shifted uneasily. She'd met Hans six months before, in a local café. He'd wanted to improve his English skills, and she her German. Back then, she'd been heavily pregnant, and their friendship had been easy. But something had changed lately. She feared he wanted more from her than she could give. It made her feel guilty. It wasn't Hans's fault Stavros had crushed all her romantic illusions forever.

"Hans," she said awkwardly, lifting the pacifier from Freddie's blanket to put it back in the fussing baby's mouth. "You know you're very dear to me…"

"And you're dear to me. So is Freddie." He looked at the baby, now sucking contentedly in the stroller. He paused. "He needs a father." He looked at her. "You need a husband."

"I—I…" She took a deep breath. The last thing she

wanted to do was hurt Hans, who'd been nothing but kind to her. *I don't think of you that way*, she prepared to say.

Then she stopped.

The only men she'd ever imagined as romantic partners had both been disasters—the three-year time-waster of imagining herself in love with Oliver, followed by the massive, life-changing fiasco last Christmas Eve with Stavros.

Maybe she should give Hans a chance. Maybe the fact that she was totally unattracted to him was actually a sign in his favor.

Because the only man who'd ever truly made her experience desire, who'd awakened her body and made her soul sing, had been a handsome, black-hearted liar who'd betrayed her before the sun rose on Christmas morning.

But as she looked at Hans's shining face, she knew she couldn't be that cruel. She couldn't destroy his illusions and ruin his life by letting him love her. Not when she knew she'd never love him—or any man—ever again.

Holly took a deep breath. It was hard, because she feared she'd lose his friendship. "I'm sorry, but you have to know—"

"Holly." The voice behind her was low and sensual. "Won't you introduce me to your friend?"

She turned with an intake of breath.

Stavros stood in the middle of the Christmas market, taller than anyone in the crowd, darkly handsome and powerful in his well-cut suit and cashmere coat. Her mouth went dry.

"What are you doing here?" she choked out. "I thought you were on your way back to New York—"

"Why would I leave?" Stavros's gaze fell longingly to the baby in the stroller. "When my son is here?"

"Freddie is your son?" Hans stammered.

He turned with a sharp-toothed smile. "Freddie?" He

lifted a sardonic eyebrow. "Yes. I'm his father." He extended his black-gloved hand. "You are?"

"Hans... Hans Müller." Shaking Stavros's hand, he nervously glanced at Holly. "I didn't know Freddie had a father. No, of course, I know everyone has a father. That is to say..."

He looked around helplessly.

"Indeed," Stavros said, his expression amused. Then he looked at Holly. "We need to talk."

"I have nothing else to say to you," she said stonily. "I'm here with Hans. I'm not going to be rude and—"

But the young man was already backing away from the powerful, broad-shouldered tycoon. "It's all right—you both have things to talk about. He's your baby's father." He looked at Holly reproachfully beneath his warm hat. "You should have told me."

"I'm sorry..." Her mouth went dry. "I never meant to..."

Hans lightly touched the top of the baby's dark head, then said softly, *"Auf wiedersehen."*

And sadly, Hans disappeared into the crowd.

Stavros said behind her, "That's the man you replaced me with?"

Holly whirled on him. "He's a friend! Nothing more!"

"He wanted more." Stavros looked down at the baby bundled up in a blanket, sucking drowsily on his pacifier. Kneeling beside the stroller, he tenderly stroked the baby's plump cheek. "My son," he whispered. "I am here. I'm your father, Freddie."

Against her will, she felt a violent twist in her heart. She took a deep breath. "Why did you come back? I told you! We don't want you here!"

Rising to his feet, Stavros glanced to the right and left. From the sweet-smelling bakery stall next door, Holly saw Gertrud watching them with a frown.

Taking her arm with one hand and the stroller handle

with the other, Stavros escorted her to a quiet spot on the other side of the massive, brightly decorated Christmas tree. His black eyes were cold. "Fine. You hate me. You don't care that I was dying. You don't want my money or anything to do with me."

"Exactly," she replied, pushing aside her feelings at the thought of him dying.

"Hating me doesn't give you the right to keep my son from me." Stavros looked down at the bundled-up baby, drowsing in the stroller as he sucked on his pacifier. "And whatever you say, I won't abandon him."

A chill went through her. "It's not your choice."

He smiled. "Ah, but it is," he said softly. "I'm his father. That means I have the right to be in his life. And I'm going to be. From now on."

She had no idea why he was pretending to care about Freddie. Out of a misguided sense of pride? Or just to hurt her?

But either way, he was correct. He did have rights, if he chose to fight for them. Fear gripped her heart as she faced him. "What do you intend to do?"

Stavros's expression was like ice. "I'm going to marry you, Holly."

Stavros hadn't intended to propose marriage like this. But it was logical. It was the best way to secure his son, and give the baby the future he deserved—with two parents in the same home.

When he'd returned to Holly's cabin an hour before, he'd intended to calmly insist on his parental rights, or perhaps threaten to sue for partial custody.

He'd arrived just in time to see Holly and the baby—dark-haired, tiny—climb into another man's car. And all his calm plans had gone up in smoke. He'd grimly had his driver follow them at a distance.

Meeting Hans in person at the Christmas market, Stavros was reassured that the man was no threat. Holly herself made that clear. There was no way the two of them had even kissed, for all the man's obvious interest in her.

But Holly was too bright, too beautiful, to be alone for long. As Stavros had watched her push the stroller through the Christmas market, her fiery red hair flying behind her, she'd looked effortlessly pretty in her black leggings and black puffy jacket. She smiled at everyone. And everyone smiled at her. She shone brighter than the star at the top of the Christmas tree.

He'd been mesmerized.

But he couldn't let her know that. He couldn't reveal his weakness. The one time he'd been weak enough to give in to foolish longings last Christmas, it had changed not just his life, but hers—permanent changes from a momentary whim.

He had a son. From the moment he'd seen his tiny, innocent baby, he'd known he would die to protect him. Just touching his cheek had made Stavros's heart expand in a way it never had before. He looked again at the sweetly drowsy baby in the stroller. He ached to take his son in his arms, but he'd never even held a baby before. He didn't know how. But there was one thing he could do: give Freddie the home he deserved, by marrying his mother.

Stavros tightened his hands at his sides.

"Well?" he said to Holly coldly. "What is your answer?"

He waited, wondering what her reply would be. Any other woman would have immediately said yes, but then, Holly wasn't like any other woman. She clearly despised him and didn't want him in her life. On the other hand, she'd agreed to marry him last Christmas. There was an even better reason for her to agree to it now. They had a child.

She stared at him, her emerald eyes wide. Then she did the one thing he'd never expected.

She burst into laughter.

"What's so funny?" he said grumpily.

"You." She wiped a tear from the corner of her eye. "Thank you for that."

"It's not a joke."

"You're wrong." She shook her head. "Do you really think I'd agree to marry a man I don't trust?"

Stavros ground his teeth. He'd been reasonable. He'd explained about his illness. He'd told her he wanted to take responsibility. He'd even asked her to marry him. What more could he do to convince her? He said shortly, "I have never lied to you."

"You lied about your illness last year."

"Damn it, Holly, what should I have done? Let you wreck your life holding my hand, watching me die?"

Her jaw tightened. "You should have given me the choice."

"Like you're giving me now, trying to cut me out of Freddie's life? I'm his father!" He narrowed his eyes. "I want to give him a name."

"He has one. Frederick Marlowe."

"No."

"It's a good name. My father's name!"

"His last name will be Minos."

"Why are you pretending to care?"

"I'm not pretending." Coming closer, he tried not to notice how her eyes sparkled beneath the Christmas lights in the festive outdoor market in the town square, with the snowy Alps soaring above. "I'm going to give my son the life he deserves. Marry me, or face the consequences."

"Is that a threat?"

"I will be part of my son's life, one way or another."

Glaring at him, she lifted her chin. "I won't be bullied into marriage. I don't care how rich or powerful you are. Family is what matters. Not money."

And as Stavros looked down at her in the cold mountain air, everything became crystal clear.

He had little experience managing tricky relationships. In the past, if a mistress ever got too demanding, he'd simply ended the relationship.

So think of it as a business deal. He coolly reassessed the situation. *A hostile takeover.* He looked down at the tiny dark-haired baby. He wanted to be a steady, permanent part of his child's life. Clearly, the best way to do that was to marry Holly. But she didn't want to marry him. She didn't want his money. She didn't want his name.

So how best to negotiate? How to win?

He could brutally fight her for custody. With his deep pockets, his lawyers would crush her. But inexperienced as Stavros was with long-term relationships, he didn't think this would ultimately lead to a happy home for their child.

How else could he get leverage?

Then he realized. She'd just revealed her weakness. *Family is what matters*, she'd said. And she'd shown that belief in every aspect of her life. She'd given up college and her own dreams, given up years of her life for that worthless sister of hers. She'd quit her job and fled to Europe when she'd thought she needed to protect her baby.

How could he use her own heart against her?

A sudden idea occurred to him. It made him feel sick inside. He tried to think of something else.

But Holly already looked as if she were ready to turn on her heel and stalk away, taking their child with her. He needed some way to spend time with her. To make her calm down and see reason. And he could think of only one way.

Since she was none too pleased with her sister at that moment, dragging her to New York wasn't an option.

But Freddie had a grandfather.

If Stavros tried to convince Holly that Aristides Minos deserved to meet the baby, he doubted her tender heart would resist. At least until she met the loathsome man. There was a reason Stavros despised his father to the core.

But a trip to Greece would give Stavros the time he needed to convince Holly to marry him. With any luck, he argued with himself, the old man wouldn't even be home.

Deliberately relaxing his shoulders, Stavros gave Holly his most charming smile. "I don't want to fight with you."

"Fine." Suspicion creased her forehead. "But I still won't marry you."

"Of course you won't," he said easily, still smiling. "You don't trust me. Because I treated you so badly."

Her lips parted. Then she narrowed her eyes. "Whatever you're doing, it's not going to work. My answer's still no."

She was too intuitive by half. "All right. So let's talk about Freddie. And what's best for him."

Holly snorted. "A father, you're going to say. But he doesn't need a father like you, who's selfish and—"

"My own father is honest to a fault," he interrupted. "Doesn't he have the right to meet his grandson?"

That stopped her angry words. She closed her mouth, then said uncertainly, "You have a father?"

Stavros gave her a crooked smile. "As your friend Hans said, everyone has a father."

"But you've never mentioned him. I assumed he was dead."

"You assumed wrong." Stavros had just *wished* his father was dead. Many, many times, after he'd divorced his mother and cut them off without a penny. After he'd ignored all of Stavros's frantic pleas for help when he was seventeen, and she'd gotten that fatal diagnosis. Pushing the awful memories away, Stavros said blandly, "I'm his only son." It was a guess. For all he knew, the man had ten other children he was ignoring or neglecting around the world. "Would you keep him from his only grandchild?"

Emotions crossed Holly's face. It was almost too easy to

read her. First, she wanted to angrily refuse. Then he saw sympathy, and regret.

"Is he like you?" she said finally. "Your father?"

"He's nothing like me."

"No?"

"Like I said. He's honest to a fault." Aristides definitely was authentic, that was true. He never tried to be anything but who he was. Social niceties like courtesy and kindness were utterly unknown to him.

"Really?" Holly said doubtfully, looking at him.

Stavros gave a humorless smile. "Really."

He tilted his head, waiting for her answer. On the other side of the towering Christmas tree, he could hear jaunty, festive music played by a brass band. How strange it would feel to see his father after all these years.

If he did, he would feel nothing. It had all happened so long ago. Stavros was no longer the boy who'd desperately craved a father's love, and been ruthlessly rejected. He was strong now, untouchable, with a heart of stone.

Taking a deep breath, he exhaled a cloud of smoke in the cold air. The tension eased in his shoulders. Feeling nothing was what Stavros did best.

Holly glared at him, gritting her teeth. "Fine," she sighed. "He can meet the baby." She paused. "Where? When?"

"He lives in Greece, I'm afraid."

"Greece!"

He gave her a smile he didn't feel. "The Minos villa on Minos Island."

"You grew up on your own island?"

"Until I was eight." Pulling his phone from his pocket, he dialed his pilot's number before she could change her mind. "We'll leave at once. My jet is waiting."

"I can't just leave," she protested weakly. "I'm the care-taker of my old boss's chalet."

Covering the phone's mouthpiece as the pilot answered the other end of the line, Stavros told her, "I'll handle it."

And he did. When she said their baby couldn't travel in the Rolls-Royce SUV without a baby seat, one miraculously materialized five minutes later. Before they'd returned to the chalet, where she packed an overnight bag for herself and the baby, Stavros had personally contacted the chalet's owner in London. The man sounded frankly astonished to get a direct call from the famous tech billionaire. "No one needs to stay there, really," he told Stavros. "It was empty for a year." And just like that, it was done.

"Does *everyone* do what you say?" Holly said resentfully as the SUV drove back over the winding road toward the private airport in St. Moritz. He lifted an eyebrow.

"Everyone but you."

"Everyone including me," she said softly, staring out her window at the snowy Alpine valley, with its picturesque, colorful chalets beneath sharp, brooding mountains. He watched her silently, hoping it was true.

She believed that they were heading to Greece for one night, which they were. What she didn't know was that, after their brief visit to his father's villa, Stavros intended to take both her and the baby back to live in New York.

He'd make her his wife. By any means necessary.

When they arrived at the tiny airport, his driver opened the SUV's door, then took their bags and folding stroller from the trunk. Holly carried the baby across the tarmac and up the air stairs to his new Gulfstream G650ER. As Stavros followed her, his gaze fell on the sweet curve of her backside in the snug black leggings, and he felt a flash of heat.

Eleven months. That was how long he'd been without a woman.

His night with Holly had been the most incredible sexual experience of his life.

She'd ruined him for all other women.

It was strange. He'd never thought of it in those terms. He'd assumed his lack of desire had been caused by radiation and chemotherapy treatments, while keeping up his workaholic schedule so no one would guess at his illness. Sex had been the last thing on his agenda.

But from the moment Holly had answered the door of that snowy chalet, her cheeks rosy and her sweater and leggings showing off her perfect hourglass shape, the whole past year of pent-up desire had exploded inside him with a vengeance.

Great, he thought resentfully. *Now* his libido chose to come alive? With the one woman on earth who seemed immune to him?

Or was she?

He looked at Holly, now sitting in an opposite chair inside the jet, as far away from him as possible, holding their baby in her lap.

The flight attendant appeared. "Would you like a drink, Mr. Minos? Your usual Scotch?"

Stavros's gaze remained on Holly, tracing the curve of her neck, her red hair curling down her shoulders, the fullness of her breasts beneath her loose sweater. Was she nursing, or had her breasts always been that big?

Holly looked up. "I'd like some sparkling water, please."

"Of course, madam. Sir?"

As Stavros looked at Holly, their eyes locked. The air between them sizzled. Images went through him of last Christmas, when she'd been naked in his bed. The heat of her body sliding against his own, her soft cry joining his hoarse shout as their mutual desire exploded. He was hard as a rock.

"Champagne," he said. "It's a celebration. A new start for us both."

Holly's eyes widened, her cheeks turning pink. Quickly, she turned her head away.

But it was too late. Because now he knew. In spite of her anger, in spite of her hatred, she was as sexually aware of him as he was of her.

And he suddenly realized there were additional benefits to taking her as his wife. Reasons that had nothing to do with taking care of their child.

He'd seduced her before. He would seduce her again. And this time, it would be forever.

CHAPTER SEVEN

SITTING IN A red convertible, as Stavros drove it down the coastal road clinging to the edge of the Aegean Sea, Holly looked out at the bright turquoise water. She felt the warm wind on her face. Felt Stavros's every move beside her. It was like torture. Holly's heart lifted to her throat.

Why had she ever agreed to this?

Guilt, she thought. Back in Switzerland, she'd convinced herself that however Stavros had betrayed her with his playboy ways and lying lips, her baby's grandfather was blameless. Now, she cursed the good intentions that had led her to come to this small Greek island.

Yes, she wanted Freddie to have a grandfather. Of course she did. She felt bad for the elderly man, who sounded like an honest, decent sort of person, to be stuck with such an obviously neglectful son as Stavros. He deserved to know he had a grandson.

Her motives hadn't been purely noble, it was true. Some part of her had hoped desperately, after Stavros spent a little time with their baby, he'd grow bored with the care of parenting a child, and decide to give up custody, and leave them alone.

But being this close to Stavros was difficult. Holly threw him a troubled glance. Every time he'd tried to speak with her on the trip from Switzerland, she'd coldly cut him off. But her own feelings frightened her. The truth was, part of her still desired him. Part of her, a very foolish part, still held on to the dream of being a family.

She'd never be that stupid again, she told herself fiercely. And they'd only be on this Greek island a single night before she returned to Switzerland. What damage could a single night do?

Hearing her baby chortling happily in the convertible's back seat, she looked back and shivered. One night could change everything.

"Almost there," Stavros murmured beside her, glancing at her sideways. She felt a flash of heat.

"Is Greece always this warm in November?" she said in a strangled voice.

"It is warmer than usual." His sensual lips curved up on the edges, as if he knew exactly how his nearness was affecting her. He lazily turned the wheel with one hand, driving the luxury convertible down the twisting road with no effort at all. Her gaze lingered on his powerful forearms, laced with dark hair below his rolled-up sleeves.

It was just the sun making her hot, she told herself. As it lowered toward the western horizon, she felt too warm in the sweater and leggings she'd worn from Switzerland. Her feet were roasting in their leather boots. "I didn't pack any summer clothes."

"Don't worry." Stavros glanced at her, his eyes traveling over her. "It's been arranged."

"You always arrange everything," she sighed.

"My assistant contacted my father's housekeeper and let her know we were on the way. She will provide anything you or Freddie might need."

Her cheeks flamed. "Uh... Thanks. I guess." She tried to smile. "What did your father say when he heard about the baby?"

He shrugged. "I didn't tell him."

"What?"

"I haven't spoken to my father for twenty years."

"Twenty—" Her jaw dropped. "Did you even tell him we were coming to visit?"

Stavros's hand tightened on the steering wheel as he drove the convertible swiftly around the thread of road clinging to the edge of the island's cliffs. He said evenly, "My assistant told the housekeeper. I presume she let him know."

Holly was scandalized. "But it's rude!"

"Rude," he growled. "What about—"

Stavros cut himself off, staring stonily ahead at the sea. "What about what?"

"Nothing."

"It's not like you to censor yourself."

"Forget it," he said abruptly. "Ancient history."

But he stomped on the gas, driving the red convertible faster along the cliff road of this small island in the Aegean.

Holly looked at him, from his tight shoulders to the grim set of his jaw. She said slowly, "Why haven't you spoken to your—"

Her voice cut off as they went past a grove of olive trees to a guarded gate. A white-haired guard approached the convertible, scowling. Then his eyes went wide. "Stavi?"

"Vassilis," he replied, smiling up at him. They spoke in Greek. Stavros indicated Holly and Freddie, mentioning their names. The guard replied, nearly jumping in his excitement, before he waved them through.

"You know him?" Holly said as Stavros drove the car past the gate.

"He was kind to me when I was young." His voice seemed strained. He roared the convertible up the hill, finally parking in front of a grand villa, whitewashed and sprawling across the cliff, on the edge of the sea. With a deep breath, Stavros abruptly turned off the engine. He stared up at the villa.

"Are you all right?" Holly asked.

He seemed almost as if he dreaded what was ahead. Which Holly didn't understand. What could there be to dread about a lavish villa on a Greek island paradise?

Unless it was the same thing that had made Stavros not speak to his father in twenty years. Holly suddenly wondered what they were getting into.

"Stavros," she said slowly, "I feel like there's something you're not telling me."

Without looking at her, he got out of the car. Unlatching the baby seat in the back seat of the convertible, Holly followed with Freddie.

They hadn't even reached the imposing front door of the villa before it flew open, revealing a plump, white-haired woman. She cried out, clasping her hands over her heart. "Stavi!"

Looking at her, his eyes went wide.

"Eleni?" he whispered.

Rushing forward, the petite, round woman threw her arms around him with a sob. She was much shorter than Stavros. Awkwardly, he patted her on the back. His expression was stricken. Holly couldn't look away from the raw emotion on his usually stoic face.

The white-haired woman spoke in rapid Greek, tears filling her eyes. He answered her slowly in the same language. She turned to the baby in Holly's arms.

Stavros said in English, "Holly, this is my father's housekeeper, Eleni. She's worked here since I was a child." Reaching out, he stroked his baby's soft dark head. "Eleni, this is my son, Freddie."

"Your son!" the housekeeper cried in accented English. She patted the baby's plump cheek with tears in her eyes. Eleni turned to Holly. "You are Stavros's wife?"

"Uh, no," Holly said awkwardly, shifting her baby's

weight on her hip. "I'm Holly, his…" His what? Baby mama? Cast-off lover? "His, um, friend."

"Friend?" the housekeeper repeated with a frown.

Turning to Stavros, she said something sharply in Greek. Lips quirking, he answered her in the same language.

The old woman looked mollified. As servants collected their luggage and moved the convertible into the nearby garage, the housekeeper turned to Holly with an innocent smile. "You must be tired from your journey, Miss Holly, you and the baby. Everything is ready. Won't you come in, please?"

"Yes, thank you," Holly replied, throwing Stavros a confused glance as she followed them into the villa, cradling her baby in her arms.

Stavros's head tilted back as they walked through the foyer. "This place is smaller than I remember."

The housekeeper's wrinkled face smiled. "It is not smaller. You are bigger."

Small? Holly's eyes nearly popped out of her head as she looked around her. It was like a palace! The foyer opened directly into a huge room with a breathtaking view of the sun lowering into the sea with streaks of orange and red. An elegant chandelier hung high above the priceless antique furniture and marble floor.

Freddie gave a hungry whimper, and Eleni crooned, "Poor baby, you are tired. I will show you to your room."

Their room? As in, Holly and Stavros would be sharing one?

No. Surely not. Holly had made it very clear to Stavros that she had no interest in spending time with him. Especially not time of an intimate nature!

"Thank you, Eleni," Stavros said. He lifted a dark eyebrow. "When can I convince you to move to New York?"

"What would I do there? You live in a hotel!"

"Anything. Or nothing." He looked at her seriously. "You

deserve to rest, after taking care of us when I was young. You were my mother's only friend when she was here. At least accept a pension?"

"Oh, no." Blushing, the older woman ducked her head. "I won't take charity."

"It's not charity. It's gratitude."

"No. I couldn't. But thank you, Stavi. If you ever need a housekeeper, let me know. You're a good boy." She smiled at him, then turned as servants passed with their luggage. "Your room is this way, if you please."

As they followed the housekeeper down a long hall-way, Holly whispered to Stavros, "What did you say to her earlier?"

He frowned. "When?"

Her cheeks went warm. "At the door when we arrived. When I said I was just your friend, she looked so upset. Until you said something to her in Greek."

"Oh." His black eyes gleamed with amusement. "I told Eleni not to worry. I will marry you soon."

His words caused a jolt that nearly made her trip. Then she rolled her eyes. "Funny."

Stavros raised an eyebrow. "You think I'm joking?"

He hadn't lost his arrogance, that was for sure. "I'll never marry you, Stavros. No way, no how."

He tilted his head with a crooked grin. "We'll see."

Holly's worst fears were confirmed when the house-keeper led them to a magnificent bedroom, with a balcony overlooking the sea. In the center of the room was a single enormous four-poster bed, and in the corner, a crib. Nearby, a changing table had been set up, with everything a baby could need. A rocking chair was placed by the windows.

"Perfect, yes?" Eleni said, smiling.

"It's beautiful, but..." Holly bit her lip as she looked around. "Where will I sleep?"

The housekeeper laughed, her eyes dancing. "I am not

so old-fashioned as to believe you sleep in separate rooms." Going to the enormous walk-in closet, she said to Stavros, "For your wife and baby."

Just hearing herself described as Stavros's wife caused a frisson of emotion to dart through Holly. She stuck out her chin. "I'm not—"

"Thank you, Eleni," Stavros interrupted as he looked into the closet. Reaching into his pocket, he pulled out a stack of bills from his wallet. "Will this cover the cost of the clothes?"

Eleni shifted uncomfortably. "It's not necessary. Your father still owes you and your mother for what he never—"

"No," he said grimly. He gently placed the money in her hands. "You know I'd never take money from him."

"I know," the woman agreed. She looked at the bills. "But this is too much."

"Keep it." With a smile that didn't meet his eyes, he said, "You made my life here endurable. For Mom, too."

Hearing the strained edge to his voice, Holly stared at him. His face looked almost...vulnerable.

What had happened in his childhood? Why hadn't he spoken to his father in twenty years?

Not even the most gossipy secretaries in the New York office, the ones who kept track of Stavros's every lavish date with starlets and models, had spoken about his childhood. Stavros's American mother had died when he was a teenager. That was all they knew.

Now Holly felt like there was some big secret. Some tragedy. She watched as the petite, elderly woman hugged him fiercely, tears in her eyes, saying something in Greek.

Stavros stiffened, then shrugged, and said in English, "It's fine. I'm fine."

"It is good of you to bring the baby here to meet him," the housekeeper responded.

"Is he here?"

Eleni looked embarrassed. "Not yet. I did tell him about the baby. He knew you were coming." Her cheeks went red. "He said he might be back for dinner, but he might not, depending…"

"I remember how he was. With Mom."

The housekeeper looked sad, then squeezed his arm as she said softly, "Your mother was a good lady, Stavi. I was so sorry when I heard she died. I wish she could have lived to see all your success."

"Thank you." His handsome face held no expression. He pulled his arm away. "There is no point in waiting for him. Perhaps we could have dinner on the terrace?"

"Of course." Eleni brightened. "Whenever you like."

Stavros looked at Holly. "Are you hungry?"

As if on cue, her stomach growled noisily. She blushed as the others laughed. But dinner wasn't what she was worried about. She bit her lip. "Er, about this bedroom—"

"We'll have dinner in an hour," Stavros told the housekeeper, who nodded and left, still smiling.

Holly turned on him. "Stavros, you can't imagine we can share a bedroom!"

Stavros tilted his head, a half smile on his lips. "Can't I?" He glanced toward the baby, who'd started to fuss. "Freddie, what's wrong?" He reached out for the baby. "Let me—"

Instinctively, Holly moved the baby out of Stavros's reach. "He's tired."

He asked quietly, "I know I don't have experience. But won't you let me try to hold my son?"

It was the first time he'd asked.

"I'm sorry, it's not a good time." Holly's cheeks went hot. She, who always prided herself on being kind, knew she was being a jerk. She was just protecting Freddie, she told herself. It was only a matter of time before Stavros realized he didn't want to be a father. He would let them down. Why pretend otherwise? Why even let herself hope?

"He's hungry. I need to give him a bath, then feed him and get him ready for bed."

"Of course," he said stiffly. Lowering his head, he tenderly kissed the baby's head. "Good night, my son."

Guilt built inside her, all the way to her throat.

He straightened, and said quietly to Holly, "Can you make your way to the terrace in an hour?"

"It's right outside that big room? By the foyer?"

He gave a short nod.

"I'll find it."

"Until then." With a small bow, he left. Holly looked after him, until the baby whimpered plaintively in her arms.

Was she being unkind, insisting on believing the worst of Stavros? Was it possible he actually wished to be a loving father to Freddie?

If he did, and Holly pushed him away from their son, then she would be the selfish one. Was she really protecting their baby? Or just wanting to punish Stavros, to make him suffer for the way he'd hurt her, by seducing and then abandoning her?

Lost in these unsettling thoughts, Holly gave her baby a bath in the en suite bathroom, then dried him off with a thick cotton towel. As she nuzzled his dark hair, breathing in his sweet newborn smell, she suddenly wished she'd never left Switzerland. All she wanted to do was be safe.

And nothing about Stavros Minos was safe. Not to her body. Not to her heart.

She shivered, remembering how his dark eyes had burned when he'd said he intended to marry her. Every moment she spent with him, every look, every innocent touch, reminded her of the night they'd conceived their child. Every moment close to him caused new sparks of need to crackle through her body.

She took a deep breath, looking out at the balcony where the sun was setting brilliantly over the Aegean Sea, past the palm trees. Oh, what she was doing on this remote Greek island, in a place that seemed expressly made for seduction?

Grabbing Freddie's old, clean footie pajamas from her overnight bag, she dressed him on the changing table and then carried him to the rocking chair near the window, overlooking the sea where the sun was falling into the water. Twenty minutes later, she tucked him into the crib, drowsy with a full belly.

Going to the en suite bathroom, Holly took a quick shower, avoiding her own eyes in the mirror. Wrapping herself in the thick white robe from the door, she went back into the closet and looked in her overnight bag. The thick hoodie, turtleneck and jeans she'd packed seemed all wrong for Greece. Snowy Switzerland seemed a million miles away.

Biting her lip, Holly slowly looked around the enormous closet. New clothes, in both her size and the baby's, had been neatly folded on the shelves and were hanging from the racks. Rising to her feet, she touched a white cotton sundress. For a moment, she was lost in a sudden dream, imagining soft fabric sliding over her skin as Stavros kissed her, his naked, powerful body hard against hers—

Electricity burned through her, making her breasts tighten and her body tremble.

No!

Holly couldn't allow herself to let down her guard. The last time she had, she'd ended up pregnant and alone.

And the stakes were far too high now. If she ever gave herself to Stavros again, either her body or her heart, he'd have the power to destroy her…and Freddie. She couldn't let that happen.

Holly lifted her chin. She was no longer an innocent girl who could be easily swayed by passionate kisses or sweet lies. She'd learned about consequences. She had a baby to think of.

This time, there was nothing Stavros could do to seduce her. If he truly wanted to help her raise their son, if his only intention was to be a good father, she would try to let him, for Freddie's sake.

She would have good manners. She would be courteous.

But Holly would never let Stavros back into her bed, or her heart. Never. Never ever!

Stavros stood out on the terrace, leaning against the white balustrade overlooking the cliff. He was still dressed in a tailored black button-down shirt and trousers that fit snugly against his body. He'd thought of changing to casual clothes, but there was no point in pretending to be casual, when the truth was, he felt anything but.

A table had been set up on the terrace, with three place settings. But he knew his father would not come.

His jaw tightened, and he looked behind him at the house of his childhood. He felt his back break out in a cold sweat. How unhappy he'd been here. He still remembered his mother's wretchedness and heartbreak. His father hadn't just been selfish. He'd been cruel to her, flaunting his affairs, just to prove his power over her.

Now, the sprawling white villa glowed gold, orange and red, illuminated like King Midas's palace by the sun setting over the Aegean to the west.

It had been a shock to return here. He wondered how long he'd been frozen when he'd arrived in the convertible, staring up at the house. He'd been stunned to see Eleni. Like Vassilis, the guard, she'd grown much older. Even the villa, which had loomed so large in his youth, had grown much smaller. Or maybe, like Eleni had said, it was just Stavros who'd grown larger.

He'd lived here until he was eight. He had strong memories of his father's violent arguments with his mother, that had left Aristides shouting insults, and Rowena weeping.

When, after years of emotional abuse, his mother could stand no more, she'd announced she was divorcing him and moving back to Boston.

In response, Aristides had coldly informed Stavros he could either remain in Greece as a rich man's son, or go to Boston to be a "nobody" and a "pitiful mama's boy."

Stavros had made his choice, and his father had been livid. He'd spoken with Aristides only once since then, when Stavros was seventeen. After months of ignoring his son's increasingly frantic phone messages, his father finally answered the phone on the day Stavros called to tell him Rowena had died.

"Why would I care about that?" Aristides had responded.

Now, every time Stavros thought of his mother's heart-break, how hard she'd tried to love her husband through his betrayals, how hard she'd worked to try to support her child when the divorce had left her with nothing but custody of him…he was furious. His mother had died from overwork and grief, as much as the cancer that had claimed her life.

No wonder, when Stavros had gotten his own diagnosis, he'd been so sure he would obviously die. How could he live, when his mother—so much better and kinder than he—had not?

Setting his jaw, he stared out bleakly at the sea. The sun was setting, leaving a red trail against the dark water that looked almost like a trail of blood.

It was a strange irony that he had lived. And now he had a son of his own. He would not abandon Freddie. He wouldn't leave Holly to raise their son alone.

But how could he convince her to let him into their lives?

When Stavros had decided to bring her here from Switzerland, he'd been sure all he needed to do was spend a little time with her to make her see things his way.

But she'd shot him down every time he'd tried to speak with her on the jet. He didn't blame her. He was totally off his game. Being back in his childhood home had thrown him in ways he hadn't expected. Now, just when he most needed to be confident and powerful to win her, he was instead feeling uncomfortably vulnerable.

He hated it.

So how could he convince Holly? What could he do or say?

Sex wouldn't be enough. He'd felt the way she shivered when he "accidentally" touched her, seen the way she licked the corners of her mouth when he looked deeply into her eyes, as if waiting for his kiss. She wanted him.

But she didn't trust him. She refused to share a bedroom with him. Bedroom? Hell, she wouldn't even let him hold his son.

No mere charm, no regular seduction, would win her now. So what would?

Leaning against the balustrade, staring out at the sea, Stavros took a deep breath. Hearing a noise, he looked behind him.

And gasped.

Holly had come out on the terrace looking like a goddess of beauty, Aphrodite rising from the sea. She was wearing a simple white sundress, exposing her bare shoulders and legs to the pink light of the setting sun. Brilliant red hair tumbled over her shoulders like fire as she walked toward him in her sandals.

His heart lifted to his throat.

Coming close, she looked up at him, her green eyes big, her dark lashes trembling with emotion. "Good evening."

"Kaló apógevma," he replied. He held out his arm.

Ignoring it, she went straight to the table, without touching him.

Following her, he pulled out the chair. She sat down, her lovely face expressionless. As he politely pushed the chair forward beneath the table, his fingers briefly brushed the soft bare skin of her back. He felt her tremble, which he'd expected.

But he trembled, too, which he hadn't.

Going to his own seat on the other side of the small table, he opened a waiting bottle. He paused. "Wine?"

"Just a taste."

He poured the white wine into two glasses, then passed one to her. His fingertips brushed hers, and again he felt her shiver. Again he held his breath.

Then she leaned back in her chair, looking away as she took a single sip of the wine, then placed it back quietly on the table.

No. Desire would not lure her this time.

Stavros lifted the silver lids off their china plates, and saw lamb and rosemary and potatoes. Sitting in the seat across from her, he sliced the lamb cleanly with his knife and chewed slowly. "You should try this. It's delicious." He smiled. "My favorite dinner from childhood. I can't believe Eleni remembered."

"She seems to think a lot of you."

"I think the same of her."

Holly ate almost mechanically, sipping mostly water, not meeting his eyes. He wondered what she was thinking about. Strange—he'd never had to wonder that about any woman before. Usually they couldn't wait to tell him. But Holly was different. Holly mattered—

Just that thought caused ice down his spine.

She mattered only because of his son. That was it. She'd never be more than the mother of his child to him. He'd never give her his heart. He couldn't, because he didn't have one.

The thought made him able to breathe again.

Biting her lip, Holly suddenly leaned forward. "I'm sorry about what you went through."

How did she know about his father's abandonment? Who had told her? He said stiffly, "What do you mean?"

Taking a deep breath, she said in a low voice, "I can't even imagine what you went through last year. Being sick. All alone."

"Oh." His shoulders relaxed. He was touched that she suddenly seemed to care. It gave him hope. "It's all right."

"No. It's not." Looking down at her hands, she said, "I just remember how I felt in the doctor's office when I found out I was pregnant." She looked up, her eyes glistening. "And that was happy news. I can't imagine going through what you did all alone. With no one at your side to help you through. To hold your hand."

A strange emotion rose inside him. Ruthlessly, he pushed it away. It was in the past. He'd battled through. He hadn't needed anyone then, and he didn't now. He was too strong for that. But he wanted to protect his child—and his child's mother.

Reaching over the table, he put his hand over her smaller one. His lips curved. "Does this mean you don't want me dead?"

An answering ghost of a smile touched her lips. "I never wanted you dead. I just…"

Her voice trailed off as she looked away.

The sun had disappeared, and the moon was rising in the darkening night. Stavros polished off his glass of wine, watching her. Wishing he could take her in his arms.

Looking up at the dark sky, Holly pulled her hand away. "The stars are bright here." She tilted back her head. "My dad and I used to look at the constellations together. He taught me a bunch of them. Orion." She pointed. "The Big Dipper, Gemini."

"He was an astronomer?"

She smiled. "A bus driver. Astronomy was his hobby. A hobby he shared with my mother." Her smile lifted to a grin.

"That made him want to learn even more about the stars to impress her. They used to go out driving at night, going outside the city to get away from the city lights. Until—"

Her expression changed and she looked down at her own still full wineglass.

"Until?"

"They went out on their twentieth wedding anniversary, and a drunk driver plowed into their car on the interstate."

"I'm sorry" was all he said, which seemed the wiser choice than "love always ends with tragedy."

"Don't be." She looked up, her eyes glistening. "My parents were happy, chasing their stars. My father always said loving my mother changed his life. She made him a husband. A father. More than he ever imagined he could be." She wiped her cheek with her shoulder. "He always said she changed his stars."

Her voice trembled with pride and love. And Stavros suddenly envied the man.

He poured another glass and took a gulp of wine. "You were lucky to have a father who loved you."

"You aren't close to yours."

Stavros barked a short laugh. "I despise him."

"You told me in Switzerland he was a good man."

"No, I said he was honest. It is not the same. He is honest about who he is. A greedy, selfish monster."

She stared at him, her face shocked.

"But perhaps you think the same about me." His lips twisted as he swished the wine in his glass. "That I am as selfish and coldhearted as every other man in my family." He looked up at the beautiful, tranquil villa. "I hate this place."

"This?" Holly looked up in bewilderment at the magnificent Greek villa, overlooking the dark Aegean Sea. She shook her head wryly. "You should have seen the house I grew up in. A two-bedroom apartment, with peeling wall-paper and a heater that broke down in winter."

"After my parents' divorce, my mother and I briefly lived in a homeless shelter in Boston."

He'd never shared that little tidbit with anyone. She looked shocked.

"How is that possible?" She pointed toward the villa. "There's no way you could be homeless. Not with a father as rich as that!"

"He cut my mother off without a penny in the divorce."

"How could he?"

"He found a way." A humorless smile traced his lips. "When my mother got tired of all his blatant cheating, he was too spiteful to even pay her the paltry amount guaranteed by the prenup. So he gave her a choice—if she voluntarily gave up that income, she could have full custody of me. He knew she'd agree." He took a drink. "The last thing she wanted was to leave me here with him."

"He cheated on your mother?"

Stavros snorted. "You think my cousin Oliver is bad? My father was worse. And my grandfather worse still. He impregnated every willing woman for miles around. My grandmother just gritted her teeth and pretended it wasn't happening." He shook his head. "I don't even know all my cousins. Oliver's mother was the result of a fling between my grandfather and one of the maids."

"Oh," she said lamely.

Looking toward the sea, he said softly, "But my mother grew up in a different generation. She couldn't put up with it forever. Seeing her suffer broke my heart. I vowed I'd never be on either side of it."

"Never love anyone?"

"Or let them love me. Love always has a winner and a loser. A conqueror and a conquered." He gave a smile that didn't meet his eyes. "I decided long ago I never wanted to be either."

Holly looked past the villa's whitewashed terrace, illuminated by light from the villa behind them, to the black moon-swept sea beyond.

"But you still hurt me," she whispered. "In spite of that."

"I know." He took another slow, deliberate sip of wine. "No wonder when you found out you were pregnant, you decided I was a cruel bastard who didn't deserve either of you."

"Was I wrong?"

Her words seemed to echo in the soft Greek night. In the distance, he could hear the roar of waves pounding the beach.

"I was selfish when I seduced you," he said slowly. He lifted his gaze to hers. "But not when I let you go. I pushed you away because I was no good to anyone, least of all you."

"Like I said, you could have told me—"

"Holly, if I'd told you I was dying, it would have only bound you to me more. You would have given me everything, all your heart and your life, until I died—and even after. It would have destroyed you."

Her lovely face looked stricken, then angry.

"You really think I'm pathetic, don't you?" She raised her chin. "You're so sure I would have fallen in love with you?"

"Yes."

"Because you think you're irresistible." Her tone was a sneer that seemed like an ill-fitting costume on her.

Stavros took a deep breath. "Because you're the most loving person I've ever known. And I couldn't ruin your life like that." He gave a small smile. "Not even me."

Her eyes were huge and limpid in the moonlight.

"I expected to die," he continued in a low voice. "But to my surprise, I lived. And now we have a child. Surely you must see that my life can never be the same."

"It doesn't have to change for you…"

"You're wrong," he said simply. Reaching out, he took her hand across the table. "I want us to be a family."

He heard her breath catch. Her hand was suddenly trembling. Nervously, she tried to pull it away, turning toward the villa. "I should check on the baby…"

"Eleni will listen for him." He was close, so close, to achieving his objective. Leaning forward, holding her hand, he urged, "Give me a chance."

Silence fell. Then she said in a small voice, "It would take time for me to trust you again."

Joy rushed through him. "Whatever time you need—"

"I want separate bedrooms tonight."

Silence fell.

Separate bedrooms? That was not at all what he wanted. What he wanted was to make love to her tonight. Right now. But since he'd just promised her time, what else could he do?

"Very well," he said stiffly.

Exhaling, Holly looked out at the sea. "It's beautiful here. Like a dream." She tried to smile. "The white puffs of cloud look like ships in the moonlight."

Stavros watched her. "I like the joy you take in life. Most people forget that when they leave their childhoods behind. If they ever even knew."

She snorted, her expression incredulous. "You think I'm a child?"

"Far from it," he said quietly. "You're the most intensely desirable woman I've ever known."

Her eyes widened. Then her lips curled in a brief, humorless smile. She clearly didn't believe a word. "That's quite the compliment, considering how many you've known."

"None hold a candle to you." He looked at her across the table. "There's been no other woman for me, Holly. Not since we were together."

She blinked, then slowly looked at him. "What?"

"I don't want anyone else," he said simply.

For a moment, their eyes locked in the moonlight. He saw yearning in her lovely face. Then, as if on cue, the lights in the villa's windows behind them went dark, and she seemed to catch herself. Biting her lip, she rose with an awkward laugh. "It's late. I should go to bed."

Polishing off his glass of wine, he rose to his feet. "Of course."

"Should we bring in the plates?"

"It's not necessary."

"I don't want someone else cleaning up my mess." Picking up her plate and glass, she paused. "What about your father's plate?"

"Leave it." He added with irony, "He doesn't have your same concerns."

Stavros picked up his own plate and glass, and the bottle of wine. As they walked back across the terrace, he felt the chill of the deepening night. A cool sea breeze blew against his skin. He looked up at the sprawling white villa.

Getting her into bed was going to take longer than he'd thought. And marrying her would be even longer.

But he didn't know how much more of his past he could share with her. Every small story was like pulling his soul through a meat slicer. He would have far preferred to seduce her.

But he'd seen the change in her. He saw it now, as they took the dishes back to the enormous, modern kitchen. The anger in her eyes when she looked at him had changed to bewilderment, even wistfulness. His plan was working.

So he'd just have to endure it.

Stavros walked her back to their large guest bedroom. Passing her without a word, he quickly grabbed his leather overnight bag. He paused only to look down at his baby, sleeping in the crib. He didn't touch him, out of fear he might wake.

"Good night, my son," he whispered.

Freddie yawned, his eyes closed as he continued to sleep, flinging his chubby arms back over his head.

Stavros turned, lifted his bag over his shoulder and started down the hall. Turning back to say good-night, he stopped when he saw Holly standing in the doorway. Her heart-shaped face was haunted.

"Do you really care about Freddie?" she said hoarsely. "You're not just doing it out of pride, or to hurt me? You really want to be his father?"

"Yes," he said in a low voice. He dropped the bag to the floor and moved close to her. "And I want you."

She looked up, her expression stricken. "You..."

"I want you. I want to hold you in my arms. I want you in my bed. I've tried to forget that night. I can't. I've thought of it for the last year."

She trembled, searching his gaze.

"You're trying to seduce me," she whispered.

"Yes. I am." Cupping her face, he lowered his head toward hers. "I want you forever..."

And in the shadowy hall outside the bedroom, he lowered his lips toward hers and kissed her, soft and slow.

For a moment, she froze beneath his embrace, and he thought she'd push him away.

Then slowly, tremblingly, her lips parted. And it was the sweetest, purest kiss Stavros had ever known. It took every ounce of his willpower to finally pull away, when all he wanted to do was take her back into the bedroom and make love to her.

But he didn't want her for just one night. He wanted her as his wife. And if he'd learned anything from nearly twenty years in mergers and acquisitions, it was to always leave the other side wanting more.

"Good night," he said huskily, cupping her cheek as he looked deeply into her eyes. And he left her.

CHAPTER EIGHT

HOLLY HAD TOSSED and turned all night in the big bed.

She couldn't stop thinking of Stavros's voice last night.

Holly, if I'd told you I was dying it would have only bound you to me more. You would have given me everything, all your heart and your life, until I died—and even after. It would have destroyed you.

Put that way, she could almost forgive him for what he'd done. Because he was right. If, last Christmas, he'd taken her in his arms and told her the truth, she would have immediately done anything, given anything, to help him.

You're the most loving person I've ever known.

He'd made it sound like a character flaw.

Maybe it was. She thought of how she'd spent all her adult life caring for others over herself. She didn't mean Freddie. He was a helpless baby.

But Oliver wasn't helpless. Neither was her sister. And for years, Holly had sacrificed herself for their needs, for no good reason. She thought of how Nicole had blamed Holly on the phone for their marriage problems.

You should be here taking care of things for him. And for me!

Maybe Stavros was right. Maybe, in some ways, Holly's need to always put other people first had been wrong. It certainly hadn't done anything good for Nicole or Oliver, who only seemed more helpless and resentful after her years of sacrifice.

And if Holly had let herself fall in love with Stavros last year, she suddenly knew she would have given him everything, too—whether he wanted it or not.

Instead, when he'd rejected her, she'd been forced to do everything on her own. She'd gained strength, and confidence she'd never had before. Both important qualities for a good mother.

And for a good father?

She shivered. She was starting to believe that Stavros really cared about Freddie, and wanted to be a family. He seemed determined to marry Holly.

Could they actually be happy together?

The idea was growing harder to resist. It would be too easy to love a man like Stavros, when he poured on the charm. She fell a little every time he spoke to her. And when he'd kissed her—

All night afterward, she'd lain awake, wondering what would have happened if she hadn't insisted on separate bedrooms. If she'd let him share her bed. Wondering, and knowing. And wishing…

Now, as Holly looked at Stavros across the breakfast table, with the morning sun shining gold from the double-story window and the sea outside a brilliant blue, her heart was in her throat.

They barely said a word to each other as they ate breakfast. She was dressed simply, in a T-shirt and jeans, while he was in his usual tailored shirt, jacket and trousers. He'd just looked at her, then kissed her on the cheek. But that had been enough to make her pulse pound.

"I know what you're thinking," Stavros said now as his eyes met hers over the table. She broke out in a hot sweat.

"Oh?" she said, praying he didn't.

He tilted his head. "You're wondering how long we have to wait. I say we don't."

"Really?" she croaked, still filled with images of him naked in her bed.

He gave her a crooked grin. "Honestly, I'm glad my father never showed up last night. I only brought you here because I couldn't think of any other way to convince you to give me a chance. I knew with your loving heart, you would feel like you had no choice but to let him meet his grandson."

Her *loving heart* really was starting to sound ridiculous. As if Holly was determined to see only the best in people, even when her positive image of them was totally untethered to reality. What she'd learned last night about Stavros's father didn't make her particularly keen to get to know him better, either.

As Freddie started fussing in her arms, she reached for a prepared bottle on the table. "You want to leave after breakfast? Without seeing him?"

"It would feel like dodging a bullet." Leaning forward, he suddenly asked, "Could I hold the baby, Holly?"

His darkly handsome face was vulnerable, his deep voice uncertain, as if he wasn't just asking her permission, but her opinion.

He still hadn't held their son yet. Because Holly hadn't let him.

Suddenly, she hated herself for that. Who did she think she was, keeping Freddie from Stavros—a man who'd made it clear that he only wanted good things for their baby?

"Of course you can," she said. "You're his father."

His dark eyes lit up. "Yes?"

"Definitely." Gently, she lifted the two-month-old into his father's strong arms, where Stavros sat on the other side of the breakfast table in the morning room. She handed him a warmed bottle. "You'll need this."

"Like this?" he asked, angling the bottle. His boyish uncertainty made her heart twist inside her.

"Tilt your elbow a little more," she suggested, touching his bare forearm. He looked up at her, and for a moment, electricity crackled between them. She saw him start to rise, as if he intended to take her in his arms.

Then he looked back down at the baby, and didn't move from his chair. Freddie wrapped his hands around the bottle, drinking with greedy gulps, his black eyes looking up at his father trustingly.

Holly watched them with a lump in her throat. The baby's sucking noises gradually slowed, then stopped altogether, as his eyes grew drowsy as he drifted off to sleep, held tenderly in his father's powerful arms.

Stavros looked up with obvious pride, his dark eyes shining.

"Look," he whispered. "He's sleeping!"

And something broke inside Holly's heart.

Stavros seemed so different now—

"So you finally came crawling back."

Holly looked up to see a wiry, elderly man standing in the doorway with two young women on his arm. The man had brightly colored, youthful clothes that did little to disguise his potbelly and skinny legs. His hair was pitch-black, except for half an inch near the roots that was white. Even from this distance, he reeked of alcohol, cigarettes and expensive cologne.

Stavros's face turned briefly pale. As if by instinct, he turned his body in the chair, as if protecting the sleeping baby. Then, as if a wall came clanging down, his expression became totally flat.

"Hello, Father." His bored gaze glanced dismissively at the two young women, both of whom looked younger than Holly, perhaps even younger than her little sister. "Friends of yours?"

"From the club." He waved toward them airily. "We

stopped to change clothes. Or at least—" he gave a sly grin "—take them off."

Holly looked with dismay at the girls, who both looked, if possible, even more bored than Stavros. They had to be a third of Aristides's age. One of them was already giving Stavros a frankly flirtatious smile that made Holly, who'd never considered herself prone to violence, want to give her a hard smack across the jaw.

The older man stepped forward, then looked down at the sleeping baby with a sniff. "Is that the baby Eleni was going on about?"

"This is my son, yes," Stavros said stiffly.

"Looks tiny. Runt of the litter."

"He's two months old."

Aristides winked back at the young women. "I'm sure you girls can hardly believe I'm old enough to be a grandfather."

"Uh, yeah," the blonde replied with an American accent, turning so that her friend could see her roll her eyes. "Look, Aristi, if we're not going out shopping like you promised then we've got to go."

"Things to see, people to do," her brunette friend agreed, giving Stavros another flirtatious smile.

"No, wait—I have gifts for you girls upstairs. Go up and wait."

"Where?"

"Up the top of the stairs. The big purple bedroom all the way at the back," he called jovially, then ran his hands slickly through his hair. After they were gone, he turned on Stavros with a scowl. "So why did you come here?"

"No reason."

"You want money, right?"

Stavros stiffened. "No."

Aristides stared at him, then shrugged. "All right, fine,

I saw the kid. Now get the hell out of here. You're nothing to me. I have no desire to be a grandfather."

Holly could hardly believe it. She tried to imagine a world in which she'd ever ignore family, or tell a son or grandson that he wasn't wanted. The thought was like an ice pick in her heart.

"Are you serious?" she blurted out. "After we came all this way?"

Aristides's rheumy, drunken eyes focused on her. "Who are you? The wife?"

"She's my son's mother." Stavros's voice was low. Holly felt, in her bones, how much he would have liked to claim her as his wife.

"Ha! So not your wife. She had your kid, but you still didn't marry her?" The man snorted a laugh. "Maybe you learned from my mistakes after all. You're more like me than I thought, boy."

"I'm nothing like you," Stavros growled, his hands tightening around his sleeping baby son.

"No?" His father stroked his chin. "You were so high and mighty when you called me after your mother's funeral. I was a monster, you said. You'd never whore around like me, you said. Now look at you."

Stavros looked speechless with rage.

Turning to Holly with a crafty expression, Aristides purred, "You're smart not to marry him. What did you say your name was?" Without waiting for her to answer, he continued flirtatiously, "A beauty like you can do far better."

With a sly glance toward his son, Aristides Minos lifted a calculating eyebrow, as if plotting what to say next; for an appalling instant Holly wondered if he was considering inviting her to join the other girls in his bedroom. Suddenly, she couldn't stand it.

"I didn't want to have a wedding while I was pregnant.

But Stavros and I are getting married soon," Holly said, meeting the older man's gaze steadily. "In a few days."

She felt, rather than heard, Stavros's intake of breath.

"Your loss," Aristides said, sounding bored. "All right. Thanks for the visit." He looked down at his son scornfully. "But don't think that this means I'll put you back in my will."

"Are you kidding?" Holly said, outraged. "Do you actually think he needs your money?"

"Shh, Holly. It doesn't matter." Holding his sleeping baby carefully, Stavros rose to his feet. He was taller than his father, and his expression was utterly cold. "Keep your money, you cheap bastard."

"Cheap!" The older man's eyes blazed. "Just because I wasn't willing to hand off my family fortune to some little waitress I met in a bar, who convinced me to marry her when she got pregnant." He scowled at Stavros. "I'm still not sure you're even mine."

"I wish to hell I wasn't," he said quietly.

"Gotten full of yourself with that company of yours? Just because you think you're richer than me now?" His father drew himself up, slicking his hand back through his skunk-striped hair. "You'd never have built that company without me."

Stavros's eyes went wide. "You say that, after what you did to Mom—"

"If I hadn't cut her off without a penny, you'd never have had the drive to make something of yourself. You should thank me." Aristides tilted his head, in the exact same gesture she'd seen Stavros use. "I should own half your stock, purely as an issue of fairness."

Stavros's fists tightened, then he looked at his baby sleeping nestled in the crook of one arm, and he exhaled.

"You're not worth another minute of my time," he said, and he turned to Holly. "Are you ready?"

"Definitely."

"Good. Go!" His father's black eyes narrowed as his voice built in rage. "Get out of my house!"

Holly looked for one last moment at the rich, horrible old man. "Goodbye. Sorry you've made such bad choices in life."

Aristides looked shocked.

Without another word, Holly turned and followed Stavros out of the villa's morning room.

"I'm sorry, too!" he screamed after her. "Sorry I wasted my time talking to you! You're not even that pretty!"

She expected Stavros to head upstairs to get their overnight bags, but instead he went straight for the front door, pausing only to talk to Eleni, the housekeeper.

Following him outside, Holly said quietly, "What about our things?"

"We'll get new ones. I'm done here."

"I understand."

"Eleni's gone to pack. She heard everything and says she can't work for him anymore." Stavros lifted a phone to his ear and spoke to his pilot. She saw how his hand trembled as he ended the call. Turning to her, he said quietly, "Did you mean what you said?"

Holly couldn't pretend not to know what he meant.

"Yes." She looked down at their precious sleeping baby cradled against his chest. "I want us to be a family." She lifted her gaze to his and whispered, "I'll marry you."

His dark gaze filled with light. "You'll come to New York?"

With a deep breath, she nodded. He cupped her cheek, running his thumb along her tender bottom lip, causing electricity to pulse through her body.

"You won't be sorry," he promised.

Shivering, Holly prayed he was right.

* * *

New York City was a winter wonderland, decorated with fresh snow and all the lights and decorations of Christmas. To Stavros, the city had never looked so beautiful. It was as if all the world had decided to celebrate.

Today was his wedding day.

His wife. Holly was going to be his wife...

Since their arrival from Greece, their wedding plans had been rushed through in only two days. Stavros wished to marry her as quickly as possible, before she had the chance for second thoughts.

Also, he had a major upcoming business deal, the acquisition of a local technology business-management firm for nearly two billion dollars, which he knew would keep him busy the last weeks before Christmas.

And as in all acquisitions, Stavros had learned from experience that speed was key. Once a man knew what he wanted, there was nothing to be gained from waiting. Better to strike fast, and possess what he wanted, before anyone else could take it. That was true in business—and marriage.

Holly had agreed to be married as soon as they could get the license. Her only request was that they invite her sister to the wedding. Apparently when she'd phoned Nicole with the news, her little sister had begged to bring Oliver to the ceremony, too. Stavros was none too pleased. He cynically expected his cousin, who'd been unemployed for months, to ask him for money. But having her sister there seemed important to Holly's happiness, and her happiness was important to his.

When Holly had said she'd marry him, Stavros thought he would explode with joy.

No, not joy, he told himself. Triumph. He'd achieved his objective. His son was secure. Or he would be, as soon as they were married today. They'd be a family. And Holly would be in his bed.

Stavros pictured how she'd looked in the moonlight, so unabashedly emotional. She didn't seem to realize how foolish it could be, to show feelings, to even have them at all: it left you vulnerable. He felt uncomfortable remembering everything he'd shared with her in Greece. He'd never been that open with anyone.

He'd only done it to achieve his objective, he reassured himself. There was no danger of him giving his heart to Holly, no matter how tempted any other man would be. Stavros's heart had been charred to ash long ago.

He'd meant it when he'd told her she'd never regret marrying him. But he'd have to walk a careful line. He wanted to make her happy, but not so happy she fell in love with him. He couldn't be that cruel, when he'd never be able to return her love. And he couldn't bear the thought of hurting her. Dread went through Stavros at the thought.

He remembered how she'd spoken so dreamily about how her parents had loved each other.

My father always said loving my mother changed his life. She made him a husband. A father. More than he ever imagined he could be. He always said she changed his stars.

Holly knew that love wasn't something that Stavros—or any Minos man—was capable of, he told himself firmly. She'd still chosen to marry him. Therefore, she'd accepted him as he was.

He might not be able to experience love, or give it, but damn it, he'd be faithful to her. He'd be a solid husband and father. He'd always provide for her and the baby.

He'd made sure of that in their prenuptial agreement, much to the dismay of his lawyers. His terms had been far more generous than needed. But he wanted Holly to know she'd never be left penniless by a divorce, as his own mother had.

If he couldn't love Holly, he'd make damn sure she was always cared for.

Stavros could hardly wait to make her his wife and make love to her. It was all he'd been able to think of on the flight from Greece. He would have taken Holly back to the jet's bedroom while the baby slept, if it hadn't been for the presence of Eleni. Nothing like a sharp-eyed, grandmotherly former nanny aboard to keep one's basest desires in check.

A judge would be arriving later today to marry them at his penthouse, which was already decorated with candles, flowers and Christmas holly and ivy. The rings had been bought, the wedding dress and tuxedo secured and the food arranged by the wedding planner.

Somewhat to his shock, Holly had let the planner sort out everything.

"You don't even want to pick out your dress?" Stavros had grinned. "You are the most easygoing bride in the world."

She'd shrugged. "It doesn't really matter."

He'd sobered. "Are you sure? If a big wedding is important to you, Holly, we can be married in a cathedral and invite the whole damn city."

She shook her head. "I had my dream wedding last year, for Nicole. And I'm not sure it made any difference for them." She lifted her gaze to his and said, "Our marriage is what I care about, not the ceremony."

Cradling her head in his hands, he gently kissed her. "But you deserve a party…"

She'd looked at him for a long moment. "I'd rather have this day just be about us. But if you really want to throw me a party, you know what I'd really like? A birthday party on the twenty-third of December, with all my friends."

"The twenty-third?" He was ambushed by the memory of that date last year, when he'd gotten his fatal diagnosis.

She'd smiled. "It's why my parents named me Holly, because my birthday's so close to Christmas." She tilted her head. "For just one time, I'd love to have a real birthday party, without Christmas taking over…"

Then she happily told him a story he barely heard, something about everyone always wrapping her birthday gifts in Christmas paper, or giving her a single gift for a combined Christmas/birthday present, or forgetting her birthday entirely. But he was distracted by memories of the shock and weakness and vulnerability he'd felt last year. He never wanted to feel like that again.

Especially now. As a father, soon to be a husband, he couldn't afford to ever feel weak or vulnerable again. He wasn't afraid of the cancer returning. His recent checkup had placed him in full remission. But emotionally, he'd have to be strong to make sure he never totally let down his walls. He didn't want to hurt Holly. Or be hurt himself…

"Of course." As she finished her story, Stavros gave her a charming smile. "The best birthday party you've ever seen."

Then they went to city hall, where a very bored-looking city employee gave them a marriage license, and an excited paparazzo took their picture as they left.

Within twenty minutes of the photo getting posted online, he'd started getting phone calls from shocked acquaintances and ex-girlfriends around the world, demanding to know if it was true and the uncatchable playboy was actually getting married. He'd ignored the messages. Why explain? Silence was strength.

But now that Stavros was about to speak his wedding vows, he felt oddly nervous. He'd told himself that he was different from the other Minos men. He was determined to be an excellent husband and father. But what if he was wrong? What if he broke Holly's heart?

He'd make sure it didn't happen. If he cared for her, respected her, honored and provided for her, how could it matter if he loved her or not? How would she even know the difference?

Stavros was distracted by a hard knock at his penthouse bedroom door. Turning, he saw his cousin, who'd arrived with Nicole an hour before, looking shifty-eyed in his well-cut tuxedo.

"I say, old man," Oliver said with an artificially bright smile. "Before you speak vows and all that, I wonder if I could have a word?"

Stavros checked his expensive platinum watch.

"I have five minutes," he said shortly.

He'd regretfully agreed to Holly's suggestion that his cousin could be best man, as Nicole had begged her to be matron of honor. It made sense, the two of them returning the favor after Stavros and Holly had done it for them the previous year.

But Stavros and his cousin had never been particularly close, and Oliver had been a very unsatisfying employee at his company. And since the other couple's awkward arrival at the penthouse, Oliver had seemed to be working up to something. Stavros had a good idea what it was. He set his jaw.

"You might have heard," Oliver began, "that I've rather had trouble finding work..."

"Because your employers actually expect you to work?"

His cousin gave a crooked grin. "Turns out I'm not good at it."

"Or interested in it." Checking that he had the wedding ring in his pocket, Stavros looked at himself one last time in the full-length mirror and adjusted his tuxedo tie. "So?"

"I never thought you'd get married, Stavros. I always figured I'd be your heir."

"Sorry to disappoint you." Since he was only a few years older than Oliver, it was a little disconcerting to realize his cousin had counted on his death as a retirement plan.

Oliver paused. "It's funny to see you in love. I never thought you'd fall so hard for any woman."

Stavros didn't bother to disabuse him of the notion he was in love with his bride. It seemed like bad form on their wedding day. "What did you want to ask me?"

"Right. Well. Since it's obvious how much Holly's happiness means to you…" Oliver gave his most charming grin. "I wonder if you'd be willing to pay me ten million dollars to stay married to Holly's sister."

CHAPTER NINE

"COME ON, HOLLY. Please! You have to help me!"

Her little sister's insistent, whining voice hurt Holly's ears as she sat in the chair of the penthouse's guest bedroom, waiting for the stylists to finish doing her hair and makeup for her wedding.

When Nicole had begged to be her matron of honor, Holly had actually hoped it was because she wanted them to be close again. Instead, she'd spent the last twenty minutes blaming Holly for her marriage problems and asking for money.

"I'm sorry, Nicole. I can't just tell Stavros to hire Oliver back." She hesitated. "We both know he wasn't a very good employee…"

"Oh, so you don't care if my marriage is ruined? If we both starve? How can you be so unfeeling? You're my sister!"

Holly's cheeks were hot as she glanced at the two stylists, who were pretending not to listen. "Fine," she sighed. "I have five thousand dollars in my retirement account. It will be a little hard to get it out but if you really need it—"

"Five thousand dollars? Are you out of your mind?" Nicole cried. "That's nothing! My handbags cost more than that!"

The two stylists glanced at each other. Holly's cheeks burned even hotter. She asked the makeup artist, "Am I done?"

"Yes." The woman put final touches on her lips. "Now you are."

"Thank you." She looked around for her bag. "I'll get my wallet—"

"We've already been paid by your husband," the stylist said, smiling at her. "And lavishly tipped, I might add."

"Congratulations, Mrs. Minos," the other stylist said warmly. "I hope you will be very happy."

Mrs. Minos. Just the name caused a flutter inside Holly's belly. As the stylists gathered their equipment and disappeared, she looked at herself. She hardly recognized the glamorous bride in the mirror, with her glamorous makeup and unruly red hair tamed into an elegant chignon beneath a veil.

She was wearing expensive lingerie, a strapless bustier and white panties, and a white garter holding up old-fashioned white stockings. The long, translucent veil stretched behind her. For a moment, she was lost in a dream, picturing a lifetime as Stavros's wife, the two of them in love forever—

In love? Where had that idea come from?

"It's easy for you to be happy," Nicole said resentfully. "With all your money." Lifting Freddie, who was whining in a similar tone, from his nearby crib, she said to the baby, "You're the luckiest kid in the world."

Lifting her simple white wedding dress from where it was spread over the bedspread of the guest bed, Holly said distractedly, "You don't believe that, Nicole. You know it's not money that makes a happy home, but love. And your money problems will work themselves out. You have a college degree. You could always look for a job yourself…"

"It's not just money." Cuddling her nephew close, Nicole closed her eyes. She took a deep breath. "Oliver's cheating on me, Holly."

Holly stiffened as she held her simple strapless white dress over her undergarments. "Oh, no!"

"He only married me because I threatened to break up with him if he didn't. But that was when he had an easy job and plenty of money. Now, he regrets he ever married me. I'm not good enough."

"That's ridiculous!" Scowling, she whirled to face her little sister. "He's the one who's not remotely good enough—"

"He's going to leave me for someone rich," she choked out, wiping her eyes. "I just know it. And I'll be all alone."

When she saw Nicole's woebegone face, Holly's heart broke for her.

"It'll be all right, Nicky," she whispered, using her old childhood nickname as she reached out to touch her shoulder. "Everything's going to be all right."

"I'm so sorry." Trying to smile, Nicole choked back her tears. "I'm wrecking your wedding day. We can talk about this all later."

But as Holly left the guest bedroom a few minutes later, and went into the grand salon of the penthouse, she still felt troubled. And not just by what she'd learned from her sister, who was dressed in a pink bridesmaid's dress, following her with yawning Freddie, resplendent in a baby tuxedo.

Holly's teeth chattered nervously as she thought of the irrevocable vows she was about to take. Just this time last year, she'd been planning Nicole's wedding. She'd never expected she'd so soon be a bride herself. Now, as she walked down the short hallway, she clutched her simple bouquet of pink peonies as if her life depended on it.

She was getting married.

To him.

Stavros stood waiting near the Christmas tree, imposing and breathtakingly handsome in front of the floor-to-ceiling windows with all of New York City at his feet. Next

to him stood Oliver, blond and debonair. On his other side
was the jocular, white-haired judge who would marry them,
smiling broadly in his black robes, and lastly Eleni, in an
old-fashioned, formal dress, beaming as if she herself were
mother of the groom.

But Holly had eyes only for Stavros.

He was wearing a sleek tuxedo that clung to his powerful, muscular body. Her eyes moved up from his black
tie to his powerful neck, his square jaw, his gorgeous face.
His dark eyes burned through her.

Their wedding ceremony was simple, lasting only a few
minutes. It seemed like a dream.

She couldn't look away from his face.

"And do you, Holly Ann Marlowe, take this man to be
your lawfully wedded husband…?"

"I do," she breathed, trembling as he slid the huge diamond ring over her finger.

"And do you, Stavros Minos, take this woman to be your
lawfully wedded wife?"

"I do," he growled in his low, sexy voice, looking at her
in a way that made her toes curl in her high-heeled shoes.
And suddenly, all her nervousness about the permanency
of their wedding vows melted away.

"Then by the power vested in me by the State of New
York, I now pronounce you husband and wife." The judge
beamed between them. "You may now kiss the bride."

Stavros's dark, hooded eyes held the red spark of desire
as he took her in his arms. As he lowered his lips to hers,
her breasts felt heavy, her nipples taut beneath the sweet-
heart neckline of the silk wedding dress. Tension coiled
low and deep in her belly.

For days, he'd been teasing her with butterfly kisses and
little touches. Now, his kiss made her forget all her doubts
and regrets. It made her forget her own name.

Then she remembered: her name had changed. From this moment forward, she was Mrs. Holly Minos.

She watched the judge sign the marriage license, followed by Nicole and Oliver, as witnesses. She saw Nicole look at her husband nervously, with pleading in her eyes. Oliver gave his wife a warm smile, put his arm around her and kissed her forehead. Nicole looked as if she was about to cry with relief.

Holly exhaled. Her sister must have been wrong. Oliver couldn't be cheating on her, not if he kissed her like that. Everything would be fine…

"Congratulations, you two," the judge said, smiling at Holly and Stavros. "Now I'll leave you—" he winked "—to your private celebrations."

Holly's eyes went wide. *Private celebrations*. She looked up at the handsome, powerful man beside her. *Her husband*.

She'd only had one lover her whole life, and for only one night. She'd never forgotten the way Stavros had made her feel so alive, or the ecstasy of his touch. The night she'd spent with him last Christmas Eve had been the most magical of her life, before it had all come crashing down the next morning.

But there would be no more rejection. They were married now. For better, for worse. For the rest of their lives…

"We'll head downstairs," Eleni said happily, holding Freddie, who looked very sleepy in his baby tuxedo. Stavros had hired Eleni as their highly paid part-time housekeeper. Holly wasn't sure it was necessary, but how could she object to Stavros giving a job to the woman who'd taken care of him in childhood?

Besides, she liked and trusted Eleni, and was grateful the other woman would be watching Freddie tonight in her new suite downstairs, giving them privacy for their wedding night.

Holly shivered. *Their wedding night.*

"We'll go now, too," Nicole said, leaning back against her husband, who cuddled her close.

"Talk later?" Holly said to her anxiously, thinking of their earlier discussion. Her little sister smiled.

"Stop worrying," she said cheerfully, patting her on the shoulder. "You need to be more selfish. You're a bride."

And everyone left at once. For the first time since Freddie had been born, Holly was alone.

Alone with her husband…

"Mrs. Minos," Stavros murmured. He slowly looked her over, making her shiver inside. Then, without a word, he lifted her up in his arms, against his chest. He looked down at her. "I've waited a long time for this night."

"Days," she sighed, thinking of the anticipation she'd felt since they'd left Greece.

Stavros looked at her seriously. "A year."

He carried her down the penthouse hall, then set her down gently beside the same enormous bed where, last Christmas Eve, they'd conceived their son. She glanced down at it, thinking how much had changed since then.

They had a future. They were a family.

Gently, he pulled off the headband of white silk flowers that held her long veil in place. He dropped it on the nightstand.

The gas fire caused flickers of white light to move against the dark shadows of his face. The room was black, gray and white. The Christmas tree lights. Through the windows, New York City at night.

Taking off his tuxedo jacket, he dropped it silently to the floor, along with his black tie. He unbuttoned the cuffs of his shirt. Never taking his gaze off hers, he reached his powerful arms around her and unzipped her strapless wedding gown. It slid down her body to the floor, revealing her white bustier bra, tiny white lace panties and white garter.

She heard the low shudder of his breath, felt the tremble of his hands as he stepped back to look at her.

"You're magnificent," he whispered.

The heat in his gaze melted her. All she could think about was that she wanted to make him hers. *Forever.*

Reaching forward, Holly yanked on his white shirt, popping off buttons that scattered to the floor. She could hardly believe her own boldness as she reached inside his open shirt to slowly stroke down his hard-muscled bare chest, lightly dusted with dark hair.

With a low growl, he grabbed her wrists. For a moment, he just looked down at her, his black eyes searing her. Then without a word, he pushed her back on the bed.

Never taking his gaze off her, her husband took off his shirt, dropping it the floor. She had the sharp image of his powerful bare chest, all shadows and hollows in the flickering firelight. She reached toward him. She couldn't wait. She had to feel his body, his weight. She had to feel him against her. *Now.*

"Stavros," she whispered, arms extended.

He moved instantly, climbing over her on the bed in a single athletic movement. She exhaled as she felt his body over hers, his heavy weight pushing her into the mattress, felt the bare skin of his chest and arms against hers. Lifting himself up on one powerful arm, he cupped her cheek, looking down at her intently.

"You're mine now," he whispered. "And I'm never going to let you go…"

He lowered his lips to hers, softly at first. Then his embrace deepened, turning hungry, almost savage. Her nipples tightened beneath her white silk bustier as his powerful muscles moved against her. As he kissed her, he stroked down her cheek, her neck, her shoulder. He cupped her breast over the silk, then reached beneath it to caress her taut nipple, making her gasp.

Pulling away, he looked down at her, his eyes dark. Sitting up, he pulled the silk off her body as if it was nothing more than a thought. Lowering his head between her full breasts, he kissed down the valley between them, all the way to the soft curve of her belly. He ran his hands over the edge of her hips, where her white lace panties clung, digging into her skin. He kissed her belly button, flicking his tongue inside it, as he unbuckled her garters. His large hands caressed each cheek of her bottom before he slowly moved down her body. Sensually, he rolled down each white stocking, soft as a whisper and elusive as a dream.

As the silk slid slowly down her skin, he followed it with kisses down one leg, then the other, down her thighs to the curve beneath her knees, all the way to the hollows of her feet. She shivered on the bed, feeling vulnerable, wearing only her tiny thong panties. After tossing the stockings aside, he pushed her legs apart. She looked up at him in the silver-white firelight, which left dancing patterns across his powerful naked chest.

She looked at his trousers, then met his eyes as she whispered like a fearless wanton woman, "Take them off."

He moved so rapidly he was almost a blur, ripping off his trousers and the dark boxers beneath. In half a second, they were on the floor, and he was on her.

Then her flimsy lace panties were gone, disintegrated beneath the force of his powerful hands. Cupping her breasts, he positioned himself between her legs. As he lowered his head, possessing her lips with his own, she felt the hard thickness of him pressing between her thighs. Her hips moved of their own volition, swaying against him, as her hands raked down his back, settling against his hard-muscled backside.

She felt his powerful body shiver. Lifting his head, he looked down at her face. For a moment, she thought he would say something, something that could either annihilate her or make her soul explode with joy—one or the other. Instead, he just lowered his head and kissed her fiercely. Pulling his hips back, he thrust inside her in a single smooth movement, making her gasp as he filled her, all the way to the hilt.

Her fingernails dug into his skin as she looked up at his handsome face. His eyes were closed, his expression one of ecstasy.

Drawing back, he pushed inside her a second time, this time very slowly, so she could feel him, inch by inch. She closed her own eyes, surrendering to the pleasure building inside her, spiraling rapidly out of control.

She gasped as he suddenly moved, rolling her on top of him. Her eyes flew open. She looked down at him.

He reached up and tenderly caressed her cheek.

"I want to watch you," he whispered. His hands moved down the edge of her throat, lazily cupping her full breast, stroking his thumb against her taut, aching nipple. "I want to see what your face is like when you're the one in control."

Stavros looked up at his bride, naked astride him on the enormous bed in his penthouse bedroom.

He was telling her the truth. But not all of it. He watched the play of lights and shadows on her beautiful face. Across the room, the artificial Christmas tree sparkled in front of floor-to-ceiling windows revealing Manhattan at their feet.

He did want to see her in control. But only because, being inside her, he'd been about to lose his own.

She felt too good. She felt too tight. After a year of rampant hunger, of repressed longing, he'd nearly lost his mind pushing inside her once. For the second thrust, he'd applied the brakes, going as slowly as possible. But that hadn't helped. He'd known, if he thrust a third time, that he would have exploded inside her.

Hardly the wedding night he wanted, or the one Holly deserved. And so he'd rolled on his back, thinking to give his willpower some respite. If she controlled the rhythm, surely he could make it last.

Instead, as he looked up now into her glowing emerald eyes, he saw the red blush on her cheeks as she bit down harder on her swollen lower lip, and his shaft, already so hard he groaned with need, flexed instinctively. She hesitated, glancing down at his naked body, now spread beneath her. She said uncertainly, "What do I do?"

"As you want, *agape mou*," he said huskily.

Her face was uncertain. Then as she looked down at him, her expression changed. Lowering her head, she whispered, "Don't move a muscle."

She kissed him, entwining his tongue with hers. A shiver went through him and he started to lift his arms around him. Punishingly, she ripped her lips away. "No." Grabbing his wrists, she pushed his arms down firmly into the mattress. "Don't move. And don't say a word!"

He started to reply, then saw her glare.

When she saw his surrender, she gave a satisfied nod and then kissed him again, lowering her lips to his. She was careful to let no other part of their bodies touch, teasing him.

It was hard not to move or speak, when all he wanted to do was wrap his arms around her. She kissed his rough, bristly chin, then down his neck, flicking her tongue over his Adam's apple, caressing down his collarbone to his muscular chest. He felt the delicious warmth of her breath on each nipple. He held his breath as she lowered her head, swirling her tongue around him, drawing him further into her warm, sensual mouth as she suckled him.

And all the while, she was careful not to touch any other part of his body. His shaft was hard, bucking and swaying toward her desperately. Glancing down at him, she smiled: a very smug feminine smile. As if she not only accepted her total power over him in this moment, but she also relished it.

"Holly," he breathed, reaching for her.

"No," she said sharply, pressing down his wrists against the pillow. "If you move again…"

"If I do?"

A strange look came over her face, and she looked him straight in the eye. "You won't feel what you're about to feel."

With an intake of breath, he blinked, then gave her a slow nod, keeping his wrists against the pillow, where she'd pressed them. Her intent gaze burned through him as she slowly lowered her head, sucking on his earlobes, then down the edge of his throat, nibbling on the sensitive corner between his neck and shoulder. She watched how his body reacted, and he saw her triumph. As she kissed her way down his body, he vowed that soon, very soon—

Then all rational thought disappeared as, never taking her eyes from his, she slowly lowered her head between his legs.

He couldn't look away from the sight of her beautiful, angelic face as her full, swollen, ruby-red lips lowered to take in his hard, throbbing shaft. Her pink tongue snaked out to lick the drop of opalescent liquid at the tip. Then she licked her lips, and murmured, "Mmm…"

He sucked in his breath, staring at her in shock. What had happened to the shy virgin of last Christmas Eve? This woman seemed sure of herself, and ready and able to torture him with his own desire for her.

He held his breath as he watched her take the tip of him into her wet, soft mouth, swirling him with her tongue. Then she took him in deeper, and deeper still. He felt her small hand run exploratively beneath the shaft, juggling him as she sucked him more deeply into the sweet heaven of her mouth. She peeked up at him, and he felt, rather than saw, her satisfied smile.

He could take no more. With a strangled groan, he reached for her, ignoring her weak protest, "I told you not to move!"

He picked her up by the hips as if she weighed nothing, lifted her over his shaft, then slowly lowered her, impaling her inch by delicious inch. With a gasp, she swayed against him, and the sensuality of even that simple movement pounded through his veins. He released her hips, to give her freedom of movement, praying she wouldn't move, praying that she would.

She answered both his prayers when she leaned forward, gripping his shoulders. She closed her eyes, holding still. But just as he started to exhale, she began to move, sliding over him, riding him slowly at first, but then with increasing rhythm. Watching her generous breasts sway over him as she moved, with their tight, deep pink nipples, was too much for him. He closed his eyes, tilting back his head, fighting to keep control. But the image remained. He was lost in the incredible sensation, in pleasure such as he'd never felt before, pleasure he'd never imagined.

She rode him harder and faster, pounding him, until he filled not just her hot wet core, but the universe itself, which began to spin all around him. Finally, gripping his shoulders, she gasped his name.

That pushed him off the edge, and catapulted him into the sky. He thrust one last time, then exploded inside her. He heard a low voice, rising to a ragged shout, crying out her name…and realized to his shock that it was his own.

She collapsed over him, their naked, sweaty, slick bodies intertwined and tangled on the bed. He held her, kissing her temple, and cradled her close. He was lost, he thought. He was found.

His eyes flew open in the darkness. As he held his wife,

who'd fallen asleep cradled in his arms, all he could think
was that he'd tasted the sweetest drug of his life. But if he
consumed too much of it, it would destroy him. There was
another name for something like that.

Poison.

CHAPTER TEN

MARRIAGE TO STAVROS was wonderful. Incredible. Better than Holly had ever dreamed.

At first.

After their wedding, they spent a few honeymoon days touring the city with their baby. They'd visited the big Christmas tree at Rockefeller Center, drunk hot cocoa, seen all the festive lights. Stavros had insisted on taking them shopping. When she'd told him they wouldn't need any winter clothes, since her former employer in London had promised to arrange for her possessions to be boxed and sent from Switzerland, Stavros had shrugged. "It's my duty to provide for my wife and child. Not just my duty— my pleasure."

He'd looked so serious and determined, it would have been churlish to refuse.

But instead of just buying her and the baby a few things, as Holly had expected, Stavros had gone as crazy as a contestant in a game show trying to throw as many items in his shopping cart as possible before the timer sounded. Only in this case, he wasn't shopping in a discount mart, but the most expensive boutiques and department stores in the city, and there were endless supplies of carts with no buzzer to stop them.

Finally, after they had more clothes than they'd need in a lifetime of New York winters, he'd taken them back to the chauffeured Rolls-Royce. Even then, instead of returning to the penthouse, her husband had told the driver to take them to the biggest toy store in Manhattan, where, like some darkly sexy Santa, he bought cartloads of toys for Freddie—baseball gear, books, games, an expensive train set, a teddy bear bigger than Stavros himself.

"Freddie's just a baby," Holly had protested, laughing. "He can't play with any of that stuff!"

"Not yet. But soon," he'd replied, kissing her. As his driver arranged for the toys to be delivered to the penthouse, Stavros looked at Holly, his black eyes suddenly hungry. Leaning forward, he stroked through Holly's long red hair beneath her pink knit cap and whispered in her ear, "Let's also get some things we can play with now."

Their exhausted baby had fallen asleep in his car seat by the time they'd arrived at a ridiculously expensive lingerie boutique. Holly had stared at the mannequins in the windows in shocked fascination, before ducking her head, blushing at the image of all the demi bras, garter belts, and crotchless panties that she might have called cheap, except they obviously were not. Aside from her wedding lingerie, which had been procured by the wedding planner, Holly had always purchased simple, sensible cotton bras and panties from places like Wal-Mart or Target.

Reluctantly walking into the French lingerie boutique with Stavros pushing a baby stroller, she'd felt nervous and out of place. When she'd looked at a price tag, she'd gasped and turned around, intending to walk straight back out again.

"Where are you going?" her husband had said, grinning as he grabbed the stroller handle.

She'd looked at him incredulously. "It's two hundred dollars!"

"So?"

"For a *pair of panties*!"

"I would pay far more than that," Stavros had said huskily, running his hand along the sleeve of her long, sleek black coat he'd just bought her at Dior, "to see you in them."

Her blush had felt like a raging fire, and she'd glanced right and left, hoping the salesgirls, all as glamorous as French supermodels, hadn't heard. Then her husband leaned forward and whispered what he planned to do to her later that night, and she was relieved that Freddie was still sleeping in the stroller so his innocent ears wouldn't hear.

"And," Stavros had said when he finally pulled away, "jewelry."

"What could I possibly need more than this?" she'd blurted out, lifting her left hand, with its huge, bulky, platinum-set diamond on her ring finger.

Her husband had given a low laugh. "Oh, my sweet wife," he'd said, cupping her cheek. He ran his thumb lightly along her lower lip, which was still swollen from their lovemaking the previous night. That simple touch made her tingle from her mouth to her breasts and lower still. "You will have rubies as red as your lips. Emeralds bright as your eyes." He'd looked at her with sensual, heavy-lidded eyes. "I will see you naked in my bed, wearing only diamonds that sparkle like Christmas morning…"

And he had.

Holly shivered now, remembering.

For the last three weeks, since their marriage, he'd made love to her every night. Somehow, each night was more spectacular than the last. She didn't understand how it was possible.

Perhaps it helped that she was no longer so exhausted from waking up multiple times with their baby throughout the night. As if even Freddie felt the new stability and security of their lives, he'd started sleeping better and longer at night than he had before. And she also had Eleni's help now.

So, almost against her will, Holly had found herself spending the holiday season as a princess in a New York penthouse, draped in jewels and expensive designer clothes, a lady of leisure whose only job was to cuddle her baby by day and be seduced by her husband at night. A life so wonderful it made her feel guilty, wondering what she'd done to deserve so much, when other people she knew had so much less.

So she'd asked Stavros if, instead of giving each other gifts for Christmas this year, they could donate money to charitable causes. He'd grudgingly agreed, seeing how important it was to her.

Holly was happy to make homemade Christmas gifts—knitted booties for Freddie, and a red felt star for Stavros, in the Marlowe family tradition. Whenever her former employer got around to sending her old Christmas decorations from Switzerland, Holly couldn't wait to add her husband's star to her family's heirloom garland.

Wrapping his red felt star in homemade wrapping paper, Holly had hidden it amid the branches of the brightly lit white Christmas tree in their bedroom, and waited for the right moment to surprise him.

But after the first delicious week of their honeymoon, things seemed to change between them. Stavros went back to work. Instead of spending all day with him, she saw him only in the middle of the night, when he would wake her up to make passionate love to her. By dawn, when Holly woke, Stavros was gone again.

Finally, out of desperation, Holly had put the baby in his stroller and gone to the offices of Minos International, hoping to see him, maybe take him to lunch. But Stavros had been deep in a conference meeting and barely spoke two words to her, seeming only annoyed by the interruption. Rejected, she'd gone to talk to her old coworkers. She'd relished the other secretaries' excited congratulations and demands to see Holly's spectacular diamond ring. They'd invited her to lunch, and she'd accepted happily.

But seated at their usual delicatessen, the conversation had dwindled. The other secretaries, who'd once been her colleagues, didn't really know how to act now she was the CEO's wife. A few were clearly trying to repress burning jealousy, while others seemed merely uncertain what to say.

Holly yearned to show them that she hadn't changed since her marriage, and was still the same person. But how?

As she ate her favorite Reuben sandwich with dill pickle, she listened to the other women talk about their problems. One had an ex not paying child support, another was falling behind on medical bills, another couldn't find good day care. Then their eyes inevitably fell on Holly's huge diamond ring, and baby Freddie, sleeping in his expensive, top-of-the-line stroller. Holly could see what they were thinking: lucky Holly and her baby were set for life.

Cheeks burning, Holly had said quickly, "If there's anything I can do to help—"

"No, no," her former friends had said, waving her off. "We'll be fine."

"Perhaps my husband could give you a raise..." But before Holly even finished her sentence, she knew she'd made a mistake. Her friends had stared at her, quietly offended.

"We're fine, Holly."

"We don't need your charity," another had muttered, sucking down the last of her soda noisily through a straw as she glared at the floor.

The lunch had gone downhill after that. When it was finally over, Holly had suggested they make plans soon. But none of her old friends seemed particularly keen to set a date.

"Don't worry," Audrey, her closest office friend, had whispered as they left. "They'll get used to it. Just give them a little time."

Holly hoped she was right. She still felt a lump in her throat, remembering that awkward lunch.

But at least she and her sister were friends again. Though Nicole hadn't told her much, apparently Oliver's financial situation had improved. Either they'd learned to live on less, or Oliver must have found a job. Either way, she was happy to have her sister back. Nicole now answered all her texts, and had even visited Holly last week at the penthouse.

But when Holly asked how things were going, Nicole had given a wan smile. "You know how marriage is. Or at least," she'd sighed, "you will."

And maybe Nicole had had a point.

Because Holly felt like something had already changed in her marriage. She and Stavros had started in such bliss, with such joyful days together. It hadn't been just shopping. She'd gotten lots of his time and attention. She'd watched him play with their baby. They'd spent hours talking, hours just kissing—in front of the fire, on the sidewalk as they pushed the stroller...he kissed her anywhere—but somewhere along the line, something shocking had happened.

She'd fallen in love with him.

It was the purest bad luck, a horrible coincidence, that the very day she realized she loved him, and started trying to find the words to tell him, Stavros had become utterly distracted at work by the acquisition of some billion-dollar tech company.

He wasn't avoiding her deliberately, she told herself. Of course not. Why would he? True, he'd told her he had some issues about fearing love and commitment, but that was all in the past. He'd married her, hadn't he? He'd promised to be faithful forever. That proved he was more than ready to open up his heart!

But Stavros had run his company for nearly twenty years. That mattered to him, too. He'd tried to explain the new technology to her, and why Minos International needed to acquire it, but Holly's eyes had crossed with boredom halfway through the first sentence.

Or maybe she just hadn't wanted to understand it. What she wanted was for him to finish the deal, so he could stop spending eighteen-hour days at the office and spend time with her and Freddie again.

Like tonight. For the umpteenth time, Holly glanced at the clock over the mantel in the great room of the penthouse. It was nearly ten now, and Stavros had been at the office since dawn. He hadn't seen his son before he left; and now, Freddie had been asleep for hours.

"Is that all, Mrs. Holly?"

Looking up from the chair where she was reading a magazine, Holly saw Eleni. The white-haired Greek woman, who'd by now become part of their family, still insisted on calling her by that formal name. "Yes, Eleni. Thank you."

She nodded. "*Kalinixta*, Mrs. Holly."

"Good night. Thank you." After the older woman headed to her suite downstairs, Holly tried to read, watching the clock, waiting always to hear Stavros at the door.

Finally, she yawned and stretched. Letting the magazine drop against her chest, she looked out at the nighttime city through the wide windows.

She just had to be patient, she told herself. After his business deal was done, their marriage would return to the way it had been during their honeymoon. He would have time for their family again.

And Holly would finally tell him she loved him.

She closed her eyes, hope rising in her heart as she pictured the scene. And then—and then…he'd tell her he loved her, too.

She hoped.

What if he didn't?

Nervousness roiled through her. She set down the magazine on the end table, then rose to her feet and paced in front of the windows. She stopped. There was nothing to be gained by being afraid, she told herself. She'd just have to be brave, and trust everything would be all right. Her husband would love her back. Of course he would.

Holly pushed away her fear. Glancing at the clock over the mantel, she saw that it was just past midnight. It was December twenty-third. Just a few minutes into her twenty-eighth birthday. She brightened.

At least she'd finally get time with him at the surprise party he'd promised her. Could it be called a surprise party when she was counting on it, longing for it? She smiled. He hadn't said a word about what he'd planned, but Holly knew it would be wonderful.

Turning off the lamp, she looked around the quiet, lonely penthouse. It was dark, except for the lights of the Christmas tree shining in the great room.

She wished she didn't have to go to bed alone. But she comforted herself with thoughts of tomorrow. As she brushed her teeth in the enormous, gleaming master bathroom, she closed her eyes in anticipation, imagining her friends and family celebrating together. They'd talk and laugh and eat birthday cake, and all awkwardness with her former colleagues would be smoothed over. Nicole and Oliver would be there. And best of all, she'd finally have time with her husband.

Looking at herself in the mirror, she came to a sudden decision.

Tomorrow at the party, she'd tell Stavros she loved him.

Yes. Tomorrow. Smiling, she peeked into the nursery to check on her sleeping baby, then padded softly back to climb into bed. Glancing at the empty bed on Stavros's side, she looked out the window and made a birthday wish that he'd finish the deal tonight, and starting tomorrow, he'd never be gone so much again. And why shouldn't it happen? Her smile became dreamy. When she woke up, they'd celebrate her birthday, and the day after that would be Christmas Eve. And sometime in the middle of the night tonight, Stavros would wake her with a kiss, and make passionate love to her.

She fell asleep when her head hit the pillow, and spent the night dreaming of her husband's hot kisses.

When she woke up the morning of her birthday, she saw the sky was blue outside, and the sun was bright and gold. She looked over at Stavros's side of the bed, and saw it hadn't been slept in. Stavros had never come home last night at all.

Holly heard echoes of Oliver's laughing voice. *Minos men are selfish to the bone. We do what we like, and everyone else be damned.*

And worse, Stavros's words. *Love always has a winner and a loser. A conqueror and a conquered.*

If she loved him, and he didn't love her back, which would she be?

With a chill, Holly knew the heartbreaking answer.

When his eyes opened, Stavros sat up straight from the sofa.

Seeing the full morning sunlight coming from the window, he gave a low curse, then stood up so fast he almost felt dizzy. His muscles were cramped from a long night spent hunched over the conference-room table, and a few hours of unsettling sleep on his office sofa had left his spine and joints out of place.

He stretched painfully, blinking with exhaustion as he looked around his spacious private office. Piles of papers covered his large, usually pristine black desk, along with empty takeout cartons, the remnants of the kung pao shrimp and broccoli beef his support staff had arranged to be delivered for the negotiating team's dinner at midnight. Stavros had brought the cartons in here to eat privately as he read through the other company's last-minute counter-offer, striking out lines with his red pen before he returned to the conference room to compare notes with his lawyers.

Sometime around 4:00 a.m., he'd realized his brain was in a fog. So he'd stretched out on his sofa. He'd only meant to rest his eyes for a moment, but now it was—looking at his smartwatch, Stavros cursed aloud—nearly eight o'clock. He was supposed to meet back with his team in ten minutes.

Stavros should have texted Holly to let her know he wouldn't be coming home. He should have—

He should do nothing. The cold voice spoke calmly in his soul. Keep his distance. Let her know that their marriage could never be more than a domestic and sexual partnership. Romantic love would never—could never—be a part of it. He wanted Holly to realize this without him having to tell her. The last thing he wanted to do was hurt her.

The first week of their marriage had been the best week of his life. Pleasure, enjoyment, friendship…and mind-blowing sex. He'd been happy with her. He'd forgotten to be so guarded. He'd spent hours with her, not just in bed, but talking about his past. About his feelings. About everything.

And he'd caught Holly looking at him with wistful longing in her beautiful emerald eyes. Something more than admiration. Something far more than his dark soul deserved.

It had shaken him to the core. He'd crossed a line he shouldn't have crossed. He couldn't let Holly fall in love with him. He couldn't. And not just because he'd never love her back.

Love was tragedy. There were only two ways love could end—betrayal, or death.

It was a thought made all the sharper today, Stavros thought now. The one-year anniversary of when he'd gotten his fatal diagnosis last year. He'd lived, against all odds. But the miracle could so easily have not happened. And though his last medical scan had showed him in complete remission, one never knew. He could die of something else. Or Holly could.

How could anyone think of loving each other, knowing it could only end in tragedy?

So he'd forced himself to turn away from all the joy and light his wife had brought to his days. He'd grimly reassembled the walls that guarded his soul. He couldn't let her love him. He had to hold the line. He couldn't be so cruel as to lure her into loving him when he knew it would only bring her pain. He had to fight it.

He couldn't bear the thought of ever seeing Holly suffer. He had to protect her—even from himself.

But how could he pull away, without making her feel the sting of rejection?

He'd grabbed onto the negotiations for this business deal with force. It was an amazing excuse to create some distance from his wife.

Although spending an entire night apart was a little *too* much distance. Going into the private bathroom of his office, he brushed his teeth, then spat out the toothpaste. He looked bleakly in the mirror.

There were dark circles under his eyes from stress and lack of sleep. He missed Holly. He missed his son. He wanted to be home.

He had to remind himself, again and again, that he was staying away for their sakes. Because if Holly fell in love with him, sooner or later she'd demand he love her back. When he couldn't, she'd ask for a divorce. And just like that, their family would be destroyed.

Or maybe she wouldn't ask for a divorce. Maybe it would be even worse. Maybe she'd stay in their marriage, trapped forever in silent desperation.

Last year, when Stavros had thought he was dying, he'd feared leaving Holly behind as a brokenhearted widow. How much worse would it be if instead, she loved him without hope for the rest of her life, making their marriage a sort of living death?

Stavros's shoulders ached as he took a quick, hot shower, trying to wash his churning feelings away. Getting out, he toweled off and pulled on the spare suit that he kept cleaned and pressed in his closet.

Quickly shaving, he avoided his own eyes in the mirror. He hurried out of his private bathroom, already late, trying to focus his mind only on the upcoming conference call—

Stavros stopped flat when he saw his wife waiting in the middle of his private office.

"Hello," Holly said, gripping the handle of the baby stroller.

"Hello," he replied, shocked. The one time she'd visited the Minos building since their marriage, he'd made sure he was too busy to talk to her.

Now, against his will, his eyes drank her in hungrily. Gone were the beige, baggy suits she'd worn as a secretary, and the casual jeans and sweater she'd worn in the Swiss chalet. Now she dressed like the wife of a billionaire CEO. She wore a sleek black cashmere jacket over a white button-down shirt, fitted black pants and knee-high black leather boots. Diamond studs sparkled in her ears. "What are you doing here, Holly?"

She ducked her head. "I was in the area. Nicole asked me out for coffee." She gave a shy smile. "For obvious reasons."

Obvious? How obvious? Then he remembered. "To thank you? So Oliver got the paperwork."

"Paperwork?"

"For the ten million."

Holly's expression was blank. "What are you talking about?"

Stavros frowned. If his financial gift to his cousin wasn't the obvious reason, what was? "The annuity I arranged."

Her lips parted. "You're giving Oliver money?"

"Don't worry," he assured her. "The contract is airtight. He just gets a million up front, and each year they remain married, he'll get another. But only if Nicole signs a statement each year that he's keeping her happy."

Instead of looking reassured, she looked shocked. "You're *paying* Oliver to stay married to my sister?"

"Just for the first ten years," he said, confused. Why did Holly seem so upset? "I know you can't be happy unless the people you love are happy, too. The money is a pittance. So I took care of it."

Her face was incredulous. "And you think paying that—that *gigolo* to stay married to my sister will make her happy?"

"Doesn't it?"

"Love is what makes a marriage! Not money!"

Stavros didn't like where this conversation was going. His fear about making Holly love him, about breaking her heart and ruining her life, started pressing against him as heavily as an anvil. Folding his arms, he said tightly, "Fine. I'll tell my lawyer to cancel the annuity. Is that all?"

"No, it's not all!" Her lovely heart-shaped face was pale as she lifted her chin. "Why didn't you come home last night?"

Her lips were pink and chapped, as if she'd chewed them for hours. Her green eyes were vulnerable, troubled with shadows. Had he put those shadows there?

The thought of hurting her made him sick inside. It made him angry. He glared at her. "I've been closing an important deal. As you know. Which is what I need to be doing now. So if you'll excuse me…"

But she blocked him with the stroller, where their baby was babbling and waving his pudgy arms. "And that's all you have to say to me? After you were gone all night? Without a single message?"

A low Greek curse rose to his throat. It was all he could

do to choke it back. "Holly, I'm working. I'm sorry I didn't call. Now please let me go."

She took a deep breath. "Stavros, we need to talk."

But the last thing he wanted to do right now was talk to her. She was blocking him from where he needed to be. And if he stayed, he'd only be forced to say things that might hurt her.

Why couldn't she take the hint that he didn't want or deserve her love? Did he have to spell it out for her?

Stavros nodded scornfully toward the sofa where he'd slept a few uncomfortable hours. "What is it? Do you think I was here all night with some other woman, making hot, sweet love to her? You think I'm like all the other Minos men—after just a few weeks, I'm already bored of my wife?"

Her beautiful face went white, then red. She whispered, "You don't have to be cruel."

Grinding his teeth, Stavros clawed back his dark hair. "Look, if you don't trust me, why are we even married?"

Folding her arms, she glared at him in turn. "Yes, why, when Freddie and I barely see you anymore?"

Exhaling with a flare of nostrils, Stavros glanced at his watch, imagining the conference call had already started. If he didn't hurry, it might cost his company millions of dollars. But that wasn't the reason he had to get away from her, from the bewildered suffering he saw in her expressive green eyes.

"Fine," he growled. "We'll talk. Tonight."

"All right." Biting her lip, she lowered her arms and said uncertainly, "I just remembered. Today is the anniversary of your diagnosis last year. How are you feeling?"

"Never better," he said shortly. "I got a clean bill of health last month. Still in complete remission."

A warm smile lit up her face. "I'm so glad. I wish you'd told me you—"

"Look, Holly, I don't mean to be rude, but can this wait? I have a conference room full of lawyers waiting."

"Yes. Yes, of course." She blushed a little, looking sweetly shy. "I'm looking forward to tonight. Will you be home early?"

"Unlikely," he said shortly, wondering why she'd be excited for him to come home tonight so they could argue, and he could tell her, to her face, what she should have already known—that he'd never love her. "I've got to go."

"All right." She came closer, her eyes glowing, her expression caught between hope and fear. "There's something I want to tell you. Something important. I—"

But as she looked at him, something made her expression change. Something made her back away.

"Never mind," she choked out, shaking her head. "It doesn't matter. I'll see you later—"

And she turned, and fled his office with the baby.

Stavros exhaled, relieved. Maybe he'd been wrong. Holly wasn't falling for him. She was too smart to give her love to a man who didn't deserve it. And what could a man like Stavros ever do to truly deserve her love and light?

He couldn't. So there was no point in trying. It would only lead to loss and darkness—

Pushing away the twist in his gut—it felt like being punched—he clenched his hands into fists. Striding out of his office, he barked at one of his assistants, "Call my lawyer. I want the deal with my cousin canceled at once."

He didn't slow down to hear the reply. Because if there was anything his illness had taught him, it was that life was short. You had to do the important things now, because you never knew if there would be a tomorrow. You had to know what was really, truly important.

And blocking out all emotion from his soul, Stavros hurried to the conference room, where a billion-dollar deal waited.

CHAPTER ELEVEN

SHE'D ALMOST MADE a horrible mistake.

Holly was still shaking as she pushed the stroller down the long city block toward the small café where she was supposed to meet her sister for coffee.

She'd been heartbroken when she'd woken up to discover Stavros had never come home last night. When her sister had invited her out for her birthday, she'd chosen a café near his office. She'd gone there with her heart on fire, half longing for him, half hurt.

And she'd nearly blurted out that she loved him. Surely, once he knew that, once he understood that he held her heart in his hands, he would treat her with greater care?

But looking at his coldly handsome face in his office, Holly had suddenly realized that he wouldn't. Because he already knew.

He knew she loved him. But he didn't want her to speak the words aloud.

Because then he'd be forced to admit he didn't love her back.

Now, hurt and grief threatened to overwhelm her as she maneuvered the stroller down the Midtown sidewalk, crowded with last-minute holiday shoppers. The windows were full of brightly decorated Christmas scenes. But in her current mood, as her eyes fell on the vestiges of melted snow in the shadowed places on the sidewalk, the city seemed gray and dirty. Just like her dreams.

Her baby gave a little plaintive cry from the stroller, snapping Holly back to reality. Stopping on the corner to wait for the crosswalk light, she caressed Freddie, even as she fiercely blinked back tears. Reaching into his blankets, she found his pacifier and popped it back into his mouth, causing him to settle back into the stroller.

Straightening, Holly took a deep breath. As the light changed, she crossed the street surrounded by happy, smiling crowds laden with holiday gifts. Looking down at Freddie in the stroller, she felt her heart in her throat as Stavros's words came back to her.

Love always has a winner, and a loser. A conqueror and a conquered. I decided long ago I never wanted to be either.

She'd thought, when Stavros married her, he'd changed his mind. But he hadn't. He just wanted them to be a family.

So did she.

Holly took a deep breath. Maybe she could love him enough for both of them, she tried to tell herself. If Stavros treated her well, if he cherished her, couldn't that be enough? As long as he was a good father, and a good husband? As long as he spent time with them? Which she was sure he would, as soon as this business deal was over.

Stavros might not be in love with her, but he cared about her. After all, he'd arranged a big birthday party for her tonight. A sort of surprise party, their first social event as a married couple. All their friends and family would be there.

She just had to focus on the positive. She was twenty-eight now, a married lady with a baby. It was time to grow up.

She could live without her husband's love.

Lifting her mouth into a smile as she reached the café, she pushed the stroller inside. She saw her little sister sitting at a nearby table, her face in her hands. Next to her on the table, there was a small birthday gift beside a large coffee mug.

Holly parked the stroller beside the small table. "Nicole?"

Her sister looked up. Tears were streaking her face.

"What is it?" Holly cried, horrified.

"I just got a call from Oliver," she whispered. "Stavros canceled the annuity. So he's leaving me."

"Oh, no!"

"He's moving in with someone else." Her voice choked. "A rich older woman who can give him the lifestyle he deserves."

Sitting in a nearby chair, Holly pulled Nicole into her arms as her baby sister cried against her shoulder.

"I'm so sorry, Nicole," she whispered, rubbing her back. "This is my fault. I told Stavros he shouldn't pay Oliver to be married to you. You deserve more. Marriage should be about love, not money." But as her sister's crying only increased, Holly blurted out, "I'm sorry."

Nicole pulled away, wiping her eyes. "This *is* your fault, Holly. Your fault for trying to take care of me, even when I didn't deserve it. You fault for always thinking I was wonderful, even when I was a total jerk. Even when I stole the man you wanted."

"Stole..." Nicole had tried to steal Stavros? Holly stared at her, confused. Then she understood and exhaled in relief. "Oh, you mean Oliver."

"I knew you had a huge crush on him as his secretary," Nicole sniffed. "But I still took him. And now the universe is punishing me as I deserve."

"You're wrong," Holly said. "Oliver was never mine. The romantic dream kept me company, that was all. It was never real. You didn't take anything from me, Nicole. You don't deserve anything but love!"

"That's what I mean," her little sister said, shaking her head as she gave a tremulous smile. "Even when I've been horrible to you, you find a way to see me in the best possible light." She wiped her tears. "When Mom and Dad died, you gave up everything to raise me. I never appreciated that. It's only now I realize how selfish I've been."

"Oh, Nicole…"

Her sister took a deep breath, leaning back into her own chair. "It's time for me to strike out on my own. The fact that Oliver has left makes it easier."

"You don't have to be alone. Come stay with us for Christmas. There's plenty of room!"

Nicole shook her head. "I'm going to visit my old roommate up in Vermont. Her family has a ski resort, you know, a little one, which they operate on a shoestring. I need some time away, to figure out what to do with my life." She paused. "Besides. You have your own problems."

"What are you talking about?"

"Like I said. You always see the best in people, Holly. Even when they don't deserve it. You see what you want to see with those rose-colored glasses. Oliver. Me." She tilted her head. "Stavros."

"You think I don't see him how he really is?" she said slowly.

Her sister's eyes challenged her. "Do you love him?"

Holly took a deep breath. The truth forced itself from her lips. "Yes."

"Does he love you?"

In spite of Holly's efforts to convince herself she didn't need her husband's love, a lump rose to her throat. She looked away.

"That's what I thought," Nicole said quietly. Putting her hand on her shoulder, she repeated the same words Holly had just said to her. "You deserve more."

Suddenly, Holly was the one who was crying. Angry at herself, she wiped her eyes. "We can still be happy. Stavros just loves me differently, that's all. He cares for me. He shows it through his actions. Like the party tonight…"

Nicole frowned. "What party?"

She smiled through her tears. "You don't need to pretend. I know he's throwing me a birthday party. He insisted on doing it, since I didn't want a wedding reception. There's no way he wouldn't invite you." Holly's lower lip trembled. She desperately needed to feel some hope. "So you can tell me about it. It's not a surprise."

"I'm not trying to keep anything a surprise. There's no party, Holly."

She stared at her sister. As a waiter came and asked if they needed anything, Nicole shook her head. Holly didn't even look at him.

"No party?" she said numbly.

"I'm sorry. Maybe he's doing something else to surprise you?" Her sister tried to smile as she pushed the small, brightly wrapped present toward her. "Here. Wrapped in birthday paper, like you always wanted." She smiled ruefully. "Not Christmas paper, which you've always had to put up with from me."

Holly looked down at the present. It was beautifully wrapped, in pink and emerald, her two favorite colors.

"What's inside is even better. Something I know you've always wanted but were never selfish enough to admit it. Open it."

Slowly, Holly obeyed. And gasped.

Inside the box, nestled in white tissue paper, was the precious gold-star necklace that had once belonged to their mother.

"Told you I'd find it," Nicole said smugly. "It was tucked in my old high-school sweatshirt buried at the bottom of my keepsake box."

A lump rose in Holly's throat as she lifted the necklace. Their mother had worn it every day. It had been a gift from their father, who'd always called Louisa his north star.

"I know you wanted me to have it, so I'd never lose my

way," her sister said in a low voice. "But I think you need it more than I do now."

Nicole's husband had left her, they'd soon be going through a divorce, but she still thought Holly needed it more? Her hand tightened around the necklace as she said hoarsely, "Why?"

"You told me love makes a marriage, not money." Nicole shook her head. "Are you really going to spend your life waiting for Stavros to love you—waiting hopelessly, until you die?"

Holly stared at her little sister in the small New York café. As customers and waiters bustled around them, the smell of coffee and peppermint mochas in the air, the heat of the café made her feel sweaty and hot, then clammy and cold.

Then she realized it wasn't the café, but her heart.

She'd spent her whole life taking care of others, imagining herself in love with unobtainable men—first Oliver, then Stavros. Even now, she'd been ready to settle for a dream to keep her warm, so she didn't feel so hopeless and alone, rather than be brave enough to hold out for the real thing.

Her gaze fell on Freddie, wrapped in blankets, sucking his pacifier in the stroller. Was this the example she wanted to set for her son? That marriage meant one person martyred by love, and the other a tyrant over it?

Love always has a winner and a loser. A conqueror and a conquered.

Which one was she?

Closing her eyes, Holly took a deep breath.

Then she slowly opened them.

No. She wouldn't settle. Not anymore. Not when her and Freddie's whole lives were at stake.

And Stavros's, too.

He'd never wanted to hurt her. He'd said from the beginning that he had no desire to be a conqueror. And yet her love for him would make him one.

Holly reached up to clasp her mother's necklace around her neck. She touched the gold star gently at her collarbone. No. She wanted love, real love. She wanted what her parents had had.

Love made a marriage. Not money. Not sex. Not even friendship. Only love.

And she wouldn't, couldn't, spend the rest of her life without it.

It was nearly midnight when Stavros arrived home.

For a moment, he leaned his head against the door, exhausted. He'd only slept three hours in the last forty-eight. But the deal was struck at last. He was done.

At least until the next deal. He was already considering a potential acquisition of a company in Pittsburgh that had developed an AI-based sales networking platform. He would call his lawyers about it tomorrow. With any luck, they could strike first, while his competitors were still lazing over Christmas presents and turkey dinners.

Entering the dark, silent penthouse, he turned on a light in the foyer. He nearly jumped when he saw his wife sitting on the sofa of the great room, staring into the pale flames of the gas fireplace. Beside her, the lights of the Christmas tree sparkled wanly.

"What are you doing up so late?" he said uneasily. It couldn't be anything good.

Slowly, she rose to face him. She wasn't in pajamas, as one might expect, but was fully dressed, and not in the sleek designer clothes he'd bought her, but the simple sweater and jeans she'd worn when they'd left Switzerland last month.

"We need to talk."

"So you said. But it's been a long day. Can we do it tomorrow?" *Or never.* He raked a hand through his dark hair, setting down his laptop bag as he gave her a small smile. "The deal is signed."

"Oh?" She came toward him. "So you're done?"

"Yes."

She paused. "So you'll be home more—"

"There's always another deal, Holly." He hung up his black Italian cashmere coat. "There's a new potential acquisition brewing. I'll need to leave for the office early tomorrow."

Her lips parted. "But tomorrow's Christmas Eve. And you just got home. We haven't seen you for weeks—"

"I'm CEO of a major corporation, Holly." His voice was more harsh than he intended, but he was tired. He didn't want to hear her complaints. He didn't want to feel guilty right now—or feel anything at all. "This is how we pay for this lifestyle. For all your jewels and fine clothes."

Holly lifted her chin. "I never asked for any of that."

She was right, which left him no room to negotiate or blame her. It irritated him. "Look, I'm exhausted. Our talk is just going to have to wait."

"Until when?"

He shrugged. "Until I have time." Which, with luck, he never would. All he needed to do was line up endless mergers and acquisitions, endless reams of work, and he'd have an excellent excuse never to have to tell her out loud that he didn't love her, or see her beautiful face break into a million pieces.

But as he turned away, he was stopped by her voice.

"Do you know what today is?"

Scowling, he glanced back. She'd better not bring up last year's fatal diagnosis again. "The day I signed a new billion-dollar deal?"

She gave him a thin smile. "My birthday."

He blinked, then a savage curse went through his mind. Of course. December twenty-third. Her birthday.

Now he felt guiltier than ever, which only made him angrier. He'd totally forgotten her birthday, and his promise to throw her a party. He was the one who'd first insisted on throwing her one, like a big shot. Now he looked like a flake. Now he'd let her down.

Stavros hated the disappointment in her green eyes—the hollow accusation there. It was the same way his mother had looked at his father when Aristides failed her, time and time again. As a boy, Stavros had always wondered why his mother put up with such treatment.

Now, he was somehow in his father's place. He hadn't cheated, but he'd accidentally lied. There was no party. He wouldn't, couldn't, bear to think of himself as the villain in this equation.

"I'm sorry," he said tightly. Admitting a mistake was difficult for him. He resisted the temptation to make excuses, to blame her for expecting too much when he'd been swamped with the business deal. Setting his jaw, he said only, "I forgot about the party. I will have my secretary arrange it as soon as possible."

"Your secretary?"

His jaw tightened further. "Would you rather have a gift? Jewels? A trip?"

She took a deep breath. He saw tears in her eyes. "What I wanted was your time."

Seeing her tears hurt him so badly, he couldn't help lashing out. "Then you had unrealistic expectations. Did you really think our honeymoon could last forever?"

"Yes," she whispered. She looked down at the big diamond ring sparkling on her left hand. It glittered like the tears in her eyes. "I love you, Stavros. Can you ever love me?"

It had finally come. The moment he'd dreaded. He wanted to avoid the question.

But looking at her miserable face, he had to tell her the truth.

"No," he said quietly. "I'm sorry, Holly. It's nothing personal. I told you. I'm just not made that way."

Her shoulders sagged. Then she looked up with a tremulous smile. "I'm sorry, too. This is what you meant, isn't it? About the conqueror and the conquered."

"Yes." His heart felt radioactive. Grimly, he buried it in lead, beneath ten feet of ice. "I never wanted you to love me."

"I know. And I was so mad when you told me this would happen." Her expression was wistful. "That I wouldn't be able to resist falling in love with you."

His shoulders felt painfully tight. "You're a good person, Holly. I don't want you to suffer." He pleaded, "Can't you be happy with the life we have? Can't you just take your love back?"

Holly stared at him for a long moment, then slowly shook her head.

"I can't. I can't pretend not to love you. I can't wish it away. I'm sorry. I know I'm putting you in a position you never wanted to be." Blinking fast, she tried to smile through her tears. "It'll be all right."

Stavros frowned, coming closer. He yearned to wrap his arms around her, to comfort her. But how could he, when he himself was the reason she was crying? "It will?"

Holly nodded. "It's time for me to grow up. To see things as they really are." She looked at him. "Not as I wish they could be."

He felt her words like an ice pick through his frozen heart. And it was then that he saw her old overnight bag, sitting by the front door.

"You're leaving me," he whispered, hardly able to believe it.

Looking away, Holly nodded. Tears were streaking her

face. "I knew what you were going to say. But I... I guess I just had to hear it aloud. To know there was absolutely no hope."

Reaching forward, he grabbed her shoulders and searched her gaze. "You don't have to leave. I want you to stay..."

She shook her head. "I saw Nicole today. Oliver's left her for another woman. In the past, I would have been scrambling to try to fix her life, to smooth her path. But she doesn't need that anymore. She's stronger than I thought. And you know what? So am I." Lifting her gaze to his, she said simply, "I've been on my own before. I can do it again."

Stavros dropped his hands. "On your own?"

"I once thought the only way I'd be loved was if I sacrificed myself for others. It's taken all this—" she looked around the elegant, sparsely decorated penthouse "—for me to realize that's not how love works. You can't earn someone's love by giving them your soul. They either love you, or they don't." She gave him a tremulous smile. "It's all right, Stavros. Truly. You'll be better off this way, too. You have nothing to feel bad about."

"Holly, damn it—"

"It's no one's fault." She tried to smile. "Thank you for telling me the truth."

"And this is my reward?" A lump was in his throat. "To have you leave?"

"No one will be surprised when we break up. You gave your baby your name. That's enough." Wiping her eyes, she gave a wry grin. "I mean, come on, a secretary and a billionaire tycoon? No one would ever think *that* marriage could last."

"And Freddie?" he said hoarsely.

A wave of emotion went over Holly's face. But he saw her control it, saw her accept it and master it.

"We'll share custody," she said quietly. "You'll always be

in his life." She allowed herself a rueful smile. "Although let's be honest. Working eighteen-hour days, Christmas included, you weren't exactly going to see him much, anyway, were you? Even if we all lived in the same house."

Stavros's heart twisted at the thought of no longer living in the same house as his baby son. But how could he argue with her?

Everything she'd said was true. Just like with her birthday party, he'd made grand promises he hadn't kept. He'd sworn he'd be an amazing father. Then he'd disappeared to the office.

He yearned to reach for her, to drag her into his arms, to kiss her senseless until she agreed to forget this love idea and stay with him forever.

But he was backed into a corner. Holly was leaving him, and there was nothing he could do about it. He couldn't lure or romance her into staying, knowing he'd be stealing her soul and giving nothing back in return. He couldn't be such a monster, allowing her to remain and look at him each day with heartbreaking hope in her eyes, yearning for love he couldn't give.

Nor could he be the spiteful, selfish man his father had been, trying to hold her against her will, by threatening to take custody of Freddie or withholding the five million dollars guaranteed by their prenuptial agreement, in a malicious attempt to punish her, or keep her down.

No.

"Where will you go?" he asked in a small voice.

"Switzerland."

"Tonight? So late?"

"I wasn't sure when you'd get home tonight." She gave a brief smile. "Or even *if* you'd come home."

His eyes tightened. "I explained why I was late."

"It doesn't matter anymore." Her smile was sad. "Freddie and I are booked on the first plane to Zurich tomorrow. It leaves at five. It seemed easier to stay overnight at a hotel by the airport. Eleni's already there with him."

He wouldn't even get to say goodbye to his son? He felt a lump in his throat, a coldness spreading to his chest. He wanted to argue, to demand more time.

Then he looked at Holly. She'd already decided. Once a woman knew what she wanted, what was to be gained from waiting?

He'd never admired her more than he did in this moment.

All he could try to do was accept her decision better than his own father had. He forced himself to ask the question. "When can I see him again?"

"Anytime you come to Switzerland."

His voice was hoarse as he said, "Take my jet."

Holly looked surprised at his offer, then gave a crooked half grin. "We don't need anything so fancy. Commercial is fine. Just a seat in economy class with my baby in my lap."

Stavros imagined his wife crammed into an uncomfortable middle seat, with four-hundred-pound men on each side of her, and their baby squirming and crying in her lap for nine hours straight. "If you don't want to take my jet, at least fly first class. You don't need to economize. Your prenuptial agreement guarantees—"

"No." She cut him off harshly. "That's Freddie's money."

"I'll always provide for Freddie. The five million is yours."

"I don't want it." Her green eyes were hard. Then she added lightly, "Anyway, first class is no place for a baby. The executives and supermodels up there would smash their champagne flutes and attack us if Freddie started crying. Which he will. His ears always hurt during take-off. You remember how it was when we flew to Greece. And New York."

Their eyes met, and he felt a stab in his chest.

"My jet will take you." He was proud of his matter-of-fact tone.

"It's not necessary—"

"Stop arguing." His voice was flat, brooking no opposition. "You don't need to sleep in a motel 'til morning. You can leave at once. Freddie will be more comfortable. You know it's true."

She sighed. "Thanks," she said slowly. Pulling the huge diamond ring off her finger, she held it out. "This belongs to you."

Reluctantly, he took it. The ten-carat, platinum-set diamond that had been the symbol of forever was now just a cold rock in his hand. He gripped it in his palm.

"I'll have a lawyer contact you after Christmas." She tried to smile. "We'll be civilized."

He'd never felt this wretched, even when his mother had died. As Holly turned to go, he choked out unwillingly, "How can you do this? If you love me, how can you leave?"

She turned back, her eyes full of tears. "If I'm not strong now, I never will be. And we'll both have lifetimes of regret. I know what your childhood did to you. I won't let our son believe all the wrong things about what a marriage is supposed to be. I won't let him grow up crippled like…"

"Like I am?" Stavros said in a low voice.

Coming forward, she kissed his cheek. He felt her warmth, breathed in the scent of vanilla and orange blossoms.

"Be happy," she whispered.

And, picking up her overnight bag, Holly left.

CHAPTER TWELVE

THE NEXT MORNING Stavros woke up to the blaring sound of an alarm on his phone. Without opening his eyes, he reached out for Holly's warmth.

Her side of the bed was cold. And he remembered. Slowly, he opened his eyes.

She was gone.

With a hollow breath, he looked down at his rumpled clothes. He'd fallen into bed last night in his white shirt and black trousers. He hadn't had the energy to change his clothes. He hadn't wanted to think. It was either fall into bed, or into a bottle of whiskey, and the bed had been closer.

But he'd dreamed all night, strange dreams where he was smiling and happy. Beautiful, vibrant dreams in which he'd held his wife's hand, and they'd been together in a wintry valley, making a snowman with their son. Stavros hadn't been afraid to love her. In his dream, he'd fearlessly given her all his heart.

The cobwebs of those dreams taunted him as he stiffly sat up in the cold light. It was Christmas Eve morning. Everything looked gray. His empty bedroom. The city outside. The sky. Gray. All gray.

Except—

His eyes narrowed when he saw a strange flash of color. Something red. Getting out of bed, he padded softly across the marble floor as he reached for something in the branches of the artificial tree. A small Christmas present, wrapped in red homemade paper with a red bow.

To my husband.

His heart twisted. For a moment, he stared at it, like he'd discovered a poisonous snake amid the branches. Then, grimly, he lifted the small box in his hand. It weighed almost nothing. He wondered if she'd gotten him the gift before she'd decided to leave him, or after. He hoped it was after. He couldn't bear to open a gift filled with all the awful hope of her romantic dreams.

He didn't want it. He'd have to be a masochist to even look. He dropped the gift back into the tree, then went to take a shower. Taking off his wrinkled clothes, he let the scalding hot water burn down his skin. He scrubbed his hair until his scalp ached.

Perhaps it was better their marriage had ended this way. Swiftly. Cleanly. Before anyone got seriously hurt. Before they realized how little he deserved their love, when he was incapable of giving himself in return.

He remembered Holly's haunted, heartbroken face.

I love you. Can you ever love me?

And his cool, factual response as he'd told her he'd never love her. Told her it was nothing personal.

Shutting off the hot water, he stood still in the shower, remembering. His heart was pounding strangely.

Going to his walk-in closet, he tried not to look at all the designer clothes Holly had left behind, many of them still unworn, wrapped in garment bags from the boutiques. Feeling hollow, he turned away, pulling on black silk boxers and black trousers. He would call his acquisition team to tell them they needed to come in tonight. Christmas Eve be damned. Business was what mattered. Building his empire for his son to inherit—

What was in Holly's gift?

Turning on his heel, he almost ran across the bedroom to the Christmas tree. Grabbing Holly's present, he ripped off the wrapping paper and yanked open the tiny cardboard box.

Inside, tucked into white tissue paper, he saw a homemade Christmas ornament, a red felt star. He heard her sweet voice like a whisper through his heart.

My parents were happy, chasing their stars.

A lump rose in his throat. Not everyone was so lucky. Not everyone could—

"You are a fool, Stavi."

The words, spoken in Greek, were more mournful than accusing. Turning, he saw Eleni standing in the doorway.

"She chose to go. I could not stop her," he replied in the same language. The elderly Greek woman shook her head.

"She loves you. The last thing she wanted was to go."

"Her quick departure proves otherwise," he said flatly. He looked out the window at the gray morning above the gray city. He knew the stars existed above the clouds, even now. But he couldn't see them. Just like his wife and child.

He wondered if his private jet had landed yet. If the sky in Switzerland right now was bright and blue above the sparkling Alpine snow. He imagined them decorating a Christmas tree. Drinking cocoa. He saw Holly, so beautiful and loving and warm, wearing flannel pajamas tonight as she put stockings on the hearth of the old cabin's stone fireplace. She believed in love. She probably believed in Santa, too.

"Oh, Stavi." Eleni sighed, making clucking noises with her tongue. "Why did you not just tell her the truth?"

Anger went through him.

"I did," he growled. "I can never love her."

The older woman's dark eyes looked back at him, and she sighed again.

"Men," she chided, shaking her head slightly. "The truth is, you already do."

Stavros stared at her.

"Love Holly?" Ridiculous. He wouldn't love anyone. Love was a tragedy that made victims out of at least one, if not two people. He scoffed rudely, "You're out of your mind, old woman."

But she didn't let his insult stop her. "Of course you love her. Why else would you send her away?"

"Now I know you're crazy." He looked at her incredulously. "Sending Holly away proves I love her?"

Eleni looked at him steadily. "You think you're not worthy of her. So you won't let her waste years of her life, like your mother did, loving someone who obviously doesn't deserve it."

Stavros stared at her in shock. His eyes narrowed.

"I'm nothing like my father."

The white-haired Greek woman tilted her head, her dark eyes glinting in the shadowy dawn. "No? It's true you don't sleep with other women. But do you ignore? Do you abandon and neglect?"

His hands tightened at his sides. "I've been nothing but good to them."

"You forget I've been living here lately." She lifted her chin. "While you have not."

Stavros opened his mouth to argue. Then he closed it again. Yes, all right, he hadn't been around much for the last few weeks. He'd barely seen either his new wife or his child. But he'd been trying to protect them. From loving him. Because he didn't want them hurt.

He'd tried his best. He'd given Holly his name. His money. They'd wanted for nothing.

Except his attention and love.

Because they deserved more. They deserved better.

Because he wasn't worthy.

Swallowing hard, Stavros stared out the floor-to-ceiling windows at the city.

"Go to her," Eleni said softly behind him. "If you do not, if you are not brave enough to fight for her, brave enough to give her everything, you will regret it all your life."

Silence fell.

He whirled around, but she was gone.

Pacing the room, he stopped, staring down at the red felt star his wife had made for him. He'd brought her to New York with great fanfare, promising he'd be a good husband, promising he'd be a good father, promising her she'd never regret it. Insisting he wanted to throw a party for her birthday.

Then he'd done none of it, and ghosted her.

Eleni was right. He'd abandoned his family. Not because of some business deal. And not even because he was trying to protect them.

He'd deliberately avoided his wife because he was afraid.

Afraid if she ever really got to know him, she would finally realize that she was the conqueror, not him.

My father always said loving my mother changed his life. She made him a husband. A father. More than he ever imagined he could be. He always said she changed his stars.

Slowly, Stavros held up the red felt star.

He wasn't worthy of her. That was true. He didn't know if he ever could be.

But he'd never let fear stop him before. It hadn't stopped him from building a billion-dollar company out of nothing. It hadn't stopped him from marrying Holly, though he'd somehow always known this was how it would end.

Could he change?

Could he be brave enough to give her everything?

Could he win her heart?

Tears filled his eyes as he looked out over New York City.

He couldn't see the stars above the clouds, but they were there. Waiting for him to see them. Waiting to guide him.

Stavros gripped the red felt star in his hand. It was as soft as her red hair. As tender as her heart.

Blinking fast, he took a deep breath.

Maybe, just maybe…it wasn't too late to change his stars.

The Swiss valley was dark and silent, late on Christmas Eve.

Outside, the stars were bright as diamonds in the cold, black night. In the distance, Holly could hear church bells ringing for midnight mass. The road in front of her cabin was empty. Her neighbors had all gone to spend time with friends and family—those who hadn't gone to sunny climes for a holiday.

She was glad she'd taken Stavros's jet, as he'd insisted. Freddie's ears had hurt, and he'd cried the whole way. So had she. Exhausted from crying for hours, her baby had finally gone to sleep an hour before. Now, she was alone in the quiet.

Holly wondered what her husband was doing right now, back in New York. She looked out the cabin's window, but all she saw was the reflection of a young red-haired woman, lonely and sad.

No. She couldn't feel sorry for herself. She was lucky to have this cabin for herself and her child. Lucky to have time and space to figure out how to start over.

Opening the front door, Holly looked out at the quiet, wintry valley. Moonlight swept the snow, and she could see the sharp Alps high above. Her breath was white smoke dancing in the air, the icy cold a shock against her lungs. From a distance, she could see a car's lights winding down the valley road toward her tiny chalet. Someone was traveling to be with family for Christmas, she thought, and her heart felt a pang.

Shivering in her thin white T-shirt and tiny knit shorts, she closed the door, turning back inside. She had family, she told herself. Her sister had just texted her from Vermont, to tell her that the ski slopes were snowy and beautiful. Yuna's family was already stuffing Nicole with Christmas cookies and eggnog.

I think I'm going to be all right. It might take a while. But the New Year is just around the corner.

Holly smiled wistfully. Her little sister had truly grown up.

Then with a shake of her head, she started tidying up the small interior of the rustic chalet. The Christmas decorations were still up from last month. Nothing had been changed. She blessed her former employer's frantic schedule for keeping him too busy to arrange for her possessions to be packed and sent to New York.

Picking up her grandmother's old quilt from the back of the tattered sofa, Holly wrapped it around her shoulders. Taking a freshly baked sugar cookie from her chipped ceramic Santa cookie jar, she bit into it and sat down, staring at the fire.

Even the fire was different here. At Stavros's penthouse in New York, the flames had been white and without heat, fueled by cold gas, over elegant stones. Here, the fire was hot enough to warm up the cabin, fueled by split logs she kept on her porch.

When her neighbors had heard of Holly's return, they'd rushed to welcome her. Elderly Horst, bright-eyed and spry, had brought her a small Christmas tree, which he'd hewn from the nearby forest. Kindly, plump Elke had brought sugar cookies, decorated by her grandchildren.

So Holly wasn't alone. Not really. And she'd tried her best to make Freddie's first Christmas special. Her eyes lifted from the roaring fire to the two homemade knit stockings hanging over it. Before she went to bed tonight, she'd fill them with the oranges and peppermints that Gertrud had brought her, and the bag of homemade candies from Eleni. Not that Freddie could eat them yet, but at least he'd know he was loved…

The car lights outside grew brighter. Holly wondered if someone was visiting one of her neighbors. Elke's son from Germany, perhaps. Horst's brother from Geneva.

Her gaze trailed to her Christmas tree, now sparkling between the stone fireplace and the small, frosted-over window. She'd decorated it with big colorful lights and the precious vintage ornaments from her childhood. The only thing she'd left untouched in her family's old Christmas box was the garland of red felt stars. The tree seemed sparse without it. But she just couldn't.

When she'd made Stavros his homemade red felt star, she'd hoped it would start a new tradition for their marriage—blending his sophisticated Christmas tree with her own family's homespun style.

She'd only remembered her gift on the plane, when it was too late to take it back. She wondered if Stavros would even notice it, tucked amid the branches of his artificial tree, or if Eleni would toss it out with his other unwanted things.

Like Holly.

A lump rose in her throat. No, that wasn't fair. Stavros had been clear all along that he would never love her. She was the one who'd tried to change the rules. She was the one who, in spite of all his warnings, had given him her heart.

She heard the sudden slam of a car door outside, followed by the crunch of heavy footsteps in the snow. Had another neighbor decided to visit, this late on Christmas

Eve? It had to be. Who else could it be—Santa Claus delivering toys for Freddie from his sleigh?

She set down the barely tasted cookie on the saucer next to her cold cocoa. Rising to her feet in her fuzzy bootie slippers, she glanced down worriedly past her mother's gold-star necklace to her old white T-shirt, so thin it was almost translucent, showing not just the outline of her breasts, but the pink of her nipples beneath. Her knit sleep shorts were so high on her thighs that they were barely better than panties. She'd dressed for solitary sobbing and brokenhearted cookie-snarfing, not to entertain guests.

A knock rattled the door, reminding her of Marley's ghost in *A Christmas Carol*. Pulling her grandmother's quilt more tightly over her shoulders, she came close to the wooden door. Quietly, so as not to wake the tired baby sleeping in the next room, she called, "Who is it?"

For a moment, there was no answer. She wondered if she'd somehow imagined the knock, by a trick of a passing car's lights and rattle of the icy winter wind. Then she heard her husband's low, urgent voice.

"Holly…"

Now she really knew she was dreaming. She ran a trembling hand over her forehead and looked back at the sofa, half expecting to see herself still sleeping there.

"Holly, please let me in. Please."

It couldn't be Stavros, she thought. Because he never talked like that. He didn't plead for her attention. *Please* was a foreign word to him.

Frowning, she opened the door.

Stavros stood there, but a different Stavros than she'd ever seen.

Instead of his sharply tailored power suit and black Italian cashmere coat, he was dressed simply, in jeans, a puffy coat and knit beanie cap. And somehow—it didn't seem fair—his casual clothes made him more handsome than ever. He looked rugged, strong. The vulnerability in his dark eyes, shining in the moonlight, made her heart lift to her throat.

"What are you doing here?" she breathed.

"May I come in?" he asked humbly. "Please."

With a shocked nod, she stepped back, allowing him entrance to the cabin. Her knees felt so weak, she fell back against the door, closing it heavily behind her.

He slowly looked around the room, at the homespun ornaments on the Christmas tree and two stockings above the roaring fire.

"It's Christmas here," he said softly. He looked at her, and his black eyes glowed above his sharp jawline, dark with five-o'clock shadow. "The Christmas I always dreamed about."

She said hoarsely, "What do you want?"

With a tentative, boyish smile, he said almost shyly, "I want you, Holly."

Her heart twisted. Had he come all this way just to hurt her? To taunt her with what she'd never have? "You came all this way for a booty call?"

Slowly, he shook his head.

"I came to give you this." Pulling his hand out of his jacket pocket, he opened it. The red felt star she'd made him as a gift rested on his wide palm.

Looking down at it, she felt like crying. Why had he come all this way? To reject her homemade gift? To throw it callously in her face? "Do you really hate me so much?"

"Hate you?" Shaking his head ruefully, he lifted her chin gently with his hand. "Holly, you had no reason to love me. I made my position clear. I was scarred for life. I had no heart to give you. All I could offer was my name, my protection, my fortune. That should have been enough."

Holly couldn't move. She was mesmerized by his dark, molten eyes.

"But it wasn't." His lips curved at the edges. "Not for you, my beautiful, strong, fearless wife." He ran the tips of his thumbs lightly along the edges of her cheekbones and jaw. "You wanted to love me, anyway," he whispered. "Even if it cost you everything, heart and soul."

Holly shuddered beneath his touch, unable to speak.

"And now…" Stavros paused, and to her shock she saw tears sparkling in his dark eyes, illuminated by the firelight and the lights of the Christmas tree. "There's only one thing left to say."

She held her breath.

His dark gaze fell to the tiny gold necklace at her throat. Taking her hand in his larger one, he pressed something into her palm. Looking down, she saw the red felt star.

"You've changed my stars," he whispered.

She looked up. His handsome face was blurry from the tears in her eyes. She saw tears in his gaze that matched her own.

"I love you, Holly." Stavros put his hand against her cheek. "So much. And when you and Freddie left me, it was like I'd lost the sun and moon and Christmas, all at once."

She searched his gaze. "You…" Licking her lips, she said uncertainly, "You love me?"

He gave a low, rueful laugh. "I think I loved you since last Christmas Eve, when I first saw you in that red dress, standing in the candlelight of the old stone church."

With a snort, she shook her head. "You didn't act like it…"

"I hid my feelings, even from myself. I was afraid."

"You didn't want to be a conqueror," she murmured.

"I didn't want to be conquered."

"Conquered?" She choked out a laugh. "As if I could!"

He didn't laugh. "When I met you, for the first time in my life, I wanted marriage, children. I thought it was just because I wanted a legacy. Because I believed I was dying. But it wasn't."

"It wasn't?"

Stavros shook his head. "It was because of you. You made me feel things I'd never felt before. And after we slept together, I knew you could crush me if you chose." He took a deep breath. "So I pushed you away. I was afraid of hurting you. But more. I was afraid you could destroy me." Cupping her cheek, he looked down at her intently. "But I'm not afraid anymore."

"You're not?" she whispered.

"My heart is yours, Holly," Stavros said humbly. "My heart, my life, are both in your hands." His voice became low as he looked down at her hands, clasped in his own. "Can you ever love me again?"

For a moment, Holly stared at him.

Then her heart exploded, going supernova, big enough to light up the entire world. Gripping his hand, she led him to the tree and gave him the red felt star. "Put it on our tree."

With an intake of breath, Stavros searched her face. What he saw there made joy lift to his eyes. Tenderly, he placed the homemade star on a branch of the fresh-cut tree. Reaching into her family's Christmas box, she pulled out her mother's garland of red felt stars, which she wrapped beside it, around the tree.

"Now," she whispered, facing her husband with tears in her eyes, "it's really Christmas."

Love glowed from Stavros's handsome face. Then his expression suddenly changed. His dark gaze lowered to her breasts.

Holly realized that when she'd bent to get the garland, the quilt had slid off her shoulders to the floor. Her husband's eyes trailed slowly over her thin, see-through white T-shirt and the tiny knit shorts. Her body felt his gaze like a hot physical touch.

"Stavros," she breathed.

Pulling her into his arms, he kissed her, his lips hungry and hard. His jacket flew off, followed by his knit hat.

And as they sank together to the quilt on the floor, bodies entwined, Holly felt not just passion this time, but true love and commitment. The cabin was fragrant with pine and sugar cookies and a crackling fire. She'd never known joy could be like this.

And as her husband made love to her that night, on the quilt beneath the sparkling tree, Holly knew that even with the ups and downs of marriage, they'd always be happy. For there was nothing more pure than true love begun on Christmas Eve, when all the world was hushed and quiet, as two people spoke private vows, holding each other in the silent, holy night.

Three babies crying, all at once.

Stavros looked helplessly at his wife, who looked helplessly back. Then Holly's lips suddenly lifted, and they both laughed. Because what else could you do?

"I'm sorry," Eleni sighed, standing on the snowy sidewalk as she held the hand of Freddie, now fourteen months old, wailing with his chubby face pink with heat and lined with pillow marks. She continued apologetically, "I shouldn't have woken him from his nap. But I was sure he'd want to meet his new brother and sister."

Holly and Stavros looked at each other, then at their hours-old babies behind them in the third row. Stella and Nicolas had both seemed to agree, with telepathic twin powers, that they hated their car seats. They'd screamed the whole ride home from the hospital. After one particularly ear-blasting screech, Stavros had seen Colton, his longtime, normally unflappable driver, flinch beneath his uniformed cap. As if they hadn't already shocked the poor man enough by trading in the Rolls-Royce for the biggest luxury SUV on the market.

And that wasn't even the biggest change. Six months before, when they'd discovered Holly was pregnant with twins, they'd decided to move to Brooklyn, of all places.

"Our kids will need friends to play with," Holly had wheedled. "And I want to live near the other secretaries from work."

"You're friends again?"

"Most of them were finally able to forgive me for marrying a billionaire." She flashed a wicked grin. "In fact, when you're grumpy at the office, they even feel a little sorry for me…"

"Hey!"

"The point is, I don't want to raise our kids in a lonely penthouse. They need a real neighborhood to play in. Like Nicole and I had when we were young."

Eventually, Stavros had agreed. Now, he shook his head. If his father could only see him now, living in Brooklyn, surrendering to domestic bliss—and liking it! Aristides would swear Stavros wasn't his son!

His father had replaced him with a son more to his liking, anyway. After Nicole and Oliver's divorce was settled last summer, his cousin had soon found himself dumped by his wealthy lover. Facing the daunting prospect of finding a job, he'd gone to visit his Uncle Aristides in Greece, and never come back.

Now Oliver would never have to work, and Aristides had the perfect wingman to help pick up girls in bars. It was a perfect solution for them both, Stavros thought wryly.

Luckily, his wife's family wasn't as embarrassing as his own. Nicole was apparently settling in nicely to her new life in Vermont, working as a schoolteacher and dating a policeman. The relationship didn't sound serious yet, but he was sure he'd hear all the details when Nicole arrived tomorrow morning for Christmas breakfast. Whether he wanted to or not.

"Oh, dear," Eleni said, pulling him from his thoughts as she peered into the SUV's back seat with worried eyes. Freddie continued to noisily cry in harmonic counterpoint to his younger siblings. "Do you need help, Stavi?"

"May I help with the babies, Mr. Minos?" Colton offered. For Eleni to offer help wasn't unusual, but for his grizzled driver to offer to provide baby care was unprecedented. The crying must be even louder than Stavros thought.

"Yes. Thank you." In a command decision, Stavros snapped Stella's portable car seat out of the base first, then Nicolas's. He handed the first handle to Eleni, who capably slung it over one arm, and the second to his driver.

"We can manage," Holly protested beside him.

"I have someone else to worry about."

"Who could be more important than our babies?"

Stavros looked at his wife. "You."

She blushed, and protested, "I'm fine."

Fine. Stavros shook his head in wonder. Holly had spent most of yesterday, her twenty-ninth birthday, in labor at the hospital, then given birth to twins at two that morning. She should have remained in the hospital for another week, relaxing and ordering food as nurses cared for the newborns. But it was Christmas Eve, and she'd wanted to come home.

"We have to be with Freddie for Christmas, Stavros," she'd insisted. "I want to be in our new home, waking up together on Christmas morning!"

Even though mother and babies were healthy, Stavros had been doubtful they'd be allowed to leave the hospital just twelve hours after delivery. But Holly had been adamant. The instant she'd gotten her doctor's slightly bemused approval, she'd insisted on coming home.

That was his wife, he thought, shaking his head in admiration. Determined their family would be happy, and letting nothing stand in her way.

"Wait," Holly called as Eleni and Colton and Freddie started up the steps of their brownstone. "I can help—"

Now it was Stavros's turn to be adamant. "No, Holly. Be careful!"

"Wait," she cried after her children, pushing herself up from the seat before he saw her flinch and grimace with pain.

Setting his jaw, he lifted her from the SUV in his powerful arms, cradling her against his chest.

"What are you doing?" she gasped.

"Taking care of you."

"It's not necessary—"

"It is," he said firmly. "You look after everyone else. My job—" he looked down at her tenderly "—is looking after you."

And he carried her up the stoop, into their five-story brownstone.

The hardwood floors creaked, gleaming warmly as the fire crackled in the hundred-year-old fireplace. Holly had decorated the house for Christmas with her family's homemade decorations. They hadn't expected the babies to arrive early. They weren't due until January. Although when, he thought ruefully, did any Minoses let other people's expectations stand in their way?

When Holly had gone into labor yesterday, she'd stared at the three stockings on the fireplace with their embroidered names, and cried, "The twins can't be born before Christmas. I haven't made them stockings!"

Now, as Stavros carried his wife past the five stockings hanging on the fireplace, he smiled with pride when he heard her gasp.

"Nicolas… Stella—you got them Christmas stockings!"

Holly looked up at him in shock. "Their names are even embroidered!"

His smile widened to a grin. "Merry Christmas, *agape mou*."

"But—" She looked at him helplessly. "How? You were with me at the hospital the whole time!"

Stavros looked down at her. "I have my ways."

"Santa? Elves?"

Lifting a dark eyebrow, he said loftily, "Call it a Christmas miracle."

She gave him a slow-rising grin. "Oh, was it now?"

"What else could it be?" He gently lowered her to her feet, then looked down at her seriously. "But not as much a miracle as this."

And putting his arms around her, he lowered his head to give his wife a tender kiss, full of love and magic, of sugarplums and sparkling stars.

After a lifetime of being frozen, it had taken a fatal diagnosis to make Stavros open his heart the tiniest crack. In that moment, Holly had gotten inside him, warming his soul with her golden light.

Once, he'd been grimly ready to die. In an unexpected miracle, he hadn't.

But Holly was the one who'd truly brought him to life.

He'd been wrong about love all along, Stavros realized in amazement. Love hadn't conquered him. It had saved him. It had set him free to live a dream greater than any he'd ever imagined. His children. His home. His wife. Especially his wife.

Being loved by Holly was the greatest Christmas miracle of all.

* * * * *

MILLS & BOON

Coming next month

THE GREEK'S SURPRISE CHRISTMAS BRIDE
Lynne Graham

'I have a proposition that you may wish to consider.'

'Did Isidore mention that I'm in need of money?' Letty had to force herself to ask, her creamy skin turning pink with self-consciousness.

'Your grandfather asked you to call him Isidore?' Leo remarked in surprise.

'Oh, he didn't invite me to call him anything,' Letty parried with rueful amusement. 'To be frank, he didn't want to acknowledge the relationship.'

'That must've been a disappointment,' Leo commented wryly.

'Not really. I wasn't expecting a miracle but, considering that my father never paid any child support, it's not as though I've cost that side of my family anything over the years,' she responded quietly. 'My mother has always been very independent but right now that's not possible for her, so I've had to step in...'

'Which is where I enter the equation from your point of view,' Leo incised. 'Your grandfather wants to amalgamate his shipping firm with mine and retire, leaving me in charge. For me, the price of that valuable alliance is that I marry you.'

A pin-drop silence fell.

'You would have to marry *me* to get his shipping business?' Letty exclaimed in disbelief. 'I've never heard anything so outrageous in my life! I knew he was an out-of-date old codger, but I didn't realise he was *insane*!'

'Then I must be insane too,' Leo acknowledged smoothly. 'Because I am willing to agree to that deal, although I also have more pressing reasons for being currently in need of a wife...'

Letty felt disorientated and bewildered. 'You *need* a wife?' she almost whispered, wondering why there wasn't a stampede of eager women pushing her out of their path to reach him and then suppressing that weird and frivolous thought, irritated by her lapse in concentration.

'Six months ago, my sister and her husband died in a car crash. I am attempting to raise their four children. I need a wife to help me with that task,' Leo spelt out succinctly.

'*Four*...children?' Letty gasped in consternation.

'Aged five and under.' Leo decided to give her all the bad news at once. 'The baby was a newborn, who was premature at birth. Ben and Anastasia were on the way to pick him up and finally bring him home from the hospital when they were killed.'

In the stretching heavy silence, Letty blinked in shock. 'How tragic...'

'Yes, but rather more tragic for their children, with only me to fall back on. They need a mother figure, someone who's there more often. I work long hours and I travel as well. The set-up that I have at the moment is not working well enough for them.'

Letty shrugged a slight fatalistic shoulder. 'So, you make sacrifices. You change your lifestyle.'

'I have already done that. Bringing in a wife to share the responsibility makes better sense,' Leo declared in a tone of finality as though only he could give an opinion in that field.

'And you and my grandfather, who doesn't really *want* to be my grandfather,' Letty suggested with a rueful curve to her soft mouth, 'somehow reached the conclusion that *I* could be that wife?'

Continue reading
THE GREEK'S SURPRISE CHRISTMAS BRIDE
Lynne Graham

Available next month
www.millsandboon.co.uk

COMING SOON!

We really hope you enjoyed reading this book. If you're looking for more romance, be sure to head to the shops when new books are available on

Thursday 28th November

To see which titles are coming soon, please visit

millsandboon.co.uk/nextmonth

MILLS & BOON

MILLS & BOON

THE HEART OF ROMANCE

A ROMANCE FOR EVERY KIND OF READER

MODERN

Prepare to be swept off your feet by sophisticated, sexy and seductive heroes, in some of the world's most glamourous and romantic locations, where power and passion collide.
8 stories per month.

HISTORICAL

Escape with historical heroes from time gone by. Whether your passion is for wicked Regency Rakes, muscled Vikings or rugged Highlanders, awaken the romance of the past.
6 stories per month.

MEDICAL

Set your pulse racing with dedicated, delectable doctors in the high-pressure world of medicine, where emotions run high and passion, comfort and love are the best medicine.
6 stories per month.

Celebrate true love with tender stories of heartfelt romance, from the rush of falling in love to the joy a new baby can bring, and a focus on the emotional heart of a relationship.
8 stories per month.

Desire

Indulge in secrets and scandal, intense drama and plenty of sizzli hot action with powerful and passionate heroes who have it all: wealth, status, good looks…everything but the right woman.
6 stories per month.

HEROES

Experience all the excitement of a gripping thriller, with an inten romance at its heart. Resourceful, true-to-life women and strong, fearless men face danger and desire - a killer combination!
8 stories per month.

DARE

Sensual love stories featuring smart, sassy heroines you'd want as a best friend, and compelling intense heroes who are worthy of the
4 stories per month.

To see which titles are coming soon, please visit

millsandboon.co.uk/nextmonth

JOIN US ON SOCIAL MEDIA!

Stay up to date with our latest releases, author news and gossip, special offers and discounts, and all the behind-the-scenes action from Mills & Boon...

 millsandboon

 millsandboonuk

millsandboon

It might just be true love...